CHAPTER ONE

CW01499559

"Look out, Bel!"

The druid heard the warning shout threw himself to the side. He felt a bul let out a great roar of pain, fearing he'd been terribly injured and would not now be able to stand and face his adversary. He could hear his friend, Duro, charging towards him, forcing his way through the thick undergrowth, cursing with every step as brambles and nettles tore and stung at his flesh.

"Are you all right?"

Bellicus, teeth gritted, levered himself to his feet with the shaft of his spear, not looking down at his injured leg for he knew that even a moment's inattention could lead to death. Their enemy was that dangerous. "I'm alive," the druid shouted, gingerly placing weight on his left leg, praying to the gods that it would not give way and leave him lying, helpless, on the grass.

"Should have brought Cai with us," Duro shouted, bursting through a juniper bush and staring around wildly.

Before Bellicus could reply, reminding him that Cai was not trained for this kind of fight, there was a grunting sound that chilled the druid to his very bones, and then came the noise that heralded the enemy's return.

"Ready?" Duro demanded.

"Aye," Bellicus replied, relieved to find his wounded leg could take his weight. He stepped back, setting himself in a defensive stance, spear levelled in both hands as Duro mimicked his movements.

"Here he comes! Be ready to move!"

The ground actually seemed to vibrate as their foe came back for the druid and now Bellicus could see it charging along an old path towards him. "By Taranis," he murmured in awe, "he's massive!"

It was no exaggeration, for the wild boar they'd come across must have weighed almost as much as the two men combined, and had it struck Bellicus cleanly on its first pass the druid would surely be dead by now. The beast did not seem to have the mental capacity to try and avoid the spear that was levelled at it, or perhaps it was simply too enraged to care, as it charged directly at Bellicus who swallowed and braced himself for the impact.

"Don't just stand there!" Duro roared. "It'll kill you!"

Staring intently at the boar, Bellicus waited until the last moment, and then he dropped his spear, jumped up, and grabbed hold of a branch, praying it would take his weight as he swung his legs desperately upwards, away from the razor-sharp tusks of the wild beast. Mercifully, it was a yew tree the druid had been standing beneath and, although the branch bent under his considerable weight, it held, and he was able to move up even further as the furious boar, oblivious to the world around it, slammed into the yew's trunk.

The whole tree shuddered, almost dislodging Bellicus who held on for dear life as, underneath, Duro ran forward and plunged his spear deep into the animal's thick, bristly hide. The boar let out a tremendous squeal and turned to face Duro. It seemed to be dazed from its collision with the tree for it stood without moving for a moment, breathing heavily as blood oozed from the wound the spear had inflicted.

"What are you waiting for?" Bellicus called down. "You're unarmed, you lunatic. Get away before it attacks again!"

Duro appeared rooted to the spot, awed by the ferocious power that emanated from the animal, but his friend's words penetrated his mind and he blinked then turned and sprinted for the nearest tree that looked like it might be used for shelter, as Bellicus's yew was doing for the druid.

As he ran, the boar came to its senses and thundered after him, the spear still stuck in its side but doing little to slow its progress. Bellicus shouted encouragement to the centurion who was a decent runner but not as fast as a wild boar, even an injured one. Just in time, Duro reached an elm and jumped, desperately grabbing for the nearest branch.

The boar had learned its lesson from before and did not slam into the elm's trunk this time, but it stopped underneath the gasping centurion, glaring up at him and snorting with terrible malevolence.

"By Mithras's balls, druid," Duro cried, arms entwined around one of the co-dominant stems of the tree, foot firmly wedged between the fork. "We've both lost our spears, and that evil big

2

THE DRUID'S PREY

by

Steven A. McKay

Book 7 in the

WARRIOR DRUID OF BRITAIN CHRONICLES

KINDLE EDITION

Dedicated to Ziggy, Sam, and Pippi. Not as big as Cai, but just as loved.

MAP OF BRITAIN

PICTS

Dunadd

Wall of Antoninus

Dun Breatann●········●Dun Edin   Britain

DAMNONII VOTADINI   c. AD434

SELGOVAE

Wall of Hadrian   Northern
                    Sea

Manu

Hibernian
Sea

Torp

Shrine of
Arawn   Tir Ambre

Durobrivae●   Garrianum

Durovigutum●   Cedrid

Duroliponte

PLACES IN THE DRUID'S PREY

Alt Clota - Strathclyde
Ard Sabhal - Overtoun/Barnhill, West Dunbartonshire
Cedrid – Chatteris, Cambridgeshire
Cibra - Castlehill Fort, Bearsden, East Dunbartonshire
Dunadd – Argyll and Bute
Dun Breatann - Dumbarton Castle, West Dunbartonshire
Dun Edin – Edinburgh
Durobrivae – Water Newton
Duroliponte – Cambridge
Durovigutum - Godmanchester
Egtved - Saksnot's birthplace. Southern Jutland (Denmark)
Garrianum - Burgh Castle, Great Yarmouth
Litana - Bearsden, E. Dunbartonshire
Manu – Isle of Man
River Bure - River Bure
River Clota – River Clyde
River Gerne - River Yare
River Vividin - River Waveney
Tir Ambre - Arminghall Henge, South Norfolk
Torp – Langthorpe, Yorkshire

bastard isn't likely to piss off until we come down. What are we going to do?"

Bellicus hauled himself up to a higher branch, frightened that his weight might snap the one he was on. He looked at the ground where his spear lay and wondered if he could drop down, grab the weapon, and use it to defend himself before the boar made it back to him and tore him to shreds. He doubted it, but, unless the gods provided some miracle, he would need to try.

Duro was still armed but with his spatha, the long sword that the Roman cavalry had originally used before the rest of the legions adopted it over the smaller gladius. It was a good weapon for fighting humans, but it would not have the cutting power to do much damage to a boar, or the reach to kill the thing before it killed Duro. Bellicus was similarly armed with his own sword which he called Melltgwyn – White Lightning – and, again, unless it somehow lived up to its name and sent a bolt of fire arcing across the woods into the animal, it would be little use as a weapon.

What were they going to do? It was a good question. "Pray!" he shouted across the clearing to Duro who gave an amazed snort in reply.

"I've been praying since the moment that beast turned up," the centurion shouted. "Why did it attack us anyway?"

"Who knows," the druid replied. "Maybe it has babies nearby and thought we were a threat."

"Oh, that's all we need. More of the bastards turning up. They could take it in turns to make sure we don't try to escape!"

Despite their predicament Bellicus couldn't help but laugh, as he often did at his friend's dry humour. His laughter turned to anxiety eventually though, as the boar did not wander off as they'd hoped, but remained in the clearing, snorting and growling with a fury that did not seem to abate even after what seemed like hours.

"My legs are starting to ache," Duro shouted over. "I can't stay like this much longer, Bel. We can't sleep in these trees either. One of us is going to have to make a run for it and hopefully get away to bring help."

It had been a hot summer day and Bellicus was glad he had a skin of water with him for dehydration was one problem he'd rather not add to all the others he faced. He took a sip now and realised the water was all gone. Looking up through the densely packed

3

branches of the yew he noted the position of the sun and knew there were still a few hours left before it sank beneath the horizon and the land cooled.

"Have you got water left?" he asked Duro.

Worryingly, the centurion's had also run out some time ago.

"This is ridiculous," Duro muttered. "After all the enemies we've faced, and beaten, it looks like we're going to end up being killed by a pig!"

The earlier jocularity of his tone was gone, replaced by anger and growing trepidation.

Bellicus closed his eyes and slowed his breathing, allowing calm to wash over him as much as possible while still keeping a firm grip on his branch. "Cernunnos," he mouthed, softly invoking the god of the forest. "Send us aid."

When he opened his eyes he was astonished to discover the sun had moved some way across the sky. I must have dozed off, he thought. That was a bad sign, suggesting the heat and lack of water was getting to him already. If they did not get down from their trees soon, there was every chance one of them would fall, and be unable to defend themselves from the boar which apparently felt as fresh as it had hours before, in spite of the spear still jutting out of its bristly hide.

"Duro," the druid called, fearing his friend might also become dazed or even incapacitated from sunstroke.

"Aye?"

From the languid reply it seemed Duro was also tiring. They had to do something now, before it was too late.

"I'm going to jump down," said the druid, moving his position within the tree, making sure none of his limbs had gone to sleep.

"All right. Then what?"

"I should be able to lift the spear. I'll try to kill the boar with it. It doesn't look tired or weak, but it must have lost a fair bit of blood. It'll be slower than before." He realised he was trying to persuade himself but did not really believe what he was saying. "Are you able to move?"

Duro grunted and shuffled about in the tree. "Damn foot has gone numb," he replied. "But it'll be fine." He rolled his head on his shoulders, freeing the tightness that had settled in his neck. "Aye, I'll be fine to move. What do you want me to do?"

4

"Run," Bellicus told him.

"Run? And leave you to face the beast alone? I don't think so!"

"I'll just try to stick the thing with the spear," the druid argued. "And then jump back into this tree. It should distract the boar enough for you to get away and bring help."

Duro thought about it, clearly unhappy at being asked to run from a fight. There seemed no other choice though. "All right," he sighed. "If you insist, old friend. May the gods be with you."

Bellicus closed his eyes and prepared for the battle that was to come – if it could even be called that. He visualised what he wanted to do, how he hoped it would play out, with him landing well, scooping up the dropped spear, and planting his feet in time to force the iron point of the pole arm into the charging boar's maw. "Cernunnos protect me," he begged, and, opening his eyes, shifted his feet for the drop onto the grass knowing full well it would likely be the last thing he ever did.

"Wait!" Duro suddenly called, interrupting his own shouting as he attempted to distract the boar. "Wait, Bel, I hear someone coming!"

Bellicus swallowed and felt a wave of relief wash over him. It might only be a temporary respite, for he could not hear whatever Duro had, but he was glad to have even a few more moments of life.

And then they spotted who was coming through the trees towards them. Or, more accurately, what.

"By the gods," Bellicus breathed in astonishment. "And we thought things couldn't get worse!"

Lumbering towards them was not a rescue party of wild boar hunters, but an enormous brown bear.

CHAPTER TWO

Narina ran along the beach, hair flying behind her as she looked over her shoulder and saw her pursuer was no more than a few paces behind. Gritting her teeth she forced herself to move faster, desperately trying to get away.

It was futile.

The queen heard laughter and, from the corner of her eye, saw the girl who'd been behind her slowly edging in front. Narina had no more to give and, as they reached the stream that fed into the River Clota she slowed and came to a stop, breathing heavily and doing her best to ignore the victorious cackle that echoed out across the glittering water.

"I…" the queen gasped, hands on her thighs. "I almost beat you that time." She finally got the words out and stretched up, looking at the sky and enjoying the warm sun that beat down upon the beach.

"Almost," her daughter, Princess Catia, replied. The blonde, green-eyed girl was twelve summers old and barely out of breath despite the race. Even in the past couple of months she had grown so she was now taller than her mother and, undoubtedly, she would continue to grow since Bellicus was her father. She might not end up over six and a half feet like the druid, but even so her long legs allowed her to run like the wind and Narina simply could not defeat her in their foot races these days. "Almost," Catia grinned. "But not quite."

"Come on," Narina said, putting an arm around her daughter's shoulders and giving her a quick, congratulatory hug before leading the way back along the beach towards Dun Breatann.

The fortress had been besieged at the start of the summer by a combined army of Picts and Saxons and, to relieve the anxiety and boredom of those seemingly endless days locked within the walls Narina and Catia had raced against one another, and eventually other challengers. The soldiers and workers had placed bets on them and it had been such a fun experience in those dark days that the queen had vowed to keep doing it now that the war was over and peace reigned over Alt Clota once again.

Narina had lost that first race, just as she'd lost every one against Catia since, but she never let it dishearten her. She was fiercely proud of her daughter – losing to her was not an issue, and Narina had not felt so strong in many years. At thirty-two she was hardly old, but she knew it would grow harder to remain fit with every passing year so she was happy to put in the work, especially since it meant spending time with Catia.

Life was good again, she thought. Alt Clota was at peace, and her family was safe and happy. Of course, it would not last forever, but she hoped in the coming months to consolidate the Damnonii position, perhaps forming new friendships or alliances with their Dalriadan, and Selgovae neighbours, while reaffirming and strengthening old relations with the Picts, and King Cunneda's Votadini people. Narina had always wanted peace for Northern Britain and she believed it was finally within reach. With Bellicus by her side they could bring all the tribes together, rather than fighting amongst themselves as they'd done for untold generations.

"By Lug, it's so hot," Narina said, eyeing her bare, tanned arms and squinting up at the sun. "I'll be glad to get inside the hall and have a drink."

"We could go for a swim," Catia suggested. "The river's right there."

Narina looked at her, noting the mischievous glint in the girl's eye. "We haven't brought anything to dry ourselves with," she protested. "And it's a long walk up the stairs of Dun Breatann."

"So what?" Catia grinned. "Like you said yourself, it's roasting hot!" With that, she ran to the river and waded into it fully clothed, squealing with delight for, although the air was warm, the water was anything but.

Narina watched her, smiling. Like Catia, the queen was wearing an undyed, calf-length linen gown similar to what the Greeks called a peplos, girdled at the waist and held together at the shoulders with brooches. It was light and airy and ideal for walking, or running, in sunshine. Not quite suited to swimming, however.

"Come on, mother!" Catia shouted. "It's lovely once you get used to it!"

A small vessel was passing in the middle of the river and the fishermen on board were watching the princess, shaking their heads and laughing at her antics. They began to cheer as Narina ran to the water and charged in, screaming at the sudden chill. It was likely the fishermen had no idea who the women in the water were or they'd not have openly called out to them but, as the boat was rowed away

7

to the east Narina waved to them and splashed Catia, berating her for egging her on to this foolishness.

A while later the pair passed through the two gatehouses that guarded Dun Breatann and walked up the many steps towards their house at the top of the fortress. Guards and workmen and women gazed at them in amusement, or amazement, as they passed, for they were thoroughly soaked, hair and gowns dripping with water and leaving a trail behind them.

"Look what you've done," Narina hissed as they reached the central portion of the great rock. "Everyone thinks I'm mad now!"

"Only now?" Catia retorted, and ran off, up the slope that led to the royal residence, laughing as her mother chased after her in mock indignation.

By the time they reached their single-storey dwelling they were almost dry, the sunshine was so hot. Still, their garments were damp and stained and they hastily changed into fresh ones, making sure their brooches were thoroughly dried out before reusing them.

"Come on," said Narina. "This morning was fun, but I'm absolutely famished now."

They walked down to the great hall, nodding demurely to all they passed, as if their earlier, sodden passage up the rock had never happened. When they went into the hall it was mercifully cool for the cooks were heating the evening meal outside. A servant hurried over to them with mugs of barley beer and Narina sipped at hers with pleasure, eyes scanning the gloomy interior of the hall.

"Where is Bellicus?" she asked the servant. "I thought he would be here."

"I haven't seen him all morning, my lady. He hasn't been here."

Narina frowned, setting down her mug and wiping her mouth with her forefinger. "He's not at the house," she murmured, still looking into the shadowy corners of the hall for the druid she'd married, at last, just a month or so ago. "And he's not here. So where is he?"

"He went up to Ard Sabhal with Duro earlier," Catia said. "Remember?"

"I do remember," Narina nodded. "But they should have been back by now."

At another time their absence would barely have registered with the queen but now, so soon after the recent war with the Picts and

Saxons, Narina remained on edge, always the fear at the back of her mind that some other raiders would come to Alt Clota and cause trouble. Of course, it was ludicrous to worry about the druid and his centurion friend – they were skilled, armed warriors simply going for a walk to gather herbs and things for Bellicus's potions and salves. What could possibly happen to them in the woods near Ard Sabhal?

Gavo came into the hall then, smiling. "You two are the talk of the place," the commander of Alt Clota's army and captain of Narina's personal guard told them. "Wandering around soaking wet and dripping water every—"

"You have Cai with you," Narina interrupted, standing up and looking at the huge mastiff that belonged to Bellicus.

"Aye," Gavo nodded, examining the queen as if she worried was going mad from heatstroke. "Bel said he was going up amongst the rocks around Dun Buic and Ard Sabhal looking for the gods know what – plants or something. He was worried Cai's feet would get burned." The captain glanced over his shoulder at the blinding sunlight coming through the hall's open doors. "I'd say he was right, and it's better the hound remained here on a day like this."

"But Bel isn't back yet?"

Gavo shrugged. "They've only been away a few hours."

"Maybe," Narina replied, swallowing, her throat dry and tight. "But he told me he'd be back by midday, and it's already well past that."

Gavo simply looked at her, uncertain what to say or do. Narina was not one to make a fuss over nothing, as she seemed to be doing here.

"What's wrong, mother?" Catia asked.

"I have a bad feeling," the queen said, biting her top lip and looking again at Gavo. "I'm sorry, but could you have some men ride up to Ard Sabhal and check Bel and Duro are all right?"

The guard captain dipped his head, nodding respectfully. "Of course, my lady," he said. "I'll go with them myself, and take the dog."

"Be prepared for danger, Gavo," the queen told him as he spun and strode from the hall, Cai at his side.

"Always," he called, and disappeared from view.

9

"What is it?" Catia asked, frowning. "You're making me nervous, mother."

Narina tried to smile but could not. "I don't know," she admitted, feeling more than a little foolish. "I'm afraid something's wrong."

Catia examined her face, now infected with the queen's anxiety. "You're just worried about the Saxons," she said, fingers idly touching the pommel of the short sword that she wore at her waist. "Worried that Hengist will come looking for revenge for what we did to his brother."

Narina swallowed nervously again, remembering Horsa, the imposing enemy jarl who'd spoken disrespectfully to her during the recent siege of Dun Breatann. Well, he wasn't so tall and imposing now that his decomposed corpse, what remained of it at least, was swinging from a rope over the topmost of Dun Breatann's walls.

Catia was right: Hengist would be outraged when he found out that Duro had defeated Horsa in single combat, and then the Saxon's body had been left to rot in full view of everyone who came to Dun Breatann rather than being given the proper funeral rites. Of course, as an enemy warrior – and one who'd treated Narina's Damnonii people with despicable cruelty – Horsa was not entitled to respectful treatment, but that wouldn't matter to Hengist. The Saxons were well known for carrying on blood feuds for generations, even when the reason for it had long been forgotten.

Narina feared what form the *bretwalda*'s retaliation would take, and she guessed those fears lay behind her current anxiety over Bellicus.

Still, she would not be at ease until the druid was safely back within the fortress's walls and the gates firmly locked behind them.

CHAPTER THREE

"Bel! I thought you were communing with the gods to get us some help! That's a fucking bear!" Duro was doing his best to climb higher up the tree that had thus far been his safe haven.

"I can see that," Bellicus murmured, transfixed by the sight of the lumbering brown animal that seemed to be heading straight for them.

There couldn't be many such beasts within these woods, surely, and the druid felt a sudden twinge of recognition stirring in his brain as the bear drew closer.

"Climb further up the tree!" Duro shouted, his usual parade-ground bellow disintegrating beneath the heat and the stress of what was happening. "The bear will reach you there!"

Bellicus was too fascinated by what he was seeing to take in the centurion's command. He was practically in a trance as his eyes moved from the bear to the enraged boar which had not noticed the arrival of the even bigger animal.

"Climb the damn tree!" Duro hissed, almost comical in his attempt to avoid attracting the bear's attention.

"Bears can climb trees," Bellicus replied absently, still staring at the two animals for the boar had now realised it might not be the most dangerous thing in the clearing any more.

The druid had been looking forward to the coming year, having finally married Queen Narina. They could live as a family with their daughter Catia at last, overseeing Alt Clota as its people recovered from recent wars. Bellicus had been planning to personally visit the Dalriadans on the east coast in hopes of forming an alliance, or at least some kind of lasting peace, as well as making the most of their new relationship with the Picts in the north. Recent years had been full of battles, adventures, death, and all the things that sounded exciting in songs and stories but were not so pleasant to actually live through. Was it too much to ask for even a few months of peace? He watched the bear lumber into the clearing where the furious boar stood and decided the gods were laughing at him.

What would the beasts do? the druid wondered. Would they work together to kill the humans that had strayed into their territory? Would the bear decide it wanted no part of whatever was happening – wanted no part of the boar's deadly, razor-sharp tusks – and lumber off, back into the trees? Or would the animals fight each other, forgetting the humans for at least a short time? If that was to happen maybe Bellicus and Duro could make a run for it. Perhaps that was Cernunnos's plan for them all along.

The bear stopped moving, taking in the sight of the boar which was peering at it in return. And then the bear looked up at Bellicus and their eyes met. The druid swallowed, knowing for certain that he had come across this very animal before – it had attacked them some years prior, not far from where they were now, badly injuring King Coroticus and Gavo and killing one warrior and three dogs. It had eventually decided to give up the fight but only once it had a spear stuck in its back and a number of arrows from the Damnonii hunters' bows. Bellicus examined its hairy pelt for evidence of those earlier wounds but it seemed to have healed well in the intervening years.

As if it recalled that battle the bear suddenly stood up on its hind legs and let out an enormous roar. Bellicus gazed at it in awe – the animal was not just enormous, it was majestic, and the thought of trying to kill it again was truly terrifying.

It seemed the boar had similar thoughts, for instead of charging at the bear, it turned and hurried off into the trees, the spear that Duro had planted in its side clattering noisily against tree trunks until, at last, it must have snapped off for there was a last, distant squeal and then only the low growling of the bear was left to fill the clearing.

"Mithras protect us, we're in for it now," Duro said, doing his best to draw his spatha while still gripping the trunk of his tree for dear life. "At least the boar couldn't get up here."

"Don't do anything," Bellicus ordered in a low voice. "Do you not recognise it?"

"Aye," the centurion nodded. "It's the same bear that almost killed us all before. You told us to let it go back then for some mad reason."

"The Bear of Britain," Bellicus said, so softly Duro could not hear him. "That's what the Merlin had called Arthur." Memories of the previous encounter with the bear were filling his mind and he remembered being in a shocked stupor as he'd stared at the bear bristling with missiles like a hedgehog. The animal had lost the will to fight that day and Bellicus had commanded those with him to let

12

it go, a decision he'd never really understood himself. For some reason he'd seen the beast as connected to Arthur, or perhaps he just didn't want any more people – or Cai, for the mastiff had been involved in the fighting too – getting injured or killed.

Whatever his motives had been, the bear stared up at him now, its round, dark eyes fixing on his own. There seemed an intelligence behind that gaze that Bellicus had not expected. Did it recognise him? Did it understand that he'd been the one that called off the attack on it and most likely saved its life after their previous encounter? Maybe. The druid knew that bears had an even more developed sense of smell than dogs, so it was possible the beast, which had dropped back to all fours now, recognised his scent if not his face.

The bear made a strange, ululating, guttural grunting sound and then simply wandered off into the trees, quickly disappearing from sight.

"Is…Is it over?" Duro gasped, sword still glinting in the last of the sunshine as he lowered himself down, hanging from a branch by one arm as he tried to see through the foliage and make sure the bear had really gone.

Bellicus grinned and jumped heavily down to the ground, lifting his dropped spear just in case anything else decided to lumber into the clearing. "Looks like it," he grinned, stretching and trying to work the numbness from his limbs. "Come on, hurry up. Let's get out of here while we can."

Duro remained on edge as they headed south, in the direction of Dun Breatann, so much so that he did not sheath his spatha and continually looked around and behind as they walked. They'd not gone far at all when the centurion grabbed Bellicus's arm and hauled him back, eyes wide. "Listen."

Bellicus did listen, and heard the sound of bushes being thrust aside as something came in their direction. Again.

In silence, the druid nodded and the pair moved apart, standing against the thick trunks of trees, one with sword in hand, the other with his spear ready to thrust at this new woodland danger. It had been a long, stressful, and frightening day, but the two men had effortlessly moved back into the warrior mindset and were ready to fight for one another, even if it meant death.

The sun had started to drop beneath the treeline now, casting long, twisting shadows as a gentle breeze moved leaves and branches this way and that. Birds and insects still flitted about, singing and buzzing, oblivious to the pent-up aggression contained within the two hidden figures.

And then another hairy beast hove into view, crashing noisily through a patch of rowan, deadly white teeth flashing in the shadows.

"Gods above!" Duro cried, and Bellicus burst out laughing, more from relief than humour, as Cai spotted them and came charging towards the druid.

"Duro!" Gavo pushed through the rowan bush next and spotted the centurion, then the druid. "You're both alive, praise Lug."

"Why wouldn't we be?" Bellicus asked, surprised to meet the grizzled guard captain along with Cai and half a dozen of Dun Breatann's finest soldiers.

Gavo shrugged. "Queen Narina seemed to think you were in danger. I didn't even try to argue with her; she seemed so sure of herself I just thought it best to come and look for you as she commanded." He grinned. "I'm relieved to see she was wrong."

"Wrong!" Duro practically squawked, thrusting his spatha back into its scabbard with some venom. "Aye, we've been having a fine time out here, haven't we, Bel?" Shaking his head ruefully he pushed past the astonished Gavo and was swallowed up by the undergrowth although they could all hear him exhorting them to hurry up and follow for he was looking forward to an ale to steady his nerves.

"What's wrong with him?" Gavo asked, turning wide-eyed and amused to the druid. "Did you piss in his aleskin or something?"

Bellicus laughed and it was a welcome release of tension. "No, nothing like that. Come on, I'll tell you all about it once we're safely back inside Dun Breatann."

The party turned and headed after Duro, Cai sensing his master had been in danger and trotting along protectively at his side.

There must have been heady scents in the air from the boar, and the bear, so the great hound did not notice the eyes of the lean young warrior staring malevolently at them from his hiding place within the foliage as they began the homeward journey.

CHAPTER FOUR

"It's just as well I enjoy sailing," Jarl Sigarr announced to his crew as their ship forged northwards towards Dun Edin, capital of the Votadini tribe. "I seem to have spent half my life on the swan's road these past few years with the likes of Leofdaeg and Horsa."

His captain, Cretta, a tough, very tall man, stood at his side, nodding slowly. He had been with Sigarr for some of those voyages and knew, as all Saxons did, what had happened to Horsa. "Where's Leofdaeg now?" he asked, easily adjusting his feet as the ship bounced on a sudden wave and Sigarr almost fell over.

The jarl pondered Cretta's question. Leofdaeg had served with Sigarr the previous year when they sailed to the far north of Britain to speak with the Picts in Dunnottar about an alliance. That expedition had turned to shit when their ship was stolen by the Pictish princess Aife, her friend Catia and, as incredible as it seemed now, Lancelot, famed swordsman of the Britons. Ultimately, the mission had been such a disaster that Leofdaeg had fallen out of favour with the Saxon war-leader, or *bretwalda*, Hengist.

"I've no idea, actually," Sigarr said, wiping sea spray from his face. Somehow, despite being part of endeavours which ended badly for the Saxons, Sigarr was held in high enough regard by his cousin Hengist that he continued to undertake important missions on the *bretwalda's* behalf.

Missions such as this one.

"Do you think the Votadini will agree to an alliance with us?" Cretta asked, quickly forgetting about Leofdaeg as the coastline of their destination came into view through the rain that had lashed at them almost continuously for the best part of the morning. "Things didn't end so well with the Picts after all."

Sigarr snorted humourlessly. He'd also been part of the joint Saxon/Pict army that marched to Alt Clota just a few months ago and besieged the fabled fortress of Dun Breatann. The Picts were led by King Drest, a rather weak individual, while the Saxons were led by Hengist's famously bloodthirsty brother, Horsa. Sigarr, a cousin to Horsa, had done his best to rein in the younger man's cruelty but his constant complaining had seen Horsa send him back south to Hengist. After that, the Damnonii army had rallied thanks to the leadership of the druid, Bellicus, and then attacked the invaders.

15

Even some of the Picts had refused to fight alongside Horsa and his vicious wise-woman, Yngvildr, so the battle was one-sided and ended in a crushing defeat for the Picts and Saxons, with both Drest and Horsa being killed in the fighting.

Like Cretta suggested, it did not exactly paint any alliance with the Saxons in a good light but that was exactly why Sigarr had been chosen for this mission to meet King Cunneda of the Votadini. Hengist admired Sigarr's sharp wit and calculating mind, but whether they would be enough to win the friendship of the Votadini ruler remained to be seen.

"Have you ever visited Dun Edin?" Cretta asked the jarl, eyeing him with, Sigarr thought, disdain. "You know it's another of those bloody hillforts the Northern Britons seem to love so much? Probably a lot of steps."

Sigarr, unlike his cousins, had not been blessed with great physical strength. He could barely run the length of the ship without wheezing. He had come to accept his limitations over the years though, so the fact that his subordinates viewed him as something of a figure of fun no longer angered him. Let people underestimate him – it gave him an advantage over them. Besides, Cretta's comment about how steep Dun Edin would be was quite perceptive and Sigarr nodded.

"I've heard there's a lot of steps," he said. "If I find it too hard you'll have to carry me up, Cretta."

He watched as the comment slowly sank in for the captain who then turned a horrified gaze on the jarl, opening his mouth to protest before realising he was being made fun of. "I'm sure you'll manage, lord," Cretta said at last, unsure whether to smile or bow his head respectfully.

Sigarr turned away, enjoying the man's discomfort. He might not be as cruel as Horsa, or even Hengist, but he was not above humiliating someone if they forgot he was their jarl and the man in command of the mission.

The port that served Dun Edin was familiar to Cretta and his crew for they traded there often, just as they had done with the Picts a hundred miles or so further north. They had soon tied up the ship and disembarked, carrying the gifts Hengist had sent for King Cunneda which were many and varied, some of them quite heavy. To pull it all they hired a wagon and an ox from an old trader at the port who was heading towards Dun Edin, and Sigarr, as commander of the party, jumped onto the wagon as it rattled towards the fortress.

"Looks a lot like Pictland," the jarl opined to no one in particular while they headed along the road, taking in the scenery around them.

"Nothing like it," the old man who was driving his ox retorted in an offended tone. The fact that he'd understood the Saxon tongue was not lost on Sigarr who guessed the trader must have come across many different peoples and cultures during his years on *Miðgarðr*.

"You understand us?" the jarl asked with interest.

"Only a little," the man replied.

"Then I shall talk to you in your own tongue," Sigarr replied using the language he'd learned in order to translate between Hengist and the native Britons. Of course, the Britons all had different dialects, and some of them were totally incomprehensible, but the trader and Sigarr were able to converse freely enough.

"What's your king like?" the Saxon asked innocently.

The trader glanced at him, one eyebrow raised in his seamed forehead. "Oh, he's a lovely person. Everyone around here just thinks the world of him."

Sigarr laughed. "I'm not asking you to incriminate yourself with some treasonous statement," he said. "Just some idea of what to expect when I meet him."

The old man peered at the jarl, appraising his clothing, and the weapons he wore. Grunting in approval, and perhaps impressed by the finery he saw, he turned back to the road and shrugged. "Cunneda is all right, as far as nobles go. Likes a good drink, and a tumble with a wench or two. Not averse to a fight either, although he's getting older and doesn't go out looking for trouble the way he once did."

"He must have been upset about his son, Ysfael, falling in battle?"

The trader side-eyed him again, too wise to fall into any traps the little foreigner in his wagon might be laying for him. "I'm not sure," he drawled at last, pulling on the oxen's halter gently, guiding the wagon around a large dip in the road that was filled with rain which had, mercifully, eased by now. "Cunneda has more than one son, and Ysfael didn't do much with his life. When word came of his death there was a feast, of course, but it wasn't a long one."

17

Sigarr was relieved to hear that, having been part of the army that killed Prince Ysfael, even if he had been banished back to Garrianum by Horsa when the actual battle took place. He'd been a little worried that someone in Cunneda's court would recognise him and the Votadini king would seek revenge for his son's death. It was unlikely, but not impossible, although from the trader's testimony it seemed Ysfael wasn't terribly missed in Dun Edin.

Sigarr noted the contents of the wagon, uttering a low oath as the rickety old thing bounced over a stone and made him fall against a sack. Vegetables, wine, cloth, the trader seemed to deal in anything he could get from the ships in the nearby port. "What does the king like to eat?" Sigarr asked.

That brought a smile to the old man's face, revealing teeth like a row of weathered, rune-carved gravestones. "Salmon," he replied. "Cunneda loves salmon, especially when its fresh. That's what's in the little barrel there. I'll make a nice profit on that lot."

"How much of a profit?"

The trader immediately sensed a chance to make money and a sly look came over his face despite his attempt to mask it. He seemed to think about the question, gauging how much he could take this Saxon jarl for. When he named a price, Sigarr suspected it was at least double the profit he could really make from Cunneda's steward but he was not in a mood to haggle, and he had been given a ride on the man's wagon after all.

"I'll buy it from you for the same price," he said, holding up a finger and wagging it sternly as the trader opened his mouth to haggle. "That's all you're getting, no arguments." His hand dropped to his sword and the old man looked at the sheathed weapon, and then at the much more dangerous looking warriors who accompanied the jarl, and smiled

"Deal," he said.

"Good," Sigarr nodded, fishing in his purse for the hack silver to pay for the salmon. "It'll make a nice gift for the king then. Get us off on the right foot."

"That it will, lord," the trader gurned, showing off his rotten teeth again. "Cunneda just loves his salmon."

They chatted for the rest of the journey which wasn't that far but took a while thanks to the slow pace of the wagon. Sigarr discovered that Cunneda felt no love at all for the Damnonii or the Picts, which was useful intelligence, and then, at last they reached the towering rock that the king's fortress sat upon.

It was steep, as Cretta had guessed, and the ox slowed even more as it trudged uncomplainingly up the winding road towards the gatehouse.

"By Woden," Sigarr said, taking in the view. "I thought Dun Breatann was impressive, but this…"

"Aye," the old trader said proudly. "This is bigger. Legends say the rock is an old volcano, whatever that is."

"Same as Dun Breatann is built upon," Sigarr murmured, fascinated by the fortress and idly searching for ways that an army might force a way inside.

They eventually reached the gatehouse which pleased Sigarr's men for they were annoyed at having to walk so slowly just to accommodate him and his poor lung capacity. It hadn't been that steep a climb and, if not for Sigarr's seat in the wagon, could have been completed much quicker.

"Cretta, grab the barrel of salmon from the cart, there's a good man," the jarl said to his captain.

"Lord," replied Cretta, muscular arms reaching out and easily lifting the barrel as Sigarr watched with a tinge of jealousy. He'd have liked to have that kind of strength but, he reminded himself, it was better that he have the power to command others to lift and lay for him.

"Farewell, my friend," Sigarr said to the trader, receiving a contented smile and a wave in return as they approached the gatehouse separately.

Word had already reached Dun Edin's guards that a boatload of Saxons had sailed into the port that day, so it was not long before Sigarr had explained the purpose of their visit and he and his men were allowed inside the walls – divested of their weapons, naturally, but not the precious barrel of fish.

"Why isn't this king more powerful?" Cretta asked quietly as they were escorted towards the great hall, where Cunneda waited to greet them. "This hillfort is hugely impressive."

Sigarr shrugged. "I'm not sure the Votadini tribe has the numbers the likes of the Damnonii do, or the tribes further south. Cunneda is just lucky enough to have this massive great rock in his lands to build his fortress upon."

19

"Is it even worth courting an alliance with him then?"

They were almost at the hall's open doors now and Sigarr nodded, feeling his stomach give a lurch in anticipation of the royal audience. "We need to make alliances with as many warlords and kings as we can, so of course it's worthwhile. Besides, this is what Hengist commanded me to do so, remember Cretta, keep your men under control. No drunken brawling, or harassing the serving women."

His captain's face fell at that but before he could complain they were ushered into the hall and Cunneda was rising to greet them.

CHAPTER FIVE

The man who'd been hiding in the undergrowth at Ard Sabhal had followed Bellicus and his companions all the way back to Dun Breatann, taking care not to lose sight of them, but making sure they did not see him or, in the case of the massive dog that looked like it would make short work of even a master swordsman, smell him. He remained downwind, tracking them as they walked, laughing and joking without a care in the world although the druid and his friend did not actually relate the story of what had happened to them in the clearing. No doubt Bellicus was planning on telling the tale that night to an enraptured audience of fawning Damnonii nobles.

Saksnot, for that was the hunter's name, curled his lip and spat as he watched his prey from a distance. There had been no need for him to follow them he realised now, for their destination could not be more obvious, dominating the skyline as it did.

Dun Breatann. Saksnot, a Saxon warrior, sat down on the soft grass, careful to make sure he was almost completely concealed by a leafy bush as the Damnonii warriors and the mastiff disappeared through a great wooden gatehouse and were lost from sight. The fortress was impressive, the man was forced to admit. Towering above the river that flowed past its southern edge, the stronghold was situated atop a great, lumpen rock that almost seemed like it had been thrown there aeons ago by some primordial god. No wonder Horsa's army had not been able to capture the place – if it was defended by even a small force of warriors it would be almost impregnable.

That made his task harder, he thought, but not impossible. Nothing was impossible to a man of his talents.

The Saxon *bretwalda*, Hengist, had heard of his brother's fate at the hands of Bellicus and the centurion Duro, and, understandably outraged, sought a volunteer to kill the druid and his friend. Saksnot was young, but he was a ferocious and skilled fighter – he it had been who'd stabbed the old Merlin – High Druid of the Britons – to death mere months before. His fame had spread as a result of that deed, and he had seen this mission as an opportunity to impress Hengist even further. Killing Bellicus would surely see many a song written by the skalds about him. So he had travelled all the way from Garrianum on a fast horse which he'd then sold at a settlement just a couple of miles away from where he stood now, since he'd have nowhere to hide the animal and there was no telling how long it might take for him to kill his two targets.

The would-be executioner's eyes roved across Dun Breatann's grey bulk now, searching for weaknesses, for a spot that might be climbed or otherwise exploited. He picked at the dry skin on his fingertips as he sat beside the bush, utterly lost in thought as he pondered ways to complete his mission.

"Are you well, boy?"

The voice startled him from his reverie and he sprang to his feet, hand resting instinctively on the sword that was hidden beneath his tunic.

"Woah, take it easy," said the man who'd addressed him, an older, weather-beaten fellow who raised his hands as if to prove he had no weapon of his own, although he was actually holding a long, curved staff. "I mean you no harm."

Saksnot did not speak the man's language, but he guessed he was a shepherd from the staff and the presence of the black dog that watched him warily from pale blue eyes. He also guessed, correctly, that the man thought he was a child.

Standing only about five-and-a-half feet tall, and with a slim, wiry build, Saksnot was often mistaken for a youth, especially since he wore no beard. Any time he tried to grow one it was a pitiful, wispy affair that was mocked by the older warriors who'd come to Britain with him. Eventually he'd grown tired of teaching those older men manners and decided to go clean shaven. People always underestimated him as a result of his boyish features and small frame, and he liked it that way. He would exploit any advantage the gods gave him.

"Are you well, boy?" the shepherd repeated. "What are you doing here in these fields? Playing in the stream?" The old man seemed to contemplate that before shaking his head, a suspicious light growing in his watery eyes now. "No, you look too old to be playing like that."

Before the shepherd could say anything else Saksnot had drawn his sword and thrust it into his chest before moving behind the man and slashing him across his throat, drawing a thin bead of crimson that quickly became a terrible gaping wound. The man's eyes

22

widened and he opened his mouth to cry out, but no sound came and he fell with a heavy thud on the grass, blood pooling beneath him.

The Saxon's stance became defensive and he braced for the dog's teeth to sink into his flesh, fully prepared to kill the animal, but the sheepdog wanted no part of the fight and, with a yelp of shock, hared off down the slope and quickly became a dark speck in the distance.

Saksnot bent and wiped the blood from his blade onto the shepherd's tunic before sheathing it again. Then he searched the body for valuables, finding absolutely nothing other than a strip of dried beef that almost broke the Saxon's teeth when he attempted to bite into it.

He stared at the dead man with great interest. He had sent men to their doom before, but in battle, where he'd been forced to move on after the kill. Now he had time to examine the effects death quickly had on the human body and it fascinated him to see how still the body was, how the skin was already changing colour, and how the open eyes did not register anything, even when he waved his hand in front of them.

He was not proud of his actions – killing an old sheep herder was not the kind of glorious deed that would win Saksnot a place in the gods' mead hall when he died himself. He turned back to stare at the fortress atop the rock in the middle distance, imagining himself within those walls, performing feats that would win him fame and glory and a high place at Hengist's feasting table.

With a last look at the man he'd murdered the Saxon started to walk towards Dun Breatann, wondering how he should approach his mission now. He could pretend to be a merchant if he had brought any goods with him to sell – thoughts of stealing such goods crossed his mind but Saksnot had no idea how merchants operated and no wagon to carry many items so such a ruse would likely just arouse suspicion.

Dun Breatann was said to be impossible to break into, with the rock being too steep to climb or, in the few places where it was not, walls had been erected and were patrolled all day. Yet Saksnot believed finding a way inside the fortress undetected would prove the easiest way to take care of the druid. Bellicus's guard would be down, and even when he saw Saksnot he would take him at first for a youth, not as a threat, just as the dead shepherd had done.

Yes, he thought, still walking towards the fortress. I must get in there somehow, and find a way to kill the druid before making my escape. He knew he must be slightly moon-touched to even contemplate such a course of action, but he was not suicidal. He wanted to perform his grisly task and then make it back to Hengist so he could enjoy the rewards the *bretwalda* had promised him back in Garrianum.

He soon reached the main road to Dun Breatann, mingling with other travellers who were going in the same direction, blending in so well that no one gave him a second glance. With it being such a hot day there were people swimming in the nearby river and Saksnot walked along the pebbled beach as if he was part of one of those groups. A short distance away was a port where sailors were loading and unloading ships, or simply lounging in the fading sun. On the walls of the fortress guards were visible – not very many, but there would undoubtedly be more within the walls, dozens at least. On the summit of one peak, the eastern one, were the dwellings and workhouses of the Damnonii. Smoke drifted from the roof holes although they were so high above the ground that no other details could properly be discerned.

Saksnot took all this in as he strolled along the beach past the ships at the port before reaching a point where he could go no further, unless he wanted to swim. That would draw unwanted attention for no one else was in the water there, but the Saxon could, from that vantage point, see another wall on the western edge of the rock, protecting the fortress from anyone who might try to break inside from that point. That particular wall was set much lower than the others Saksnot had seen so far. So low, in fact, that he was quite certain he could climb up to it without much trouble. He was slim, some would even say skinny, but stronger than he looked and agile too. Still, reaching the wall was one thing, getting over it safely another. He would need to plan carefully.

A guard walked to the end of nearby wall, helmeted head glinting in the sunshine before turning and making his way back to the other end of the walkway. Saksnot stood, trying to be as inconspicuous as possible as he waited to see if any more guards would come to patrol the wall. One did but there was a gap between the new one and the first one, and Saksnot knew he could exploit that gap, if it was a regular one.

He turned and walked back the way he'd come, kicking the odd shell or pebble like a child would do, drawing only disinterested glances from those he passed. His mind raced as he moved, making plans, trying to decide if he needed equipment such as a rope or a disguise. He would certainly need the former if he wanted to leave Dun Breatann by the same route as he hoped to get in – a rope would allow him to climb down much, much faster than if he was searching for hand- and footholds. As for a disguise, he did not think it necessary. All being well he would sneak into the fortress, take care of any guards quietly, and then make his way to wherever the druid could be found.

Where might that be? he wondered. Well, he would need to know if his plan was to be a success, but how could he find out? Who could he ask that would understand his Saxon tongue?

One of the ships at the port was crewed by tall, fair haired men with impressive beards.

"Where are you from, friend?" Saksnot asked, stopping beside one of the sailors whose hair was more grey than fair. He had a kindly face and sparkling blue eyes that spoke of humour as much as they did a lifetime downing mead.

The man looked at him in surprise and Saksnot knew immediately that he had guessed right – this was a Saxon ship. That was confirmed when the sailor replied, "You speak our tongue?"

"Ja," Saksnot confirmed with a crooked smile. "I travel with an old trader from a village to the far south. He is a Saxon, and so am I."

The sailor looked around for the trader but, seeing no one, returned his gaze to the beardless youngster. "Your master comes at a good time, for the Damnonii have just fought a war and need supplies of all kinds. That's why we're here. We hail from Jutland originally but settled over the western sea from here, in Hibernia."

Saksnot nodded as if he approved of the sailor's life choices although he secretly thought the man a coward, forsaking a glorious life of raiding for that of a peaceful sailor. "Have you been in the fortress?" he asked, shading his eyes as he looked up at Dun Breatann's peaks. "My master is away in to talk with," he shrugged and smiled stupidly, "whoever buys his wares. I would have liked to go with him, but the guards told me to stay out here. I was hoping to see the druid everyone talks about – Bellicus? Have you heard of him?"

"Oh, *ja*," the sailor said, nodding his head vigorously. "A giant of a man, and his dog is almost as big! I was in the fortress once, and saw him in passing."

"He lives in there?"

"He does. He has a house halfway up, between the two peaks. Cosy little place, although he shares it with some Roman legionary." The sailor pointed to the lower, eastern peak. The man leaned in and said in a lecherous tone, "Word is, the druid's just married the queen. Lucky bastard. The queen is a beauty, especially when you spend all day, every day, looking at the ugly bastards in my crew. Wouldn't mind ploughing that field myself, lad, know what I mean?" He cackled, breaking off when a fit of coughing struck and he ended by hawking a great ball of phlegm onto the beach. An angry shout came from the ship behind him and he called something back before saying to Saksnot, "I have to go. Sveinn is complaining about me not working hard enough again. Farewell, lad. I hope your master treats you well."

Saksnot smiled and waved to the man before wandering off, eyes fixed on the distant dwellings on Dun Breatann, trying to imagine what the druid's house would look like and, more importantly, how he could get inside it.

CHAPTER SIX

"By all the gods, Merlin, are you insane?"

The newly elected High Druid of Britain, a white bearded Pict called Qunavo, smiled and shrugged at the warlord's question. "Perhaps, Arthur, but my proposal is not mad. It makes perfect sense, lord, as you would see if you'd only take a moment to think about it rationally."

Arthur, a wiry man of around thirty with a neat brown beard and long, wavy hair that was slightly receding, stroked his chin irritably. Not a king, Arthur was a warlord, given command of an army by the rulers of central and southern Britain and charged with protecting their lands from invaders, most notably the Saxons. He looked from Qunavo to his three closest friends and advisors, Lancelot, Bedwyr, and Kay. "What say you three?" he demanded. "Is our new Merlin's plan a mad one, or not?"

Qunavo had only become Merlin in the spring, when the previous High Druid, Nemias, was murdered during the terrible raid by the Saxons. Arthur had been very close to Nemias and it had been a terrible blow for the young warlord to deal with the death of his friend and confidant. It was also proving difficult for him to warm to Nemias's replacement – not because Qunavo was particularly hard to get along with, but simply because he was not Nemias. It would take time for Arthur to trust and accept the Pictish druid fully into his inner circle but both men were, supposedly, working towards the same goal of uniting the tribes of Britain and defeating the Saxon invaders who served Hengist.

Qunavo had come to Arthur that morning with this new proposal that Arthur was finding so hard to accept: that Arthur and his warriors befriend those Saxons who had settled peacefully within Britain's villages, and even seek to recruit them in the army.

They were all sitting outside in the summer sunshine, enjoying the warmth and the gentle sounds of nature all around them. Arthur was not a king, and had no fortress of his own, but he was generally welcomed by the Britons wherever he went with his army and at the moment they were in Duroliponte, helping the local king to strengthen his defences against Hengist's encroaching Saxons.

"It seems a little like welcoming the fox in to guard the henhouse," Lancelot said, echoing Arthur's own thoughts on the matter. "I fucking hate the Saxons, and I wouldn't trust any of them, even those who have supposedly settled peacefully here."

Arthur nodded. Lancelot was his best friend, and the greatest swordsman of all the Britons. He also had good reason to despise the invaders after being enslaved by one of them for a time, suffering inhumane treatment at the hands of the Saxon jarl Leofdaeg before he was freed by Princess Catia of the Damnonii and Princess Aife, now Queen, of the Picts.

Kay grunted agreement with his companions. He generally went along with whatever Arthur suggested and he proclaimed now that he did not want to befriend any Saxons. This despite the fact that he looked just like one of the sea-wolves and could, indeed had, passed for them on occasion.

Bedwyr hailed from Powys like Kay, but he was a more thoughtful man, less likely to react instinctively than the others, and perhaps more open to unorthodox ideas such as that put forward by the new Merlin. "I think it might be worth trying," he said with a shrug. "The Saxons aren't going away; they're here to stay, and there's nothing we can do about it." He held out his hands as if imploring Arthur to think more on Qunavo's suggestion. "By all accounts many of the Saxons have integrated perfectly well with our own folk. Living and working side by side peacefully, and even intermarrying."

"They're still Saxons," Lancelot growled. "And always will be. Trusting them, letting them serve in our army, would be folly."

"Trouble waiting to happen," Kay agreed.

"It's trouble waiting to happen no matter what we do," Qunavo argued. "Some of the men who came here from Saxon lands to settle will live in peace no matter what. Those who are not warriors but farmers, labourers, craftsmen, builders. We need not worry about them – the opposite, in fact, for they will prove valuable members of our communities."

Arthur listened thoughtfully, occasionally sipping wine that had been cooled in the brook that babbled close to where they sat.

"Then there are the men who came here as warriors before growing disillusioned with the life of a soldier. Perhaps they'd seen too many friends die in battle, or they fell in love with a local girl, or they simply realised life would be easier – and longer – if they laid down their axes and lived peacefully alongside our people."

The other men took in Qunavo's words, starting to understand where his thoughts had led him.

Lancelot batted a wasp away from his face and stood up, wandering to the brook and lifting the amphora that lay cooling in the water. "Those Saxons will always be a threat," he said, filling his cup and replacing the amphora before coming back to take his seat again. "Is that what you mean?"

The Merlin nodded emphatically. "Precisely. While we're at war with Hengist, those former warriors of his could potentially be a threat to us. At any moment they could take up arms once more, their ties of blood and birth drawing them back to support their *bretwalda*."

"So we befriend them," Bedwyr said. "Make them loyal to us?"

"Aye," Qunavo replied. "Even if they don't want to fight for us, at least it might make them think twice about fighting against us should Hengist call on them."

The men sat in silence, sipping their wine and thinking over the ramifications of the High Druid's plan. On a day like that – with birds singing in the lush green foliage, sun beating down, and only the normal, peaceful sounds of a village at work to disturb their gentle inebriation – it was hard to think of the brutality of war. Yet all of them, including Qunavo, had seen the effects of Hengist's sea-wolves at close hand, had seen friends and companions hacked apart by Saxon swords and axes, and they knew that the peace in Duroliponte would not last forever. Hengist's influence was on the rise again as he took control of more and more land with each passing week and the possibility of peaceful Saxon settlers being reactivated as marauding sea-wolves was a threat that could not be ignored any longer.

"You're right," Arthur said, and, as was so often his way, now that he'd been persuaded to a course of action his eyes shone with the possibilities and thoughts of a glorious future. His friends knew this trait well and Bedwyr and Kay laughed while Lancelot groaned and shook his head while running a hand through his hair.

"Still not convinced?" Qunavo asked the blond swordsman.

"I just have an aversion to befriending Saxons," Lancelot admitted with a wry smile. "I've lived amongst them, remember. I know what they're like."

29

"They're not all the same," Bedwyr said. "I understand why you feel the way you do, my friend, but you were a slave for a vicious, cruel bastard."

Lancelot nodded bleakly. "Leofdaeg was certainly that."

"But we're talking about normal people who just want to live an easy life, not bloodthirsty sea-wolves intent on conquest and winning renown in battle."

"Even normal people can become bloodthirsty when they're part of an army," Lancelot returned, blue eyes searching out those of his companions who all looked away uncomfortably, knowing he was right.

"Then we must stop them from joining Hengist's army," said Qunavo firmly. "And the best way to do that is to make them feel welcome in our lands, not to shun them and make them always feel like outsiders."

"I do believe he's right," Arthur put in. "Let's give these settlers a chance to become good Britons, and live with us as equals."

Lancelot sighed. He'd suffered greatly during his time as Leofdaeg's thrall – not just physically from the beatings and starvation he'd been subjected to, but mentally. Being kept as another's man's slave was no way to live for a proud warrior like Lancelot. He would never be able to think of Saxons as anything other than a vicious people. He was outvoted though, and his usual easy smile returned to his face as he shook his head and downed the last drop of his wine. "Fine," he shrugged. "We'll do as Qunavo says. I just pray to the gods that we don't live to regret it."

"Regret? I don't think so," Arthur said happily, clearly pleased to have won over his closest friend. "We could even win a few hardy new recruits to our army, and Taranis knows we're always needing more men."

"Indeed," Qunavo smiled. "It worked for the Romans, after all, and look at their mighty empire. It lasted for aeons, and all thanks to the way they recruited other peoples to their ranks."

"Like Duro," Arthur said, grinning almost triumphantly over at Lancelot. "You're friends with the centurion, aren't you? Duro fought for the Romans, but now he fights for us. The Saxons in our settlements will do the same, I have no doubt of it."

Lancelot didn't reply and Kay moved the conversation on by asking how, exactly, Qunavo saw them doing what he suggested.

"Send men out to the towns and villages in the east," the Merlin told them. "See if we can recruit some of the Saxons who've settled there. They'd be the first ones Hengist would look to for aid if he needs it, so they should be the ones we target first too."

Arthur looked to Bedwyr who was the ideal man for a job such as this, being competent, methodical, friendly, and clever. He was also a fearsome warrior when called upon, a quality that might just be needed. "What do you think?" the warlord asked him.

"I'll do it, of course, lord," Bedwyr replied. "In fact, I'll start right here, in Duroliponte. I know there are foreign settlers here and this is as good a place to begin as any. Will you, come with me, Merlin?"

"Me?"

"It was your idea," Kay reminded him.

"Yes, but—"

"I'll probably need an interpreter," Bedwyr added. "I can speak a little of the Saxons' tongue, but you druids know all sorts of languages, don't you?"

Qunavo laughed, knowing he was beat. "Fair enough," he said. "I'll come this first time, but I have duties beside advising Arthur. I can't simply go riding around all the towns in eastern Britain. You'll have to make do with your own grasp of the Saxon tongue after this, or we'll find someone else to travel with you who can speak fluent sea-wolf."

"All right," said Bedwyr happily. "Let's go then."

"We should visit King Hywel first," the Merlin suggested as they moved off towards the town. "These are his lands, and he'll probably know any Saxons living and working within Duroliponte. He can tell us where to start."

"Good luck," Arthur called after them, receiving cheery waves in reply.

"I really hope you know what you're doing," Lancelot said gloomily as their companions disappeared amongst the low buildings to the north.

"Stop worrying," Arthur told him. "I have a good feeling about this. Things will work out well, you'll see."

31

CHAPTER SEVEN

Night fell and a sliver of moon occasionally appeared from between the clouds that had rolled in with the setting sun. Saksnot thanked Woden for the darkness, since a full moon would perhaps have made him visible when he began the climb up Dun Breatann's rocky face. The thought made the blood thunder in his veins and he moved swiftly and silently across the beach towards his destination.

When it had started to grow dark the Saxon managed to steal a length of rope from one of the fishing vessels hauled up on the shore a short distance from the fortress. He'd tied a thick piece of timber around one end of that rope and fervently hoped it would allow him to climb up the section of wooden wall that ostensibly protected Dun Breatann from the likes of Saksnot. If it did not, he would need to come up with another plan.

At this point, another, less confident man, might have realised he was placing too much in the lap of the gods, trusting one-eyed Woden to guide him and ensure his mission was a success. Saksnot was brash and arrogant, though, and his faith in the gods was as strong as that of any of the Germanic wise-women known as *volur*. The gods had brought him all the way from Garrianum to Dun Breatann without trouble after all, so why would they abandon him now?

He paused as a man shouted, half drawing his sword in preparation for a fight, but it was just a drunken sailor, reeling across the deck of a nearby ship that was moored out on the river. Saksnot looked at the vessel, shaking his head in disgust at the inebriated fool who was probably supposed to be guarding it while his shipmates spent the night on shore.

Moving onwards to the nearby wall again the Saxon hoped the guards in Dun Breatann would be similarly lax, although he rather doubted they would be drunk.

He reached the spot he'd selected for his ascent, praying it would prove suitable. He'd not been able to get too close earlier for fear of drawing attention to himself so it was only now, in the darkness, that he was able to inspect possible handholds and discover if he would even be able to make it up from there. Voices from above made him press his body against the wall and he froze, holding his breath.

It soon became apparent he'd not been spotted creeping along in the gloom, but the low voices overhead did not fade as he hoped. There were guards up there, and it seemed like they were in no hurry to move off on patrol. Saksnot waited patiently, the crescent moon traversing the sky while he stood there as still as a corpse, but it eventually became clear that the guards were not going to move.

Has to be a shelter or something, he thought. A place the guards retired to for a break from patrolling, or before their shift began. Even if Saksnot was able to climb up there he would, it seemed, come over the wall and be met by at least a couple of Damnonii soldiers. He did not doubt he could kill them in a fight, but the alarm would surely be raised and his mission would be over before it had even begun.

Abandoning his plan, he decided to move further westwards, to the very end of the wall. It would certainly be quieter there, although it meant he would need to sneak further back to reach the centre of the fortress. There was nothing else for it however, so he walked and eventually came to the river which lapped right up against the rock at this point.

No wonder there were so few guards at this section of the fortress – the water provided a natural barrier that would stop any army from progressing. Still, Saksnot was not an army, he was just one man, and he had Woden on his side.

By now it was fully night and even the drunken sailor had fallen silent. Waiting for more clouds to hide the moon's meagre light the Saxon crept back along the beach, squinting into the darkness until, at last, he found an old coracle that had been left behind. He lifted it and moved back the way he'd come until, when he felt he was far enough away from prying eyes, he put the little boat down and examined it with his hands. Had the thing been abandoned because it had a hole, or some even worse structural defect?

Saksnot could find nothing obvious in the darkness so there was only one way to find out if it was seaworthy, and he wasted no time in placing it into the water. Unfortunately there had been no paddle with the coracle so the young warrior was forced to use his hands to power it along the river. The water was not deep here but the incoming tide pushed him back towards the shore continuously and he feared the bumping of the tiny vessel against the towering rock might attract the attention of the guards.

No shouts disturbed his slow, bobbing progress though, and he eventually came to a point that he thought would be ideal for him to make his climb. His hands reached out and sought for crevices, or weeds to grab firm hold of and, in spite of the gloom, he was able to locate some that he judged would support his weight.

Taking a long, excited breath, he slowly, carefully, climbed out of the coracle and started his ascent. It was not a particularly difficult task, but it was slow going as he constantly had to readjust his weight and once even lost his footing, almost falling into the water below. Sweating profusely, he righted himself, breath shuddering and a low chuckle escaped his lips before he resumed the climb, wondering when he would finally come to the smooth wall that would provide his greatest obstacle.

Suddenly the rock above him lit up and the steady thump of shod feet came towards him. A guard was on patrol, and carrying a torch which seemed almost blinding to Saksnot's dark-accustomed eyes. The orange flame cast flickering shadows on the rock both above and below, and, when the Saxon glanced down Saksnot could see his stolen coracle drifting away towards the centre of the Clota. There would be no return to shore via that little vessel, he thought, but caring little about the prospect of a hasty swim once he'd completed his mission and returned here to make his escape.

Overhead, the guard stopped almost directly above him and looked out along the night-enshrouded river and the few distant lights that were visible on the far shore. Saksnot stared unblinkingly up at the Damnonii warrior who muttered something to himself before the flickering torch moved suddenly off, back towards the main gates, leaving that section of wall in darkness once more.

Saksnot had hoped to stay there, waiting for the next guard to come along so he had some idea of the timings of their patrols, but his calves were burning from trying to balance upon the slim rock edges, and his fingers ached from the unaccustomed exertions. He knew he must make his move now, or he'd end up crashing into the water and probably to his doom. He guessed he was thirty or forty feet up and a fall of that distance would surely be injurious if not fatal.

Doing his best to slow his breathing he pushed aside thoughts of falling and carefully took the looped rope from his shoulder. He gathered it in his hands and looked up, trying to remember exactly where he'd seen the guard moments before. And then, with a plea to Woden, he threw the line upwards.

There was a clatter, shockingly loud in the silence, as the length of wood on the end of the rope knocked against the wall, and then Saksnot braced himself, realising he'd missed his target. Desperately he tried to haul the falling rope into his body but he was far too slow and, again, the wood cracked against the rock, this time below, jarring the climber's arms and drenching his body in sweat as he hung on for dear life, all the while dreading the return of the flickering, orange glow of the guard's torch that would herald his discovery, and death.

"Gods protect me," he almost sobbed, his earlier exuberance now completely gone. Who knew it would be so difficult to climb up to this lower section of wall?

He drew in the rope once more, checking with his hands to make sure the piece of wood had not been damaged. It seemed intact, and no running feet came to investigate the noises his poor throw had produced, Woden be praised.

Steadying himself, he tried once more, launching the rope into the air. There was another clatter as the wood hit the wall but this time it did not fall back down and, when Saksnot pulled gingerly on it his muscles tightened as it held fast to something above. He had done it!

Throwing caution to the wind now he gripped the rope, gave it one more hard tug to be certain it was securely lodged in place, and then he started to climb.

His arms protested as he moved and he gritted his teeth, forcing himself to keep going, wishing he could see how much further he had to go. Surely he was nearly there, he prayed. He had to be, for his strength was almost gone.

At last his right hand grasped only air and he almost cried out in relief, grabbing the top of the wall and dragging his body over it. He fell with a low thud on the walkway, disoriented and shaking from exertion, but he stared, wide-eyed in the direction he expected the next patrol to come from and drew out his sword.

If a guard had appeared then Saksnot would have been unable to protect himself for he was completely spent and he knew it. He hauled himself over to the rock face which stretched into the night, pressing himself against it and sucking in deep, steadying breaths as he tried to calm his churning thoughts. He allowed himself a few moments to simply rest, relieved to feel the searing pain in his thighs and biceps receding at last, and then he went back to the wall and pulled up his rope, stashing it behind a boulder beside the walkway.

He could see practically nothing, but he cast about the ground carefully with his palms, finally understanding that the wall was attached to a wooden walkway but, beside that, there was a narrow strip of grass that butted up against the ascending rock face. He felt along it until he came to a place where the rock projected out just about a foot or so, and he pushed his body against it, hoping it would conceal him from the next guard who came to check that this section of the fortress was free of enemies.

He had done it! He was inside the apparently impregnable fortress, and he was alive, uninjured, and undetected.

Now all he had to do was make it up to the middle, and the house the old sailor had told him housed both the druid and the centurion. Soon, Saksnot thought with a triumphant grin, Bellicus of Dun Breatann, and his friend Duro, would be dead.

CHAPTER EIGHT

The Saxon closed his eyes as he heard the slow, repetitive thump of a guard's feet coming towards him. He visualised how the fight should go, with his sword slipping easily into the enemy's back, incapacitating him if not killing him immediately. It would be over in a heartbeat and Saksnot would be free to move deeper into the fortress, unscathed. He played out the scene in his mind, allowing himself to imagine things that might go wrong and how he would deal with them. His breath was calm and steady and his body felt strangely rested after his torturous climb. The advantage of being young, he smiled, wondering how old the guard he was about to kill might be.

He drew in a breath and let it out, opening his eyes, gripping the handle of his sword and watching as the walkway was illuminated by another torch. The scent of burning fat filled the air, its acrid smoke preceding the guards, suggesting the wind was blowing westwards. Saksnot was pleased, knowing he was downwind of his enemy but quickly realising it mattered little – even the great dog that had been with the druid earlier in the day would be unlikely to smell him over the stench of the torch.

His idle, almost pleasant thoughts were rudely disturbed when he heard a man speak on the walkway nearby, and, shockingly, another voice responded.

There were two guards coming on patrol this time, not just one.

Saksnot's mind raced as he pondered the significance of this development. Had someone noticed him climbing the rock, or heard his clumsy first attempt to hook his rope on the wall? Was that why two guards had been sent here? Were there even more than two?

The Saxon didn't have long to fret for an instant later the first Damnonii soldier stepped into view, heavy leather boots clumping along on the wood. They were not attempting to conceal their approach, Saksnot thought, so that meant they did not know he was there. He waited a moment longer until the second guard came into view and then, without a sound he thrust his sword out, into the man's side. In the bright torchlight the guard stared at him in amazement, before his expression turned to horror and he opened his mouth to cry out. Saksnot smashed his head into the guard's nose

37

and, instantly, sharp pain flashed in the Saxon's own skull for the Damnonii soldier was wearing a helmet.

"What the—?" the first guard spun at the sound, staring, dumbfounded at the sight of his companion on his knees, groaning, and a stranger holding his forehead, a long blade dripping with blood in his hand.

Saksnot forced himself to move despite the blinding pain that threatened to make him pass out, lunging with his sword at the guard holding the torch.

The man dodged backwards, having, at last, understood the mortal danger he was in. He seemed unsure what to do with his torch though – should he drop it and free both his hands for the fight even though it would plunge the wall into darkness and possibly even start a fire?

Before he could make his mind up Saksnot's sword flashed through the air, slicing deeply into the guard's right arm. The man grunted and instinctively lashed out with his other hand – the one holding the torch.

Saksnot screamed as the flames engulfed his face and he punched his blade into the Damnonii soldier's side once, twice, three times, before kicking the man backwards to slump against the wall. The torch fell from lifeless fingers but it did not go out, the animal fat that fuelled it continuing to cast an eerie glow on the scene as Saksnot sucked horrified gasps through his teeth, wondering how badly injured he was.

He looked down at the first guard he'd stabbed. The man was still moving so Saksnot stabbed him again and then, with quite some trouble, lifted him over the wall and dropped him with a resounding splash into the water beneath.

"Woden's balls," Saksnot sobbed, terror filling him at the thought that such a loud splash, never mind his own scream as the torch burned him, would be heard by the other guards further along the wall. He knew he couldn't leave the second corpse lying there however, no matter how much noise it would make when tossed into the river. The next patrol to come along would raise the alarm when they saw their comrade's body and that would be it for the Saxon's mission. So, with even greater difficulty, for this guard was older and fatter than the first, Saksnot pulled him up and somehow shoved him over the wall too, cringing at the splash the corpse produced.

He lifted the torch then, frightened it might set alight to the whole walkway. It had left a black burn mark on the wood but that was the extent of the damage, mercifully, and he dropped it into river, the sudden return of total darkness momentarily disorienting him.

He stood catching his breath, touching his face gently with his left hand and whimpering at the pain he felt there. He knew that pain would only grow worse if he did not tend to the burns, but there was nothing he could do about it unless he abandoned his mission and, after getting this far, Saksnot was loath to give up.

The burns hurt terribly, but he did not think they would kill him. He had to go on, for he would never get the chance to break into Dun Breatann like this again. Woden had carried him that far, it would be wrong to turn back when he'd done the hardest part.

The waves seemed to crash invitingly against the beach below as he made his way cautiously along the walkway. He imagined immersing his seared face in the cool water and told himself he'd wallow in it just as soon as he'd killed the druid and the centurion.

Another light came into view as he rounded a bend and he guessed this must be where the little guardhouse was located. He could not hesitate for time was of the essence now that he'd made two of the guards 'disappear', so he crept ahead, towards the wooden hovel where he could hear guards talking in low tones.

Could he kill them like he'd done the others? Maybe. His face pained him, but he was otherwise uninjured. Still, taking on more than one man at a time was a risk – one might not even fight, just run for help, and that would mean disaster for Saksnot. So, he slipped up to the small guardhouse which, he saw now that he was close, could only really shelter three or four men at most and was lit up by not a torch, but a brazier. He crouched behind the building and listened.

There were two voices, no more, which was something of a relief, and they sounded bored, even sleepy. Evidently they were not alarmed, yet, by the fact their companions had not returned. Saksnot waited until one of the men let out a long, exaggerated yawn, and the Saxon took the chance to move on, past the squat building, hugging the shadows until he reached a great central staircase that had been built right up between Dun Breatann's twin peaks.

He sheathed his sword for it would immediately draw attention if he was spotted, and hurried up the steps. There were a lot of them and, on top of his earlier exertions, he was soon quite tired. On top of that, dismay threatened to overwhelm him when he realised there was yet another guardhouse at the top of the steps, with another brazier at the side. There was no way to get past and onto the middle portion of the fortress without passing through the light from that accursed brazier and Saksnot was becoming desperate, so he hastened upwards.

"Woden bless me," he whispered, eyes fixed on the new guardhouse which was even smaller than the one further down. One man was in it, but he was dozing and, without slowing, Saksnot crept past, expecting to be challenged at any moment. No sound escaped the drowsing guard's lips however and the Saxon reached a flat pathway that led off in two directions.

Almost crying with relief he eased himself into the shadow of two tall trees and crouched to regain his breath and his composure. Gods, it had been a long night, but he must – must! – be near his quarry by now. He thought back to his conversation with the old sot on the ship earlier, and the man's assertion that the druid, Bellicus, lived in a low house right here in the centre of the fortress.

Casting his eyes along the path, Saksnot could see to his right yet more stairs leading upwards to the western peak, while at the end of the path to the left stood a large hall that the Damnonii people must use for feasting, and there, just a few paces from where the Saxon crouched, was a low house with a strange stone head attached to the door frame.

No one seemed to be around, hardly surprising at this time of the night, so the Saxon moved forward for a closer look at the stone head. It was just visible in the light from the brazier at the nearby guardhouse and the sight made Saksnot shudder for it depicted an incredibly sinister face with shallow holes for eyes and a hideous, gaping mouth, but no other features. The young man guessed it was supposed to represent some eldritch god the Damnonii druid worshipped – quite a difference from the likes of heroic Woden or Thunor!

A low voice split the silence and Saksnot shrank back into the shadows beside the house. He grimaced at the sound and the facial movement reminded him of the damage to his face. Angrily, he gripped his sword, vowing to kill anyone who challenged him.

The voice had come from a guard, but the man was simply greeting his comrade in the nearby guardhouse. When he received a reply from the dozing occupant of the guardhouse the man moved off, up the next flight of stairs to continue his patrol. Clearly, the alarm had not been raised yet over the two soldiers that were now floating in the Clota.

Steeling himself, Saksnot crept back around to the front of the druid's house, glancing once more at the stone head nailed there but assuring himself that his own Saxon gods would protect him from any malevolent force. He hesitated for just a moment, suddenly remembering the enormous dog that had accompanied the druid earlier that day and wondering if the hound was within the low building. That was all he needed – dog bites to go with the blistered flesh on his face!

He was right at Bellicus's door though, and there was no turning back, no matter what awaited him inside the house.

He gently lifted the latch, praying the door would not be bolted on the inside. There was a soft squeak as metal grated against metal, and then the latch was free and the door swung open.

Saksnot slipped inside, fearing another patrol would come along and spot him. He could hear soft snoring from the corner on the right of the house and he wished he knew the layout of the place. Was it simply one long room, as he expected? Or was there a partition in the middle to give druid and centurion privacy? Were there chests or tables or other obstructions on the floor that he might bump into and alert the inhabitants to his approach?

He could not linger and there was no way to light his path so, with an indrawn, almost joyful breath, he stepped softly through the house until he stood beside a bed with its snoring occupant sheathed his sword, and drew his knife for the bloody work to come.

CHAPTER NINE

It was not completely pitch black within the house. Saksnot's eyes had grown used to the meagre light cast by the torches and braziers dotted around the fortress but now that he'd been inside the unlit house for a few moments he was able to discern dim shapes and outlines. There was only one bed, only once occupant in spite of what the sailor had claimed, and Saksnot could just make out the head of the man Hengist had sent him there to kill.

This was not ideal – he would need to dispatch the druid, and then somehow find a way to kill the centurion as well. How, though? No matter, the druid was his main target, and Hengist would surely be perfectly happy with that one's death if things went awry.

The Saxon knew he should simply draw his blade across the sleeping figure's throat and make his escape, but pride stayed his hand temporarily. He'd imagined this moment, even dreamt about it on his long, lonely journey here from Garrianum. Murdering a man when he was asleep was far, far too little reward for what he'd endured to get in here. And this was no ordinary man either, not some filthy shepherd like the one he'd killed earlier – this was Bellicus of Dun Breatann, the man who'd foiled Saxon plans so many times over the years, and killed many proud sea-wolves.

Saksnot wanted the big bastard to know he was about to die, and who it was who wielded the blade.

"Hengist commanded me to kill you, druid," he hissed, grinning with excitement as his victim's eyes flared open, startlingly white in the gloom. "Tell the gods it was Saksnot of Egtved who sent your soul screaming to the afterlife!"

He punched his blade into the man's body, feeling warm blood coating his hand. The immediate sense of triumph was fleeting however, as he felt a beefy fist crash into his jaw with unimaginable power. He fell back, the dark room seeming to become instantly blindingly bright as stars exploded in his vision. Desperately, he began hacking at the air in front of him, fearing a second punch like the first. His blade bit home again and he heard a small cry of pain before he managed to thrust the knife into something more substantial, perhaps the druid's chest or guts, and then, knowing he must escape before the guards came to investigate the commotion, he ran to the door and peered outside.

There was no one around on the path or near the guardhouse, and the druid lay wheezing and gasping for breath as he bled out on the bed. Saksnot had done as Hengist commanded and taken the druid's life, but now he had to make it back to his *bretwalda* and claim the rewards he so richly deserved.

There seemed little point in stealth now, the Saxon simply had to get back down to the lower wall and ascend his rope to the river. Thoughts of moving on to hunt for the centurion were gone now – speed was of the essence, and he knew his route back to the bottom of the fortress was only lightly guarded so he threw up the hood on his cloak and started walking. The knife had been more appropriate within the cramped confines of the druid's quarters, but he put it away now and drew out his sword, feeling more secure out in the open with the longer blade in his hand.

The blood was thundering in his veins from the fight in Bellicus's house and he was in no mood to even attempt to sneak past the nearby guardhouse. Instead, he approached it without masking his footsteps, as if he was a Damnonii guard doing his rounds, and then looked into the tiny wooden building at the man who was supposed to be watching for invaders. The guard was not dozing this time, he was wide awake and their eyes locked momentarily before Saksnot plunged his sword into the enemy's heart.

It was a good, mortal blow and the Saxon quickly turned and half walked, half ran down the steps that would take him to freedom. He stared at his destination, feeling as if it was never growing closer until, thank Woden, he reached the bottom and paused once more.

He was breathing heavily but the rush of blood from his killings was beginning to fade and he became slowly aware of the toll his exploits had taken on his body. The skin on his face felt like it was still on fire and he feared he would be terribly scarred for life. On top of that, the thunderous punch the druid had landed must have broken his jaw and the pain from that was, somehow, even worse than the agonising burns. He was only twenty years old, yet this mission would leave him as battle worn and used up as a grizzled warrior of fifty.

He was alive though, dammit!

He could not allow himself to give in to despair so, with tears blurring his vision, he crept to the back of the lower guardhouse, avoiding the pool of radiance cast by the brazier in front of it. He could hear a man within the structure murmuring a low tune to himself, but there was no conversation as there had been the first time Saksnot passed by. That suggested the second guard was patrolling and, since he hadn't come up the stairs leading to the druid's house, that must mean...

"Raise the alarm!"

The Saxon could not understand the words the man was shouting but he could guess. As Saksnot feared, this guard had gone looking for his missing comrades and must have spotted the blood on the walkway. Now the entire garrison would be roused, and escape would be impossible!

Panic filled the young man and tears rolled down his cheeks, the salt making his burns sting even more. He readied himself to launch one last, desperate attack on the two guards, knowing it was his only chance, but all was not lost yet, for, as one man ran up the steps shouting for help, the other ran down towards the main gatehouse to rouse the warriors there.

Saksnot's path to the river was clear!

Relief washed over him and he ran as fast as his tired legs would carry him, west, along the walkway towards his stowed rope. Shouts filled the air above, beneath, and behind him but it only took moments to reach the end of the wall. He scrabbled around at the rockface, hunting for the rope, terrified that someone had found and removed it; if they had, he would need to jump over, into the river, and he knew there was a good chance he would not survive such a fall in one piece.

At last, questing fingers fell upon his hidden salvation and, thanking the gods loudly, he ran to the wall and wedged the piece of wood into one of the crenelations, dropping the rope down to the Clota.

Even with the rope to climb down, and although this was the lowest wall in the fortress, descending was still a daunting, frightening prospect and his palms began to sweat at the thought. The sliver of moon had poked out of the clouds momentarily and its pale light showed the rippling waters lapping against the rock beneath.

Everyone within Dun Breatann must be awake by now, Saksnot guessed, and he heard the sounds of many soldiers running up and down the stairs. When the thumping of boots shook the walkway he was standing on, the Saxon pushed himself up on shaking arms and climbed over the wall.

He gripped the rope fiercely as he began the descent, eyes constantly facing upwards, watching as a torch approached the spot where his rope was attached to the wall. He glanced over his shoulder, realising he was almost at the water, and pushed his feet against the rock with every ounce of strength he could muster.

He swung out into the night air and let go of the rope. A moment later he hit the surface of the Clota and the breath was blasted from his lungs at the shock of the icy water. Terrified, he wasn't sure which way was up, and he worked his arms and legs in desperation, finally – oh, praise Woden! – breaking the surface and sucking in air.

He'd made it out of the fortress! Now all he had to do was get out of the river and evade capture. A face was peering down at him from the wall above, flickering torchlight revealing the hatred in the Damnonii warrior's features before it turned and disappeared, the orange light tracing its way hurriedly back towards the centre of the fortress.

The garrison would soon be converging on his position, commandeering boats and searching the land all around Dun Breatann for him. The pain in his jaw and his face was almost unbearable as he came to the conclusion that he would never make it back to Garrianum, and then something struck him in the side of the head.

Gasping in fear and trying without much success to draw his sword from his scabbard under the water, he turned to face his attacker and burst out laughing. It was only a momentary joy for agony flared as he opened his mouth and he quickly closed it, thanking the gods again, for it was not an attacker that had hit him.

It was his stolen coracle, and within moments he was inside the little vessel and paddling with his hands southwards, towards the lands on the other side of the Clota and, surely, freedom.

CHAPTER TEN

"What's going on?" Bellicus asked, groggily knuckling sleep from his eyes as he sat up and reached for his staff which was propped beside his bed as always. "What's all the shouting?"

Catia appeared from behind the partition that separated her bed from her parent's, looking just as bewildered and sleepy as the druid.

Narina was standing at the open door to the house they'd been sharing ever since they were married two months ago. Her back was to him and her white tunic contrasted with the darkness outside as Bellicus admired the shape of her figure.

"I don't know," she admitted, turning and eyeing her daughter with concern. "But we'd better go and see."

Bellicus was already on his feet and had shrugged on his brown robe. He reached across the bed and grabbed Narina's cloak, helping her into it before they went outside. There were two guards stationed at their door but they knew no more than Bellicus or the queen about what was happening.

"Come with us," Narina ordered them.

Bellicus didn't think they needed the guards, especially with Cai beside them, but he knew his wife had been on edge ever since the war with the Picts and Saxons ended so he did not argue and the six of them hurried down the slope towards the great hall in the middle of the fortress.

"Intruder!" one of the guards called, pointing vaguely downwards as he saw the royal party coming.

"Just the one?" Bellicus asked, noticing Gavo, striding up towards them.

"Aye, we think just the one," the captain confirmed. "But the bastard has done some damage. Killed at least three of our men."

"Where is he now?" Narina demanded, face pale in the dim light. The sun was not visible on the horizon yet, but dawn was on its way and the fortress was not quite shrouded in the near total darkness of a short time before.

"He escaped," Gavo admitted sourly. "It seems he climbed down a rope over the south-western wall and fell into the river. We have men out hunting him now."

"Any idea who he was, or what he wanted?" the queen asked. They were now on the path that led from the main, central steps to the great hall, and soldiers were marching everywhere, searching for other intruders or signs of the mischief the one who'd escaped had got up to.

"No, my lady," Gavo said. He looked mortified by the whole situation, as though it was somehow his fault even though, from the look of him, he'd been tucked up in his bed when the enemy came over the wall. "If he spoke to anyone, they're dead. And the guard who saw him in the Clota couldn't see him well enough to even get a description for it was too dark."

"Where the hell is Duro?" Bellicus wondered, eyes casting about the fortress right up to the opposite peak where soldiers could be seen poking spears into the undergrowth. "Surely he's not slept through this uproar?"

They all turned to look at the low house that had once been Bellicus's but now was home to the centurion. Everyone knew that Duro would normally have run to find Bellicus when the alarm was raised, so the pair could face the danger together as they always did.

"Cai!" the druid said, pointing. "Find Duro."

The dog charged off towards the house and the others ran after him. Cai nosed the door wide open and went inside, Bellicus following moments later.

"Oh gods."

"Is he all right?" Narina demanded.

The druid didn't answer, he was standing over the bed which was coated in blood, Duro lying there unmoving. Bending, the druid placed his ear near to the centurion's mouth and listened. At last, trying to remain calm, he straightened and spoke to Gavo. "He's breathing, but only just. Have a servant bring hot water, cloths, bandages, needle and thread, and wine."

"I'll go," said Catia whose eyes were brimming with tears. She sprinted off, the sounds of her feet scrabbling for purchase on the stones of the path quickly receding. Narina also went outside and returned moments later with an oil lamp she must have collected from the nearby guardhouse. It was not as bright as a torch but more suitable for the low interior and cast enough light for them all to see the stricken centurion.

"Duro. Duro, can you hear me?"

There was no response and the druid looked about, finding the centurion's own knife and using it to cut away the tunic that Duro had been sleeping in. The material was saturated with blood and, when the bare torso was revealed Narina gasped at the wounds there.

"By the gods," the queen whispered, eyes wide. "Is he dying?"

Gavo reached out and gently took the oil lamp from her shaking hand, carrying it over to better let the druid see what he was doing.

Bellicus swallowed but forced himself to think positively. "I hope not," he said. "Duro's a fighter."

"Can I do anything for him?" Narina practically begged.

"Find out what's keeping Catia," the druid replied although the girl had only been gone a short time.

The queen went outside again but came back soon with the princess and the medical supplies. As Bellicus took a length of bandage from the pile Narina asked again, "Is there anything else we can do to help?"

"Pray for him," the ashen-faced druid replied, and set about what looked like the impossible task of saving his best friend's life.

* * *

Gavo was absolutely furious. With the guards who'd been killed by the intruder, with himself, with the gods, and even, ludicrously, with the centurion for not defending himself better.

"How the fuck did the bastard even get in here?" the captain raged at the two guardsmen who'd been on duty in the guardhouse beside the walkway the interloper had escaped along. "Were you two dreaming? Drunk?"

"We weren't drunk, sir," one of the guards protested. "We were carrying out our duties as normal. Never heard or saw any sign of anyone that shouldn't have been here."

"We think he must have climbed up the wall round there," the second guard added.

"The same way he left?" Gavo asked, trying not to take out his frustration on these men who had somehow been lucky enough to survive the night's events.

"Aye, lord. It was me who saw him in the river. He climbed down a rope wedged into one of the battlements. I reckon he must have come up the same way."

"Where's the rope?"

48

"Still where he left it, lord," the guard said. "I thought I should leave it there so you could see it for yourself."

"Come on then," Gavo growled, leading the way along the walkway. It had grown lighter by now and the bloodstains on the wood were visible where the two Damnonii guards had been attacked. Gavo was pleased to see the guard had not actually left the rope hanging down over the wall for any other possible intruders to climb up, but had looped it around the battlements, only leaving the wooden wedge in place so the captain could see exactly how it had been attached. "Simple but effective," he said, taking the thing out and tossing it aside.

"He must have climbed up the rock," the guard surmised, peering over the wall and pointing at the various places he thought might have been used as hand- and foot-holds. "And then thrown up the rope when he reached the wall, which would have been too smooth to climb."

Gavo nodded, agreeing with the guard's assessment. "And you saw the bastard in the water?"

"Yes, sir, but it was still nighttime and all I could make out were his eyes and his teeth. Sorry, sir."

The captain sighed and turned away from the river. "You did well, lad," he said. "All that could be expected of you. We'll need to make sure no one can ever get into the fortress this way again but, for now, you should go and get some sleep."

The guard saluted and hurried away, clearly relieved that his ordeal was over for now.

Gavo gazed out over the wall again, seeing his men rowing boats up and down the Clota as they searched for the man who'd caused so much trouble. They had not found him yet, that much was obvious, and Gavo wondered if he might have drowned. He'd been in the water, the guard had seen him there, and it would be freezing cold at that time of the morning. To have swum to shore would have been a feat in itself, but to then, in soaking wet clothes, have run away to safety…It seemed improbable.

Part of Gavo hoped the intruder hard not drowned, for he desperately wanted to question him, find out his motives for doing what he had. Who was he? Why attack the centurion in his bed? Surely this was no simple thief.

"Found him yet?" he bellowed hopefully as one of the boats came close to the wall.

"No sign, sir," a soldier shouted back.

"Check the far bank," Gavo called. "Just in case he made it over there."

"Will do!"

The boat turned and the rowers powered it away from Gavo, southwards, to the opposite side of the river. The Clota was not particularly wide here, but it would have taken a fit man to swim all the way to the far shore after his night's exertions. The captain didn't really think the soldiers would find anything there, but he wouldn't rest until they located some sign of the intruder, be that a body or just a trail Damnonii hunters could follow.

He cast his mind back to the sight of Duro covered in blood, stab wounds gaping like hideous gasping mouths in the centurion's torso. Whoever had done that would pay, Gavo vowed. They would find him and, if he was still alive, they would bring him back to Dun Breatann and make an example of him – show the world what happened to those who thought they could bring death and despair to Gavo's fortress!

He examined the wall that had been climbed and decided he would have the carpenters add a section of planking to the bottom that would stick out and prevent anyone else from climbing up that way. He'd have them hammer spikes into it as well, just in case. It astonished him that anyone had managed to get into the fortress this way at all, but at least it had only been one man, as far as they knew, and not a full invasion force.

The captain shuddered at what might have been and was just about to head off to find woodworkers to add his modifications to the wall when a shout caught his attention. It came from across the Clota and he squinted, lifting a hand to shield his eyes from the rising sun.

The boat he'd commanded to search the far bank of the river had made it there and the men were wandering about looking for signs of the intruder. Another shout came across the water and Gavo saw one of his soldiers waving his right arm while, in the other, he held something up.

The captain wasn't sure what it was at first but then he understood. The circular shape and apparent light weight suggested it was a coracle and for some reason the man who'd found the little vessel believed it was connected to the intruder.

"Damn it," Gavo hissed and strode back towards the centre of the fortress. Somehow the fugitive had made it all the way to comparative safety! Well, if he thought that was it, the piece of filth could think again.

"Cian!" the captain roared to one of his sergeants as he came down towards the barracks that housed Dun Breatann's garrison. "Gather a warband to ride for the ford. We're going to catch this bastard, and teach him a lesson."

CHAPTER ELEVEN

Sigarr found Cunneda to be more impressive than the Pictish ruler, Drest, had been. A tall man, the Votadini king had a bushy red beard, wore his hair closely cropped and his clothes, jewellery, and weapons were finely crafted. His wife was a pleasant looking woman with very pale skin and an easy smile; she also knew her place, Sigarr was happy to see, and sat on Cunneda's left side without taking part in the conversation.

The Saxons were welcomed with some trepidation but also respectfully and Sigarr appreciated the king's warmth as they sat making small talk about the voyage to Dun Edin, the recent war with the Damnonii, and the quality of the food they were being served. Of course, Cunneda was probably worried that his lands might be the subject of an invasion from the Saxons – Votadini territory was on the east coast of Britain after all and, although it had mostly been spared raids, everyone knew the sea-wolves were constantly looking to expand their sphere of influence. Dun Edin might be unmolested thus far, but once Hengist had conquered the coast to the south he would surely turn his gaze northwards.

Sigarr guessed Cunneda would be thinking all this as they sat in the hall enjoying roast meats, summer vegetables, smoked fish, and strong ale. The jarl decided to set his host's mind at ease soon after the first course was devoured.

"I am not here," he said, wiping grease from his mouth with the back of his hand, "to cause you any trouble, my lord."

Cunneda glanced at him and could not hide the scepticism from his face. He masked it by lifting his cup to his mouth and sipping slowly.

"Rather," Sigarr went on, "I've come from Garrianum to seek an alliance, and a trade agreement with you. Hengist, my cousin and *bretwalda*, believes it's time we became friends since we are, essentially, neighbours."

Cunneda's eyebrows lifted and he set down the cup, fixing Sigarr with an unwavering gaze. "Trade agreement? But we already trade, and have done for a long time."

Sigarr nodded. "True, but that is all done informally. Random ships sail between our ports and the merchants haggle over prices.

Sometimes your people come off best, sometimes ours, and taxes are never honestly paid."

"That's how trade works," Cunneda replied, almost as if he thought the jarl an idiot which, of course, he did not really.

"But we can make a binding agreement between our two peoples," Sigarr told him. "We can agree prices for different things, and we can have our officials collect taxes from the merchants which will come directly to you and Hengist."

Cunneda's brows rose again but this time he was intrigued. "I like the sound of that, I must admit," he said. "But what exactly are you expecting in return?"

"An alliance," Sigarr said, tilting his head as he spoke. "We will both benefit from such a trade agreement, and, by becoming allies it will cement the relationship and mean neither side is likely to attack the other."

Cunneda eyed him shrewdly. "Was Hengist planning on attacking my lands?" he asked coolly.

"No. We have our hands full defending ourselves from the likes of Arthur, there's no need for us to go searching for other wars to fight, my lord, trust me." Sigarr gave a sardonic laugh and Cunneda joined in although it was obvious the Votadini king was not naive enough to accept everything the Saxon was saying as the complete truth.

What Sigarr was not telling him was that Hengist planned to send ships filled with warriors to attack the Picts at some point in the not-too-distant future. Those lands were pitifully defended right now after losing two wars in quick succession, and the *bretwalda* wanted to take advantage of their weakness. If Hengist could capture Dunnottar and make those far-flung northern wilds his it would mean Cunneda's lands would be stuck in the middle. Sigarr did not think the Votadini ruler would be too pleased to know about those plans, so he of course kept it to himself. The trade agreement he was proposing was a genuine one – Hengist really did want to keep Cunneda on good terms, at least until Pictland could be conquered.

Cunneda really had no reason to refuse Sigarr's offer: a trade agreement with terms beneficial to both parties made sense. And the Votadini would probably hope that becoming friends with Hengist would save their strongholds from being attacked in the great Saxon expansion. And so it would, for a time at least. Hengist was incredibly ambitious though, and it was surely only a matter of time before his armies spread all across Britain.

Cunneda, of course, knew that. He prised a piece of beef from between his front teeth and then said, "You call it a trade agreement, then mention the word 'alliance'. Would Hengist be expecting me to send him soldiers to help him fight his war against Arthur, and whoever else he might get embroiled in a battle with?"

Sigarr smiled. "Maybe, eventually. But for now an alliance would simply mean we keep out of each other's way. If you were to attack, say, the Damnonii for how they treated your son, we would not raid your lands while your army was away in the west. In fact, we would be likely to send men to help you, for Hengist hates the people of Alt Clota."

Cunneda's face darkened at the reminder of his boy Ysfael's humiliating time as Queen Narina's husband – word of the recent wedding between Narina and Bellicus had not been slow in reaching Dun Edin and it confirmed the rumours that had been doing the rounds for years about them being secret lovers. It was said that Ysfael had been an arrogant layabout, but he was still Cunneda's son and a Votadini prince, and Sigarr guessed the whole affair must leave a bitter taste in the king's mouth. The fact that Ysfael had been killed while fighting for Narina would only make matters worse.

"Similarly," the Saxon went on smoothly, "when our forces are away from Garrianum, you will not send raiders to steal cattle and take our people as thralls from our settlements on the coast."

Cunneda looked shocked at the suggestion he would send men on such a raid but, of course, he had done just that in the past. The Picts were notorious for such raids up and down the eastern edge of Britain, but the Votadini did so too, often disguising themselves as their northern neighbours by painting their skin with blue symbols.

Despite his look of innocence, Cunneda did not insult Sigarr by denying anything. "All right," he said, bringing Sigarr out of the pleasant reverie he'd been falling into, the result of strong Votadini ale and the warmth of the firepit that crackled and sparked beside them in the centre of the hall. "My steward, and my druid, will look at the agreement you're proposing and, if the terms are as favourable as you suggest, you will have a deal."

54

"Excellent," the little Saxon replied with a broad grin, thoroughly pleased to have completed the mission his cousin had given him. "Let's drink to it!"

They clattered their cups together and downed their ales, both content with how things were going and both, no doubt, believing they were smarter than the other.

"Speaking of druids," Sigarr drawled, thoroughly at his ease now. "Where is yours?"

Cunneda waved a dismissive hand and rolled his eyes. "Some villagers are having trouble with their livestock," he said. "So the druid's gone to sort it out. He probably won't be too happy when he hears I've agreed to an alliance with you Saxons."

"Oh?" Sigarr asked innocently.

"Your warlord, Hengist, tried to wipe out all the druids not so long ago, did he not? They are rather upset about it, understandably."

"Well, your druid won't have anything to worry about now. We'll leave him well alone now that we're to be allies."

"Good," the king nodded. "What about cementing our relationship some other way? Make it even more binding?"

"How?"

"A marriage," Cunneda suggested. "I have more sons than Ysfael."

"Hengist has no daughters," Sigarr said, shaking his head.

"Do you?"

Sigarr actually laughed then. "No; not as far as I know anyway. But even if I did, Hengist is a law unto himself, especially now that Horsa is dead. I'm afraid a marriage between our peoples would not provide you with the security you're looking for, my lord. Mutual dislike for the Damnonii people, and the Picts too, should be enough, I believe."

Cunneda shrugged and the conversation moved onto other matters. As musicians struck up a tune and the king's guests, including the Saxons, began dancing and singing, Sigarr pondered his future. What he'd told the king about Hengist was true – the *bretwalda* had jarls like Sigarr and Leofdaeg to help him in his quest to conquer Britain, but they were very much subordinate to him. No one would ever really admit that, of course, for the Saxon noblemen liked to believe they were all equals – they followed a king or a *bretwalda* out of choice, not because they were inferior to those rulers. Sigarr and the other jarls helped Hengist pursue his goals, and they were rewarded for their loyalty with protection, gold, gifts, land, and so on.

But Sigarr was under no illusions that, even if he was Hengist's cousin, he might be cast aside at any time by the *bretwalda*. Sigarr was no warrior, and he had not really done much of note in Britain so far – would Hengist grow tired of him soon and banish him from his inner circle? Or what if Hengist died either in battle or from natural causes? Sigarr was highly unlikely to find favour with his cousin's successor.

He thought of Jarl Leofdaeg, undoubtedly his closest rival for Hengist's favour. Leofdaeg would surely try to step into Horsa's place as the *bretwalda*'s right-hand man. Sigarr must do all he could to take the position for himself in the coming weeks and months, or forever lose the opportunity.

From being pleased at securing an alliance with the Votadini king, and nicely inebriated from his host's ale, Sigarr grew suddenly maudlin as he pictured himself as an old man, wheezing terribly, regretting a life of being pushed around by those who were physically stronger and more imposing than himself. He noticed Cunneda eyeing him suspiciously – his behaviour must seem rather odd to the king, he realised. Doing his best to appear like all the rest of the drunken fools singing tunelessly in the hall, he plastered a stupid grin on his face and said, "I hope you enjoy the salmon I brought for you, my lord. I heard it was a favourite of yours." He fully expected Cunneda to thank him profusely for the expensive gift, for the king to tell him he was looking forward to tasting it. The reply when it came was unexpected, and most unwelcome.

"Salmon?" Cunneda asked, mouth drawing down in a disgusted frown. "I can't stand the stuff." He laughed and turned away to watch one particularly attractive noblewoman dancing to the music.

Sigarr watched her too, but he felt no lust, no pleasure in her lithe movements. He felt only disgust at himself for being taken advantage of yet again. The old trader would be riding his ramshackle old wagon back to the port now, cackling away at how he'd fooled the skinny Saxon jarl and essentially stolen his hacksilver.

Was this to be the pattern of his life?

Upending his ale, he drained the cup and slammed it down on the table, gesturing angrily for a servant to refill it.

Cunneda was no longer bothering with him thanks to the drink and other distractions in the rowdy hall, so Sigarr sat fuming in his own little world, taking no notice of anything around him. This gloomy, self-pitying state of mind was quite unlike the jarl, at least in recent years. When he'd been younger it had bothered him that he was weaker than other men, but he'd risen to his current high status on his own merits, using the talents he did possess.

"Are you all right, lord?"

Sigarr started violently and his captain, Cretta, laughed uproariously at the reaction.

"*Ja*," the jarl replied, forcing himself to smile in return. "I was lost in thought."

"You want to dance with the men?" Cretta asked, his oafish face irritating Sigarr who did not want to leave his seat. Still, he knew warriors appreciated a leader who made merry with them rather than one who brooded in the shadows so, with even more effort than he expected, he got unsteadily to his feet and followed Cretta between the benches of sweating Votadini revellers to join his men as Cunneda cheered him on.

The Saxon warriors' idea of 'dancing' was completely different to the serpentine, rhythmic swaying of the Votadini lady who'd earlier entranced Cunneda. It consisted mostly of a vigorous shuffling of the feet, kicks, and swaying from side to side often bumping against one another. Some of the men put a lot of effort into it and ended up sweating and breathing heavily, but Sigarr simply went through the motions, barely moving but smiling at his men if they met his gaze.

He thought those warriors who'd sailed to Dun Edin under his command liked him well enough. Maybe it was time he came out of Hengist's shadow and sought to build his own warband.

Or maybe that was just the ale making him overconfident. He was not sure, but he accepted another cup of the stuff from Cretta and the two men lifted their voices in a bawdy drinking song, fully determined, in their own ways, to make the most of the visit to Cunneda's lofty stronghold.

CHAPTER TWELVE

Gavo had one of Dun Breatann's best trackers with him as they rode towards the ford on the Clota that was a short distance east of Dun Breatann. Harnesses clanked and rattled, and the sun beat down on them, the scent of leather and sweat filling the air even at that time of the morning, but the captain wanted to waste no time in searching for Duro's attacker.

Bellicus had clearly been torn when Gavo told him they suspected the fugitive had made it across the river. The druid wanted to go with the horsemen and help locate the enemy soldier, whoever he might be, but Duro was so terribly injured that he would need constant care if he was to survive the rest of the day. The ensanguined bedclothes had not even been stripped for the druid did not want to move his friend unnecessarily, so it was a gruesome sight as Gavo wished him well in his efforts to save the centurion and then left to meet the men at the gatehouse.

There were five of them, plus Gavo, all on nimble horses that were much smaller than Bellicus's stallion, Darac, but they could carry the men all day if needed, and cover a wide radius far quicker than a man on foot. Hopefully they would soon find their quarry but, given the person had somehow managed to get in and out of Dun Breatann without being killed, Gavo feared their task might prove unsuccessful.

There was a pleasant breeze rolling off the Clota on their right as they galloped towards the ford, barely slowing as they urged their mounts into the river. Flashing hooves pounded through the water, splashing a couple of travellers who were coming from the other direction.

"Have you seen a man?" Gavo demanded as they passed. "Probably quite badly injured?"

The people, a middle-aged man and a woman, shook their heads sullenly, clearly annoyed at being soaked by the riders.

The Clota was narrow at this point and it was not long before they were across and moving along the opposite riverbank, searching for signs of the escaped attacker. They had to move slower now for fear of missing a clue but even the tracker's keen, trained eyes did not see anything of interest and Gavo drew the party up when they were directly across from Dun Breatann.

"Get to work, lad," he told the tracker and the man jumped down and began scouring the beach.

"Don't move from there just yet, lord," barked the tracker as Gavo made to ride off to resume his own search. "You might disturb something and confuse the trail, although the earlier searchers have already made a bit of a mess."

"All right," the captain replied, nodding towards the other riders to also hold their position. It was hard, for Gavo was desperate to examine the beach himself, but he was no expert in hunting down animals or men and so he held himself in check, contenting himself with scanning the horizon in hopes of spotting a figure stumbling away from them.

There were villages not far from where they were and Gavo wondered if he should split his party into two or even three groups, riding on in pairs to cover more ground. Really, his head was spinning for he'd not long gone off duty and fallen asleep when the fortress had suddenly erupted in shouts of alarm.

The fugitive might be badly injured, but he might not be and, if he was a local, trying to locate him could prove impossible. To make matters worse, they only had one witness who had even a vague idea of what the attacker looked like: Duro.

And Gavo did not believe the centurion would survive his injuries.

Rage threatened to overwhelm him at that thought, and shame too, for it was his place, ultimately, to defend Dun Breatann from invaders and he had failed in that duty. Thankfully, the tracker suddenly called out in excitement and Gavo gladly turned his attention back to the man.

"Here," the tracker said, lifting a battered coracle from behind a tuft of grass.

"Aye, our men found that earlier," Gavo told him. "Does it tell you anything?"

The tracker had wandered some way to the west but Gavo, remembering not to disturb the terrain, remained atop his horse as the man examined the tiny boat closely, nodding to himself before saying, "Bloodstains. Not many though, and there's no way to tell if it's his blood, or that of the men he murdered."

"Can you see where the goat-humper went?" Gavo asked impatiently, eyes turning once again to the windswept land around them.

Silently, utterly focused on his work, the tracker padded away across the stony beach, eyes scanning all around. Gavo believed the man was even sniffing the air like a dog, as if he could detect their fugitive's scent. Maybe he could, thought the captain, for this particular tracker was well known for his skill.

"This way. He went this way."

Gavo smiled grimly at the tracker's call and followed his gesturing arm, the horse easily picking its way across the stones and onto the grass of the river bank.

"Look, you see where the grass is pressed down? He came this way." The tracker straightened and looked up. Smoke curled into the morning sky less than a mile away and they hurried in that direction.

Everyone in the search party knew there was a collection of scattered farms around here, and Gavo felt a thrill of fear at what the man they were hunting might have done to the people living there. If he could brutally murder armed soldiers what might he do to simple farmers and their families?

"You keep following his trail if you can," the captain said to the tracker, kicking his heels into his mount and galloping forwards. "I'm going to check on the farm up ahead." He turned and pointed at three of his men. "Follow me. The rest of you stay with the tracker and remain alert – the bastard we're after is dangerous!"

The hooves of the four horses pounded across the soft grass, still damp with morning dew, and Gavo felt bile rise within his throat as his imagination brought images of slaughtered farm workers to mind. Still, as they approached the nearest of the houses everything seemed normal. There was smoke, aye, but it was the usual smoke curling out of the chimney hole and filling the nearby air with the pleasant scent of burning wood. They rode past a pen with a large pig, and another with some hens which squawked and clucked in alarm at the sight of them.

All looked normal, the captain thought, allowing himself to relax somewhat. If their fugitive had come this way he must have passed on by without–

"Sir!"

Gavo turned to see the rider on his left pointing at a ramshackle barn a short distance away to the east. At first the captain could not see what his soldier was drawing attention to, but then he noticed the feet sticking up from the grass and cursed, guiding his mount around.

It was obvious as soon as they came close that the farmer was dead. He was a middle-aged man with a thick brown beard, and his eyes were open, staring up at the clouds as what remained of his blood spilled from the stab wounds in his chest.

"There's nothing we can do for him," one of the soldiers muttered, staring at the farmer sadly.

"Help me!"

Gavo was out of the saddle and running into the barn before the strangled cry was completed. He had his sword in his hand and praying the man that had caused his people so much trouble would still be within the wooden building.

"Help." The gasping voice came again and Gavo looked around, trying to see where it emanated from in the gloom. There were bales of hay stacked around, and stalls with a pair of horses, both eyeing him fearfully, the smell of blood and possibly the sight of witnessing their master being butchered making their nostrils flare.

"Where are you?" he demanded, anxiety and battle-fever making him hoarse.

"Here."

The voice was already weaker and Gavo headed for it, his men moving slowly along behind him, weapons drawn, faces grim, knuckles white.

A woman lay on the hay. Her skin was pale and bore the marks of a lifetime of hard, mostly outdoor work. Gavo noticed the lines beside her eyes and knew she must have spent much of her days in laughter.

She was not laughing now.

"Is my brother safe?" she asked.

Gavo noticed her resemblance to the dead man outside and he knelt beside her, seeing blood staining her frayed tunic. "Aye," the captain lied, unable to tell the woman the truth. "He's outside. He'll be fine, and so will you. Who did this?"

"A young man," she replied, voice little more than a wheeze. "I thought it was a child at first. He took out a sword and stabbed..."

61

She broke off, coughing uncontrollably for a long moment. When she was finally able to speak again her eyes were glassy and Gavo knew she would not last much longer.

"Where did he go?" he asked. "We'll find him, and make him pay for what he's done."

"He took my horse," she said, trying to lift her hand and point at an empty stall.

"Which way did he ride?"

It was a stupid question to ask Gavo realised. How would she know the answer when she'd been lying here bleeding to death when her attacker was outside, galloping away on her own horse.

It did not matter – the woman could not answer anyway.

"Fuck!" It was not Gavo who shouted but one of his men, eloquently putting into a single word exactly how they all felt at that moment.

"Where's that tracker?" demanded the captain, reaching out to gently close the lady's eyes before turning to look through the barn's open doors.

"Here." The man appeared, framed in the pale sunlight, taking in the scene of death with a shake of his head.

"The bastard has a horse now," Gavo told him. "Find out which way he went. I'll not let him get away to kill more innocent people. We can't be that far behind him."

The tracker disappeared from view and the captain hurried out after him, heading for his horse with a last, angry glance at the other dead farmer. Who the hell was this crazed murderer stalking Alt Clota? What did he want? And, most importantly, where was he going?

"Maybe we should split up, sir," one of the soldiers suggested. "We know he's alone so he's no great danger, and we'll cover more ground that way."

Gavo snorted humourlessly. "'No great danger'? Are you mad? Have you not seen what he's done? No, we stay together and hope the tracker can lead us to him. When he does…Well, we'll see how hard the bastard is when he has all of us to deal with."

CHAPTER THIRTEEN

"You want to befriend the Saxons who live in my lands?" King Hywel seemed a little taken aback by the Merlin's suggestion, but he nodded thoughtfully. "I don't see why not. They're good workers and don't cause any more trouble than some of our own people."

Qunavo shared a smile with Bedwyr. This was a good start. "Where can we find them then, lord?" asked the Merlin.

"They stick together," Hywel said, stretching out his legs and placing his head against the back of his throne. His great hall was not as impressive as most Qunavo had seen, but it was sturdy and homely with swords and shields hung on the walls and even a couple of fine tapestries the high druid judged as dating back to the days of the Romans. "You'll find them on the northeast edge of town. Don't antagonise them, please. I could do without an angry group of Saxons coming to complain – when they get together in numbers there's inevitably much drinking of mead, and you know how that ends."

Bedwyr gave a shallow bow. "We're going to make allies of them, with any luck," he said. "Not start a fight."

"You think we can trust them if they swear not to follow Hengist should he call on them?"

King Hywel chewed his lip as he thought about Qunavo's question. A log cracked in the fire, sending sparks shooting up towards the chimney hole but the king never even flinched. Eventually he gave a shrug. "I don't know. Some might, some might not. But there's no harm in approaching them, if done right. You have gifts for their leaders?"

Qunavo glanced at Bedwyr. They did not have anything like that – it would be an expensive venture if they were forced to pay off every Saxon chief in Britain.

"No," admitted the high druid. "We're offering them our protection, and a place in our communities, as equals. That should be enough."

"Ha!" Hywel's laugh was little more than a bark. "You may be right, but in my experience men respond better to bribes than vague promises of future prosperity or the suggestion that they follow lofty ideals."

"Maybe he's right," Bedwyr murmured, but Qunavo shook his head.

"You can't buy a man's loyalty or respect solely with possessions. No, they'll get the same treatment as any Briton who fights on our side."

"Meaning?" Hywel asked.

"Meaning the Saxons will be rewarded with plunder and silver if they ever fight beside us against Hengist's forces, and we win."

Hywel frowned and turned away, staring at one of the brightly painted shields decorating the wall beside him. "You're the Merlin," he drawled, keeping his voice neutral. "You're the wise one, not me. I do think you'd be better offering the Saxon leader a bribe. Keep at least the most powerful of them on your side."

Qunavo responded with a nod. Perhaps the king was right. "We'll speak with them and see how things go," he said. "If it seems like offering the chief a shiny bauble as an incentive will do some good, that's what we'll do." He turned to Bedwyr, an eyebrow raised expectantly.

"Fine," the warrior replied. "But if this is how we're going to do it we'll have to ask the kings and warlords of Britain to send Arthur more of a tribute each year, and we all know they won't be pleased about that."

"If it keeps us safe from the Saxons it'll need to be paid," Hywel said firmly.

"Good, I'm glad you feel like that, lord," Bedwyr replied with a broad smile. "You won't mind providing us something to bribe the local Saxon chief with then, eh?"

King Hywel's face darkened as he realised he'd been backed into a corner by his own words, but after a moment where the atmosphere in the hall grew frosty, Hywel slapped the arms of his throne and gave a loud bellow of laughter. "You're even more cunning than the druid," he cried. "How can I refuse your request? I can't, can I? Very well, I'll have my steward find something for you to take to the chief."

"Thank you, lord," grinned Qunavo, thumping his staff on the floor to emphasise his pleasure. "If our meeting with the Saxons goes as well as this one I think we'll be off to a fine start, and Hengist will have at least one group of countrymen fewer to call upon for his war!"

* * *

The Saxon warrior knew he couldn't continue riding much longer. His injuries were agonising now that his battle fever and the fearful excitement of the chase had worn off. He was safe from being captured by the soldiers from Dun Breatann, for now at least, having ridden for some time on the stolen horse. It wasn't the fastest beast in *Miðgarðr*, but it was strong and fit and took Saksnot well away from the Damnonii fortress. Undoubtedly the ride had saved his life, but the constant up-down motion of the horse jarred his injured jaw and the wind whipping into his burned face made the raw skin fiercely painful. He was a soldier, he reminded himself for every agonising thump of his mount's hooves – he would endure.

But he had endured for long enough, he thought, with a last glance over his shoulder. Seeing no sign of pursuit he brought the horse to a walk, almost sobbing with the pain coursing through his body. What should he do now? He might be a warrior, a soldier, a killer, but he was also young and inexperienced. He'd never been injured like this before, and he didn't know how to heal himself. He knew that burns could become infected if not properly treated, and a broken jaw would probably lead to all sorts of problems. He was not entirely sure what those problems might be, but that uncertainty made him frightened and he felt his breathing become fast as anxiety flooded him, rising to panic.

Stop it! he told himself furiously. Warriors did not panic, they dealt with their problems. His injuries might eventually become life threatening but, for now, he was alive and able to fight if needed. He simply had to find a healer.

Looking back at the road behind him again he reassured himself that no one was following. He had time. He took a deep, calming breath and dashed away the tears that had filled his eyes – how embarrassing! What kind of man cried when he was wounded after battle? It wasn't as though he was lying on the ground with his guts spilling from him, by Woden!

He scanned the horizon, looking for signs of a settlement. A farm like the one he'd stolen the horse from would be a start – even if the people living there didn't have the skills to heal him, they'd surely know someone who could. He'd just have to pretend to be a child again, and he was good at that when he had to be.

He shuddered as he realised his smooth, youthful skin might not look quite so fresh by the time the burns healed. Damn that guard with his torch! If Saksnot could kill the bastard again he'd take his time over the task and make the Damnonii scum suffer for what he'd done.

He smelled woodsmoke and turned, eyes travelling from one side of the land to the other, sniffing as he did so, trying to discover the source of the wonderful, homely scent. There! Half a mile or so to the west. He urged his horse to walk in that direction, the smell evoking memories of the house he'd grown up in back in Jutland. The thoughts made him nostalgic, and his smile was bittersweet as he pictured the faces of his parents.

His father had been a skilled carpenter, helping to build houses, ships, and even their jarl's mead hall. His mother was a seamstress, making clothes, sails, and tapestries for the wealthy men in their community. Saksnot's childhood had been a happy, peaceful one and his family were quite well off. The boy had always been competitive however, enjoying beating his peers in foot races. He'd been too slight to win wrestling or boxing matches but his skill with a spear was quickly recognised by the jarl's men when the village youths became old enough to train with simple weapons.

Every man in Egtved who was old enough to stand in a shieldwall had to learn how to fight for there were always raids by neighbouring warlords to worry about. Naturally, not every young boy had an aptitude for battle, but Saksnot had a vicious streak within him and an athleticism that marked him out to the leaders as someone to look out for. Within months of his fourteenth birthday, and to his mother's dismay, Saksnot went on his first raid, sailing with the jarl to attack a settlement forty miles up the coast to the north. From there, his fame grew and he joined the warband on more raids, relishing each fight he took part in, and thoroughly enjoying himself when he could wipe the smirk from the face of an enemy soldier who looked at him and saw a weak boy.

Saksnot had never been a weak boy – he was a ruthless warrior, and Woden guided his sword once he had finally earned one on his third raid. Soon he owned a coat of mail known as a *brynja*, a helmet, and enough silver to buy his own ship had he wished to. His jarl had answered the call of Hengist, though, informing his people that he would sail far along the whale road to plunder the lands of the Britons with the self-styled *bretwalda*. Saksnot had gladly gone with his jarl who had not lasted long once they'd reached their destination.

The Britons proved to be fierce fighters, with a leader in the warlord Arthur who was every bit as wily and brutal as Hengist. Saksnot's jarl, along with most of the warriors who'd sailed there from Egtved, had been cut down after the first few months' fighting, but Saksnot himself caught the eye of the Saxon *bretwalda* and was given a place amongst Hengist's own hearth-warriors.

For one so young it was a terrific honour and Saksnot had done what he could to repay Hengist. Stabbing the Britons' High Druid to death was the greatest achievement of the young soldier's life, earning him battle-fame that far outstripped that of most veteran Saxon warriors. Now, he'd also taken the life of Bellicus of Dun Breatann, and every scop and skald on that damp isle, and back in Jutland too, would sing songs and lamentations of Saksnot's deeds!

The young man smiled dreamily, utterly lost in his imagination, seeing a mead hall lit by firelight, populated by Hengist and dozens of other mighty Saxon noblemen, with Saksnot himself in the place of honour. He no longer felt the agony of his burned face, or the pain of his rapidly-swelling jaw, but that was all right, wasn't it? He was a hero.

He was still smiling as his legs relaxed and he slipped sideways from the horse's back to land with a heavy thump on the grass. He could see the smoke from the low dwelling he'd been riding towards, rising languorously into the pale morning sky, and he saw bare ankles and sandaled feet striding towards him, and then all was darkness.

CHAPTER FOURTEEN

"What happened?"

Gavo jumped down from his horse and handed the reins to a stableboy. His face was like thunder and he kicked an empty wooden bucket as he strode towards Queen Narina. The thing went flying, clattering against the living rock of Dun Breatann.

"I take it you didn't find him?" Narina asked, an eyebrow raised in surprise. It was not often that her captain showed such a naked display of emotion.

"No, my lady, just the two men he threw over the wall into the Clota. I can only apologise."

"That's enough of that," the queen barked, chopping her hand down, silencing him immediately. "This is not your fault. No one expected a lone enemy warrior to climb into this fortress and attack our people. By Taranis, Gavo, you were asleep at the time, how could it be your fault? But enough of this for now, come." She looked around, seeing the guards on the walls and the stablehands all watching them. It was not seemly to conduct such a sensitive discussion in public. "Follow me up to the hall. We'll talk more there."

Realising they'd been noticed, the soldiers around them turned away, pointedly staring in any direction other than at Narina and Gavo.

"The tracker couldn't find his trail?" she asked as they walked up the many stairs leading to the central portion of the rock where the great hall was located.

Gavo sighed, eyes looking upwards as if the thought of climbing so many steps was deeply unpleasant. It probably was – he'd had a punishing morning, and he was in his early forties now after all. Fit and strong, but not as young as he'd once been. Narina slowed her pace, allowing him to take it a little easier.

"Oh, we found his trail," the captain told her, shaking his head disgustedly. "We followed him to the farm directly across the Clota from here. The bastard had killed two of the farmers – a lady and her brother – and made off on a stolen horse."

"Gods, more death," Narina muttered, breathless not from the exercise but from sheer rage. In times past she had spoken with the brother and sister who lived in that farm and could hardly imagine a less threatening pair.

"I know." Gavo gripped the hilt of his sword as they reached the top of the stairs and began the walk towards the hall. The path took them directly past the house where Duro had been attacked and Narina saw her captain's anxious glance towards it.

"He's still with us," she said grimly. "For now."

"Any better?"

"Well, Bellicus stopped the bleeding and cleaned the wounds. The centurion's still unconscious though." She let out a long, shuddering breath and looked directly into Gavo's eyes as they reached the hall and the pair of guards opened the doors for them. "I'm not sure he'll ever wake up. His injuries…" She trailed off and they went inside, the familiar bustle of servants tidying up and preparing things for the next meal making Narina feel a little more at ease.

The hall doors were left open at Narina's request for it was pleasantly warm in the hall. Cai came sauntering through them now, nose high, sniffing and eyeing the cauldron of bubbling stew over the firepit in the centre of the room. Narina lovingly stroked his soft ears as he came to sit beside her and then the huge silhouette of her husband momentarily blocked the light coming through the entrance.

"There's Bel now," she told Gavo. "Pray he brings good news."

They watched the druid striding towards them and Narina could see he was utterly exhausted – far more tired looking than even after a battle. She knew the mental toll of Duro's suffering was a heavier load than any physical pain for him, and she stood to guide him onto the bench beside Gavo.

"How goes it?" asked the guard captain gruffly.

"As well as can be expected," Bellicus replied, blinking and rubbing his eyes. He shook his head when Narina asked if he wanted anything to eat, but nodded vigorously when ale was offered and drank it down almost in one go when a servant brought it to him.

"Will he live?" Gavo asked, too much of a soldier to be anything other than blunt when it came to such a question.

Bellicus could only shrug and Narina reached out to place an arm around his broad shoulders.

"It's in the hands of the gods," the druid admitted. "I'll perform a ritual to Sulis Minerva in a little while, begging her to heal him. I'll offer something to Mithras too, since the war god is Duro's patron. I've done all I can though. If only Ria were here, she was always more skilled at healing than me."

Narina felt a pang of jealousy at Ria's name but she ignored it. Bellicus may well have been the Pictish druidess's lover for a short time, and possibly still harboured feelings for her – she was a stunningly beautiful woman after all, even Narina couldn't deny that – but Bel had chosen to marry Narina, not the Pict. And Ria was indeed a gifted healer, as the queen had witnessed herself after the recent battle for Dun Breatann.

"I'm sure you've done as much as anyone could," she said, taking her arm from Bellicus's shoulders as he accepted a second cup of ale from the serving girl. "Your fingers may not be quite as nimble as Ria's, but your friendship with Duro will have made you work with even more diligence and care than usual."

Bellicus nodded, clearly unconvinced, and the trio fell into a maudlin silence, nursing drinks as the servants moved about, completing tasks as unobtrusively as possible.

"I'm guessing you didn't find the man who did it?" The druid's clear baritone startled Gavo who looked to Narina as if he might fall asleep right there at the bench.

"No," said the captain grudgingly. "We chased him for miles, but lost the trail eventually. He stole a horse and must have pushed it mercilessly so…" Shrugging, he looked away from Bellicus and back into the depths of his cup as if he might divine the fugitive's location within the dark, cloudy ale.

"Any indication who he might have been?" the druid persisted. "Or why he came here?"

Gavo rubbed his face and Narina took pity on the guard captain. He'd been roused from his sleep long before he was due to be back on duty, and then spent the day chasing around Alt Clota on horseback. He was clearly tired. Besides, he was friends with Duro too.

"It's hard to think straight," the queen said, drawing the men's eyes to her. "But I'd suggest our attacker was sent by Hengist to avenge his brother's death. His target was Duro, or perhaps you, Bel. The other soldiers he killed simply got in his way."

70

"That makes sense," the druid agreed. "We always knew the Saxon *bretwalda* would seek revenge for what we did to his brother."

The queen nodded. "We had no idea what form his vengeance would take. We expected him to send a warband here, or even an army. None of us expected a lone warrior to scale the wall of Dun Breatann."

"Well, Hengist will be disappointed in his lackey." Bellicus laughed gloomily. "Since I'm completely unhurt, and Duro, well, if I have my way, Duro will survive his injuries."

Narina saw Gavo frown and she understood her captain's disbelief. She'd seen the blood Duro had lost, and the terrible gaping wounds in his body. It would take strong healing magic to bring the centurion back from the Otherlands.

"I suppose you're right," said Gavo, lifting his ale and tossing it back almost cheerfully. "It might not matter that we didn't catch the attacker – when he returns to Hengist and the truth comes out, there's a chance the Saxon warlord will kill him for failing his mission."

That thought raised the spirits of them all and Narina emptied her cup too before standing and holding out her arm to Bellicus. "Come, husband," she said. "You should get a couple of hours sleep. You can perform your healing rituals later. And you, Gavo. Go and rest. I want you both fresh and thinking clearly. The danger may be over, the attacker long gone from our lands, but we must remain vigilant. I won't stand for a repeat of last night's events."

Gavo was instantly on his feet, arm raised in salute. "Yes, my lady," he barked. "I'll—"

"You'll go and grab some sleep," Narina interrupted. "That's an order. Go on, off with you, man. We'll talk later, and make sure we're ready should Hengist decide to send his army here to finish what his warrior failed to do."

71

CHAPTER FIFTEEN

The patrol moved quietly through the woods, treading lightly despite the weight of their armour and weapons. The sun was almost at its zenith, making long shadows of the trees, momentarily blinding the warriors each time its brightness appeared from behind the trunks as they marched.

There were fifteen men, all seasoned soldiers with combat experience and the scars to prove it. They would be deadly if it came to a fight with the enemy foraging parties that had been reported in the area, and none more so than their leader, Lancelot.

The handsome, blond swordsman had volunteered for this duty when word had come to Arthur of a growing Saxon presence around Cedrid. At first, the warlord had been reluctant to let his friend and most valued advisor accept the mission, but Lancelot was not the type to go off on diplomatic duties the way someone like Bedwyr could do. If there were enemy forces near Cedrid, Lancelot would drive them back to Garrianum and their stolen lands on the Saxon Shore. Besides, as the messenger had told Arthur, the reports were only of a few marauders, perhaps a single warband or foraging party, not a great army – the danger would be minimal.

He slowed and held up a hand for his men to rest awhile. Although the canopy of trees kept the worst of the sun from beating down upon them it was still warm and muggy for the patrol. Lancelot removed his helmet and wiped the perspiration from his brow before putting it back on unhappily. It had felt good to let the gentle breeze play through his damp hair, but it was rather more important to avoid an arrow shattering his skull than to keep his head cool. He took the waterskin from where it hung from his belt, unstoppered it, and took a long drink. The liquid was not cold, but it refreshed him, and he felt ready to move on as he turned to glance back at his men.

There had been no sign of any enemy soldiers since they'd started out this morning, working their way southwest into the woods beside the small settlement of Cedrid. It was frustrating, for the Britons had hoped to find at least some evidence of a Saxon presence here, but there had been nothing. It made Lancelot wonder if the reports had been wrong, and he'd come there for nothing, wasting his time chasing thin air while Hengist's jarls sacked some town miles away.

Birdsong and the gentle buzzing of bees were the only sounds within the woods and a carrion crow landed on a branch not far from Lancelot, tilting its head and regarding him from black, intelligent eyes.

"Ready?" he asked, turning away from the bird and addressing his men. They nodded, and he began to walk again, quite sure there was no one – either Saxon or Briton – anywhere nearby. Still, he kept his hand close to his sword hilt as he stepped carefully across moss and lichen covered rocks, ever alert for danger. There might not be enemy warriors in the woods, but there could be bears or wolves and, although it was unlikely animals would attack so many men, it was better to be prepared for anything.

Or at least, that was what he'd always believed. He wasn't quite so sure now, as the sweat trickled from his armpits and the small of his back, that wearing a mail-shirt and a leather cuirass had really been necessary. He looked up through the leaves of the towering oak overhead, wondering when the sun might finally begin its downward descent and let the earth cool for a while.

The slight breeze wafted into his face and Lancelot blew out a breath, wishing the wind was stronger. Something tickled his brain then, a memory or…He stopped walking and held up his hand, mind working furiously to make sense of what he'd noticed, and then he realised it was a smell, carried on that cool breeze.

Stale sweat.

His hand was on his sword, drawing it from its scabbard as a man stepped out from behind one of the trees just ahead.

"Draw your weapons!" Lancelot roared. "To me!"

His warband was spread out behind him and it soon became obvious they'd stumbled into an ambush, as the sound of steel on steel, iron on wood, and cries of outrage and agony filled the trees.

"Shit," Lancelot breathed, allowing himself a quick look behind to make sure there were no enemies sneaking up on him. What he saw was not pleasing and he had a sudden, terrible flashback to the time when he'd led men into a similar ambush in the Saxon-occupied settlement of Garrianum. "Shit!" he repeated, and lunged at the man ahead of him.

73

His opponent was bigger and broader than he was, a confident, black-toothed grin peering out from behind a grizzled beard, but Lancelot was fast. His sword was knocked aside by the enemy warrior but Lancelot easily spun to the left and bent beneath a counter-attack. As he swivelled around he dragged his blade across the Saxon's hamstrings. There was a horrific shriek as the bearded man collapsed onto the forest floor but it was cut short when Lancelot's boot smashed into his face.

"Where the hell did they come from?" Lancelot gasped as he stood up, eyes scanning all around for nearby threats. Two men were coming towards him, stepping gingerly across the tree roots as they approached, iron axe heads glinting in the light that filtered through the leaves. Snarling, Lancelot moved to engage the closest one, a skinny youngster with no front teeth and lank hair.

"Take care! He's dangerous!"

When Lancelot had been held as a slave by Jarl Leofdaeg he'd managed to pick up some of the harsh Saxon tongue. He understood the shouted command but, as he quickly glanced at the man who'd shouted it, the blond swordsman's blood ran cold.

Leofdaeg! It was the very jarl who'd captured Lancelot and made his life a living hell, treating him worse than an animal, chained, beaten, starved, spat on, and almost completely broken. Only a miraculous rescue by the princesses Aife and Catia had saved Lancelot from the life and eventual death of a thrall, but Leofdaeg's face remained with him in his nightmares.

"Leofdaeg, you piece of shit," the swordsman roared. "Come and face me!"

The skinny young Saxon was upon him now and he let out a high-pitched battle cry as he swung his axe, but Lancelot easily moved aside and thrust his blade into his enemy's side. He could feel the steel grinding against ribs and then plunging into the soft innards of the screaming man before he drew the weapon free and moved on without a backward glance, heading for the hated jarl.

Leofdaeg's sword-arm had been smashed in the first meeting between them at Garrianum, when Lancelot hurled a rock at him. It had been a terrible injury and Leofdaeg's limb had never properly healed, forcing him to learn to fight holding his sword in his left hand. He had not learned very well however, and the jarl knew it. He hung back, screeching orders at his men, too fast for Lancelot to

74

follow but from the gestures it was obvious Leofdaeg was directing his warriors to attack the Briton.

Lancelot's heart sank for he could not see any of his own men still standing. The battle had been short but horrifically brutal and now only Lancelot remained alive. His thoughts churned as he contemplated his options – what he wanted to do was gut Leofdaeg, but there were too many Saxons closing on him, and he would never reach the jarl. Either he stood there and fought to the death, or his enemies captured him and made him Leofdaeg's thrall again.

The thought of that utterly terrified him, far more than the prospect of death. The second of the Saxons who'd been closest to him had finally come within range of his sword and Lancelot thrust it out. He hadn't expected to strike the man but the tip of the blade caught him on the shoulder and the Saxon fell back, bellowing Woden's name as blood bloomed on his tunic.

"Come on then, you whoresons!" Lancelot was heavily beset now, with four enemies around him and more quickly closing in. Surprisingly, none of them launched an attack as Leofdaeg continued to bellow orders. Another of them reeled back after taking a step too close and feeling Lancelot's blade tearing open his forearm. Still, not a single Saxon seemed to have the courage to attempt to kill him, and the Briton laughed in triumph as he caught yet another, stabbing the man in the groin and probably killing him, judging by the amount of blood that quickly saturated the warrior's breeches.

What are you waiting for, you fool? A voice in Lancelot's head shrieked at him. As the Saxons continued to surround him without attempting to land a killing strike, Lancelot begged the gods' forgiveness for his cowardice and, with one last thrust at the nearest foe, spun around the trunk of a massive yew tree and sprinted into the deep woods.

CHAPTER SIXTEEN

Saksnot's face still ached, especially his jaw. During the night was the worst, even a full week after his raid on Dun Breatann. He would wake up, his whole mouth – not just the jaw – aching so badly, so frustratingly, that he would squeeze his eyes shut and sob into his arm, praying that the gods would just let him pass out again that he might have a few hours respite.

"Another hard night." It was a bald statement, not a question, and Saksnot groggily looked up at the plump, middle-aged woman who'd been his nursemaid for the past few days.

When he'd fallen off his stolen horse he had not cared what would happen to him. All he wanted at that moment was to sink into oblivion, and that was exactly what had happened. Coming to hours later, he'd found himself in a cramped, round hovel, with a small, moustached man of about forty years, and the plump woman. They were, Saksnot discovered, Damnonii crofters, and married. He could not properly understand their language, nor they his, but they managed to converse after a fashion, mainly with gestures.

It seemed that Saksnot had not followed any main road during his flight, but had instead been carried off the beaten-track by his mount, up a low hill to this small dwelling which sat beside a stream. There was a more well-used road on one side, but no other dwellings visible nearby, and the Saxon warrior realised that the gods had guided him here, to the perfect place for him to rest and recover from his injuries. He even had a willing nursemaid, for the overweight woman seemed to view her part in his restoration to health as a task given to her by her own household gods. Or at least that's what Saksnot believed, from the hand waving and gazes up to the sky the woman had shared with him.

He had no idea if the woman had any real knowledge or training in the art of healing, but there was nowhere else for Saksnot to turn, so he let himself be tended to. For his burned and blistered facial skin she'd mixed up some salve which she'd handed to him, using her hands to show him that he should apply it liberally. It stank of wild mint and much, much worse things the Saxon could not place, but it did soothe his pain and he was happy to smear it all over his burns.

His broken jaw proved well beyond the woman's skill though, and all Saksnot could do was try not to move it, or to laugh – easy enough in the hovel with the dour Damnonii husband and wife – and to eat only liquids. To that end, the man went out gathering ingredients from the land nearby, or from the garden he tended beside the house, and cooked up broth or pottage which all three of them ate. There was no meat so the flavour was terribly bland to the Saxon who was used to devouring plenty of pork and beef or even fish, but it was just as well for he'd never be able to chew in his condition. Besides, apart from breaking wind more often than usual, Saksnot thought the food was doing him good.

He could not chop wood or perform any other onerous physical tasks to earn his keep, but he helped out by milking the single cow the crofters kept, gathering firewood, and by helping tidy up around the hovel. Slowly the burns began to heal, or at least the pain lessened somewhat, but Saksnot was glad there was no reflective surfaces within the circular dwelling that might show him how his youthful good looks had been ruined forever.

He tried to remind himself that warriors always carried the scars of their fights, that his new look would impress Hengist and the other Saxon noblemen far more than his boyish features had, but deep down Saksnot was devastated. He'd always felt older than he actually was, and now he would look it too, with his face all lined and wrinkled, the rough skin splitting no doubt if he laughed or even smiled too hard.

He was alive though, and his fears of dying eased with each passing day. There seemed to be no infection as a result of his injuries, and no one had come searching for him from the fortress. Soon he would mount his stolen horse which had been as well cared for as Saksnot himself, and he'd take the road south back to his *bretwalda*, and glory, just as soon as he felt capable of riding in a day or two.

That morning a man came along with a wagon. It was drawn by a massive ox that moved slowly but steadily, giving Saksnot plenty of time to notice its approach and conceal himself behind a bush close to the hovel. When the man was near enough the crofters came outside and greeted him warmly – clearly the three knew each other well, and Saksnot watched as the traveller unloaded some things from his wagon and placed them outside the building.

Supplies, the Saxon realised, brought from some larger village or town nearby. Perhaps even Dun Breatann itself, with its busy port. The three people disappeared inside and Saksnot waited, not willing to show himself to the trader. He had to hope the crofters didn't mention him either, for if word got around that an injured foreigner was there it would certainly bring soldiers hunting for him.

The trio seemed to linger inside the hovel for a long while, the sound of loud conversation and laughter spilling out through the chimney hole along with the bland smell of vegetable broth. The chattering grew even louder over time, suggesting the old wife's freshly brewed barley beer had been dished out and Saksnot began to grow impatient. Eventually the talking faded in volume and the laughter stopped completely, which seemed even more disturbing to the hiding Saxon. Ominous.

At last, the trader came out and waved farewell to the middle-aged couple, calling out in the Britons tongue as he climbed up onto the wagon and lashed the ox into a slow trudge along the track. There was space to turn the rickety vehicle, but it seemed the driver was moving on with his wares rather than turning back whence he'd come. Saksnot gave him some time to rumble off before he shoved through the bush and headed to the hovel.

It was obvious the man and woman had been given news that worried them. The man sat staring into the fire, fingers fiddling with his long moustache and refusing to look at Saksnot, while the woman's eyes did fall upon him, but only fleetingly.

"What's wrong?" Saksnot asked in his own tongue, jerking his head upwards to punctuate the question.

The crofters may not have been able to understand his words, but his demeanour and the frown on his scarred face made it quite clear what he was saying.

"What's wrong?" he asked again, this time using what he thought were the correct Brythonic words.

The woman looked at him, and then at her husband, and then back at Saksnot. She gestured to the north and shook her head, muttering a sentence which the Saxon strained to hear. He could only pick out a couple of the words, but one he knew quite well: "attack". The trader would be a source of news and gossip as much as of food and other goods, and evidently he'd brought the crofters word of Saksnot's daring raid on Dun Breatann.

From their reactions, it seemed the man and woman suspected they were harbouring a dangerous criminal, but they did not know what to do about it. A chill ran down Saksnot's spine as he realised they might have told the trader about him, and soldiers would soon be converging upon the hovel to capture him.

He forced himself to remain calm, and to think rationally. The trader had not appeared anxious at all as he rode off on his creaking old wagon. So it was likely that the crofters had kept Saksnot's presence in their home a secret, perhaps to save their own skin. Who knew how the laws worked in Alt Clota? Perhaps the crofters would be in trouble for taking care of the Saxon.

"Was anyone killed?" he asked slowly. He knew the proper word for 'killed', or perhaps, 'died', for the woman had used it many times while ministering to him over the past few days. He decided to throw caution to the wind – if these two were going to turn him in to the Damnonii authorities there was nothing he could do about it. He might as well get as much information as possible from them. "Bellicus?" he demanded.

Again, the crofters shared an ominous glance that held more than a hint of terror. They knew exactly who they were sharing their house with now. The woman shook her head however, and looked up at him almost triumphantly.

"No," she replied. "The druid lives."

Another thrill of anxiety ran through Saksnot as he tried to translate her statement in his mind. Had Bellicus survived the attack? Was that what she was telling him? It seemed incredible – impossible!

The woman noticed his consternation and nodded, smiling gleefully. "Duro, the centurion, he was attacked. Almost killed. But he lives too."

Saksnot had to take a moment to absorb the words, and to make some sense of them. He was confused and sat down on a storage chest against the eastern wall, gesturing for the woman to bring him some ale and food. She quickly brought him a brimming cup and a piece of bread on a broken old plate that had been repaired long ago with copper wire, watching him warily to see what he would do next.

Hengist had sent him there to kill Bellicus, that was his primary mission, and, if it was possible, he was to kill the Roman centurion called Duro too. Had he really managed neither feat? After so much effort, and injury to his own body?

What would he do now then? He did not know. His plan had been to ride south, back to Hengist in Garrianum, and there to proclaim his success in murdering the giant druid of Dun Breatann. Saksnot realised now that it must have been Duro he had actually stabbed in that benighted house in the fortress, not Bellicus. And he had not even managed to kill the bastard!

A cold sensation ran up both his forearms as he realised what would have happened to him had he rode back to Garrianum, proclaiming himself a great hero, only for Hengist to discover the embarrassing truth. It did not bear thinking about. Not only had he failed in his mission, but he'd suffered terrible facial injuries that he would carry for the rest of his life in the process.

By Woden's cock, he thought to himself, lost in the depths of his ale cup. *I cannot ride south now. I must go back to Dun Breatann and complete my mission!* The thought terrified him – how would he possibly get to the druid and his centurion friend now? It had been a miracle that he'd somehow made it into Dun Breatann and back out again mostly in one piece, and he doubted it could be done again. The guards would be much more alert for intruders now, there was no doubt of it. And they'd be eager for blood too, after what Saksnot had done to their comrades already.

Frightened, anxious, and utterly enraged, the young warrior downed the last of the ale in the cup and thrust it towards the woman, ordering her to refill it.

As she hurried to obey, completely subservient now, a stark contrast to the open, friendly nursemaid's demeanour she'd worn throughout his recuperation, Saksnot eyed the male crofter. The man did not directly meet his gaze, but he was obviously watching and listening to what was happening. He was also, the Saxon noted, wearing a knife sheathed on his belt, a new addition to his daily attire.

Saksnot took the refilled ale cup from the woman with a grunt of thanks and sipped it slowly, mind whirling as he tried to imagine a scenario where he could get close enough to Bellicus and Duro to kill them, while avoiding death himself. He imagined many different scenarios, but he was no fool – he knew it would be almost impossible to complete the mission he'd been given now.

It was incredible that he'd attacked the wrong man, but, even so, by Frigg's tits, how had the centurion survived his injuries? Saksnot had stabbed him multiple times, or so he believed. He touched his jaw, remembering the brutal fight in the dark little house in the middle of Dun Breatann's towering twin peaks and his mind rebelled at the thought of taking on such a man again. Clearly the centurion was protected by the gods, and as for the druid?

The ale gave him courage though, and he swallowed the rest, once again demanding a refill from the woman who hesitated, no doubt fearing how the drink would affect him. "Hurry up," he commanded, waving the cup in her direction. She moved to obey reluctantly, almost sadly, and Saksnot knew in that moment that he could not leave the crofters alive.

They might not have told the trader about him, but the moment he left their hovel they would report him to Queen Narina's soldiers. It wouldn't matter so much if he was heading south as he'd planned, but now that he would have to circle back to Dun Breatann he could not leave anyone alive to warn the druid and the centurion that he was coming for them again.

Sadly, he watched the woman filling his cup with shaking hands. He was not a monster, he truly appreciated what the crofters had done for him, taking him in and nursing him back to health. But he could not allow them to live if he wanted his mission to succeed.

As the woman came to him with the ale he reached out, forcing himself to smile although it felt more like a rictus grin and she visibly shuddered as he took the cup from her. And then he felt something smash against the back of his skull and he was falling to the ground as the woman screamed in fear.

CHAPTER SEVENTEEN

It felt like a bolt of lightning had come out of the sky, straight through the crofters' thatched roof, and struck Saksnot right in the back of the head. Stars exploded in his vision as he hit the ground, but it took only a moment before he understood what was happening. No god had struck him, it had been the crofter who was putting down a small, dented pot, and Saksnot remembered now the knife the man had worn on his belt all day.

Throwing his body to the side – any side! – and kicking his legs wildly as he did so, he was rewarded by a sudden cry of pain as he felt his heel strike something. There was a thump then, and another shout, and the prone Saxon saw the shining blade of an unsheathed knife clattering across the hovel floor.

He could feel warm blood oozing out of the back of his skull, running down his neck and making the collar of his tunic sticky, but he could not afford to worry about that. He had more pressing matters to attend to.

"You Saxon bastard!" The crofter got to his knees and tried to scrabble across the rushes to where his knife had fallen. "I'll kill you!"

Saksnot could only understand some of the words, but it didn't take a native Briton to know what the man's intentions were. Closing his eyes for just a moment to try and regain his equilibrium and to clear the points of light that continued to dance before his eyes, the Saxon drew out his own sword, gritting his teeth as he gripped the stool he'd been sitting on and used it to lever himself back to an upright position.

The crofter had managed to reach the knife by now and he came at Saksnot in a blind rage, swinging the weapon wildly. The man was not a skilled fighter, but even so, that slashing blade would cut Saksnot to bloody ribbons. Ducking to the left, the Saxon hooked his foot around the legs of the stool and kicked it into the crofter's path. The man cried out as it struck his ankle and he tripped again. As he fell, Saksnot lunged forwards and thrust the point of his sword into the side of the crofter's neck.

Blood sprayed immediately, shockingly, across the floor of the hovel, and Saksnot stepped back, trying not get any of it on himself.

He watched in grim fascination, pleased with his handiwork as the life pumped out of the gasping, wide-eyed crofter.

And then a terrible pain consumed the right side of the Saxon's body and he screamed, instinctively throwing himself in the opposite direction and striking the far wall with a thump. He gaped at the woman who'd tended his wounds in recent days and saw her standing with an empty pan in her hand, steam rising from the iron. Only then did Saksnot realise she had filled that pan with her boiling vegetable broth and thrown it all over him.

Shocked, he glanced down, seeing the thick, scalding liquid coating his arm and leg, bits of carrot and cabbage stuck to his skin and clothing. A wave of black fury flooded him and, before he even knew what he was doing, he'd covered the space between him and the woman. She was so terrified that she did not even attempt to lift the pan either in defence or as a weapon, and, in an instant, her opportunity was gone as the sword, coated with her husband's blood, slipped into her belly and was ripped upwards.

She slumped to the floor, her accusatory gaze never leaving him until her head thumped against the ground and she lay there, breath rasping in her chest for what felt like an age to Saksnot before, finally, the hovel was silent.

Crying openly, the young warrior felt his own legs give way and found himself half lying, half crouching between the crofters he'd slaughtered. They had shown him kindness and he'd repaid them with terrible brutality.

His guilt quickly faded as the battle fever wore off and the searing agony of fresh burns filled his consciousness. He did his best to wipe off the sodden vegetables clinging to his bare flesh, gasping and whimpering at the agony the movements engendered, and then he was forced to simply sit for a time, trying to catch his breath and calm his roiling thoughts.

What now? he wondered, piecing things together in his mind. He should probably take his horse and chase after the trader – the man's wagon couldn't have travelled that far, could it? And there was always a chance the crofters had told him about Saksnot.

The Saxon's mind rebelled at the mere thought of performing such energetic actions and he dropped his head in his hands, eyes shut, looking for solutions to the multitude of insurmountable problems that assailed him, or at least seemed to in those terrible moments.

The sun had sunk below the horizon outside by the time his fear abated and he was able to think clearly again. The pain had not gone, far from it, but the anxiety had passed and he believed he would have at least the night to recuperate from his latest injuries. Even if the trader did make it to the Damnonii authorities, it would take them some time to reach the hovel. Finding it in the dark of night would not be easy, especially if he made sure there was no fire to see.

That gave him something to do and spurred him to his feet, groaning from the pain. He would douse the fire, but first he would find the salve the woman had made to treat the burns on his face and slather it all over his newly scalded flesh. And then he would eat some of the broth and get as much sleep as possible before taking his horse and leaving in the morning.

As he went about his tasks some of his old steely resolve returned. At least, that's what he tried to tell himself as he gritted his teeth and tended to the peeling skin on his right forearm but, in truth, Saksnot was not at all sure he wanted any part of Hengist's mission any more.

CHAPTER EIGHTEEN

"You're happy with the agreements then?" Sigarr asked as he and King Cunneda stood looking out over the Votadini ruler's lands from Dun Edin. "You believe things will be mutually beneficial?"

Cunneda glanced at him and a small smile played about the corners of his mouth. It was enough to remind Sigarr that the king was no naive fool. Any agreement might benefit both parties, but only until one decided they wanted more, or wanted something different and, in the case of Hengist's Saxons, that kind of thing could happen at any time.

For now though, Cunneda seemed genuinely pleased.

"Aye," he said with a slow nod, the very picture of a powerful man at ease in his own hard-fought place in the world. "I'm happy enough, and so are my advisors. As long as your people pay us your share of the taxes taken from traders, and keep your warriors out of our lands, everything should work out nicely for me and Hengist."

"And I'd say the same of you, my lord," Sigarr returned lightly. "This alliance will only work if both parties are fair and honest."

Cunneda's lip curled again but his smile was openly cynical this time and he simply replied, "Indeed", before walking slowly on, past a small herb garden to a bench surrounded by colourful roses, foxgloves, and other flowers Sigarr did not recognise.

"Very pretty," the jarl noted as the pair sat down amidst the vibrant pinks, blues, and yellows.

Cunneda laughed. "Don't think it makes me any less of a warrior," he warned, although his eyes danced with good humour. "This is my wife's favourite place to sit on a sunny day. She makes sure the gardeners keep it neat, and plant only the most colourful of flowers."

"Nothing wrong with a bit of colour," Sigarr smiled, forgetting himself for a moment and reaching out to draw one of the unfamiliar blooms towards his nose, breathing in the sweet scent before letting go and finding the Votadini king watching him with some amusement. The jarl mentally berated himself for letting his guard down – hard warriors did not sniff blooms, by Tyr, what was he thinking?

Yet Cunneda did not seem to judge Sigarr any less of a man, for he too reached out and breathed in the scent of a small, green leafy plant. "Mint," he said. "It smells nice, but has to be grown in its own pot or it will spread, choking the roots of the other things growing in the garden." He eyed Sigarr coolly as he said this, and the jarl got the distinct impression that Cunneda was comparing the invasive plant to the Saxon people. Well, he'd been compared to worse things in his life. It seemed the king had had enough of flora for one day though, as he said bluntly, "So you'll be sailing south, returning to your *bretwalda*, and then? Will you attack the Picts, or that Damnonii bitch Narina first?"

Sigarr did not react, doing his best to give nothing away in his demeanour. He could not tell Cunneda what Hengist's plans were in case the information reached the wrong people, forewarning them of what was to come. Instead, he turned to smile at the king, shrugging as he did so. "I'm not privy to such plans," he said. "But I can promise you my *bretwalda* will be grateful for your support."

Cunneda returned his smile although without much warmth. "That's fair enough, I suppose," he replied. "And if you need soldiers to invade Alt Clota, I'll gladly lend you some."

"I should be going then, my lord," said Sigarr, smiling and holding out his hand for Cunneda to grasp it in farewell. "Thank you for your hospitality, and for your wisdom. May our two peoples prosper!"

"Indeed," the king replied, standing and looking down at the jarl with a genuinely friendly expression. "I'll look forward to Saxon wealth flowing into my coffers."

A short time later Sigarr and his retinue had made their way down the long sloping road from Dun Edin, back to their ship which lay waiting for them. Cunneda had given them silver or bronze arm-rings as gifts, with another cast from gold for Hengist as a symbol of their new alliance.

As the rowers powered the sleek Saxon vessel away from the shore and out into the open sea, Sigarr looked back with pleasure, waving to the Votadini soldiers who'd escorted them to the port. He was proud of himself, and rightfully so. This was the kind of mission he could excel at, where someone who was more of a simple warrior – like Horsa or Leofdaeg – would fail miserably, getting into drunken brawls or worse. Hengist would be pleased with Sigarr, and with the agreement he'd brokered with King Cunneda, and his success would surely bring him more power and influence.

One day, he thought, if he could continue to prove himself worthy, he could rise to become an influential jarl in his own right, and then? Who knew what he might do with more of the Saxon people behind him? Some of these Britons weren't bad people too – maybe he could even work together with them, instead of just attacking them all…

* * *

"I'm telling you, there was something strange about the whole situation." Lancelot shook his head, staring off into the middle distance without even noticing the raw recruits that were being trained there by Arthur's sergeants.

"What d'you mean?" the warlord demanded, frowning as he filled a cup with fresh, cool stream water and handed it to his friend.

Lancelot turned to look at him directly, brow furrowed even deeper than Arthur's. "The Saxons killed my men easily enough. We had no chance really. They were hiding, waiting for us to come along."

Arthur shrugged. "It sounds like a bad business," he admitted. "Especially for those killed by the sea-wolves. But I don't understand what's so strange about it. They must have got wind of your coming and laid the perfect ambush. Don't take it so badly, old friend, it could have happened to anyone."

"No," the blond warrior replied. "This wasn't like that." He trailed off, eyes drifting across in the direction of the training soldiers in the field nearby. He had returned from his ill-fated patrol just an hour before, having travelled through much of the night to escape from Leofdaeg's Saxons. He'd only stopped to rest when the sky had clouded over, obscuring the stars and robbing Lancelot of any sense of direction. He was fairly sure he'd put a fair bit of distance between himself and the enemy warband however, and had allowed himself to catch a couple of hours' sleep amongst a stand of trees, hoping the twigs and branches strewn about the ground would snap if anyone tried to sneak up on him. Either no one had come close during his slumber, or he'd been in too deep a sleep to hear them, for he'd awoken at first light, groggy, still exhausted, and still reeling from the bloody loss of so many of his men.

"Why was I not killed by the Saxons too?" he'd asked himself as he resumed his journey back to Arthur's camp, and he asked the same question now. "It was as if the bastards were too frightened to come close to me."

"Maybe they were," Arthur suggested, motioning for Lancelot to drink some of the cool water. It was a warm day and he had run for a long time - dehydration was the last thing he would want to incapacitate him after his great escape.

"I was greatly outnumbered," Lancelot protested. "And those men of Leofdaeg's were not all untried, beardless youths. There were hardy, seasoned warriors among them – I mean look at how easily they slaughtered the rest of my patrol! What made me so special?"

Arthur pondered the question but offered no solution. Instead, he turned the question back on Lancelot. "Well, what do *you* think? What *did* make you special? Why did you escape while the others were killed?"

The swordsman drained his water and ran a hand through his long hair. He was extremely tired and found it difficult to gather his thoughts, but he'd had long hours to think of reasons why he'd not been cut to ribbons by the enemy warband and he'd come up with a deeply troubling answer. "Leofdaeg wanted to take me as his thrall again," he growled. "He ordered his men not to kill me, or injure me seriously, so he could put me in chains and work me to death as he'd hoped to do before."

Arthur shuddered. The idea of living a life of slavery was anathema to anyone, but especially a proud warrior, and everyone knew how badly Lancelot's time as a thrall to the Saxon jarl had affected him. Still, he did not seem totally convinced by the argument.

"You shattered Leofdaeg's sword arm," the warlord reminded him. "And made him look a fool when two girls helped you escape his clutches." He raised a hand, smiling. "Oh, I know, I've heard all about those two and how tough they are, but still…Leofdaeg's men would have mocked him terribly for that little escapade. When you take it all into account are you really sure he would be so desperate to enslave you again that he would take the chance of allowing you to escape, as you did?"

Lancelot pursed his lips and helped himself to some more of the water. He sipped it slowly, enjoying the coolness in his mouth as he tried to make sense of what had happened the day before. "It's true, the horrible bastard hates me. I experienced the force of that hatred every day when I was his prisoner, forced to work for him, eat the soiled food that was all he'd provide, drink the water he'd spat in more often than not…"

"Precisely!" Arthur said, nodding vigorously. "And he must hate you even more now than he did then. Every day you're alive he's reminded that you escaped from him." He shook his head. "I cannot believe he would risk you escaping again when he could have killed you yesterday. The fact that his men were too wary of your blade isn't really all that shocking is it? You have a well-earned reputation after all. Only a fool would come at you recklessly."

"But their numbers—"

"Meaningless," Arthur interrupted. "Of course, they could have swarmed you and cut you apart, but your sword would have killed some of them too. The fear of that held them back more than it would with an unknown opponent."

"Maybe," Lancelot conceded, beginning to think the warlord might be right. The whole battle was slowly fading from his memory now, becoming a blur, and he wasn't sure he'd fully understood what was happening even at the time. It had all happened so fast, and the loss of his men had been a terrible shock. Arthur's scenario did make sense and, besides, even if Leofdaeg had wanted to recapture him, it had not happened, and Lancelot had escaped to fight another day.

Next time he hoped he'd be close enough to the despised jarl to finally pay him back properly for all he'd suffered as the Saxon's thrall…

"Maybe you're right," he said at last, doing his best to ignore his misgivings and the little kernel of doubt that continued to nag at him and suggest that something had been strange about the Saxon ambush. He changed the subject, moving the conversation onto another topic. "How is Bedwyr getting on? Has he persuaded any of the sea-wolves to join our cause?"

Arthur smiled and wagged a finger at him in rebuke. "Don't look so smug! I know you think it's a ludicrous idea to befriend our enemies, but the truth is, those Saxon settlers are not our enemies. And, to answer your question, aye, he's had some success."

"Well, that's good, I suppose," Lancelot replied dryly. "Let's hope the followers of Woden and Thunor don't return to Hengist the next time he calls upon them."

"The ones who do would have done so anyway. Maybe this way a few of them will ignore his call and, perhaps, even fight on our side."

Lancelot's laughter pealed out so clearly that the recruits being drilled in the nearby field turned to see what was happening.

"Fight on our side?" the blond swordsman chuckled when his mirth had subsided enough to let him speak again. "That will require a miracle, Arthur, and I'm afraid I just don't see it ever happening."

"Maybe not," the warlord replied, but his confidence in Merlin and Bedwyr's powers of persuasion was not shaken, judging by the smile on his face. "We shall see when the time comes, but I think you'll be surprised and, one day, you will come to think of the Saxons as friends."

Lancelot did not laugh this time. He could not ever see any Briton calling the likes of Leofdaeg a friend. "The Saxons will never see us as equals," he warned. "They are too arrogant, too proud, and too filled with their own sense of superiority."

"We shall see," said Arthur. "We shall see."

CHAPTER NINETEEN

Bellicus was preparing some herbs he'd collected from the small garden that grew on the northern side of Dun Breatann's towering rock. Sometimes he used the produce to craft potions and salves for his work as a druid, taking them to the people of Alt Clota if they called on him to help them recover from some malady or other. Healing was a huge part of any young mystic's training and Bellicus felt more comfortable with this aspect of his duties than, say, mending a broken bone or sewing up an open wound. His great hands and fingers were simply not as well suited for such tasks as the likes of Ria, the druidess who was now the main advisor to Aife, Queen of the Picts.

Still, he thought with some pride, he'd done a decent job of tending to Duro's injuries, and his poultices, bandaging, and prayers to Sulis had, it seemed, staved off any infection.

He was not using his gathered herbs this morning to mix up a healing unguent or elixir though, he had gathered thyme and rosemary and, after washing them, was chopping them up for use in a marinade the fortress's cook would use to season trout caught in the waters of the twin rivers that flowed around its great bulk, the Clota and the Leamnha. The powerful smells filled his nostrils and he smiled as he chopped the herbs in a rear section of the great hall, mouth beginning to water as he imagined how the cooked fish would taste.

He heard heavy footsteps coming through the hall, the rushes doing little to muffle them. Whoever was approaching was doing so in haste, and that made Bellicus grip the bone handle of his knife tighter as he turned, ready to greet the newcomer. It could not be an enemy, he knew that with relative certainty, but the recent attack on the fortress had set everyone on edge and it would be a long time before the inhabitants would again feel truly at ease even within its high walls.

It was no Saxon who appeared through the doorway into the partitioned section though, it was Gavo, and he looked even more irritated than usual.

"What's wrong?" the druid asked immediately, still not setting down the knife for instinctively he could tell some danger was at hand.

"Our fugitive," the captain replied.

"The Saxon who attacked Duro and the others?"

"Aye, him," Gavo confirmed, lip curling hatefully. "He's struck again."

"You mean on his way back south?"

Shrugging, the captain's angry expression faded to be replaced by uneasy uncertainty. "Who knows?" he said. He sat down on a rickety stool that had been in the kitchen area for so long that it had become deeply stained from the years of cooking fumes. "A trader had visited a couple of crofters in the middle of nowhere. He went past their place regularly, dropping in to barter his goods and to carry the latest news to them."

Bellicus nodded, setting down his knife and rinsing little slivers of thyme and rosemary from his hands in a bowl of water. The scenario Gavo was describing was a familiar one, one that had played out up and down the length of Britain for aeons and would continue to do so for generations to come.

"The trader had told the crofters – a man and his wife – about our trouble here in Dun Breatann. He'd noticed that they seemed terrified and perhaps even guilty upon hearing his news, but he didn't know them quite well enough to pry, so he went on his way to the next village. On his way back he noticed the crofters' chimney wasn't smoking, something he'd never seen before, even in summer, so he went in to check on them."

Bellicus gritted his teeth, guessing what was coming.

"They'd been brutally murdered," the guard captain reported. "Their bodies left to rot within their own home."

"But why?" the druid demanded.

Gavo gave a shrug and blew out a long, tired breath. "Some militia men from the nearby village visited the house and it seemed to them like there had been three people living there for at least a few days. There was evidence of an extra, recently slept in pallet, three cups sitting out, that kind of thing."

"They must have taken him in and helped him heal from the injuries he suffered here," Bellicus guessed.

Nodding, Gavo went on. "And when the trader visited, the Saxon realised he'd told the crofters about the attack here, and that the fugitive was on the run. They'll have understood immediately who he was."

92

"And the sea-wolf couldn't let them report him to us," said Bellicus sadly. "So he killed them, just as he did the farmers across the river. Gods below…!"

"Aye, it's a bad business," Gavo muttered, sniffing and brightening for just a moment as he took in the scent of the freshly cut herbs and realised his dinner later that day would be especially tasty.

"The perpetrator escaped again, I assume? He'll be halfway back to Hengist by now if he still has the horse he stole, or a new one."

"He escaped, aye. He was long gone by the time the militia men turned up to look for him. I don't think he's going back to his *bretwalda* though. They found hoofprints, but they weren't heading south, they were going north."

Bellicus frowned and idly began to move his chopped herbs into a small wooden bowl. "You think he's coming back here? Why?"

Gavo held up his hands. "I'm not sure, Bel, but think about it. If the trader told the crofters that Duro had survived the attack, and the Saxon overheard, or otherwise found out…"

"By Taranis," the druid breathed. "What kind of a lunatic are we dealing with, Gavo? He must have been badly injured here – I found lacerations on Duro's fist, he punched the bastard with some force, and you know the centurion, he's as strong as an ox."

"That's not his only injuries either," the captain replied, smiling nastily. "The militia men found a badly dented pot on the floor of the crofters' house. Neither of the two dead folk had injuries matching that, so it seems our Saxon got cracked across the skull with it."

"Ha, good on them," Bellicus chuckled humourlessly. "With any luck he won't make it here, he'll die on the road and the worms can feast on his worthless carcass."

They were silent for a time, digesting everything, and then Gavo murmured, "What kind of man is this, Bel? Not only did he make it inside these walls and almost kill Duro, but he escaped and, despite being injured, still doesn't give up."

Bellicus grunted but he had to grudgingly admit some respect for their foe. Either they were incredibly brave, or incredibly stupid, although sometimes the druid wondered if those were the same anyway.

"He's a killer," Bellicus said at last, moving back to finish off preparing his herbs. "Hengist chose him for this mission because he has certain skills – climbing, fighting, stealth, courage, recklessness, arrogance…"

"He's dangerous, Bel," Gavo grated. "And he's coming for you. We must be prepared for him."

"He won't get in here again, will he? You've had the defences overhauled, especially at that section of wall he made it over." Bellicus lifted the bowl of herbs and walked over to place it beneath the unshuttered window with a plate over the top so they didn't dry out before the cook had a chance to use them in the marinade.

"True," the captain agreed. "He'll find it impossible to get in here again, even if he can fly."

"Well, then," the druid told him, stretching up and patting the knife in his belt. "We'll need to make things a little easier for him, won't we?"

Gavo looked at him in surprise but then he grinned and slowly nodded. "I like your thinking. Let's bring the skulking rat out of the shadows, and give him the justice he richly deserves."

CHAPTER TWENTY

Saksnot had arrived back near Dun Breatann that morning, unrecognised of course, since no-one who'd seen him committing any of his crimes was still alive, well, other than Duro, maybe. His hood masked his scalded face, still smeared with the salve the crofter woman had mixed up for him to soothe those parts in particular that oozed pus. He was still forced to eat only soft foods that didn't need to be chewed, or liquids, for his jaw continued to ache terribly and had given him yet another near-sleepless night.

He was in a pretty bad way, he thought, but, despite his wounds and his burns, and his exhaustion, he felt strong enough to fight, and to best the men he'd come there to kill. So he'd lounged around on the road near the gates to Dun Breatann until midday, lost amongst the rest of the travellers who went to and from the fortress, or the port on the Clota, or the market that seemed to operate most days during these summer months. None remarked on Saksnot's presence for they were all busy with their own tasks and what was one more cloaked, hooded man amongst many? It was still warm and sunny, true, but lots of people – both men and women – wore hoods or shawls to protect their heads against the heat so Saksnot blended in easily enough.

From his position he could not have missed the sight of an absolutely enormous man striding out through the gates of the fortress. Shaven headed, almost seven feet tall with broad shoulders to match, and a long, heavy staff topped with a metallic eagle, there could be no doubt Saksnot was looking at Bellicus, fabled warrior-druid of Dun Breatann. Beside him walked a man of above-average height and build, and he too was unmistakable for he wore a crested helmet and a breastplate the Saxon knew were of Roman design.

Now that was a surprise. The centurion had not only survived his attack, but was walking here with the druid? True, the Roman moved slowly and did not stand fully upright, almost shuffling along beside his huge companion, but still. To have recovered from so many stab wounds so quickly was incredible.

Saksnot shuddered, realising there could be only one possible explanation: the druid had called on the gods of the Damnonii to heal his friend, and they had answered. It showed not only Bellicus's power, but that of Taranis, or Sulis Minerva, or Cernunnos, or whoever of the Briton's strange pantheon of deities had healed the dying centurion. Perhaps it had even been the bull-slaughtering god of Roman soldiers, Mithras.

The Saxon reached up and touched the silver amulet he wore around his neck, silently beseeching Woden to protect him in the coming hours and days. He would need all the help he could get, that was clear, but he would manage. He was Saksnot, after all, legendary Merlin-killer, or at least that was what he'd told himself as he turned away and hurried back to his horse. He'd remained amongst the crowd until druid and centurion went past, now mounted on horses of their own, and then Saksnot had jumped up and nudged his mare into a trot.

The young warrior knew he couldn't follow his targets too closely for the traffic thinned out the further away from the fortress they got. Bellicus and Duro might not know what he looked like, even the centurion had only fleetingly seen him in darkness after all, but his presence behind them would surely arouse their suspicions. So he allowed them to move far ahead – there was only one road here anyway, so they were unlikely to lose him. It seemed the pair were repeating their previous visit to the wooded area that overlooked Dun Breatann, where the furious boar had chased them up into the trees.

Even at a distance, Saksnot could easily pick the riders out as they ascended the hill, the druid especially being impossible to miss for his black warhorse was just as oversized as he was himself.

Why would the pair be going back to such a dangerous place? The Saxon could see they were not armed with the long spears that would be effective against either of the deadly beasts that roamed this area. It did not matter, the Saxon thought. All that mattered was remaining out of sight until he could get close enough to ambush them. After what had happened with the dangerous beasts before it was possible, likely even, that soldiers had come from Dun Breatann and hunted down the angry boar and the lumbering brown bear, hence Bellicus and Duro's apparent lack of apprehension as they rode up the steep road towards the woods.

Perhaps they were simply out riding to help the centurion recuperate from his wounds. Fresh air was always a good way to heal the mind and body, or so Saksnot had heard the wise-women say. He'd had plenty of fresh air in recent days though, and his face still felt like it had been shoved in a blacksmith's forge so…

He watched the pair until they disappeared from view, gave them a few more moments to put some extra distance between his position, and then he followed. They had looked relaxed enough, he thought, although it was hard to tell without seeing their faces and demeanour up close. Why would they not be at ease, though? These were their lands, and they were noblemen, probably heavily armed, and certainly skilled fighters. Perhaps the very best the Damnonii had to offer. It would take something like an enraged boar or a pissed-off bear to cause them trouble they couldn't handle.

They thought they were safe. Saksnot's mouth twitched but he stopped himself from smiling, knowing it would hurt his skin if not his jaw as well. He was pleased however, content in the knowledge that he would soon be riding triumphantly for home.

The possibility of failure, or even of being killed, was always there, but the young Saxon was arrogant – he knew it too, even revelled in it – and, although his faith in the gods and his own prowess had been somewhat shaken in the past few days, he felt sure he could win the coming battle. He would take his time, prepare thoroughly if given a chance to do so, and only strike when the odds were in his favour, preferably by picking the two men off singly, rather than challenging them at once.

He pegged his horse to the ground and fed it some oats he'd taken from the crofter's house. He liked the animal, and it seemed to like him. Gods willing it would survive the long journey back to Garrianum once his job here in Alt Clota was completed.

Leaving the horse hidden amongst a small copse of trees the Saxon began to walk, senses straining for any sign of his quarry.

It was cool there as the trees were fully laden with summer foliage that rustled softly and seemed to deaden the sound around him as he walked. It was a strange place, this, as he'd noted on his previous visit there. There was something ethereal about it, something he couldn't quite put his finger on.

There was a noise to his right and he stopped, drawing his sword in a quick, fluid motion, nostrils flaring as he prepared to defend himself. It was just a female blackbird though, rooting about in the undergrowth for insects. It sensed his attention upon it and paused in its task, small brown body completely still, pale yellow beak turned to the side as it examined him for a moment and then disappeared into the trees.

Wish I could move as fast as that, Saksnot thought as he pushed on, still alert for signs of his quarry. He did not have to strain his hearing for long, as the distinct sound of cheery voices filtered through the foliage from a short distance ahead. Slowing his pace, and watching the ground so he could avoid any obstacles or dry twigs that might snap and give him away, he crept closer to the chattering people.

The voices were male, and there were only two of them. It had to be Bellicus and the centurion. Stopping and pressing himself against the rough bark of a pine he watched and was soon rewarded with a view of the druid. It was impossible to miss the man, given how prodigiously large he was, and Saksnot felt a shiver of fear run through him as he contemplated the possibility of facing such a foe in open combat. The Saxon might have a burgeoning reputation amongst his own people, but Bellicus's name was known all throughout Britain, by natives and immigrants alike – he truly was a legendary warrior, fast and skilled, as well as enormous.

Saksnot breathed through his nose and let it out through lips that were dry despite having been liberally spread with healing salve just a short time before. He would not have to face the druid. Hengist didn't care whether the big bastard was stabbed in the front or the back – the *bretwalda* simply wanted him dead. Besides, Saksnot could easily make up some grand tale about his own courage once he'd killed Bellicus since no one was there to report the truth, whatever it turned out to be. Saksnot would invent some tale that painted him in a glowing light, and add to his fame.

The centurion was not in sight and the hidden Saxon listened, hearing Duro's voice growing fainter as the druid's became louder. They were splitting up! This was exactly the scenario that Saksnot had prayed for; this was his chance to complete the mission. His breath became faster as he pictured the outcome: by the time this day was out he would be known as the man who'd killed not one, but two men that the Britons had called 'Merlin'.

CHAPTER TWENTY-ONE

Bellicus walked with his head down, ostensibly scanning the ground for herbs, mushrooms, or whatever else a druid might collect on a foraging trip like this. It was the fourth such trip he'd taken in as many days, although this was the first time he'd returned to Ard Sabhal since that incredible encounter with the two wild beasts. A wry smile pulled at the corners of his mouth as he remembered that day, and the fright he and Duro had felt. Their panicked climbing of trees while praying to the gods for help seemed amusing to the druid now, although it had been anything but at the time. Still, they'd both survived that adventure, and the centurion still clung to life in Dun Breatann despite the best efforts of his Saxon attacker.

This day's 'foraging' was a ruse to try and flush out that lackey of Hengist's. When Gavo had delivered the news that the Saxon seemed to be heading back in the direction of Dun Breatann to finish what he'd started, Bellicus suggested they draw their foe out by offering themselves as bait. With the Damnonii fortress being locked up as tight as a bodhran drum they had to give the would-be killer an opportunity to complete his mission. Riding or walking out, just the two of them, would hopefully draw their enemy's attention and draw him from his hiding place.

Bellicus knew that Dun Breatann was being watched. He had felt it even when he was safely tucked up in bed beside Narina with guards posted at the doors outside and extra patrols on the lookout for invaders sneaking around the twin peaks. Whether his sense of being observed was his imagination, or some gods-given sixth sense, the druid was not entirely sure – perhaps he was simply paranoid about the possibility of his kith and kin being attacked again. Bellicus did not think so, however. He had spent most of his thirty years honing his senses, opening himself to the otherworld, being alert to things that were outwith the ken of most normal people. He had felt eyes upon him in recent days, human eyes that gazed upon him with cold malevolence.

The man that Hengist had sent to kill him was in Alt Clota still, and nearby, the druid was certain of it. They simply had to bring him into the open and make an end of him.

He spotted a rare herb growing in the lee of a thick, sprawling yew and bent to pick some. He listened for movement nearby, fully aware that Hengist would not have sent an unskilled fighter on such a dangerous mission – there was every chance Bellicus would be defeated by the man, especially if he allowed himself to be complacent.

Hopefully their quarry had followed them there and saw this as the perfect opportunity to strike, with the two Britons separated. Of course, Bellicus was not too far from his friend, as they had agreed, but the Saxon would not know that, with any luck.

The druid straightened and gently tucked his leafy prize into one of the pockets sewn into his cloak for this exact purpose. His herbs and spices could be used to barter for goods and services with those who understood their value and…

Something, a movement in the air perhaps, alerted Bellicus to danger and he tried to spin away behind the thick trunk of the yew, ducking and grabbing at the lower branches to steady himself. He was not quick enough and something struck him, causing him to let out a sharp cry of pain. Glancing down he saw a short knife lying on the hard earth and thanked Sulis that he'd decided to wear a mail coat beneath his cloak.

Drawing his sword, Melltgwyn, the druid was just in time to parry the cut of a gleaming blade that sliced through the air, around the tree towards his midriff.

"You killed Horsa," growled a surprisingly youthful, whip-thin warrior. He spoke in the Saxon tongue, which Bellicus could understand quite well, and was clad in good quality, if not ostentatious clothing consisting of a long-sleeved, pale grey tunic with brown piping, brown shoes, and leggings wrapped at the ankles. The druid had no doubt the Saxon wore a coat of mail like his own beneath the tunic which was held in at the waist by a belt.

"I did not kill Horsa," said Bellicus stepping out from behind the tree to give himself room to stand up straight. He was rewarded by a widening of his opponent's eyes as the young warrior realised just how massive the druid was up close, standing well over a full head taller than the Saxon himself. "Horsa was killed by my friend, Duro. The centurion you tried, and failed, to kill."

The Saxon parried a blow from Melltgwyn and stepped back, eyes flashing angrily.

"How could you not kill a sleeping man?" Bellicus asked mockingly, aiming another thrust that was easily parried by the lithe young warrior. "I see you suffered some injuries of your own too. How's your face? Looks painful, boy." He barked a laugh and pressed forward, launching a flurry of blows which, again, the Saxon managed to parry without too much trouble. As Bellicus had expected, Hengist had sent someone well-versed in battle for this task and, although the Saxon looked barely older than about sixteen, he was wielding his sword with practised ease.

"How are your friend's wounds?" the youth demanded. "Could a mere boy have done the things I did? Killed the Damnonii soldiers I did?" He came forward, blade cutting through the air this way and that, forcing Bellicus to defend for his life. "My name is Saksnot," spat the Saxon. "And I am the Merlin Killer."

Bellicus recognised him then. He had seen this enemy before, just a few months ago at the druid moot in Caer Legion. "You," he breathed, eyes smouldering at the memory of the beardless boy who'd struck down Nemias, High Druid of Britain.

"*Ja,*" smirked the Saxon. "And now I will claim my second Merlin and then find your friend and finish him off properly. I'm amazed he can even walk after what I did to him, but he won't put up much of a fight with all those bandaged stab wounds, eh?"

He fell for it, Bellicus thought with grim humour. He thinks it's Duro with me, patched up and unable to fight.

"Gavo!" he suddenly bellowed. "To me!"

The Saxon's brow furrowed and Bellicus could see the wheels spinning in his head as he tried to figure out who, or what, Gavo was.

"Duro is safely back in Dun Breatann, healing," said the druid. "Gavo is the captain of Queen Narina's guards, and he will help me send you to your Woden now."

Understanding lit up Saksnot's boyish features – he was not facing the druid and a near-invalid, but instead there would be a second powerful, fully fit, warrior along any moment to attack him!

Bellicus laughed and stepped forward again, confidence filling him. He was able to see the Saxon's burned face clearly now that there was a brief respite in the fight, and he could imagine just how painful those burns must be. There was an unnatural set to the lad's jaw too, and, although he could not see a wound Bellicus remembered Gavo's suggestion that the dead crofters had also done him some damage before they were murdered.

"Come, boy," Bellicus said, making his voice low and persuasive as only a trained druid could do. "You cannot beat me, and my friend will join us soon. Lay down your weapons and I'll let you live."

Saksnot gazed at him, uncertainty in his eyes but, surprisingly, no fear. For all his youth, the lad was either stupid, arrogant, or supremely confident in his own abilities – maybe even a mixture of all three.

"Lay down the sword," Bellicus commanded, his tone making the Saxon words come out harsh and clipped and dripping with dread promise of what would happen if he was not obeyed.

The only reply from the young warrior was a hissed oath and a renewed attack, this time with even more urgency. Bellicus was forced onto the back foot, impressed once more by Saksnot's speed. His foe was nowhere near as strong though, and each parry must have rung through the Saxon's slim arms with increasingly painful force. The druid purposely hammered Melltgwyn against his opponent's blade, gritting his teeth and laughing each time he noticed the smaller man wincing.

The supreme confidence that had shone from Saksnot's eyes began to fade as the bout drew on and it seemed like he was gaining no advantage. Both men were fit, neither seemed to be tiring, and neither had drawn blood yet, but it soon became obvious Bellicus was easily a match for the Saxon and, if he wanted, might even be able to dispatch Saksnot if he chose to commit himself fully.

Indeed, the druid had no intention of sacrificing himself on this boyish killer's blade. He might feel in control of the duel at the moment, but any small slip might lead to a thrust or a slash that proved fatal. No, he would wait for Gavo to appear and then the pair of them could quickly make an end to another of Hengist's most valued hearth-warriors.

Bellicus felt himself slipping into the familiar battle trance, his movements becoming utterly instinctual, crisp and fluid, while his opponent's blade appeared to slow, giving the druid plenty of time to dodge it or knock it aside. He felt like laughing, like crying out to the gods in sheer joy as the killing fury descended over him. It seemed the easiest thing in the world to pierce Saksnot's defence and thrust Melltgwyn's tip into the shocked Saxon's side.

Gavo's thundering footsteps reached the combatants then and now Saksnot's arrogance was completely gone. He looked like a frightened youngster, no longer prideful and confident as the reality of his own mortality became horrifyingly apparent. His eyes grew wide as he quickly glanced down at the tear in his mail coat and the blood that was oozing out.

The druid held out his enormous arms and roared like a wild beast, fully aware of how imposing and, frankly, terrifying he would look with his sword outstretched and coated in Saksnot's own blood. His animal display worked even better than expected, as the Saxon drew in a deep breath, stared venomously at the Damnonii mystic, and then turned and sprinted in the opposite direction.

"Where is the bastard?" Gavo finally appeared through the trees and stared at the surprised druid. "What happened?"

"I got him," Bellicus replied like a man waking from sleep and gesturing with his bloodied sword. "He's ran off, the craven scum. Come on, we can't let him get away again, this way!"

"He won't get far if you injured him badly," the guard captain breathed as they raced into the trees.

"Not that badly," Bellicus admitted. "Drew blood, but I doubt I hit anything major. He'll survive, if he gets away and tends to the wound, so hurry up!"

His long legs pumped but the trees were densely packed here and the ground was strewn with old fallen branches and other woodland detritus so his stride gave him little advantage. The fleeing Saxon was also out of sight so they had no real idea which direction he was moving.

"There!" Gavo called, not waiting to see if his companion had heard him.

Bellicus changed direction to move to the left but slipped on what he suspected must be the only damp patch of grass for miles. He lost his balance momentarily, cursing as he grabbed hold of a nearby sapling and hauled himself around, using his momentum to power himself after Gavo.

"There he is!" the captain roared, putting his head down and charging in a straight line as both pursuers heard the unmistakable sound of a horse's harness jingling and then the heavy thump of hooves moving away from them.

"Shit!" Bellicus gasped as Saksnot rode off through the trees, quickly finding the main trail and picking up speed. "The bastard's escaped us. Again!"

CHAPTER TWENTY-TWO

"What do you mean? This is insane!"

Queen Narina stared down, for once, at Bellicus as he rooted about in the chest that sat against one wall of the royal residence on Dun Breatann's lower peak. He grunted as he finally found what he was looking for: a bundle of warm, winter clothing he'd not had to wear since March of that year.

"I have to go after the Saxon, and I don't know how long I'll be gone. I might need these." He looked from his wife to the thick undershirt, tunic, trousers, leg wraps, and woollen socks. "Garrianum is a long way."

"Are you mad?" Narina hissed, shaking her head at the pile of clothing as he shoved it all into a sack that could be attached to his horse's saddle. "You said yourself the Saxon ran away from you. That he could see he was no match for you. He's gone, Bel!"

"For now, aye," the druid agreed, standing up and facing her with a grim, portentous expression on his face. "He lost all his confidence when he realised he wasn't the master swordsman he believed himself to be. When he realised I was more skilled than he was." He lifted his eagle-topped druid's staff and leaned down to kiss her on the lips. She resisted for a moment but then relented, grasping his broad shoulders and returning his embrace with almost desperate passion.

"Gods below," she murmured when the kiss was finally over. "I knew when I married you that you were impulsive and couldn't let things go once you started – I've seen it so many times over the years – but this seems foolish. Why do you need to chase after this man? We have a fortress filled with competent soldiers like Gavo. Why does it always have to be you?"

"I know the road," he reminded her with a small, reassuring smile. "Remember, I followed it when Horsa abducted Catia. I know the way, I know many of the people in the settlements leading there, and I know I have the beating of Saksnot. As does he! I am the only choice for this task. Besides," he pushed open the door and stepped out into the sunshine where he was greeted by Cai who ambled across from the nearby wall and pressed against his legs. "I'll have this one with me."

Narina eyed the big mastiff with some concern. "Are you sure he's up to a long journey, Bel?" she asked, reaching out to gently touch Cai's ears. "He's not as young as the last time you went chasing across the length of Britain."

The druid smiled. "He's young enough yet for a journey like this. The exercise will do him good." His pleasant feelings evaporated then and he turned to gaze down the slope towards the house that used to be his. "I just wish Duro was coming with us."

Narina looked in the same direction and even Cai, recognising the centurion's name, gave a soft whine. He'd missed Duro as much as anyone.

"Aye, Duro would look after you, my love," the queen said, grasping his arm in hers. "Why don't you take someone else with you. Gavo, perhaps?" Her suggestion was hesitant and it was clear she did not relish the thought of both her highest-ranking military men leaving Alt Clota.

"Gavo's place is here," Bellicus replied. "Hengist hates us. Who knows what else he might have in store for Alt Clota? No, we need Gavo in Alt Clota to look after things and to lead our army should it be called upon."

"You think—?"

"No," he broke in, shaking his head firmly. "I don't really believe the Saxons will send an army. One man was supposed to be enough. But you never know with the likes of Hengist, especially when he's grieving his brother. By all accounts they were like chalk and cheese, completely different personalities, but they loved one another. So perhaps it will come to us fending off an army of sea-wolves one day, but, for now, Narina, don't fret too much over that possibility. Better to have Gavo here just in case though. Hengist isn't the only one who could cause us problems after all."

The queen nodded resignedly. Most of the surrounding tribes had been subdued in recent months and years, their kings and warlords killed or defeated or simply biding their time until they were strong enough to make yet another play for the wealthy lands of the Damnonii people. "All right," she conceded. "Gavo remains with me. But there must be someone else amongst our garrison who could travel with you."

Bellicus shook his head. "I travelled alone before, and I'll do so again this time. Besides, Saksnot is only one man, and the lands I'll pass through are still owned by Britons. With Darac to carry me, and Cai to guard me, I will move quickly and dispatch Duro's attacker without too much trouble."

"You told me the Saxon had been foolishly overconfident," Narina said, looking up at him with one eyebrow arched. "Don't fall into the same trap."

He chuckled wryly at the advice. "Don't worry, I'm not stupid."

"So you say," Narina smiled noncommittally. "But chasing a beaten man all the way to Garrianum seems like folly – stupid male pride! – to me."

"Gods willing I won't need to go anything like as far as that to catch up with him," the druid said. "And we can't just let him escape. If we do, we'll never rest easy, fearing he might return to finish what he started."

Narina examined his face, taking in every line and furrow although there weren't many of those. "You want vengeance for Merlin, don't you?"

Without hesitation Bellicus nodded sharply. "I do. Nemias was my friend, and that Saxon whoreson killed him. I would see him face justice for that heinous crime. The thought of the sea-wolves singing songs about Saksnot's prowess makes me sick to the stomach. We need to show them what happens to those who attack our High Druid."

Sighing, the queen laid her head against his bicep and he bent to kiss her soft brown hair, breathing in the scent of her and committing it to memory.

"Please be careful," Narina whispered. "We've only just been wed. I don't want to lose a third husband, Bel."

The thought of leaving her alone in this life sent a shiver down the druid's back. "I will come back to you safely, Narina," he promised. "You can count on it. Saksnot was not the great fighter he thought he was, and he's nursing more than one injury now on top of that."

"No match for you, eh?" she asked, just a hint of bitterness in her tone at his charging off alone again. "Mighty Bellicus, Warrior-Druid of Dun Breatann!"

"Exactly," he replied lightly. "So don't worry about me. I'll return long before I need to start wearing those winter clothes I packed. Come on, I should get going before the Saxon puts too much distance between us. I've tarried too long as it is."

"I'm surprised you came back here at all," Narina said as they started the walk down. "Knowing how impulsive you can be."

"I had to collect Cai, and my supplies," he said. "And Darac will certainly be faster than the stolen nag Saksnot is riding."

"Let's go then," a new voice piped up as they passed the piece of ground that was used for sparring and training the soldiers.

"Catia!" The queen glared at the princess who was wearing a coat of mail that had been made for a smaller sized warrior, and carrying her sword. She also had a full pack over her shoulder that undoubtedly contained food and other supplies. "What do you think you're doing, by Dis?"

The girl did not look at her mother, instead observing Bellicus as if daring him to argue with her. "I heard about you and Gavo fighting the Saxon in Ard Sabhal, and him escaping from you. I knew you'd be going after him, and, since Duro is not able to travel with you, I thought I should come."

Bellicus stifled his smile. He was so proud of his brave daughter, willing to retrace the route her cruel abductors had taken a few years before. She certainly had inherited traits from both her parents and would be an extremely formidable noblewoman one day.

Not yet, though.

Bellicus started walking again and Catia fell in behind them.

"You can't come," he said over his shoulder. "I'm sorry, Catia, but, like Gavo, you are needed here. Your place is with your mother, not on the road with me."

"Don't be daft," the girl protested, patting her sword hilt. "I'm armed, and you know I can use it as well as any man."

It was true she was skilled with her short sword, although still too slight to truly match a seasoned warrior in battle, but that hardly mattered. "That's why you must stay here," he replied, not wanting to belittle her or hurt her feelings. "You must protect your mother if Hengist sends an army to complete the mission Saksnot failed in."

That silenced the princess for a moment although she continued to follow them as they passed the house Duro was still recuperating in and moved down the main flight of stairs towards the stables and gatehouse.

"But"—

"You're not going," Narina said firmly, cutting off her daughter's half-hearted attempt to continue the conversation. "Without Cai and Bel here I need every available sword to protect Alt Clota. If it comes to it, that will include yours, Catia."

The princess eyed her parents suspiciously, apparently not sure whether they were genuine or simply making excuses for her not to go with the druid. A year or two before she'd have known fine well it was just a way to silence her arguments, but now she couldn't be certain. She genuinely was a fine swordswoman and, in the event of another siege like the previous one, if the enemy managed to breach the walls, she could prove valuable.

The small party reached the lower section of the fortress and made their way to the stables where a groom had brought Darac out, saddled and loaded with provisions for beasts and man. Bellicus attached his pack of winter clothing and turned to his daughter. She returned his gaze stoically and he was glad to see she'd accepted their decision not to let her travel with him. It was a shame, he thought, for he truly enjoyed Catia's company, but this was no mission for a girl of twelve summers. For all the druid had played down the dangers to Narina, Saksnot could not be taken lightly, and who knew what other enemies might lie in wait on the long road to Garrianum and the Saxon Shore?

He reached out and took the girl in an embrace. She was tall for her age, taking after him, but still he dwarfed her and she grasped him the way any child hugs a beloved parent. "Duro will want to see you around when he awakes and starts to regain his strength. If I'm not back, you should spar with him if he's up to it. Also," he spoke to Narina too as he went on, "I'm assuming Saksnot is returning to Hengist, but he might decide to double back and come here for yet another attempt at completing his mission. It's highly unlikely, but don't let your guard down."

Queen and princess both nodded solemnly and then Bellicus drew his wife into his arms and kissed her farewell as Catia grabbed Cai's massive neck, hugging the mastiff tightly.

"You look after my father," said the girl, turning her head to look up at Bellicus. "And you look after Cai. I won't be happy if anything happens to either of you."

Narina laughed although there were tears in her eyes. "Agreed," she said. "Come back soon, and safely, both of you."

Bellicus mounted Darac and headed for the gates which the guards opened on his approach. With a last, lingering look over his shoulder he left Dun Breatann and, when the road was clear enough, kicked the big black into a gallop.

CHAPTER TWENTY-THREE

"I've heard that you do impressions of us. Is this true?"

Bedwyr swallowed a sip of mead and glanced at the Saxon chieftain, wondering if his answer would lead to outraged violence. Who could tell with these warlike people?

Qunavo had returned to his usual duties as the Merlin, but Bedwyr, with two guards, had continued to travel around the towns and villages in central Britain that had accepted Saxon settlers into their midst, living and working alongside them in relative peace. There had been around five or six households in each settlement, including farmers, craftspeople, potters, weavers, smiths, cobblers and more. He'd met many of the most powerful men in those immigrant communities, some of whom had seemed genuinely eager to pledge themselves to Arthur, or at least to not answer Hengist if he called them to battle. Others were clearly unwilling to align themselves to the warlord of the Britons, perhaps still feeling a sense of loyalty to their own *bretwalda* or at least their kinfolk who remained in Hengist's army. Even those Saxon leaders did not outright refuse Bedwyr's request for parley though – they were no fools, no matter what propaganda had been spread about the sea-wolves by the natives. Openly rejecting Bedwyr would have marked them as possible, or even probable, future enemies, and that might bring the wrath of Arthur down upon them.

So Bedwyr had journeyed unmolested about the various settlements made up of Britons and Saxons, being received with various degrees of enthusiasm but never with open hostility. Today, he was in a small place called Durovigutum and he'd found his Saxon host quite unreadable up to this point. They were sharing horns of mead in what was little more than a large, sturdily built house but seemed to be used as a meeting hall by the new settlers. There were some benches for men and women to sit at, although only a handful of people occupied them at the moment, everyone else being out hard at work in the village. A very old man, whose duty seemed to be taking care of this hall, brought the drinks and some food to Bedwyr and the Saxon chieftain who was called Taki and built like the side of a barn.

"Impressions?" Bedwyr asked, glad that he had two of Arthur's best warriors with him, both of whom could speak the Saxon tongue almost as well as Qunavo should an interpreter be required.

"Aye, you can do our accent," Taki replied, staring hard at Bedwyr, eyes like lumps of coal in his pale face. "Let me hear your Briton tongue but with our accent."

Taki was broad and muscular and bore two separate, old scars on his face that had been earned in battle. He might be a farmer nowadays, or so he'd told Bedwyr when they'd met that morning, but he had surely sailed along the whale road to Britain as part of Hengist's invading army originally.

"What makes you think I can do your accent?" Bedwyr asked, still oblivious as to whether Taki was hostile or friendly.

"We heard you were coming here," the Saxon replied. "Yesterday. Some of the Britons in town were talking. I asked them about you. One of the men said they'd been in a warband with you, and heard you talking like one of us. You were very convincing apparently."

Bedwyr knew exactly what the villager had been talking about – more than once his friend Cador, Arthur's cousin, had pretended to be the leader of a band of marauding sea-wolves in order to frighten the native Britons into improving their settlements' defences. When a dozen or so invaders appeared near one's village, heavily armed and apparently out for plunder and rape, well, it tended to make people see the sense in building sturdy walls and gates. Somehow, Bedwyr had been mistaken for Cador, who had actually been killed in Garrianum when Lancelot was captured by Jarl Leofdaeg.

Taking a chance that Taki was genuinely intrigued and not looking for a fight, Bedwyr did his best to mimic the Germanic accent as Cador had once been so good at, and said in Brythonic, "What would you like me to say? That Hengist is a fool, and Arthur will reward you well for fighting on our side?"

The chieftain's eyes lit up and, for the first time since they'd met, he grinned. Slamming the bench he laughed heartily and raised his mead horn in salute. "I like it," he said, and his accent sounded very much like the one Bedwyr had adopted. "Although I'm not so sure Hengist is a fool."

Bedwyr shrugged, feeling relief and pleasure at the sight of Taki's laughter. "Maybe not, I don't know him well enough to be certain. But he will not win this war he's brought to our shores. Even you must have seen that, to give up the life of a warrior and settle here as a farmer."

Taki nodded slowly but without much conviction and jerked a thumb over his shoulder towards the wizened caretaker. "Like Fritigern there, I am too old to be a warrior now. Not physically weak, like him," he clarified, sitting up straighter on the bench and puffing out his impressive chest. "But in here." He tapped the side of his head and smiled ruefully. "I no longer care to see my friends cut down in their prime, all to earn a bronze arm ring or a fine new seax."

Bedwyr diplomatically did not mention the fact that Taki was proudly wearing such arm rings, of silver as well as bronze, allowing the man to continue.

"Battle fame and glory is all very well," noted Taki wisely. "But I would like to see my fiftieth winter without losing a limb, or an eye, or my life. So," he shrugged. "I settled here with those who thought like me. I would not like to fight anyone else's battles, Lord Bedwyr, whether it's for Hengist, or your Arthur. Let the younger men, those full of dreams of plunder and of songs being sung in their honour, fight. I will plant my seeds here." He paused to take a sip from his horn although his eyes remained on Bedwyr, twinkling with amusement. "If you know what I mean," he finished, winking suggestively.

Bedwyr blinked, realising what the chieftain meant but unsure how he felt about it. A Saxon mating with a woman of the Britons? Lifelong prejudices rose within him and outrage bubbled to the surface, but he forced himself to think rationally. Why should this man not start a family with a native woman? If there was anything that would make Taki, and others like him, fight on the side of the Britons, it would be familial ties to the island and its people.

"I'm glad that you no longer wish to be a warrior," he said to the Saxon, raising his horn in another salute to the chieftain. "But the day may come when you will have to choose a side. I would like you to make that choice now, and swear allegiance to Arthur, or at least swear not to raise your hand against we Britons for Hengist."

Taki's humour faded and he peered at Bedwyr and his two silent companions coolly.

"What would you do," Bedwyr asked, "if a Saxon warband attacked this village right now? If Hengist and his men began destroying the buildings, killing the men, and raping the women? Maybe you've got your eye on a particular woman, with thoughts of marrying her?" He could see by Taki's reaction that he'd struck a nerve so he forged on with it. "Whose side would you take if a Saxon warrior dragged that woman you like, a Briton, into the road, ripped off her tunic, and began to beat her and rape her? Would you join in?"

His tone was deliberately hard, even accusatory, and Taki's jaw tightened as he stared at him.

"I am no raper," he breathed with barely controlled anger.

"Then what would you do? Would you join in with your fellow Saxons and destroy this village that you've made your home? Or would you defend the people who've accepted you into their community?"

It seemed a very simple choice to Bedwyr, and Taki had come across like a decent man, but the hypothetical scenario had clearly rattled the Saxon and made him deeply question himself. This was the exact problem the new Merlin had foreseen and wanted to deal with now, before it became a reality.

"Well?" Bedwyr prompted, returning Taki's angry stare unblinkingly. "What would you do? Would you, and the rest of your Saxon settlers, fight to save this village you now call home, or would the bonds of kinship between your fellow sea-wolves draw you back to fight, and burn, and kill, alongside them once more?"

When Bedwyr and his two guards first started visiting Saxon immigrant communities they had trod very lightly, but, as they gained in experience of dealing with men such as Taki they had learned that harsh words often gained the best results. The Saxons appreciated blunt, direct speech just as much as they enjoyed riddles in the game they called flyting. It might anger them to be harried like this by the emissaries, but, in a strange way, they respected the Britons for it.

Taki turned and examined the old Saxon man who was busy repairing the leg of a damaged bench nearby. Bedwyr wondered if the hall's caretaker would frown on Taki if he sided with the Britons rather than his own people. Replying in a low voice that was barely more than a whisper, Taki confirmed Bedwyr's thoughts but,

114

thankfully, the chieftain said, "I will defend this village, and the people in it. All the people in it, not just Saxons."

Bedwyr and his two companions shared happy smiles. Keeping his own voice low, Bedwyr said, "That is good. Thank you. Will you swear it to me?" He held out his arm and the Saxon stared at it as if unsure he was making the correct choice.

After a long, breathless moment when even the old caretaker's thumping seemed to fade into the background, Taki at last reached out and grasped Bedwyr's forearm. "I swear it, by Thunor," and he touched an amulet that hung around his neck on a leather thong. To Bedwyr's eye the amulet depicted a bearded figure and he knew it must symbolise the Saxon thunder-god.

"Then I will swear to Taranis that you will be rewarded by Arthur if the day ever comes when you are forced to honour your oath." Bedwyr nodded solemnly and the two men drew their hands back to grasp their mead horns, raising them in salute to their newfound alliance.

Taki swallowed his drink and didn't seem to know whether he should be pensive, pleased, or something else. The emotions rolled across his face like cattle gathering in the field before a storm and Bedwyr watched, still not entirely sure whether he'd made a friend or an enemy. At length, the Saxon smiled and said, "So, where are you going next to spread your message of peace and companionship?" He laughed, a great bark that filled the modest hall. "You're not Christ followers are you? We've seen far more of them in Britain than at home."

Bedwyr shook his head. In truth, he didn't know much about the new religion that was rapidly growing all across Europe, or so he'd heard. "No, we follow the old gods. It was our High Druid's idea to reach out to your people. As for where we're going next – Durobrivae. It's just a few miles north of here."

Taki nodded. "I know the place. I sell grain and meat there at times."

"There are Saxons living there?"

"*Ja*," the chieftain said. "Not as many as there are here in Durovigutum, but a few."

"Hopefully they are as accommodating as you, friend." Bedwyr beamed, very happy to have concluded business in such a positive manner. Standing, he reached out to grasp the chieftain's forearm again. "May the gods shine on you, and your farm, and on your family, should you be lucky enough to have one someday."

"Oh, I'm sure there will be little Takis wandering around the streets of Durovigutum before long, my lord," the Saxon replied with a glint in his eye. "The gods protect you too." He nodded to Bedwyr's companions who murmured their own blessings and thanks for Taki's hospitality and then the Britons went outside into the sunshine. Bedwyr could feel the hard eyes of the old caretaker watching them as they left, and an involuntary shudder ran through him. That man had also been a warrior once, Bedwyr thought. A warrior who had killed Britons and believed his gods would reward him for it in the afterlife.

These were different times now, though, and a new era was being ushered in by Arthur and the Merlin and those who served them.

"Well," he said to his men, who both looked merry after the mead they'd all shared. "It's not too late. Let's forge onto Durobrivae and see what we find there, eh?"

"More of that mead hopefully," one of the men replied, prompting an appreciative chuckle from Bedwyr.

"Aye, that, and more Saxons as open to peace as Taki. Come, lads, let's get our horses and ride on. I have a good feeling about the coming days!"

They strode away, smiling happily and none looked back at the hall doors or they would have seen old Fritigern the caretaker stonily watching them go.

CHAPTER TWENTY-FOUR

"Into these bastards!" Hengist did not always lead battles from the front but recently, since his brother Horsa's death in fact, he'd found that cleaving the skulls of Britons was therapeutic, so he stood in the foremost rank of the Saxon shieldwall, swinging his axe and crying out for the glory of the war god, Tyr.

The blade of his weapon stuck fast in a Briton's shield and he instinctively tried to yank it free. The poor wretch holding the shield stumbled forward for Hengist was a strong man and, when he did so, Hengist rammed the spiked boss of his own shield into the Briton's face. The pointed iron tip was thrust with such force that it pierced the enemy's skull, dropping him instantly to the ground.

"Into them!" Hengist repeated, holding his arms aloft in triumph. So caught up in bloodlust was he that he didn't even see the spear tip that was aimed at his chest. Had it not been for one of his hearth-warriors knocking the shaft aside just before the leaf-shaped tip plunged into him the *bretwalda* would surely have been killed.

"Have a care, lord!" the warrior shouted, shoving his own spear point into the massed ranks of the enemy shieldwall.

Hengist roared with laughter, parrying another attack and grabbing a spear from one of the men in the rank behind. It felt good to fight, his conscious mind almost going to sleep as his body was moved by instinct or the gods, defending, attacking, stepping forwards and back, ducking, and rejoicing as his weapon stole the life of another foe.

"I warned you ugly she-goats what would happen if you didn't agree to my demands," the Saxon warleader cried as he ripped open the arm of a Briton. "You should have done as you were told! Now your village will burn along with everyone in it!"

At that moment, with the thrill of killing coursing through him, if Hengist had the power to call down a lightning bolt from Thunor to raze the land to ashes he would have done so without a thought for the innocent women and children he would be consigning to the funeral pyre. He was not normally a cruel man, but battle fury did strange things to him and he fought on with sheer savagery, reddening his spear point until the shaft itself became slick with blood and slippery in his fingers.

He saw his axe still sticking out of the shield that had claimed it. It was lying on the ground close to him and, pulling it free, he realised that, despite the intense, brutal fighting, the opposing shieldwalls had not actually moved positions much. And then he wondered just how long ago he had lost the axe – it felt like hours but perhaps it was mere moments. It was impossible to tell.

Without thinking about it his left arm came up and his round shield batted aside a sword that was slicing through the air towards his shoulder. He barely registered the dull tremor that ran all down that left side of his body and then, teeth gritted in fury, he smashed the reclaimed axe down on his opponent's head. The Briton must have been a lower-class levy for he wore no helmet, merely a cloth cap that offered no resistance whatsoever to the hardened iron of Hengist's axe. There was a crunch and the light in the man's eyes instantly flickered out as he died.

"They're running!"

Hengist had moved back into a defensive stance, drawing in quick, sharp breaths, eyes wide as he surveyed the hideous wreckage he'd made of the Briton's skull. It took a long moment before he was able to take in the shouts of the men standing either side of him in the Saxon line.

"They're running! The cowards are running!"

Reality momentarily returned to Hengist – the reality of everyday, mundane life, and of the situation there in Britain, most relevantly his situation and that of his army. It flashed through his mind that sparing the frightened natives might make him seem more benevolent, and persuade future opponents that the Saxons were not the brutal savages they were often portrayed as.

He pictured Horsa though, imagining his brother's body swinging like the carcass of a butchered cow from the towering walls of Dun Breatann, and any merciful feelings evaporated like frost when the sun comes up in the morning.

His men were watching him and he smiled grimly, pleased at the discipline he had ingrained in them. When they'd first arrived on these shores his followers had been wild and fought in entirely separate units formed by bonds of family or birthplace – now they looked to him for orders, eager to be unleashed upon the fleeing Britons. This was not a large settlement but there would be plenty of plunder, and women, within its now undefended walls.

Massacring the beaten defenders would be the first task though, should Hengist allow it.

"Get them!" the *bretwalda* screamed, leaning back and gazing at the sky, feeling the power of Thunor being channelled through him and into the legs that began pumping as he raced after their enemies, jumping over corpses and crying, sobbing, injured men who begged for mercy and their mothers even as their pale faces were ground into the earth by dozens of booted feet.

Hengist ran with his men, leading from the front as any good leader must do, although there was little danger to him now. The Britons had no fight left in them, and even if they did most of them had thrown down their weapons. They wanted to run away from the battlefield as quickly as possible, and, in their terror, they were heading for the safety of their settlement's walls.

"Sigarr!" he roared, noticing his cousin tarrying near the rear of the Saxon tide sweeping across the churned-up field.

Sigarr heard the call and looked about, trying to see where it came from. Hengist cursed, annoyed at having to slow, but even in his excited state he did not judge his cousin too harshly, knowing Sigarr was not physically as capable as other soldiers. He was a jarl though, and knew how to lead.

"Take your men to the right, there," Hengist shouted, pointing his spear where he wanted Sigarr to head for, a section of the settlement's walls which the Saxon scouts had reported to be in a state of disrepair before the battle started. Indeed, the Britons must have known their feeble walls could not protect them, which was why they'd deigned to come out from behind them and face Hengist's army in the open. It had been a brave decision, and one taken no doubt to try and save the women and children from their enemy's depredations. Perhaps those same women and children had been running away while the battle raged. That would not be ideal, for Hengist's folk always needed new slaves, and it was a warrior's right to take his pleasure with the women of those they'd slaughtered in battle.

Sigarr could not have known all of this was spinning through his cousin's head at that moment, but he heard Hengist's command and understood what was required of him. He split off from the rest of the army, exhorting his own troops to follow him. It was a mark of his rising influence and the respect he was earning for himself that those warriors obeyed him almost as soon as they'd heard his orders. Hengist smiled. Sigarr was no replacement for Horsa, but he was kin, and he was ambitious, and he would always do his best.

As the wheezing jarl took his warband away to the eastern side of the settlement to force their way through the rotting walls, Hengist pushed forward again. He was no longer near the front ranks and somehow that dampened his lust for blood. The fury that filled him had dissipated as he communicated across the battlefield with his cousin and his rational mind began to assert its dominance once more.

He slowed, watching as the surviving Britons reached their village and tried to push the gates closed. There were too few of them though, and Hengist's rabid sea-wolves threw themselves against the wooden barriers, their combined weight enough to keep the defenders from dropping the locking bars into place until more Saxons arrived and the gates were thrown open with such force that one literally ripped away from its hinges.

The *bretwalda* felt a momentary thrill of fear for the occupants, particularly those too weak, young, or old to defend themselves. Hengist had seen this scenario play out many times before and he knew an army revelling in a bloody victory on the battlefield were no longer men, they were savage animals. No Briton would be safe now, especially as Sigarr's warband was spilling through the wall they'd made short work of knocking down.

Already screams were rising into the air alongside smoke and burning embers.

Hengist stopped moving completely and just stood, leaning on his spear as he caught his breath and watched the village become a flaming charnel house.

He should have commanded his men to hold back rather than allowing them to charge into the settlement and put the place to torch and sword. What good did this rampant death and destruction do for Hengist's cause? For the Saxon expansion into Britain?

He was no longer worried about the suffering of the villagers – they'd been given the chance to surrender in return for swearing him allegiance, and they had thrown his offer back in his face. Hengist could hardly be blamed for what happened now. No, his annoyance lay in the fact that those Britons could have been useful – they'd have worked the land, created goods and furniture, hunted, and done all the other things they'd been doing throughout their miserable lives. The only difference would be that they'd pay Hengist taxes instead of one of the fat native lords.

Now, or at least very soon, there would be no taxpayers left, for they would be used up and burned to ash with the rest of the village. The smell of roasting meat was already blowing back towards Hengist and he wrinkled his nose, feeling hungry and nauseated in equal, confusing measure. What a waste of resources this all was. He knew it was necessary, but still, it was wasteful.

Of course, wiping this village from the face of *Miðgarðr* along with its occupants would send a message to the next Britons Hengist's army came up against. Perhaps it would make them less likely to stand against the Saxons, but it might have the opposite effect. Certainly, it would not make the natives look on Hengist with anything but hatred and terror.

Did he want to subjugate the entire population of Britain, killing all who opposed him, no matter how great their numbers were? Would he rule a barren wasteland? Or would it be better to integrate with the people, as Sigarr had often advised. He had been inclined to see his cousin's point of view until Horsa's disrespectful treatment in Alt Clota, and now…

"Well, we won, but it hardly feels like a triumph, lord."

Hengist had become lost within a daydream, shutting out the world around him, and he realised now that Sigarr was standing beside him. Irritation flared within – he did not need this little weasel reminding him that there were alternative ways to conduct a war than simply crushing everyone in your path. "Are you not joining in with the celebrations, cousin?" he demanded. "There must be a girl in there you could take a fancy to, surely. Or at least help gather any plunder before the buildings collapse upon themselves."

Sigarr shook his head. "The smoke affects my breathing," he admitted, and he was already wheezing even more than normal, his lungs making that unpleasant crackling sound that told every warrior in the army how weak the jarl was.

"What a sad life you must lead," Hengist said, tilting his head thoughtfully. "What little joy you take in things – even a victory such as this." He raised a hand as Sigarr opened his mouth to reply. "I agree, cousin, this is a waste. But our borders have moved another

121

few miles further west and our territory continues to expand, despite Arthur's efforts to push us back."

Sigarr had closed his mouth and was watching his charismatic, powerful cousin somewhat enviously, although Hengist did not detect any jealousy. He knew Sigarr was a realist, accepting his own weaknesses while admiring the strengths of others and aspiring to greater heights himself. The thought gave Hengist pause and he eyed his cousin suspiciously, seeing him with new eyes.

Was Sigarr the type of man to attempt to become *bretwalda* himself? To supplant Hengist? A year or so ago the very idea would have seemed ludicrous, but Hengist had given him more responsibility in recent months and Sigarr had performed admirably, earning the respect of not just his cousin, but of many of the men in the army too. A taste of power often made jarls greedy for more, but Sigarr with his physical weaknesses would surely never be accepted by an army of taller, stronger men as their commander. Would he?

No, Hengist knew his cousin. Sigarr was ambitious, surely, but he had never seen himself as a warrior, and only a great fighter – or someone who had once been such and built a great reputation – could ever be *bretwalda* of their warlike people. Angles, Saxons, Jutes, Franks, Danes and so on did not sail across the whale road from their homes to serve unimposing men like Sigarr who could barely run up a flight of steps never mind carve a bloody swathe through massed ranks of Britons.

Hengist had nothing to fear from his cousin.

"Come," he said, placing a fraternal hand around Sigarr's narrow shoulders and leading him away from the burning settlement, back towards the Saxon camp. "Let us share a horn or ten of mead, and discuss our next moves."

CHAPTER TWENTY-FIVE

The first time Saksnot attempted to kill Bellicus and Duro he escaped directly to the south, across the Clota from Dun Breatann and onwards, riding his stolen horse. This time the Saxon had chosen a different route, and it was a familiar one to Bellicus, for it was the same way Catia had been taken by Horsa, Aldred and the other abductors four years previously. Presumably someone who had been part of that earlier warband had given Saksnot detailed directions so he didn't get lost but, as the druid tracked the fugitive old, unpleasant memories were stirred up.

He vividly remembered the fear he'd felt for the princess, stolen away by dangerous, evil men, and each section of the journey threw up another mental image of the people he'd met and the places he'd visited during that earlier chase. The old woman who'd pointed him towards the ruined Roman fort at Cibra; the walls of that fort as he'd climbed them and gazed out across the sweeping landscape; the people of Litana who'd offered him hospitality that night before, despairing that he'd lost Catia's trail, he performed a ritual and the gods rewarded him by showing him exactly which direction to ride.

All these images and sensations returned to him, fuelling the anger he felt for not only Saksnot but all of his warlike people, especially Hengist. The *bretwalda* had come to Britain with blade and fire, stealing land from the natives, killing, enslaving, and raping them in the process. And yet Hengist had the gall to act offended when the Britons fought back and killed his brother! His brother, indeed, who'd been attempting to invade Alt Clota!

The arrogance and entitlement of the sea-wolves astonished Bellicus. Even the Picts and the Dalriadans were not so blatantly narcissistic.

What made them behave in the way they did? Bellicus wasn't sure, suspecting more than one reason. The people who made up what he called 'Saxons' – Jutes, Frisians, Angles, and so on – were large and physically more imposing than the average Briton, which, as the druid knew from personal experience, naturally made one feel superior. The invaders also came from hard, unforgiving homelands where snow and ice was as common as sunshine – not perhaps those who sailed from Jutland, which Bellicus knew was about as temperate as Alt Clota – but certainly those who came to Britain from even further north, like the Suiones or those from Norvegia. Warriors used to living in freezing temperatures would not balk at the relatively cool climate they found on the eastern coast of Britain, being happier to fight battles and travel in winter than the native tribes. The Saxons also worshipped hard gods like Woden, Thunor, and Tyr, all of whom could be ruthless, cruel, manipulative, and bloodthirsty in the tales Bellicus had heard of them. Where the Britons believed they would be reincarnated after their death, the Saxons warriors sought to die well in battle, expecting their gods to reward them with a place in some mythical mead hall where every day would be spent feasting, fighting, and fornicating.

Not such a bad afterlife, Bellicus conceded to himself with a wry smile as Darac cantered past Drumcrew, another town laced with memories of his previous hunt for sea-wolf raiders.

The Saxons were not simply warriors, though. Their craftsmen made wonderful things, especially from wood, and they appreciated poetry, games of skill like tafl, and many of their myths had great depth.

All of these aspects of Saxon life unsurprisingly made them see themselves as stronger and better than the people they raided. Physically, morally, culturally, spiritually – Hengist, Sigarr, Leofdaeg, Thorbjorg, Horsa, all believed they were destined to rule.

That strong self-belief made them formidable opponents, and not ones to surrender easily.

"You, boy!" The druid tore his mind away from musings about sea-wolves and called to a youngster who was idly watching some sheep in a field beside the road.

The youth, a barefoot lad of about ten summers wearing a simple grey tunic and a stained cap to keep the sun from his head, looked up at the druid on his great black horse and swallowed. "Aye, lord?" he asked breathlessly.

"Have you seen another man riding past here recently? A man with a red, scarred face?"

The child nodded instantly, eyes wide. "Aye, lord," he repeated. "A couple of hours ago. He didn't look very healthy."

Bellicus smiled grimly at that. "Did he just continue along the road?"

The boy shrugged, seeming to grow in confidence as he saw the druid's good humour. "I didn't go after him so I can't say for sure, but he stayed on the road until it took him out of sight. Are you going to kill him?"

"What makes you ask that?" the druid asked, genuinely curious and impressed by the boy's perception.

"Well, he looked frightened and upset, and here you come along a little while later looking angry with your hand on that fine sword." He shrugged again, bony shoulders rising and falling as though his deduction had been a simple one. "Seems to me like you two have had a fight, and he's come off the worst for I don't see any injuries on you. Is that your dog? He looks friendly. Can I pet him? My dog isn't so big, and doesn't like being petted."

Bellicus couldn't help but laugh at the youngster's simple vitality and he reached into his cloak, drawing out a piece of hacksilver and tossing it to the little shepherd. It spun, glinting in the sunshine, before the boy plucked it nimbly out of the air and made it disappear almost as fast as if he'd been trained in sleight-of-hand by the druids themselves.

It was amusing how Cai seemed friendly to people that weren't a threat. He had no doubt Saksnot would not find the mastiff so approachable when they finally caught up to the fleeing Saxon.

"He's friendly enough, but we must be going. We have to catch up with that other man."

"Good luck, my lord," said the boy with surprising brevity and a final pat of Cai's head over the dry-stone wall that kept the sheep penned in and stray dogs from wandering into the field. "I hope you catch him, he looked mean!"

"Oh, I'll catch him, my friend," the druid promised, urging Darac into a walk and waving cheerily at the little shepherd. "You can be sure of that."

* * *

The sun was not particularly hot that day as it was later in summer now, but there was barely a cloud in the sky so the heat had been relentless and it was taking a terrible toll on Saksnot's injured face. The salve the old woman crofter had been mixing for him was all used up by now and he mentally berated himself for killing her before she could make another batch. He wondered what ingredients she'd used for it, and whether he could gather them himself. For a time he looked at the foliage as his horse carried him along, wondering what each plant and herb and leaf might be used for. The *volur* collected such things and made all sorts of poultices, drinks, food flavourings, even things to make a person think he was flying or walking with the gods in some strange other world. The damn druid he'd been sent to kill would no doubt know exactly which things to collect for a salve to relieve burns – better than the stuff the crofter had made too.

A bird, Saksnot had no idea what kind, made a strange, loud screeching sound beside him and he jerked upright in the saddle, staring at the thing as it spread great wings and took off into the sky, languidly soaring out of sight, long pointed beak making it seem like some instrument of war to the young swordsman.

As the bird faded from sight Saksnot realised he'd been lost in a pleasant daydream and had even forgotten for a time about the pain in his face. The burning returned with a vengeance then, and he let out a low, tortured moan, grasping his side where the Damnonii druid had stabbed him for that wound ached too.

When he'd escaped from the druid and his fake centurion friend, Saksnot did not stop riding for a long while, putting plenty of distance between himself and any pursuit, guiding his mount along streams to hide their scent from that huge mastiff Bellicus roamed about with. When he was sure that no one could be trailing him he'd stopped, feeding the horse and allowing it to drink before doing his best to bandage the bleeding gash in his side.

His inexperience was apparent then, as it had been more than once on this ill-advised trip, for he had no real idea how to deal with his injuries. Of course he'd seen healers tend to those cut or maimed in battle, and he felt certain that the wound Bellicus had inflicted upon him should be stitched shut, but he did not know how to go about it, and he never had the equipment for it anyway.

What a fool I am, he thought sadly. He'd travelled all the way from Garrianum to Dun Breatann with little more than a pack of food and his weapons, safe in the knowledge that he was a mighty warrior who had little to fear from any enemy. The idea that he might be stabbed had barely crossed his mind and he inwardly raged at the older warriors in Hengist's retinue who never thought to advise him of his own stupid arrogance. Why had they not given him needle and thread to stitch wounds? Shown him how to use them? Why had his parents never taught him such skills, useless bastards that they were? He was sure one could use fire to seal a cut, remembering vividly the stench of burning meat and screaming of men who'd been 'healed' in just such a fashion after the attack that had seen him kill the Merlin, but he had no intention of doing that to himself.

He looked down and pressed his hand against his mail coat where it had been torn through by the druid's blade. When he took it away the palm was slick with blood and he groaned again, glaring up at the sky as he thought to rail against Woden and the other gods who seemed to have forsaken him. He bit his tongue however, knowing that would simply anger them further.

Since no one had ever bothered teaching him how to heal himself, and the gods were not inclined to help, there was only one other option: he would need to find more people to help him, like the crofters that had taken such good care of him before.

He turned to look over his shoulder, noticing the saddlecloth was also stained red as his lifeblood oozed slowly out of him. The road behind was not empty, but the only travellers upon it were merchants with wagons, or small groups of people walking between villages on whatever errands filled their miserable little lives. No one was coming after him. He had time to pause and persuade someone to heal him; all he had to do was find a man or a woman with the skills, and the inclination to do so.

With that decision made Saksnot felt a lightening of his load and his slumped shoulders rose a little. Things did not seem quite so gloomy now for there were houses, and settlements small and large dotted all along this road – he would find someone to stop the bleeding and he would persuade them to do it, one way or another.

He stroked his horse's neck, murmuring words to soothe himself as much as the animal which seemed content enough. Pondering his injuries had made him feel even more of a failure – his face had been burned, his jaw broken, his skull dented by an iron pot, and now he was bleeding slowly to death from what he believed was a fairly shallow stab wound. He felt terrible, almost wishing he would die and find some respite from his shame and chronic pain.

He thought back to that dark, low house in the middle of Dun Breatann and remembered how he'd frantically stabbed the dozing centurion. He'd done all he could to kill the man, yet Duro had somehow survived the attack and, if Bellicus's claims were to be believed, was healing well.

I'm a failure, the Saxon thought bitterly, and he welcomed the warm tears that spilled from his eyes and soothed his blistered cheeks for at least a few moments.

CHAPTER TWENTY-SIX

"Haven't you just got married, Aesus?" Bedwyr asked the younger of his two escorts, a tall, lean man in his mid-twenties. "Why would you volunteer for this job?"

Aesus raised an eyebrow as he turned in his saddle to look at the captain. "I got married two years ago, lord."

"Two years!" Bedwyr whistled and shook his head ruefully. "Where does the time go, eh? Seems like just yesterday you were talking about it. Oh, well, two years married, I guess that answers my question about why you wanted to come with me on this mission."

The second escort, an older fellow in his early thirties, laughed at that. "Aye, this must be a nice rest, eh?"

Aesus smiled along with them, but he very clearly did not really share their amusement. "Actually, I've not seen her in weeks. She's living with her mother and father in the south. She's given birth to my son too, but I'll not get to see them for a while now."

"The life of a soldier," Bedwyr murmured, nodding sadly. "Arthur will see you well rewarded for your loyal service though, Aesus. You'll be able to take care of that boy of yours when we complete our mission, and hopefully that won't take too much longer."

"Aye, I was told I'd be well paid for this so that's why I volunteered. You're not bad company anyway, lord."

"Ha, glad to hear it," Bedwyr replied. "What about you, Motius? You here to get away from a nagging wife or because you love my conversation?"

"My wife is no problem," the escort said fondly. "She even likes my battle scars."

"Scars?" Aesus demanded, pointing at the older man's head. "Half your ear is missing!"

"Aye, I can thank the Saxons for that," Motius replied, a hint of pride in his voice. "I'm still here though, and, like I say, the women love a good scar, especially if you have a heroic story about how you got it."

"And you do, no doubt."

"Oh aye, Bedwyr," replied Motius. "More than one!"

"So you're just here for the extra pay too then?"

"Aye, and I thought it would be good to see a bit more of the country. I'm from the southeast and don't really know these lands. Besides, I thought it would be safer than standing in the shieldwall when Arthur next engages Hengist's raiders."

"Safer?" Aesus scoffed. "I thought you liked earning battle scars."

"I did," Motius agreed. "But I've got enough now. Don't want to get too many, my wife might think I'm ugly if I keep getting more all the time."

"I doubt she'd mind. Poor woman must be near blind anyway if she thinks you're handsome."

The older man took the jibe in good humour. He was not an attractive man, with or without his scars, and he knew it. He had a bulbous nose, a mouth that was too broad for his face, and protruding eyes. He looked like what he was: an experienced soldier, veteran of dozens of battles, and he was quite content with his lot.

"You might be a pretty boy now," he grinned, revealing surprisingly intact, mostly white teeth. "But if you survive another ten years or so and reach my age, you'll look just like me, lad."

"By Dis, I think I'd rather be cut down by the Saxons than end up like that!"

It was all said in jest, and taken as such, and Bedwyr laughed along with the two men who he could tell had been friends before they'd taken on the job of escorting him. He was glad to have them with him for it would have been a much less pleasant journey with quieter, or less amusing companions and they were both incredibly gifted with languages which he was not.

"You men are glad you came along then?" he asked them.

Motius removed his helmet and nodded. His head was wet with perspiration but they all knew the importance of being ready for anything. Hengist's foragers were not the only threat in these lands – brigands were always a problem, and probably always would be. A sweaty head was preferable to a skull cracked by some slinger hidden in the undergrowth. "I'm fairly enjoying the mission," he admitted. "What's not to like?"

Aesus was in full agreement. "I've always enjoyed riding, and, so far at least, the Saxons we've been meeting have treated us with respect."

"That mead of theirs is something else, eh?" Motius said wonderingly. "I'd like to get the recipe from them, get my wife to brew me some."

"Bit strong for me," Bedwyr complained. "A horn of that stuff is like two mugs of ale. It's too easy to end up falling over your own feet and lying abed with the room spinning around you."

"Don't drink more than one horn then," Aesus chuckled, licking his lips. "I'm with Motius, it's good stuff."

"Their food is tasty as well," Bedwyr noted, realising it was about time they stopped for a rest and something to eat.

"It's different to what I'm used to," said Motius. "But, like the mead, I'm getting a taste for it."

"They know how to take a piece of fish and make it interesting."

"Exactly, Aesus!" Bedwyr agreed enthusiastically. "Although, in saying all that, let's give the horses a breather and fill our bellies. We might not have a barrel of mead and platters of smoked fish to share, but bread and cheese will be more than welcome."

They guided their mounts off to the side of the road, riding down a slope that was fringed with trees and would hide them from other travellers. They may be hard men, and heavily armed, but there were only three of them after all, so there was no point in advertising their presence if it wasn't necessary.

When the horses had been tethered and given water from a shallow dyke that flowed nearby, the men sat and enjoyed a meal together. They were in the middle of a war that could last for generations, but moments like this always proved to the optimistic Bedwyr that the gods were with them, and life was filled with much to enjoy.

* * *

At first, Bellicus thought he recognised the small settlement beside the river as the light began to fade and he knew he'd have to rest up for the night. He soon realised he was mistaken though, and this was a place he'd never been to before, only passing it by on his previous journey to Garrianum. This was his tenth day in the road and he must have travelled a good two hundred miles from Dun Breatann by now.

The sun was setting, making long shadows of the few buildings up ahead, and turning the nearby river a fiery orange that rippled and danced with the tide. He would find a warm welcome here, he hoped, and perhaps even enjoy some nice smoked trout or salmon given how close the village was to the water.

Cai had stopped to relieve himself and Bellicus turned Darac to look back at the hound, waiting patiently for him to finish. Before they moved on the hairs on the druid's neck seemed to stand up and, instinctively, he kicked his mount's flanks, forcing the horse to jump forwards, almost into the undergrowth that flanked the road. Just as they moved, something whistled through the air, narrowly missing Bellicus's shaved head.

Hauling the reins to the right, the druid turned and pulled his staff from its place on Darac's saddle. "Cai!" he roared, charging along the road towards a startled man who held a leather sling in his right hand. "Attack!"

"What? No!" The words were barely out of the slinger's mouth before Cai's jaws were around his forearm and the weight of the dog had dragged him to the ground, screaming and ineffectually trying to kick the animal away.

There were two more men standing in the shadows beside a house, tall enough to reach the thatched roof although no longer in youth's full bloom. Still, they were both armed, one with a hatchet of the type used for chopping firewood, the other with a simple sword. Sliding down from Darac's back, Bellicus kept his eyes fixed on the armed men, pleased to see they didn't move as he strode towards Cai.

"Come," he commanded, and the dog obeyed immediately, letting go of the slinger's bloodied arm and loping across to stand defensively beside his master. The druid stepped forward, towards the mewling slinger, and slammed the butt of his staff into the man's head. The agonised cries stopped immediately but the violence outraged the pair in the shadows and they came ahead now, brandishing their weapons and growling as if they were dogs themselves.

Bellicus held his staff of office in both hands, ready to parry any attack, and he saw his foes' eyes examining it. Although he wore his sword, the staff was just as deadly in his hands, being a length of ash topped with a finely cast bronze eagle – it was as impressive as it was dangerous.

"Why are you attacking me?" he demanded, powerful, trained voice ringing out and making the villagers visibly blanch. "Speak! Is this how the people of this settlement welcome travellers? Is this how you welcome a druid?"

The mouths of both men dropped open and they glanced at one another fretfully, the anger they'd shared disappearing in an instant. When they looked back at Bellicus it was plain they had no idea what to do next.

"Answer me!" the giant druid demanded, taking a step forward menacingly, Cai coming with him like a shadow, bristling with barely restrained ferocity. "Why did this fool try to smash my skull open with his slingshot?"

The villager with the sword, surely the leader of the pair hence his more expensive armament, swallowed and finally spoke up. "We know who you are," he said in a high voice that sounded close to cracking. "You're a murderer, and a thief, and you've come here chasing after an innocent young boy."

Bellicus digested that for a moment, not wanting to make the situation more volatile than it already was. He did not want to hurt these men, simple farmers from the look of them, who had clearly mistaken him for someone else. Still, the similarities to his real story, and his real reason for being there, were too much to be coincidence, surely.

"Is that 'innocent boy' here?" he demanded.

"No," the man with the hatchet replied instantly but the shared look between him and his companion suggested a lie. "He rode off hours ago."

"I am no thief, or murderer," Bellicus said, breathing slowly and doing his best to be patient although he was growing angry again when it seemed his quarry must be nearby, probably in one of the buildings just a few feet away. "I am Bellicus of Dun Breatann, once High Druid of Britain, and husband to Queen Narina."

"That's what you say," the villager with the hatchet retorted. He did not seem as intelligent as the one with the sword, and his stupidity not only made it difficult to reason with him, but apparently made it hard for him to see just how much danger he faced.

"That is what I am!" Bellicus cried, thumping his staff on the road. "Look at my staff! Do you see many normal folk just wandering around carrying one of these?" In all honesty, he was rather disappointed, and more than a little put out, that the villagers had not recognised him – a large part of a druid's power came from the stories that people told about them, and the songs of their exploits. It was galling to know that people just a few days ride from Dun Breatann had no idea who he actually was.

"I know who Bellicus is," the man with the sword said though, cheering the druid a little before he went on. "But Bellicus is said to be eight feet tall, with a dog…" He trailed off then, understanding finally lighting his face.

"Oh, shit," murmured the man with the hatchet as he too realised at last that this enormous newcomer, with a powerful war-dog and a black stallion, was not likely to be anyone other than the real, fabled Damnonii druid.

"Aye," Bellicus growled. "'Oh shit'. Now, I'll ask you again, and make sure you tell me the truth this time: is the young man you spoke of still here? He's no innocent youth, he killed Damnonii soldiers and tried to murder my friend, Duro, while he slept in his bed. He's a Saxon warrior on a mission from the warlord Hengist, and he is highly dangerous."

The reactions of the two villagers was quite different. The one with the hatchet scoffed and commented that the lad was far too young to be what Bellicus claimed, while the sword wielding man cried out, "He's what? But my wife is with him!" and gaped at the druid imploringly.

CHAPTER TWENTY-SEVEN

"Does he know I'm here?" Bellicus demanded, bending to touch Cai soothingly, reassuring the mastiff that there was no immediate danger from the two men now.

"Aye," the villager replied. "He had one of us watch the road for you all afternoon. He told us you were some thief who'd broke into his family's house somewhere to the north and killed them all, apart from him. He'd just been knocked out cold, he claimed, and when he came to you'd set alight to the house and he was burned in the fire before he broke out through the walls and escaped on his horse with you chasing after him."

"Ha," the druid laughed coldly. The Saxon's tale wasn't a thousand miles away from the truth, although he had never been the innocent party in any of the real events. "So you've left him alone with your wife? Where?"

"My house," the man whined, pointing at a building on the eastern edge of the settlement that was a little larger and sturdily put together than the other dwellings. A village headman's house, no doubt about it. "My wife is tending to his injuries. Whatever you did to the fellow, you almost killed him."

"Shame I didn't," the druid grunted. "But the only one of those wounds I inflicted was the stab wound in his side. The rest were given to him by the innocent people – women included – that he attacked and killed."

"Oh, Taranis protect us," the headman gasped. "I had no idea, my lord, I swear to you. You must help us. Don't let him hurt my Lucilia!"

"Where are we anyway?" the druid asked, jerking his head towards the nearby water. "What river is that?"

"The Ure," said the headman. "Our settlement is called Torp."

Bellicus looked at him, and then back at the house where Saksnot was hiding away with the headman's woman completely at his mercy. What should he do? If he just burst in through the door the whoreson might well kill Lucilia – he'd already murdered at least two other women that Bellicus knew of. But what other choice did he have?

A sudden thought struck him then and he felt foolish for not thinking of it earlier.

135

"Hang on," he demanded, eyeing the villagers suspiciously and gripping his staff a little tighter as more of the local men and women appeared from their homes, gathering around to see what was happening. "The Saxon doesn't speak our tongue. I conversed with him, and I had to use his own language. So how, by the balls of Dis Pater, were you able to get his story from him?"

"Puck," the man holding the hatchet replied.

Bellicus stared at him, expecting more than that single, meaningless word but nothing was forthcoming. "Puck?" he prompted irritably. "What does that mean?"

"Puck lives there," said the headman, gesturing wildly at the house closest to them, fear for his wife's safety making him lose his composure even more. "He's a Jute."

"What?" The druid was amazed. A Jute living here, in this little rundown village miles and miles away from the Saxon Shore and the rest of his own people?

"Puck was hit on the head not long after arriving here fifteen or so years ago," the man with the hatchet said. "He was in a battle and almost died. From what we can get out of him he thinks he wandered for months or even years after that, living off the land and hiding from people he thought would kill him."

"And he just wandered here?"

"Aye, my lord," the headman confirmed. "He's been living here for, oh, over ten years now I'd say. He must have been a great warrior before his head was thumped. Perhaps even one of their jarls, for he's clever, when he makes sense at least. Picked up our language pretty easily."

"Where is he now?" Bellicus asked.

"In the house with my wife and the boy."

"Of fucking course he is," the druid muttered, heart sinking as he walked towards the dwelling that sat beside the glistening waters of the Ure. "So now there isn't just one sea-wolf to worry about, there's two!"

"Puck isn't a threat," one of the villagers protested. "He's moon-touched, but he's not dangerous. I like him; we all do."

"He's a Saxon," Bellicus murmured. "That makes him a threat, no matter what you people believe."

"Look," the headman said, hurrying to keep pace with the druid's long strides while also warily keeping his distance from Cai. "That

136

boy with the burns on his face can't be that dangerous, can he? He's only a lad."

"He killed my friend Nemias. Have you heard of him? No? Well, he was better known as Merlin. That's right, the sea-wolf scum in your house murdered the High Druid. He might look young, and he might be able to act like an innocent simpleton, but he's as dangerous as any of Hengist's warriors." Bellicus drew closer to the house and quickly walked around it, noting the windows and single door that might offer Saksnot means of escape.

He noticed a pair of eyes watching him from between a set of shutters that had been partially opened. Saksnot.

"I see you out there, druid!" the Saxon shouted. "Leave now, or I'll kill this bitch!" He pulled open the shutters fully to reveal a woman that must be Lucilia. He was gripping her by the hair and he had his sword in his hand, its blade appearing almost black in the shadows cast by the rapidly setting sun.

"Don't hurt her!" the headman screeched, not understanding the words but easily able to comprehend Saksnot's intentions. "We helped you, you little prick!"

"Leave this place, druid," the Saxon repeated, giving Lucilia's hair a hard jerk to emphasise his words. "Leave or she dies."

"I'm not going anywhere," Bellicus returned in a firm, level tone, setting his feet as though he was taking root in the earth. "I'll wait here until you come out. If you harm the woman there will be nothing to stop me coming in to get you, or simply burning the place down about you."

Saksnot absorbed the druid's threats and then he shoved Lucilia across the room so she was out of sight but could still be heard sobbing, even over her husband's tortured whimpers. There was more shouting from within the house, and a second male voice answered Saksnot this time, although the words were spoken so fast and in such harsh tones that the druid couldn't make out what was being said. At length, another man appeared at the open window.

"Puck!" the headman shouted pleadingly. "Tell him to let Lucilia go!"

The man gazed out from the house from oddly disinterested eyes and Bellicus assumed the story about him suffering a terrible head injury in some decades-past battle had been true. Some part of Puck had died in that fight, yet here he was, still functioning and able to

137

communicate with Saxons and Britons alike. He was quite tall, wiry, and certainly had the look of an old warrior. Was he dangerous? Any man could be dangerous, the druid knew that, and one who was openly viewed as moon-touched doubly so.

"He says you've all to go away," Puck called out to them and his voice was clear and almost melodious. "Go away, or he'll start cutting bits off the woman, starting with her fingers and"—

His words were drowned out by not just the headman's anguished cries, but everyone else that had now gathered outside the building.

"You have to leave," the man with hatchet shouted at Bellicus, prompting a warning growl from Cai. "Your appearance here has just caused trouble. Go, druid, and let us sort this out ourselves."

Cai's teeth were bared now, saliva dripping from his mouth, and the villagers all moved back, staring at the mastiff nervously. Bellicus wasn't sure what he should do. He could leave, and simply ride on to the south, lay an ambush for Saksnot a mile or so away. Of course, the young warrior would be expecting it, but the druid would still have the advantage.

If he did leave though, would the Saxons let Lucilia go? Well, why not? With Bellicus gone, the danger would be gone too, and Saksnot would have no reason, or need, to harm the woman.

"Please, my lord," said the headman, wringing his hands, eyes darting from Bellicus to his house, back and forth repeatedly. "Go."

Grasping Cai gently by the scruff of his neck Bellicus nodded and began to back away from the house. Everyone watched him, including Saksnot who stood in the window beside Puck, teeth bared in a triumphant grin.

He reached Darac, the horse standing patiently where he'd been left just at the edge of the houses. Perhaps surprisingly, the slinger Cai had mauled before Bellicus knocked him out cold with his staff was still lying, unmoving in the road. "You might want to see to this man," he called in disgust to the villagers. "Before he chokes on his tongue."

No answer came, and no one moved as the druid hauled himself into the saddle and gave them all a final glare, his eyes meeting Saksnot's for a long moment before he kicked his heels in and Darac trotted southwards, Torp quickly disappearing from view as sunset's shadows swallowed the settlement up behind him.

When they'd gone about half a mile Bellicus could feel eyes watching him and he glanced down at Cai. It seemed, incredibly, that the dog returned his gaze with a disappointed frown, and he smiled grimly. "Don't worry, boy," he reassured the animal. "We're not finished with that Saxon wretch yet, not by a long way."

They rode on for another half mile or so, Bellicus doing his best in the fading light to scan the surrounding terrain for signs of hidden tracks that might be used to bypass the main road. Luckily, all along this stretch the River Ure flowed nearby on the left, but it would be possible to travel on the opposite side of the road if one wished to push through undergrowth. On foot, it would be fairly simple, but on horseback? No, if Saksnot was to continue south, towards Garrianum, it was most likely he would come this way. He would not abandon the horse that had served him well, not unless he wanted to add days to his journey time.

"We'll stop here," he murmured to Cai and Darac, drawing up and dismounting before leading the big black into a thick stand of trees and pegging it to the mossy ground.

What would Saksnot do now that the druid had gone? What would Bellicus do in his position? He made sure his animals could not be seen from the road and then found a good spot to sit and watch for travellers, hood pulled up, blending into the shadows and undergrowth.

The Saxon would not want to spend the night in the settlement. He must be exhausted from his exertions in recent days, and would likely be weak from loss of blood. Aye, he would need to sleep, but not in the village. How could he rest there? The only person that might possibly protect him was Puck, and that fellow had been living happily amongst the villagers for ten years or more. Could he be trusted to defend a sleeping Saksnot from the headman and the simpleton with the hatchet? Maybe, but Saksnot could not be sure, and would be a fool to take the chance.

Cai made a small snuffling sound beside him and Bellicus was glad to see the dog had fallen asleep. He remembered Narina's fears over such a long journey, but Cai was not old yet. Still, he would need plenty of rest after covering so many miles in just a few days and the druid was happy to let him lie, for who knew when he would be called into action again?

Saksnot would force Lucilia to treat his wounds, feed him, and refill his pack of provisions. Then, with his horse also fed and watered by the villagers, the warrior would ride off, perhaps taking the woman with him for a short way just to make sure no one attacked him. Ultimately, Bellicus thought, Saksnot would be heading southwards sometime during the night, perhaps in as little as an hour or two.

Would he suspect an ambush? Yes, of course he would. But what other options did the druid have? Bellicus hoped the Saxon would come this way, ready for an attack or not, but then another idea hit him. What if Saksnot enlisted Puck to travel with him for a time, and act as a bodyguard? Bellicus had no idea how dangerous the older man might be, but two against one would certainly even things up a little.

The druid cursed and then looked apologetically at Cai whose dark eyes were now gazing back at him. It was impossible to know what Saksnot would do – if he chose to ride northwards and search for a different route to Garrianum Bellicus would be stuck here all night, awake, alert, and all for naught! But there was nothing else he could do, except pray the gods would deliver his quarry to him.

He closed his eyes for a moment but had not even begun to formulate a plea to Taranis before the sound of approaching hooves reached him and he was on his feet, staff in hand, Cai bristling at his side, both ready for a fight to the death.

CHAPTER TWENTY-EIGHT

As Bellicus stood, staff in hand, staring into the darkness, he felt a wave of relief wash over him for he could only hear one set of hooves thumping along the road. Saksnot was alone, and the Saxon would be just as exhausted as the druid after their long journey and lack of proper rest. At least it would be a more even fight.

He glanced down at Cai and a humourless smile curled his lip. Well, perhaps not such an even fight after all.

The horse came closer but it was in no hurry and Bellicus cursed inwardly. Saksnot must know he was waiting for him in the shadows – not here, perhaps, but somewhere along the road an ambush had been set, and the Saxon would not gallop blindly into it as Bellicus had hoped.

It seemed to take forever, druid and wardog standing with their patience slowly ebbing away, before their enemy at last came into view, a great, black shape against a dark background.

How to engage the bastard? Bellicus had hoped to spring out upon a fast-moving target and halt their progress with the large branch, but that would not work now. He would simply need to bide his time until Saksnot was level, and then use his staff to push the rider from the back of the horse. The fight would not last long after that, for Cai would make short work of the stunned, grounded Saxon, especially with the dog able to see far better in the inky darkness than either man could.

"Taranis, guide my staff," Bellicus breathed, looking upwards and feeling the strength of the gods filling him, removing the heavy weight of tiredness that had settled across his shoulders like a blanket over the past hour or so. He bent and whispered to Cai, "Ready, boy," just as their quarry at last reached them.

Silently, without wishing to give Saksnot any advantage whatsoever, the druid stepped into the road and thrust the butt of his staff up and out, towards the rider's head. The horse let out a startled whinny and jerked upwards, its front hooves coming off the ground. Bellicus cursed for he did not feel his weapon strike home. There was no one atop the panicked horse though, and the animal, not trained for war, broke into a gallop, continuing in the direction it had been walking but this time at a full-blown, noisy gallop.

The druid's surprise was immediately replaced by a panic of his own, as the unmistakable glint of oiled steel suddenly appeared, flashing in the starlight mere inches from his face. It was all he could do the whip his staff up, knocking the blade to the side just before it tore him a second mouth.

He stepped back into a defensive stance, the eagle on top of his staff thrusting out, pushing back his opponent. There was no sound of growling, or snarling, as Bellicus expected – no sounds from Cai at all, and he wondered with mounting fear where his loyal friend was. Something must have happened to the mastiff for him not to be ripping the Saxon to shreds.

Moving into the road, circling the Saxon, Bellicus was forced again to parry the long blade of his enemy's sword and only then did he see Cai. The dog was lying in the centre of the road, the great body almost tripping the druid before he noticed it.

Saksnot saw the prone animal at the same time and, laughing with glee, rushed towards the limp body, sword held high to make sure Cai could never attack another Saxon again.

"Back, you whoreson!" Bellicus roared, the trained druid's Voice filled with so much rage and command that it momentarily startled his foe, making the man pause and then jump hastily backwards as the staff swept out in a wide arc, questing, seeking for ribs, limbs, or a skull to shatter.

The combatants glared at one another and, although it was dark, Bellicus realised at last that he was not facing the man he'd chased all the way there from Dun Breatann. It was not Saksnot standing, sword in hand, in the road near the prone body of Cai, it was Puck.

"What are you doing here, you stupid bastard?" Bellicus demanded, quickly glancing over his shoulder to make sure Saksnot was not sneaking up on him. "I could have killed you!"

The Saxon's grizzled face wrinkled as he shot a malevolent grin at the druid, and then the oiled blade that Puck knew how to wield all too well was thrusting towards Bellicus and the deadly dance started again. The ash wood of the druid's staff was hard, but it splintered away as Puck's sword hacked at it, each thump or harsh crack sending more fine shavings into the air as each man sought to incapacitate the other.

Puck was a more skilled swordsman than Saksnot had been, and he had the advantage of not being exhausted from days on the road.

Although Bellicus was younger, stronger, and faster, the fighters were evenly matched, especially as the druid knew he had to be wary of Saksnot suddenly appearing from the shadows around them.

"Why are you doing this?" Bellicus asked. "You would put your life at risk for what? A stranger?"

Puck's lip curled but he did not answer. There was a wild, untamed look in the man's eyes, as if he'd been raised by wolves, and Bellicus realised that, whatever his motives, the Saxon would not stop fighting until he was unconscious or dead. Whether he'd taken Saksnot's place out of loyalty to his Saxon people, or from hatred of Britons, or druids, or some other reason, Puck had made his choice and was utterly committed to it. He was not simply trying to distract Bellicus so that Saksnot could somehow escape – he was actively trying to murder the druid.

And he almost succeeded, as the shockingly sharp sword sliced through Bellicus's sleeve and cut deep into the bracers the druid was wearing. Had he not been protected by that thick leather the arteries in his forearm might have been slashed open and the fight would be done. As it was, the Saxon assumed he'd landed a mortal strike and, drawing even more confidence from it, lunged forwards, bringing up his knee to catch the giant druid in the groin.

Bellicus grunted in pain but thanked the gods for his height, for the blow had not struck him fully between the legs, as Puck had hoped. Still, it was a delivered by a trained warrior, and Bellicus stepped back, knowing his mobility would be hampered for at least a few heartbeats.

The Saxon was chuckling, enjoying the fight and knowing full well he'd hurt his opponent. His eyes narrowed in disappointment however as he noticed Bellicus's torn sleeve and the ragged leather underneath. The crazed, mocking laughter faded, but still Puck's eyes glittered merrily.

Before the druid felt confident enough to launch another attack, Puck suddenly turned to the side and lunged across the road, directly towards the still form of Cai.

"No!" Bellicus watched that sleek, oiled Saxon blade raise into the air, glinting like ice in the pale moonlight, and despair filled him. Cai might only be a dog, but he had been a loyal friend and ally to Bellicus, and the bond of love that bound them together was as strong as steel.

As the sword arced down, Puck giggling viciously, Bellicus drew back his right arm and launched his staff with every ounce of strength he could muster. His massive bicep tensed and relaxed as the length of ash streaked through the air and, just as Puck's blade was about to hack into Cai's ribcage, the bronze eagle that topped the druid's staff struck the Saxon just behind his ear.

The maniacal laughter was silenced as Puck's head jerked to the side and his limbs simply gave way. He fell to the ground, flopping down in a heap, legs and arms splayed out around him.

Breathing heavily, more from the shock of almost losing Cai than from the exertions of the fight, Bellicus drew out Melltgwyn, and stalked across the road, eyes on the downed Saxon. Puck was silent, and there was a great, oozing wound where the druid's staff had struck his skull, but his chest continued to rise and fall slowly.

"Dis Pater take you," Bellicus growled, thrusting his sword into Puck's chest. Withdrawing it, the druid wiped it clean on the dead man's ragged tunic and glanced about once more for signs of Saksnot. The night air was still and Bellicus guessed his quarry was long gone or else he'd have come to Puck's aid while the fight was raging. No, Saksnot must have sent his fellow Saxon here to keep Bellicus busy while he made his escape by some other route.

"The river," murmured the druid, remembering just how close to the road the Ure's fast-moving waters flowed. The chase would have to wait, he thought angrily, focusing his attention on Cai who, worryingly, was still immobile.

The druid knelt on the ground, eyes quickly becoming moist as he remembered the last time he'd lost a dog during a fight with Saxons. *Eolas*, he thought, picturing his old friend in his mind's eye and recalling that heartbreaking moment when he'd held the hound's body in his arms and knew Eolas had passed into the Otherworld. *Please, Cai, don't leave me. Not yet.*

He reached out and stroked the mastiff's head, silently praying to Sulis Minerva for some healing magic to flow from the earth into the prone dog. Bellicus had not understood what caused Cai to end up in this position, but he understood now as he saw a large bump had formed on the animal's forehead. Puck's mount must have struck Cai with one of its hooves when the fighting started and the horse reared up in fright.

Such a blow, from a beast as powerful as a horse, could very easily kill, and Bellicus felt a wave of despair wash over him. He had caused this. He should never have brought Cai here – Narina had even warned him about the dangers! Despair quickly became guilt and he rested his head gently on the mastiff's neck, a lump forming in his throat.

"Wake up, Cai," he murmured. "Wake up, the chase isn't over yet."

There was no obvious sign of Sulis Minerva's healing magic flowing around them but there came the sound of a low, deep, growl, and Bellicus jerked his head up, gazing down at the dog with desperate hope. The druid was not sure if he'd imagined the growl, or if it had been Cai's final gasp before he loped off into the Otherlands to run and play once more with Eolas, but Bellicus had not prayed so fiercely for the gods' help in a long time.

Dashing tears from his eyes, Bellicus saw Cai came slowly awake, groggy, frightened and clearly uncertain of where he was, but alive. Alive!

There could be no suggestion of continuing the hunt for Saksnot that night – Bellicus and Darac were spent, and Cai would need rest to recover from his injury. Despite the fact that the murderous Saxon had escaped his clutches again, it did not seem terribly important as the druid set up a hasty camp. He made sure his animals were comfortable and settled before lying down next to Cai and stroking the soft fur to reassure himself as much as his canine friend that all was well.

As he lay there looking up at the stars the name of each twinkling pinprick of silver light drifted into his mind and he drew the constellations in his mind eye. He remembered teaching little Catia the names of those constellations – her favourite was the Great Bear, which the Romans knew as Arctos. Bellicus remembered pointing out the shape that the stars made in the sky and telling his daughter the mythology behind it, and a sudden homesickness came over him.

He was surprised, for he could not remember ever feeling the sensation so strongly before – he desperately wished he could transport himself, Cai, and Darac across the miles, back to Dun Breatann so he could be with his wife, child, and friends. Was Duro recovering from his terrible injuries? Gods, how Bellicus would like the centurion to be there beside him, alert for danger, protecting the druid while he slept…

Shame flowed through him then and he berated himself mentally for his childish weakness. Was he not Bellicus, warrior druid of Dun Breatann? Yet there he lay, feeling sorry for himself, melancholy threatening to overwhelm him. It was ridiculous! He forced himself to clear his mind and put aside all feelings of guilt, sadness, despair, or anything else, and to think rationally.

He was exhausted, it had been a long, long day, and he'd almost lost Cai – it was understandable that his mind was rebelling and reminding him of his beloved companions back home. Yet, although he told himself that, the idea of continuing to hunt Saksnot when the sun rose on the morrow did not seem important any more.

So what if the beardless, sly warrior escaped? Hengist was not likely to reward him for his failed mission anyway – in fact, there was every chance the *bretwalda* would punish Saksnot, perhaps even with death.

It did not take very long for Bellicus to make up his mind after that; Saksnot was gone, maybe many miles along the Ure by this point, and far out of the druid's reach. There was no point in chasing him any further, not when Narina and Catia needed him back at home. It was one thing to risk one's life in a quest that might prevent a death, or to stop a war, or some other lofty goal; it was another thing entirely to put oneself, and one's companions, in mortal danger simply to gain the satisfaction of vengeance.

In the morning they would turn back, and ride north instead of south – home to Dun Breatann. Bellicus's quest to kill Saksnot was over, and that thought brought great relief, allowing the druid to fall into a deep sleep almost instantly.

CHAPTER TWENTY-NINE

Queen Narina sat slowly chewing a piece of buttered bread – her favourite meal – and gazed into the fire that was burning low in the central pit of Dun Breatann's great hall.

"You think Cunneda has done this because of what happened to Ysfael?" Gavo asked. "I can see no other sensible reason for it."

That morning news had come from the Votadini king that he would no longer be trading with Narina's Damnonii – a great surprise for the two peoples were neighbours and both benefited from the previous arrangement that had been in place for generations. Even when they were actively at war with one another the merchants had continued to trade. With the Damnonii being on the west of the country, and the Votadini on the east, different goods flowed into their ports from lands across the seas and there was money to be made transporting them across land to be sold in their neighbours' markets.

"I think Ysfael's death probably played a part in Cunneda's decision," Narina nodded, setting down her bread and wiping her mouth with a frown. "From his point of view, we didn't treat Ysfael with the respect a Votadini prince deserved."

"The man was an arse!" Gavo protested. "He tried to destroy us, and brought about the whole war with the Picts!"

"I know that," Narina replied. "And Cunneda knows it too. Still, Ysfael was his son and it must rankle that he was treated essentially as a prisoner for his last months alive, before being killed in battle. Cunneda has many children and was not particularly fond of Ysfael, but I can see how the whole affair would be viewed by a man – a king – as proud as Cunneda."

Gavo muttered gloomily and idly chewed his own bread, a wonderfully fragrant, soft loaf that had been freshly baked that morning yet might have been a week-old, stale lump from all the pleasure the captain seemed to derive from it. "You said Ysfael's death maybe played a part in Cunneda's ceasing trading with us. What else d'you think influenced the decision?"

Narina looked pointedly at him. She'd lost her appetite completely but took a sip of water and cocked her head, raising her eyebrows as she asked, "Really? Take a guess."

Gavo pursed his lips and shrugged. "I'm not sure. I would expect the Votadini must have some new source of revenue to fill their coffers, or they'd not be so quick to turn away our money."

"Exactly," Narina agreed. "And whose ships ply the whale road off the coast of Cunneda's lands?" She did not wait for him to reply, answering her own question. "Hengist."

"But they've always traded," Gavo protested.

"So they have," Narina nodded darkly. "But Hengist must have offered a better deal to Cunneda. Perhaps even made him swear to cease trading with us in return for a better agreement with them."

Gavo took his queen's words in and his expression, naturally dour, grew even more grim as the implications and possibilities struck home. "Cunneda and Hengist have formed an alliance," he growled, taking his hands from the table and sitting straighter, as if he expected an attack at that very moment.

"I think that most likely," said Narina, who had picked up her buttered bread and was eating again, resigned to the fact war was never far from their borders. "How are our new recruits faring?"

Gavo did not smile as she seemed to change the subject, but Narina could tell he was pleased as he pondered her question. A very good sign indeed, for it took a lot to impress her bluff captain. "They're doing well," he said with a hint of paternal pride. "Many of them obviously saw action in the recent fighting, and even the youngsters were involved in the war effort, helping out with logistics, feeding the troops, caring for equipment and things like that. War is a terrible thing, but when you've seen it as much as we have here in Alt Clota…well, everyone learns how to deal with it just that bit better than people who enjoy long years of peace."

"We're in a good position," Narina said. "In spite of everything we've had to deal with in recent years. And, as you say, we know how to fight a war now, and handle the tribulations that go along with it other than the actual fighting. Well, when autumn comes, step up our patrols, Gavo, and use some of those young recruits. Get them a proper taste of what it's like to face enemy raiders, or at least to feel the fear of the possibility."

"Oh, there are always enemy warriors pushing their luck, stealing sheep and cattle and things like that from the settlements on the edges of our lands."

"The Dalriadans are growing in strength again," Narina noted sourly. "And in confidence."

"Indeed," Gavo murmured. "They have a new king, or a warlord at least, named Domangart mac Nissi, in Dunadd. If you agree, I'll start using our recruits more in those patrols that are likely to face actual fighting on that western border. Get the youths some experience." He paused and drank some of his water, eyeing Narina over the rim of the cup. "Do you fear Hengist or Cunneda will send an army here, my lady?"

The queen took a deep breath and let it out in a long, heavy sigh. "I do now. Cunneda's decision to cut off trade marks yet another deterioration in our relationship, and I think it wise to prepare as best we can for whatever is coming our way, Gavo."

The captain accepted her thoughts and rose to his feet. "Then I will make sure our soldiers are ready, our patrols alert, and our gates and walls in good repair."

"I know you will," Narina told him with a fond look. "Thank you."

Returning her smile, Gavo threw the lady a crisp salute and strode from the room. Narina watched him go, reassured by his stoic, powerful presence. Of all the soldiers under her command, Gavo was the most fiercely loyal, and the most competent. He would do everything in his power to make sure Alt Clota was ready to face the next enemy who sought to conquer the Damnonii. Would that truly be Hengist with his sea-wolf hordes? It had been bad enough facing Horsa and his moderately-sized Saxon warband; the idea of Dun Breatann being besieged by the full might of Cunneda, and the *bretwalda*'s army, was terrifying.

For a long moment she pondered the situation in Britain. Hengist was angling for supremacy and would surely turn up in Alt Clota eventually, especially if he had formed an alliance with King Cunneda. But Hengist was badly beset by Arthur's forces at the moment – the Saxons would not be marching upon Dun Breatann that summer. Perhaps it would be sensible to neutralise the threat of Cunneda's Votadini warriors now, rather than waiting for them to join up with the sea-wolves...

Narina stood up and nodded her thanks to the servants before heading for the doors, plans brewing in her mind.

* * *

Fritigern had watched the Britons converse with his chief, Taki, wishing he was still young enough to chase them from the hall and the settlement. He cursed the failing eyesight, creaking joints, and breathlessness that had overtaken him as he passed his seventieth winter and had been forced to give up the life of an adventurer. He had been old even when he joined Hengist's sea-wolves to sail along the swan's path to Britain, but he had still been capable of standing in a shieldwall, using his decades of experience to guide the untried younger recruits, and his natural ferocity to compensate for his slowing reflexes. Hengist and Horsa both liked him and the *bretwalda* had been sorry when Fritigern sadly decided it was time for him to put down his axe and live peacefully amongst those other less warlike Saxons who'd settled in the new lands.

There were few men or women of his age in the world, and even fewer warriors who'd seen as many battles as Fritigern, yet he found himself accepted into the Saxon community in Durovigutum without the fanfare or pleasure he'd envisaged. In his mind, the settlers would welcome him with open arms, offer him the highest seat in the mead hall, beg him breathlessly to regale them with tales of past glory, and view him as something of a beloved patriarch.

The reality was far different. Taki had agreed to his staying with them gladly enough, for Taki had fought alongside him, or at least in the same warband, more than once in previous years. But it had become clear Fritigern was there to live out his last years on *Miðgarðr* not as a valuable, productive asset, but as a drain on resources. The old man could not help to build houses for he no longer had the strength in his limbs; he could not hunt, for his eyesight was not good enough to spot a hart never mind a deer before the thing noticed him; and he had never learned skills such as cooking, mending clothes, or tanning.

He'd complained to Taki more than once that he was not being treated with the respect his years and experience deserved, but he was quickly told by the chief to pipe down and find some way to earn his keep. In his youth he would have smashed Taki's teeth out, but now he was forced to hold his tongue or face being banished. The thought of that terrified the elderly man and he had decided to make himself valuable to the rest of the Saxons in the community

150

by entertaining them with stories of his long life. Everyone loved an exciting tale after all.

Or so he had assumed, until Taki ordered him to stop regaling the folk in the mead hall with his brutal stories.

"But why?" Fritigern had demanded, coming close again to lifting his hands in fury to the chief. "Our people have always been roused by songs and poems and tales of adventure."

"That's the problem!" Taki had retorted, staring down at Fritigern as if he was a father scolding a stupid child. "I do not want to 'rouse' our people! We have been accepted by the Britons here in this village and must live peacefully alongside them. We do not need to hear about you caving in the skull of some native warrior before you raped his sobbing wife and took her children as slaves! Are you stupid, old man?"

Fritigern had raised his fist then, so enraged was he by the chief's disrespectful words, but Taki had simply batted the blow aside and shoved the old man into the road. That had not helped Fritigern's already fading sense of self-worth, especially since he'd landed on a pile of ox shit and been pointed and laughed at by not only Saxon children, but Britons too.

When he'd cleaned himself and calmed down, Fritigern realised that, although he wanted to slit Taki's windpipe while the chief slept, any attempt would not end well for the grizzled warrior.

As much as it pained him, Fritigern had been forced to become subservient to Taki, and, eventually found himself crafting or mending small tools and pieces of furniture – folding tables, stools, chests, doors, brooms, and so on. He was not very good at it for his hands were not steady enough for intricate work, but he could chisel out a new leg for a stool or a table and hammer them into place with a mallet.

It was enough to earn his keep, but it was a miserable existence for a once proud soldier.

Then the emissaries from Arthur, warlord of the Britons, had turned up in Durovigutum and Taki had not only welcomed them into the mead hall, but he had even ordered Fritigern to serve them. He, Fritigern, scourge of the Britons just a few years ago, now reduced to carrying meat and drink to them like some serving wench or thrall! It was humiliating and unconscionable and the old man had raged within himself as he sat there listening to Bedwyr talk to Taki about fighting against Hengist when the time came.

Had it come to this? Saxons now selling themselves to the likes of Arthur so they would be left alone to live a life of planting and ploughing? The only ploughing Fritigern had ever done was of maidens, willing or no. Taki had once been a proud, and brutal warrior too, yet now he gladly parleyed with Bedwyr, selling his soul to men not worthy of cleaning Hengist's armour.

When the Briton had told Taki where he planned to travel next Fritigern listened carefully, making a mental note of the name of the place and now, well, now he would put his knowledge to good use.

"Where are you going, greybeard?"

The question startled Fritigern from his bitter musings and he jerked upright, staring with rheumy eyes at a tall, lean soldier with a sparse red beard.

"I asked where you were going, you old fool," the warrior barked, leaning his face closer to Fritigern's. There were no lines on the man's forehead, no crow's feet crinkling around his eyes, and the nervous excitement of youth radiated from him.

"Help me down," Fritigern returned irritably, grasping the younger man's shoulder to support him as he slid down from the cart that had brought him there to Garrianum. "Ride on, baker," he called to the man in charge of the rickety vehicle. "Find me here before you leave, eh? I'll need a ride back to Durovigutum."

"Fine," the baker called without enthusiasm. "I'll unload the loaves and cakes, get my payment, and then wait for you. Don't be long, eh?"

"Last time, greybeard, before I knock you out and toss you in the river"—

"Where am I going?" Fritigern finished, a grim smile curling his lip as he glared up at the young soldier. "I'm going to see Hengist. I have some news he'll want to hear, so you'll shut your mouth, boy, and lead me to the *bretwalda* if you know what's good for you."

CHAPTER THIRTY

A sound woke Bellicus and he opened his eyes, staring up at the glittering stars in the black veil of the sky. He felt completely refreshed even though he must have only been asleep for at most an hour or two and that worried him – to have woken him from such an incredibly deep, healing sleep, the noise must have been very loud. His hand slowly moved to Melltgwyn at his side, fingers wrapping reassuringly around the cool handle of the sword. He could not hear anything that suggested danger was close at hand, and he could not hear either Darac or Cai showing obvious signs of alarm. Alert, but feeling the sense of danger slowly passing, a new sensation crept over the druid and he suddenly realised that not only was the night utterly silent, but the stars were very slightly different to those he knew so well, with one or two even being completely alien to him. Having studied astronomy in great depth all throughout his life, as all druids did, he knew every shining speck in Britain's night sky so he understood that something unusual was happening.

He rose to his feet, no longer grasping his sword. Looking down he could see Cai was watching him and, glancing to the trees behind them, so was Darac. Neither animal appeared frightened or anxious in any way and, in fact, Cai drifted back to sleep as the druid turned and walked slowly across the road. A pale, almost invisible blue light seemed to come from where Bellicus had left Puck's corpse and, as he approached, a portly, balding man came into view.

"Peredur!"

The rotund man waved to him and then peered down at the body of the Saxon, pale and quite horrific in the starshine. "Bad business that," Peredur growled. "You've been lucky to survive the journey this far, but I've always admired your resilience, Bel."

They grasped forearms, smiling at one another and, despite the strangeness of the whole situation, Bellicus felt completely at ease. Usually he met Peredur during the course of a ritual, when the druid's consciousness would fade from the real world and pass into the Otherlands for a time. Peredur would come to him and they would converse like old friends, sometimes with the portly man offering some piece of sage advice that might not make sense until long after the druid had completed the ritual and was fully awake once more.

153

In truth, Bellicus had no idea if Peredur was, or had ever been, a real man. He was the hero of many old tales told around campfires and in great halls all across Britain and no doubt beyond. Was he really there, talking to Bellicus? Was it all just a dream – a result of exhaustion and the tribulations the warrior druid had suffered before finally falling into a deep sleep beside Cai?

Who could say? Did it really matter? Over the years Bellicus had come to value these fleeting moments he was allowed to spend with the mythical figure and he turned his full attention on Peredur now, intent on taking whatever he could from the strange meeting.

"You did not travel all this way to kill him, did you?" the balding man was asking as he gazed down at Puck's corpse. "You were hunting another."

"Aye," Bellicus agreed somewhat gloomily. "Saksnot was the man I sought. He sent this one in his place and, I assume, made his escape on the Ure. He'll be long gone by now."

Peredur's eyes searched his face intently, as if he could see into the druid's soul and draw out the true feelings concealed there. "Will you follow his trail in the morning?" he asked.

"Trail? What trail," Bellicus asked in disgust. "A boat leaves no trail any man, or even dog, could follow. And speaking of dogs, Cai was almost killed in the fight with the dead Saxon there. It's made me realise that this was all a mistake. Putting myself and my animals at risk simply to avenge what Saksnot did to Duro was foolish."

"Perhaps," Peredur shrugged.

"You don't agree?"

"Maybe," the mythical hero hedged, shrugging noncommittally once again.

"You think I should go after Saksnot then? How? He'll be miles away by now – the river flows fast and he might leave the boat anywhere. Shit!" He suddenly realised that he'd not taken the horse that Puck had been riding – the beast had run off and Bellicus, too tired to think straight, had simply fallen asleep. If the horse continued along the road Saksnot might well find it and be able to continue his journey to Garrianum much faster than he would have managed on foot. But the horse had come from the north, he thought, not the south. Surely it would make for home…?

"I think you should ruminate more on your options, Bel," said Peredur seriously. "Sometimes the sensible choice is not the right one."

The druid thought about that. It was strange advice, but what could one expect from a man who was perhaps nothing more than a figment of his own imagination?

"Anything else I should think about?" he asked with a wry smile.

"Aye," Peredur replied and his expression was not as jovial as the druid's. "I'd advise you to wake up, my friend. There are people coming to kill you."

CHAPTER THIRTY-ONE

Bellicus sat up, stunned to discover he was still lying on the grass beside Cai who was also alert, ears twitching as though the mastiff had heard something. Darac stood, still pegged to the ground, but appeared nervous and the druid slowly rose, pressing himself against the trunk of the tree he'd been sleeping beneath. Drawing Melltgwyn, he slowed his breathing and simply tried to make sense of what was happening.

Whether Peredur had really been there or not, Bellicus could not say. He knew that he felt completely rested though, even though he'd not slept for very long, maybe a couple of hours, for it remained dark. He was also sure that the mythical hero's warning had been legitimate – Cai and Darac's demeanour was proof that someone, or something, was prowling about not too far away. Bellicus looked around, taking in the dense trees on this side of the road, the dry-stone wall that flanked the far side where the body of Puck still lay, and the road itself, a Roman construction that had been a marvel of engineering when laid and was still in good condition even now, decades or even centuries later.

It all seemed mundane and as it should be, and the towering druid began to feel a little foolish. He'd had a vivid dream and spooked not only himself but his animals and now they were all standing, awake, instead of catching up on much-needed rest. He could not hear talking or sounds of anyone traversing the land close to them and, sheepishly, he patted Cai's back and placed the point of his sword on its sheath when a crack reverberated off the trees beside him.

It was not a loud noise, but in the still of the night it was shocking. No fox or pine marten would be so clumsy as to snap a dry twig while they were out hunting, but a man certainly would, especially if they were not experienced enough.

There was a hiss of irritation as someone berated whoever had trod on the twig, and Bellicus let out a sigh. There was more than one person looking for him in the dead of night, probably from the settlement Puck had come from.

That thought gave him pause. Puck had obviously not returned home to Torp – perhaps the villagers had come to find him. Surely he wouldn't have told them he was working with Saksnot to cause trouble for the druid...

Any thoughts that the villagers might not be hostile quickly faded from Bellicus's mind when a cry of outrage came from the other side of the road. Someone had come through the field on the other side of the dry-stone wall and discovered Puck's corpse lying out in the open. The villager who'd spotted the body clambered clumsily over the wall, cursing as he came, before standing and gaping down at Puck unhappily. It was the fellow with the hatchet that Bellicus had spoken with before, and he was visibly shaking.

"The bastard's done for old Puck!" shrieked the man and suddenly the hatchet was in his hand again and he was casting about, eyes probing the darkness for the druid. "He must be nearby! Call out if you see him!"

"Watch out for that dog of his," came an answering cry from amongst the trees behind Bellicus, and then at least four more men shouted advice or threats of their own. From what they said, and the fury in their voices, it was clear they would not want a calm, civilised conversation when they found the druid.

Mind racing, Bellicus wondered what to do. He did not fear the villagers for, although they outnumbered him, they were not warriors, and Cai seemed to have recovered from being knocked unconscious. The problem was, those men hunting him were Britons – they were not Saxons or enemies from some other tribe. They were simply men who had, like him, experienced an unusual night and were now outraged that their friend Puck had been killed.

It would not be right to kill them too.

He sheathed his weapon and moved silently across the soft ground, stepping carefully so as not to make the same mistake as the man who'd snapped the twig. He reached Darac – patient, silent, proud – and pulled out the peg that tethered him in place. Nimbly he jumped up onto the horse's back, thanking the gods that he'd not set up a camp so had nothing at all to pack or abandon. Gesturing, he beckoned Cai to stand beside the horse and then he sat in silence once more, trying to figure out where his hunters were.

"There he is!" The man with the hatchet must have heard Bellicus, or perhaps Darac or Cai, for he'd come stalking directly across the road towards them and now, despite the trees casting long shadows all around them, had spotted the trio.

"Get him!" This shout came from the druid's left and, with a start, he realised his attackers were far closer than he'd expected.

"Move!" the druid roared, powerful voice filling the air just before Darac's powerful legs pushed them away from the trees and they were charging towards the road, sending the man with the hatchet flying, a wild oath on his lips.

"Stop them!" someone roared, and Bellicus laughed, for how could they possibly catch him now? Darac was powering away from the wrathful villagers and Cai was sprinting alongside seemingly with ease.

It was not exactly the proudest moment of the druid's life for running from a fight was not in his nature, but this was far better than cracking the skulls of Britons.

A white face appeared suddenly in front of him and Darac slowed, rearing and moving to the side but the big black could not quite avoid a collision and Bellicus saw the man hurled aside with terrific force, a yell of pain following them as they picked up speed once more.

"Gods, how many of them are there?" It seemed the entire population of Torp had come out to search for the missing Puck and some of them must have been in boats, disembarking when they heard the commotion and running to the road to try and block Bellicus's escape. Mercifully none were armed with swords, but five or six of them had formed a line across the road ahead and the druid could see more of their fellows appearing from the trees on the left.

The villagers might not have had swords, but knives were visible in some of their hands, while others had small axes or rudimentary, but quite lethal, spears.

Bellicus hauled on the reins, slowing Darac while he called on Cai to match their reduced pace. Glancing back, he could see they had put a bit of distance between them and the folk coming along behind them. What to do? If he was to charge directly into the wall of villagers some might get injured and, even worse, Bellicus or his animals might well feel the bite of those blades he'd noticed, or feel the bone-crushing power of an axe head.

If he dismounted and got into a fight it would be a bloodbath however, and, with so many people against them it was more than likely the druid's party would come off worst.

To the right the dry-stone wall stood around four feet high, a mighty obstacle for a horse with a rider, even a thoroughbred like Darac. Ahead, and behind, were the irate, murderous people of Torp, while on the left lay the Ure and numerous trees with—

"Shit!"

Another white face suddenly emerged from the clustered trunks and a hand reached up, grasping the druid's cloak and tugging. Bellicus kicked out, another oath erupting from his lips, but his foot missed the man and he began to slide out of the saddle. Desperation flooded him as he saw the villagers ahead grinning maliciously and hurrying towards them.

"Cai!"

The mastiff reacted instantly, large, powerful body moving with incredible speed around the hindquarters of Darac and lunging at the villager. The man screamed, a terrible wail that brought outraged shouts from his kinfolk, and then Bellicus felt the grasp on his cloak disappear.

"Kill the big bastard!"

"Druid thinks he can do what he likes! Get him!"

"Smash his skull in!"

"Watch out for that crazy dog!"

It was a monumental effort for Bellicus not to give in to the red mist that was quickly descending over his mind. "Come, Cai!" he shouted, and kicked his heels into Darac's flanks, urging the horse into a gallop.

There was hardly any distance between them and the stone wall on the right side of the road, but Bellicus could see no other option: they would have to try and jump it, or die at the hands of the villagers.

Cai's quick canine mind understood his master's intentions immediately and streaked ahead, accelerating even faster than Darac. Bellicus watched, heart in his mouth, and then gasped in relief as the muscles bunched in the hound's back legs and then pushed off against the road, powering Cai up and easily over the wall.

"Your turn, old friend," the druid breathed, knuckles white as he grasped the reins so hard that the leather cut painfully into his palms. The stone barrier that had seemed no great obstruction when Bellicus was standing beside it, now appeared enormous as he was carried towards it ever faster. If Darac misjudged the jump, or did not have enough space to build up the speed required to clear it, the wall would maim the horse, send the druid crashing to the ground, and, ultimately, see them both dead.

The villagers had seen his desperate bid to escape and they were sprinting through the gloom towards him, screaming, howling, calling down the very gods Bellicus represented. They were not just hurling words in his direction though; an axe smashed off the wall in front of them, sparks flying from the iron head as it hit home and Bellicus felt a pang of fear at what the weapon would have done had it struck his head rather than the stone.

"Jump!" The druid was not sure if he had shouted out loud or simply screamed the desperate cry in his own head, but up Darac went, and Bellicus's stomach seemed to drop terrifyingly, before they came down on the other side of the wall, hooves thundering ahead without missing a beat and Bellicus found himself cackling with maniacal laughter yet again.

It all happened in an instant but time had slowed for the druid so it felt like an age. Now, everything was moving at breakneck speed again as Darac and Cai raced across the open field to the southwest, away from the road, and the villagers who were scrabbling clumsily across the wall behind them without hope of ever catching up to them.

"Well done!" Bellicus cried, patting Darac's neck and grinning down at Cai who seemed to smile back at him, tongue lolling as they slowed to a less tiring canter. "By the bones of Dis, that was close." He looked up and thanked the gods for seeing them safely across the wall, and Peredur for waking him in time to escape the villagers' malevolent clutches.

What now? the mythical hero seemed to ask. *Would you still ride homewards, Bel? Knowing the poison Saksnot carries within him, infecting even a settlement full of Britons?*

The first light of dawn was just beginning to illuminate the rolling field they were traversing, and it seemed also to show Bellicus the path he should take.

No, he would not ride for Dun Breatann after all – he would continue the hunt for Saksnot. For whatever reason Peredur – be he real or some facet of Bellicus's own mind – wanted him to follow the road southwards, so that was what he would do.

160

Saksnot might believe himself safe, but Bellicus would find him, even if it meant he had to travel all the way to the massive walls of Garrianum itself.

CHAPTER THIRTY-TWO

Bedwyr and his two companions were in a fine mood as they rode through the countryside towards their next destination. After visiting Taki in Durovigutum they continued to travel from settlement to settlement, speaking with headmen, and Saxon chiefs if there were any living in the area. The meetings tended to go much as they had with Taki – the chiefs would usually be hard men, former warriors themselves who carried enough authority and physical presence to lead their fellows into their new life of peace alongside the native Britons. Such men would rise to a challenge if Bedwyr presented one, but he quickly learned to deal with the chiefs with respect and to seek their co-operation in a humble, although never deferential manner, if he wanted to achieve a favourable result. Promising those proud men loyalty and friendship in the coming years was a far better way to form alliances with them than threatening them with Arthur's army.

"How did you become friends with Arthur anyway?" Aesus asked as they headed towards their next destination. Motius glanced across as well, interested to hear the reply.

"I grew up with him," Bedwyr told them. "Me, Kay, and Lancelot all had fathers who were friends with Arthur's foster-father. We would visit one another often and get up to the usual things young lads do."

"I'll bet you did," Aesus chuckled, staring ahead dreamily as though picturing his four superior officers running wild around the countryside.

"Never got into too much trouble," Bedwyr laughed. "Merlin – Nemias, I mean – was around Arthur from a young age, guiding him, making sure he didn't stray and became the warlord we know now."

"You three were trained to be Arthur's captains from childhood then?"

"Aye," Bedwyr confirmed. "Merlin had a plan for all of us." His smile faded, remembering wise old Nemias, cut down by the Saxon raiders so recently.

"Well, our mission is going well, eh?" Motius noted, quickly changing the subject as they approached the next village on the western road.

Bedwyr put aside his melancholy and nodded happily at his escort in agreement. "Indeed. Qunavo was right about these foreign settlers – they might have been bloodthirsty killers when they arrived here in Britain, but time and age have mellowed them. They're ready for a civilised life. A life of hard work alongside their neighbours, reaping the rewards of their toil and enjoying the company of people who don't simply live for death."

"Why would any man live just to kill and plunder?" the second escort asked. "I mean, look at these lands. There's enough room for us all to live in peace, surely."

"Some men don't want to just live in peace though, Aesus. Some want to own more than everyone else, and they'll take it by force. You've both fought in the shieldwall, you've felt the thrill of battle."

"And the fear," Motius murmured.

"Aye, the fear is always there," Bedwyr admitted. "But that just makes the battle fever stronger when the fighting is over. That feeling of glory is what so many of the sea-wolves crave. That, and the wealth they can steal."

"Stealing is easier than working your fingers to the bone," said Motius.

"More dangerous too," Bedwyr grunted. "As Hengist's hordes have found out, and will continue to find out as they attempt to push further out from the Saxon Shore and into central Britain!"

"That's fighting talk!"

The three riders paused, shocked by the unexpected voice that came from the trees on their left. Bedwyr felt panic rise within him as he replayed the words in his mind and it dawned on him that they'd been spoken with an unmistakable Saxon accent.

"Who's there," he demanded, drawing his sword an inch or so from its scabbard as he glared into the trees but saw only shadows for the leaves were thick and blocked out most of the sunshine. "Show yourself!" Part of him expected – hoped – this was some joke, but it became immediately clear that the situation they now found themselves in was no laughing matter.

"You think you are a danger to us?" The source of the voice stepped out from behind the trunk of an old beech tree, revealing himself to be a broad-shouldered man with a long blond moustache and hard, blue eyes.

"Who are you?" Bedwyr asked, trying to remain calm as both Aesus and Motius drew their swords and nudged their horses around to face the newcomer who was very plainly not a fellow Briton.

"I am—"

"Leofdaeg!" Bedwyr's blood ran cold as he noticed the Saxon's lame right arm which everyone in Arthur's army knew had been broken by Lancelot; the stories of that whole terrible affair had become part of the folklore amongst Arthur's warriors, as had the brutality of Jarl Leofdaeg.

"You recognise me!" The Saxon appeared pleased, revelling in his fame amongst the Britons.

His smile quickly turned to a snarl though, as Aesus spat, "Everyone knows about you and your bent arm."

Self-consciously, the jarl drew back his right arm and unsheathed his sword with his left hand. It was not a natural, fluid movement, and Bedwyr was surprised at the awkwardness for the man had been injured a couple of years ago yet still did not seem at ease using his left hand instead of his right. Did he never practice? Spar? For a man as warlike as Leofdaeg it seemed incredible that he must be a poor fighter, but he was a jarl after all, and maybe that status allowed him to retain control of his hearth-warriors.

Bedwyr saw those men now, Leofdaeg's private warband – all in service to Hengist, but under the near-crippled jarl's immediate command. They had come out from amongst the trees, ten of them, armed with spears which they levelled now at the three riders, making the horses step back nervously.

"Circle them," Leofdaeg barked in his own language, gesturing with his lame arm so Bedwyr was able to easily understand the command.

"Don't let them surround us!" he shouted, kicking his heels into his mount in a desperate attempt to get away from those levelled spears. He had not turned his horse to follow Leofdaeg so he was still facing along the road and his sudden action took the Saxon warriors by surprise, allowing him to break through.

Motius and Aesus were not so lucky – their horses, startled by Bedwyr's sudden bid for freedom, also tried to gallop away but the trees were too thick to allow them easy ingress and Leofdaeg swung his sword at Aesus, who was nearest to him. The attack was clumsy but the blade was sharp and easily cut right through the flesh on the

Briton's leg and into the bone, drawing a horrific scream of pain that panicked the horses even more.

There were no more commands, or even intelligible words, just gasping and groaning, perhaps the beginnings of a shrieked oath from Motius that was viciously cut off, ending in a gurgle as two spears tore through his mailcoat and blood erupted from his mouth.

Bedwyr had looked over his shoulder and saw his escorts – friends now, after their time on the road together – slaughtered before his eyes. He was not in the clear either, however, and he found himself falling from his saddle before striking the ground, head reeling, desperately trying to get back to his feet but having no control over his own limbs.

What had happened? How had he ended up in the road, unable to even reach out for his sword that lay nearby having slipped from his grasp?

The sound of laughing came to him, growing louder as someone approached. An enemy warrior, slim, with the sides of his head shaved and a beard braided into a plait swaggered into view. He grinned and called something to Leofdaeg which Bedwyr could not understand, but then he bent down and lifted a hand axe that was lying beside the Briton's own sword. The Saxon cackled and shook the axe at Bedwyr, gloating no doubt over the fact that he'd used it to knock Bedwyr out of the saddle.

The sounds of bodies being stripped of armour and valuables reached the injured Bedwyr and tears of rage and impotence blurred his vision. He could not see his escorts' bodies being defiled in death, but his mind unhelpfully created a picture for him.

"So," said Leofdaeg, walking across and staring gleefully down at him. "You still think you are a danger to us? To Hengist's mighty sea-wolves? I think not, Briton." He reached out and touched Bedwyr's skull where the axe had struck him, sending a shock of searing pain lancing through him. He was wearing a helmet, or at least he had been, he was too dazed now to tell whether it was still in place or not. Either way, the helmet might have saved his life, but he may have a serious wound that might kill him eventually. Especially if his captors did not have a healer in the ranks.

He almost laughed himself then, but lacked the strength to do so. 'Captors'? Why would he think of these rabid dogs as his captors when they were so ready to kill his two escorts without hesitation?

Surely he would suffer the same fate. Why would they waste the skills and resources of a healer on a man one of their own number had injured?

He felt his arms grasped and roughly dragged behind his back and he gasped, trying desperately to curse whoever was behind him. The Saxon ignored him, or perhaps didn't even hear his hoarse whisper, and set about binding his arms together.

"What's this?" Leofdaeg stalked before him again, seeming to appear as if through a mist as Bedwyr slowly began to lose consciousness. "Oh, very nice," said the jarl and unbuckled the sword belt around Bedwyr's waist, holding it up to examine the attached scabbard with gleaming, greedy eyes. "This reminds me of the helm I took from your friend, Lancelot. Similar superb workmanship."

Bedwyr's tongue felt huge in his mouth as he tried and failed to rail at the Saxon. Like the helmet Leofdaeg had referenced, the priceless scabbard had been a gift from the former High Druid, Nemias, consisting of a poplar core covered with red leather embossed with a wonderfully detailed hunting scene, while the scabbard's throat and chape were both of polished bronze.

"I'll have this. Thank you," Leofdaeg smirked, buckling it in place around his own waist without even bothering to remove his own. "I'll wear it with Lancelot's helm, to remind me of how I bested not one, but two of Arthur's captains."

"Didn't best Lancelot." Finally Bedwyr found his voice, grinding out the words with terrific effort. "He's still alive, and he'll find you one day, you ugly whoreson."

Leofdaeg's upturned mouth became a hard line and his left fist flashed out, smashing into Bedwyr's cheek. "Hengist will be very pleased with me when I bring you to him. Very pleased. He might even make me his new second-in-command!" The jarl grunted in satisfaction and turned away, shouting to his men as Bedwyr felt himself lifted like a sack of grain and thrown over the back of a horse. He was then tied in place so he wouldn't slip off. He could see Motius and Aesus, stripped naked and spreadeagled in the road for travellers to view and the birds and foxes to feast upon. Already the excited cawing of crows could be heard swirling in the air overhead as they looked forward to filling their bellies with human flesh.

Bedwyr was too dazed, too numb, to feel much sorrow for his friends. All he could think about was the fact that he had been right, it seemed, to think of Leofdaeg as his captor. The jarl had stolen his belt with its exquisite scabbard, but he had not killed him. They had strapped him to this horse and were now moving back along the road to the south.

He was a prisoner of Leofdaeg, the man who had enslaved Lancelot, brutalising the blond swordsman so badly, dehumanising him to the point where he had wanted to die. Was that what lay in store for Bedwyr?

Perhaps, but even in his befuddled state, Bedwyr knew it was no coincidence that the Saxon warband had been hiding in the trees waiting for them to come along. Leofdaeg had come looking for Bedwyr personally, and was probably taking him now to Hengist.

Why? What fate did Hengist have in mind for him, to go to all the trouble of ambushing him and carting him off across the countryside rather than simply killing him and parading his mutilated body before Arthur's army?

Bedwyr had no idea, but he knew that whatever was coming to him would not be pleasant. He bounced up and down on the horse's back and wished for death to save him from Hengist and Leofdaeg, and he was glad when his eyes closed and darkness swept over him.

CHAPTER THIRTY-THREE

Saksnot was very pleased with himself. He had not even needed to persuade Puck to help him deal with the Bellicus – the moon-touched Saxon had suggested it himself!

"That big bastard will be waiting for you on the road," Puck had told him when the two were stood in the headman's house, the woman still whining although Puck had been strangely kind to her, Saksnot thought. Perhaps that was why the people in the settlement had allowed him to live amongst them for years. They could see he was a warrior, anyone could see that, but if he was pleasant and helpful they'd be more likely to accept him into the community, as they clearly had.

Saksnot wondered what went through Puck's mind as he lived and worked amongst those rustic Britons. The Saxon was not particularly old, he could still have fought alongside Hengist's men – from his bearing and the way he moved it was plain that Puck would be an asset to any warband. Yet he lived there, with farmers and labourers and weavers and maybe twenty or thirty other oafs, content to plant their crops and scratch a poor existence from the soil. How could Puck stand it, when he could be winning riches and renown with his kinsmen, pillaging the towns along the eastern coast of Britain?

The warrior was not quite right in the head though, Saksnot could see it in his face. There was a strange light burning in Puck's blue eyes, a light that warned of a madness that could erupt at any moment. Apparently nothing had set the man off since he'd been living in the village, although Saksnot wondered if perhaps Puck had gone abroad of an evening, visiting nearby farmsteads and villages and giving free rein to his madness. Perhaps tales had gone around the surrounding lands of missing people – women and children most likely – taken in the night, never to be seen again.

The little boat hit a sudden swell and Saksnot grasped the sides in alarm before it righted itself and he paddled furiously to bring the craft closer to the centre of the river. The mostly gentle ride along the Ure had sent him into a near trance and set his imagination running wild. What did it matter if Puck was a killer? So was Saksnot, and his fellow Saxon had seemed eager to take his place riding south to spring the ambush Bellicus would have undoubtedly laid for Saksnot.

Woden-willing, the murderous instincts Saksnot had dreamily ascribed to Puck would make the druid's night a most unpleasant one. The young man beamed at the thought and it felt good, at least until the burns on his face crinkled painfully, reminding him of his recent troubles. Still, he was happy and pleased with how things had turned out. The river had carried him southwards with no fear of Bellicus catching him and there was a possibility the druid would not be able to continue hunting him when the sun rose. Even if Puck only managed to injure him, or his horse, it would slow the big whoreson enough for Saksnot to put many miles between them.

"You can take my boat," Puck had told him, and that was a couple of hours after Bellicus had left the village. Puck had stood watch in the headman's house, keeping the woman calm but still a hostage, while Saksnot caught some desperately needed sleep. Then, at last, Puck woke him, set the woman free to go back unharmed to her man, while Saksnot was shown to the little boat, his pack of provisions refilled, and set on his way along the river.

Why had the strange Saxon helped him so much? Saksnot guessed he would never know. A combination of his youthful looks, their shared Saxon blood, and perhaps a desire in Puck to relive his glory days of fighting enemies like Bellicus of Dun Breatann. Some of that must have played into the fellow's actions, and probably more besides which Saksnot was not sufficiently moon-touched to comprehend. Maybe the gods had finally stepped in to help Saksnot, using Puck as their agent? That was possible, and it was about time, for his mission had been particularly ill-omened up until he'd met Puck.

Who knew how the gods operated? It made sense that in Alt Clota the druid's gods would be the most powerful. But, as Saksnot and Bellicus travelled further away from there, drawing nearer to Garrianum and the *volva*, Thorbjorg, perhaps the Saxon deities' influence would become stronger. In that case it made sense for Puck to be here, ready and willing to help Saksnot escape the druid.

The thought cheered Saksnot even more as he rowed the boat along, keeping it away from the shore as the current carried him back to Hengist. He had no idea how far south the river went, and Puck admitted he'd only ever used the boat to cross to the other bank or to fish. Looking ahead now, however, Saksnot could see the course of the river curving eastwards and he decided it was time to disembark and make his way on foot once more. It had been a nice change riding the river but, since he had no idea where it flowed from, he thought it best to take the familiar road again. It was not easy rowing against the current anyway and he did not want to waste any more strength.

He paddled the water on the left of the boat, slowly but surely drawing closer to the western shore until, at last, he felt the bottom grinding against the stones and silt and, with a jerk, he came to a stop. He pulled the small craft up onto the riverbank so it would not float off when the tide came in and Puck could retrieve it at his leisure. With a last satisfied glance at the water, he headed for the road.

This was the same way he'd come on his northward trip to Dun Breatann so, although he couldn't be completely sure, from certain landmarks he believed he was around halfway back to Garrianum. The prospect of walking hundreds of miles on foot dampened his good humour and he looked along the road in both directions, praying that the gods would continue to look favourably upon him and provide a horse he could steal. Some old pedlar or merchant riding a sturdy palfrey would be ideal he thought, but there was no one at all in sight and, with a sigh, he started to walk.

Travellers did pass him, in both directions, as the sun came up and the world came alive and men and women went about their business. Some were on foot, some on ox-drawn wagons, some riding horses or donkeys. None were suitable targets for the Saxon to rob of their transport, however; either their animals did not look up to the task of carrying him to Garrianum at a fast pace, or there were too many people – witnesses – around to make a violent theft risky. So he walked, glancing back over his shoulder continually, fearing Bellicus would come riding after him at any moment.

The sun reached its highest point, beating down on Saksnot and making him sweat profusely. He was glad he had a full water-skin and was able to fill it at a stream halfway through the morning, but, more worryingly, the dampness of his feet and between his buttocks meant that his skin grew more chafed the further he walked. As midday came and went he began to limp, his backside stinging and the beginnings of blisters making every single step painful.

His face, already burned by the Damnonii guard's flaming torch, also stung terribly as the sun seared him anew. At that point he stopped praying to Woden for a horse to steal, and wished simply for a wide-brimmed hat to keep the harsh sunshine from his skin. He tried putting on his hood but it did little to help. His earlier good mood had dissipated, and he even contemplated finding a shady spot to simply rest and wait for night to fall, but he feared the druid and his damned wardog catching up to him so he did his best to block out the discomfort and focused only on putting one aching foot in front of the other.

So much for the gods, he thought bitterly, staring down at the road, wondering how many more days of this he would have to endure. Would it rain on the morrow? He bloody hoped so, and then he realised that squelching through mud in the sections of road that had disintegrated would lead to even worse issues with his feet.

A voice hailed him then, and he looked up anxiously, hand falling to his sword. It was not the vengeful druid however, but a middle-aged man riding an ox-drawn cart. Saksnot could not understand what the fellow had said, even when the words were repeated, until the carter patted the seat beside him and smiled kindly.

The young warrior grinned, a genuine, happy expression as his heart filled with relief that he would be able to rest his weary body for a time. Even a few minutes respite would be welcome, and he pulled himself up beside the man with a grateful nod.

The carter could obviously tell that Saksnot did not understand his language so they rode in silence, taking in the scenery which was rather pleasant along this stretch. The Saxon looked inside his pack and found some bread that Puck, or someone, had given him. He took it out and shared some with the carter who greedily consumed the lot in moments.

"For a skinny old bastard you certainly enjoyed that," Saksnot murmured, smiling at the carter who laughed uncomprehendingly and turned his attention back to the road.

Saksnot leaned against the back of the cart and tried to rest but it was simply not comfortable enough. He was glad to take the weight from his feet but, if anything, sitting on the hard wood beside the carter was making his chafed arse crack sting even more and they were actually travelling slower than Saksnot had been walking. He imagined Bellicus on that big black horse of his, charging along the road behind them, growing ever closer, the bloodthirsty mastiff growing hungrier for Saxon flesh with every passing mile.

He knew it was a foolish notion – Puck would certainly have given the druid a great deal of trouble and it was quite possible there was no pursuit at all. But the thought of facing the enormous Briton in his weakened state continued to prey on Saksnot's nerves until, at last, his neck became sore from looking over his shoulder and he decided enough was enough.

"Thank you," he said to the carter, nodding to him and then jumping down onto the road and continuing on foot. There was a small farm to the left and Saksnot pointed there, as if that had been his destination all along. The carter nodded kindly and waved, but it seemed to take an age for the ox to drag the old vehicle and its occupant away.

The road was deserted for now, apart from the slowly receding cart, and the Saxon looked around, made sure he was not being observed, and then slipped along the hedge-lined track that led to the farm. There had to be a horse, or even a donkey here, surely. He would simply do what he'd done before and help himself. If anyone was foolish enough to stand in his way he'd make them regret it.

The farmhouse was in poor repair, so Saksnot deduced that it was owned by someone older. Someone without the time or inclination to make the repairs that a younger person would keep on top of. Someone that would not be able to stop him stealing whatever he wanted. Still, he would not be hasty – the woman at Torp had sewn up his injured side and rebandaged it, but it would not take much to open the wound again he guessed.

Slowly, moving low and keeping himself hidden behind bushes, trees or outbuildings, he circled the farm house, scanning the area for workers, or dogs that might be kept to herd sheep and deter intruders. There appeared to be no-one around although there was a pile of hay with a fork in it that someone must have been working not too long ago, dragging some of it into a barn with open doors that probably housed cattle and, hopefully, a horse. Everything pointed to Saksnot's appraisal of the place being correct: this farm was owned, and worked, by no more than one or two people, probably quite elderly, and they'd taken a break to escape from the blazing afternoon sun. The warrior continued his scouting, completing a full circle and coming back to the road before creeping slowly towards the front of the house.

He could not see into the single-storey building, but he imagined what it would be like inside. There would be cool water or ale laid out on the table, with milk and cheese produced by the animals of that very farm, and perhaps other wonderful foods to eat. Freshly churned butter! He pictured it, imagining spreading it on some barley bread, mouth watering as he tasted it in his mind, and then he thought he might spread some of it across his burns to ease them. Maybe…No, slathering butter between his arse cheeks did not seem like such a good idea. He doubted it would ease the chafing. Probably make it worse!

Sniggering at his own silliness he crept across the open ground to the side of the house, eyes fixed on the door. Although it was a fairly large home there was only the one entrance, and the windows were shuttered, probably to block out the sunshine and keep the interior nice and cool on this scorching late-summer day.

He reached the wall and pressed himself against it, carefully moving towards the door, listening intently for anyone inside. This part of the house was in direct sunlight and he had to squint to protect his eyes so he was a little worried he might be caught by surprise, but he made it to the door without issue. He placed a hand on the latch and raised it, pushing the door open and stepping inside. He could see the building was split into two rooms by a thin wooden wall, and he moved to the left side first.

A woman sat at a table, white-haired and wizened although he could only see the back of her head and her hands. She had not heard him come in, either deaf from old age or simply engrossed in enjoying the meal that was set before her. Saksnot could smell milk, and the glorious smell of berries, and his stomach growled noisily.

The lady was not so deaf after all, for she began to turn her head towards him. Cursing softly, the Saxon stepped quickly across the space between them and slammed the pommel of his sword into the back of her skull. There was a thump but no other sound as the woman's head fell onto the table.

Saksnot muttered another oath as her white hair landed in the bowl of blackberries, turning the pale strands to vivid purple. He sheathed the sword and lifted her head, pulling the bowl away and greedily popping berry after berry into his mouth. He looked around again, still wary that there would be someone else in the farmhouse although he could hear no movement. Checking that the woman was either unconscious or dead – no threat either way – he put the bowl down and took out his sword again, moving towards the second room.

There had to be someone else nearby he mused. That old woman couldn't work a farm like this by herself. Better be careful.

As he went into the second, slightly bigger area of the building his eyes took in the furnishings. Good quality items – a sturdy chest made from oak, comfortable bed large enough for at least two people, a bronze figurine that depicted some strange god of the Britons, and, on the wall, a long-handled axe that had clearly been designed for battle rather than chopping wood. There was no one in the room so he went to the weapon and examined it. Although it was still in good condition with the shaft appearing to have been oiled recently, the blade was free of nicks. It had likely belonged to the old woman's husband and seen action many decades ago, but it was merely an ornament now.

Still conscious of the fact that there must be someone else around – someone stronger than the old crone in the adjoining room – the Saxon lifted the bronze figurine and shoved it into his pack. It was clearly valuable and would pay for a new mail shirt when he eventually made it back to Garrianum.

Then he went back to the dining area and grabbed whatever he could carry: salted meat, a block of cheese, and a couple of apples. There were more berries but they would simply make a mess of his pack, so he crammed them all into his mouth, glorying in the harsh, slightly bitter taste, not caring that he got the dark purple juice all over his mouth, his fingers, and his trousers. There was a jug of beer, too heavy to carry but too inviting to ignore, and he quickly swallowed it down in long gulps.

He found the butter but, when he smeared it across the cracked burns on his face he realised what a terrible mess it was making, and became aware of what a bizarre sight he would present when he returned to the road. His fellow travellers would mark him instantly and, if Bellicus came asking for him they would know where to direct the druid.

He did his best to wipe away the greasy yellow mess from his skin, wondering if it might even attract flies or wasps and shaking his head at the thought. That was all he needed after everything he'd suffered so far!

A sense of urgency came over him then and he closed his pack and headed for the door, sword in hand. The old woman was still not moving and he was sorry for hurting her, but he put thoughts of her aside and went out to the courtyard, squinting as the blinding sun hit him.

The butter had certainly worked, he thought, easing the dryness of his burned face. The speed with which he'd downed the beer also meant the heavy, dark liquid was taking effect already and he felt better than he had in days as he headed for the barn to search for a horse. He grinned, realising that he'd almost forgotten what he'd come to the farm for in the first place.

It was a shame the horse he'd stolen back in Alt Clota was gone. He hoped Puck would take good care of the animal for it had served him well. Gods willing there would be a similarly sturdy beast within the barn, and it would carry him quickly back to the *bretwalda* on the Saxon Shore.

Before he reached the large outbuilding he slowed. Something was different. He wished he hadn't drank the beer so fast as his mind worked sluggishly to put things together, and then it suddenly hit him: the fork that had been stuck in the bale of hay was gone. Had Saksnot lifted it himself? It took him a moment, but he was eventually quite sure he'd never touched the thing. Why would he?

Someone else was around after all, and probably in the barn.

He crouched behind the hay, listening, but there was no sound from within the gloomy interior. Suddenly he felt shame and wondered what Bellicus would do in his position. Would the towering druid be hiding behind a bale of hay, frightened to face some farmhand despite being armed with a sword and trained in its use? Wasn't he supposed to be one of Hengist's most feared and trusted hearth-warriors? He pictured Bellicus standing tall, striding proudly into the barn as if he owned the place himself, caring little whether one enemy or ten awaited him there.

He seemed to leave his own body for just a heartbeat, seeing himself as though from above, a slim, anxious young man, unsure of what to do next, scarred, burned, sweaty, tired, and aching from multiple wounds and abrasions.

Rising, his face transformed into a confident scowl and he strode towards the wide doors of the barn. It looked just like the one that he'd taken his horse from in Alt Clota, and he remembered how he'd made quick work of that little adventure. He was Saksnot of Egtved, killer of the Merlin, and none could stand against him!

He stood in the entrance, arms outstretched, blade glinting impressively in the sunlight, imagining the sight he must be to anyone standing inside. His eyes scanned the interior, seeing only hay, a single cow penned up on the left, a horse on the right, and little else. He glanced up at the storage loft but saw no one there either.

"Just as well," he murmured to himself, sheathing his sword and swaggering across to the horse. The animal's tack equipment hung on the wall beside the stall and Saksnot took it down and set about readying the horse to leave.

A sudden, anguished cry filled the still afternoon air, and the Saxon jumped, startled. He left the horse, making sure to close the stall door so it didn't wander off, and took out his sword once more, sidling across to peer out in the direction of the farmhouse. He was sure that was where the shout had come from, and he was proved correct when a large, muscular farmer of around thirty summers appeared in the doorway. Not only was he built like an ox, he was armed with the axe that had hung on the wall of the house and, from the way he was holding it, he would not struggle to wield the thing.

Where had the big bastard come from? Saksnot guessed the farmer had been in the barn then left to do something at the rear of the farmhouse, the two men passing each other without realising it. The Briton had spotted him staring out from the barn now and, with a feral growl, lumbered towards him.

It crossed Saksnot's mind to make a run for it. He was not in the best shape after all. Then his old pride returned, magnified by inebriation, and he stepped out beside the hay bale, swinging his sword expertly, showing his opponent just what he was up against.

"You murdered my mother!" the farmer bellowed, and, although the Saxon did not understand the words he hardly needed to. The man's rage and murderous intent was quite evident, and he raised the big axe and brought it down with surprising speed.

Saksnot threw himself to the side, knowing he could not parry a blow from the farmer's heavier weapon which would surely smash his sword if the two came together with such force.

Rolling nimbly back to his feet, chafed backside and blistered feet momentarily forgotten, the Saxon lashed out expertly and laughed in delight as his blade caught the farmer on the bicep. It was a deep cut and the livid red line quickly became a shocking scarlet stream that ran down the man's arm and dripped from his elbow. Before the farmer could attack again, Saksnot danced forward and thrust the point of his sword into his foe's guts.

Shrieking in fear, the farmer collapsed on the ground, grasping the terrible stomach wound as blood continued to ooze from his slashed arm, quickly turning the hay-strewn ground red.

Saksnot revelled in his easy victory for it reminded him of who he truly was, and what he was capable of. His confidence had taken a bit of a beating during his travels but now the beer and this simple triumph restored his arrogant self-belief. He contemplated mocking the dying farmer but decided the clumsy oaf was not worth the time. He had to finish preparing the horse and get back on the road before more Britons turned up. A farm, even one as small and quiet as this one, generally had a stream of regular visitors coming and going, taking produce away or bringing in animals and equipment.

With a last sneer the proud warrior returned to the barn and completed tacking up the horse before he led it out into the sunshine. The animal was skittish for it had seen the men fighting and was clearly not used to violence, but Saksnot kept the beast in check before jumping easily onto its back. He winced, his backside still stinging, but at least the weight was off his aching, blistered feet now, and he would soon be back with his comrades and be able to bathe and set about healing his battered body. By Woden's eye, he'd earned a rest!

It was good to be mounted again and Saksnot took a little time to make sure his pack was firmly attached to the horse's blanket and wouldn't slip off when they eventually picked up some speed. Satisfied all was safe, and he had taken enough provisions from the farmhouse, the warrior urged his steed into a walk and headed towards the road.

The combination of the heat and the alcohol gave him a strange kind of tunnel vision and he was so focused on the path his horse was picking out that he did not notice that the farmer was no longer lying, bleeding out beside the hay bale. Turning to search out the injured Briton, Saksnot was shocked to see the man had somehow climbed up on the hay and now towered above horse and rider, axe held high, teeth gritted in anguish.

Utterly defenceless, for he had sheathed his sword, Saksnot gaped up at the farmer as the man launched himself through the air, bringing down his great axe as he came.

The horse had spotted the attack and, although it must have known and perhaps even loved the farmer who had fed and cared for the beast, no animal would stand still in that situation. It tried to bolt, and its sudden movement saved Saksnot from taking the axe head directly in the top of his skull.

The blade hissed through the air, missing the Saxon's head but striking the horse's rump. It was only a glancing blow, but the weapon was heavy and it caused the animal to rear and lose its footing. Saksnot cried out as he felt himself falling, and then there was a terrible pain in his leg as he was pinned to the ground beneath the horse.

The Briton had landed behind him and he was sobbing uncontrollably, desperately trying to grasp the axe handle. It had fallen from his grasp when he struck the ground and Saksnot, also crying in pain and confusion, tried to draw his sword. It was stuck fast, trapped between his waist and the ground and he did not have the strength to pull it free. He stared, terror stricken, as the dying farmer gripped the axe and began pushing himself to his knees for another wild swing.

The horse was up again though, and galloping towards the road, leaving Saksnot on the hay-strewn ground. He'd given up on the sword and instead pulled out his seax which was sheathed closer to the centre of his belt. As the burly farmer reared up, blood, snot, and tears covering his chest and arms, Saksnot threw his knife, a scream of supplication bursting from his lips, wordlessly begging the gods for help.

Almost in disbelief he watched the seax strike the Briton in the throat. It had been a desperate throw however, and the blade did not hit the farmer point-first. Instead, the seax twisted in its flight and it hit the man side on, bouncing off rather than hammering fatally home.

It was enough to unbalance the mortally wounded farmer though, and, with a last desperate cry, he fell backwards, not landing flat on his back but sticking half upright on his haunches, breathing raggedly for a few heartbeats before, at last, he fell silent, staring at the Saxon from unseeing eyes.

Saksnot watched, fearing to believe the fight was truly over. He gasped for air, filling lungs that had been instantly emptied when the horse threw him to the ground, and he continued to whimper and sob for a long moment before the shock of his near-death finally overcame him and a sense of calm took over.

He was alive, praise Woden!

Relief replaced fear and he saw the horse had stopped before reaching the road and was watching him warily, confused and unsure what to do next. All was well – he had defeated the farmer, he still had his pack of possessions, and the horse would take him home to his *bretwalda.*

He thought of Hengist then, wondering what the warlord's reaction would be when he found out Saksnot had not killed either of his targets. He'd generally found Hengist to be a wise, realistic man – surely he would not think badly of Saksnot for failing his mission? To make it inside Dun Breatann, find the centurion, and injure him terribly was no mean feat. Saksnot was just one man after all. He smiled, reassuring himself that Hengist would reward him for what he'd achieved.

With a low, almost maniacal laugh, he leaned on his palms and pushed himself up. A sudden, searing pain ran the length of his left leg, from his toes to his hip, and he collapsed on the ground, gritting his teeth against the scream that was ripped from his throat.

Damn the gods! He should have known he would not simply walk away unscathed from this fight; the entire mission to Alt Clota had been cursed from the moment he'd arrived there!

Glancing down he gingerly used his fingers to probe the bones of his leg. He was terrified that something may have snapped completely in half – he'd seen injuries like that in battle and knew there was a good chance they would prove lethal, especially to Saksnot who had no business being in that farm and could hardly expect aid from any locals after the crimes he'd committed. No bones were protruding through his skin though and he guessed – hoped! – that his injury, whatever it was, would prove to be minor, despite that horrific pain that had torn through him like a bolt of lightning when he tried to stand.

He called out to the horse, trying to make his voice as pleasant and reassuring as possible. "Come here, boy! Here!" It came out as a strangled squawk and the horse, which could surely not understand his language anyway, continued to eye him warily.

He had no choice - grabbing the farmer's axe, he used it to lever himself up to his feet and, sweating profusely, he hobbled towards the waiting animal. Still skittish, the horse danced away from him, but not far, and, at last, cooing and calling softly to it, he was able to grasp the reins.

Usually he would jump easily up to ride, but with his injured leg he did not even try. Instead, he was forced to put his arms around the horse's neck, the axe falling with a thump, and use his arms to clumsily drag himself up. It was humiliating for the young warrior, and the task was not made easier by the anxious horse beginning to walk when he was only half in position but, eventually, he was up and riding towards the road, every muscle in his body crying out for respite. In his distress he did not even think to collect his seax.

A couple of men were passing when he reached the main road and they looked at Saksnot with raised eyebrows. He must have looked terrible, but their eyes fell to the sword sheathed at his waist, an expensive weapon that only trained, and powerful, warriors would carry. They glanced at one another with a mixture of amusement and trepidation then continued on their way, northwards, with only the occasional backward glance, probably to see if he'd fallen off his horse and might be safely robbed.

A sense of security settled over him as he was carried away from the farm and the corpses he'd left there. The horse was calm and Saksnot's strength returned with each hoofbeat, and with each bend in the road that hid the scene of his most recent crimes from view.

How many people had tried to kill him now in his nineteen summers on *Miðgarðr*? Too many to count, and many of them had been in the past month, yet he remained alive and mostly intact while his enemies were now food for the crows. Whether the gods favoured him or not, he had proved himself a formidable warrior and the old, familiar pride swelled within his chest. He could hardly wait to reach Garrianum and regale Hengist's hearth-warriors with his incredible tales of daring. Bellicus and Duro may yet live, but

180

Saksnot had carved a bloody swathe through the Britons and his Saxon comrades would enjoy hearing all about it, he was sure.

As the sun finally began to set the perspiration dried on the Saxon's body and he took his cloak from his pack, throwing it around his shoulders and huddling against the horse. His backside was not so painful, nor were his feet, and his leg did not hurt so much at the moment although he was not looking forward to dismounting. All things considered, he was in a good position. Long shadows were cast by the trees as he rode and he began to look forward to stopping for a rest. Sleep would be most welcome.

He watched the terrain, searching for somewhere secluded that would offer protection from a possible shower and hide him from prying eyes of fellow travellers. There were not so many folk on the road now that the light was failing, and he gaped around at the pleasant countryside, already growing drowsy.

Then he glanced over his shoulder and came instantly, fully awake. Staring back at the road behind he knew he was not imagining it – there was a lone rider in the distance.

A lone, hooded rider, accompanied by a massive, loping dog.

CHAPTER THIRTY-FOUR

Bedwyr had regained consciousness hours after he'd been captured by Leofdaeg. Fully awake, his body naturally tried to adjust to the motion of the horse he was stowed over and, before long, his chest, belly, and ribs ached terribly. When the Saxon warband stopped to set up camp for the night he'd been given only a small amount of food and water and then ordered to keep his mouth shut and go to sleep.

He'd hoped his captors would spend the evening downing ale and getting rowdy, making so much noise that perhaps one of Arthur's patrols would find them. It was a desperate hope, not very realistic, and, of course, no one came to his rescue. The Saxons did nothing to draw attention to themselves anyway, displaying a professionalism that Bedwyr could not help but be impressed by. They drank only a little ale, took turns to watch over the camp throughout the night, and kept their voices low the entire time. The way the sea-wolves went about their business only made Bedwyr more pensive – these were no loutish raiders, riding abroad to rape and plunder whatever easy targets they could find. These men had been sent by Hengist to complete a particular mission and return with their prize – Bedwyr – as quickly and quietly as possible.

It was a terrifying prospect for Bedwyr, especially since he was unarmed, and remained bound hand and foot, only allowed to move when he had to relieve himself.

His imagination fed him all sorts of images of what the *bretwalda* had in store for him, and naturally this only made him more frightened. He was a soldier himself, and he'd stood in the shieldwall, bravely facing the bellowing enemy hordes who sought to rip him apart with axes, spears, and swords. Those had been terrifying, but at least he had his comrades to stand with him, and his arms and armour to defend himself. Gods, if it came to it, he could even have run from the field of battle – it would have been humiliating, and he'd have been branded a coward forever, but the option was always there.

Now, Bedwyr had no options. No weapons, no way to defend himself, no chance to run. He could do nothing but lie there on the cold ground waiting for dawn and the journey to resume.

He had never been so afraid in all his life.

Despite the old adage that time always flowed quicker when one was enjoying oneself, the miles seemed to pass in the blink of an eye as Bedwyr was carried on the backs of horses to the eastern coast of Britain. He was not ill-used other than the occasional kick from Leofdaeg, but neither was he treated with kindness or respect. It was clear he was to reach the Saxon Shore alive and in one piece, but his captors had no interest in talking to him, not even to gloat, and he spent the days in silence until, at last, he knew from Leofdaeg's demeanour that the trip was coming to an end.

They had reached Garrianum, and now Bedwyr would discover why he'd been captured.

From his position on the horse that was carrying him like so much cargo, Bedwyr could not get a proper look at the old Roman fortress as they approached. He twisted his neck to try and take in the view but it hurt too much and he ended up simply staring at the ground just as he'd done for most of the ride. He caught glimpses of the massive stone walls the legions had erected, but they were soon through the old gatehouse and within the interior of the fortress. Men called out to Leofdaeg and his warband, greeting them cheerily and praising Woden and Thunor for the success of their mission. More than one of the fort's inhabitants came to laugh at Bedwyr and some even spat on him or slapped the back of his bruised head as he passed.

He bore it all in silence, for what else could he do? He did not want to talk to the Saxons, and he was sure they would do more than slap him if he became a nuisance anyway, so he held his tongue and stared at the grass moving past below until, at last, the horse stopped moving and he was unceremoniously cut loose to slide with a painful thud onto the ground.

Had his limbs been free he might have tried to stand up, to make some effort to protect himself from potential attacks, but he remained bound and his entire body ached from the ride anyway. So he simply rolled onto his back and lay staring up at the sky, praying that his face did not show his captors how frightened he was.

His stomach rumbled loudly, a natural and uncontrollable reaction any man might have when they'd barely eaten for days and arrived in an army camp where multiple cooking fires were roasting meat, simmering stew and pottage, and baking loaves.

"Ha! Hungry, Bedwyr?"

The voice seemed somewhat familiar to him and he moved his head to look up at the man who'd addressed him. Tall, muscular, and with the unmistakable bearing of one used to wielding great power, Bedwyr knew him immediately.

"Hengist," he murmured, pleased that his voice held firm and did not crack.

"*Ja*," the Saxon warlord confirmed with a broad, disarming smile. He looked genuinely pleased to see Bedwyr, and that only made the Briton more nervous. Suddenly, his attention was drawn away, to Leofdaeg, and the fine new sword that adorned the jarl's belt. "What's this?" the *bretwalda* asked, eyes shining greedily.

"The Briton's sword," Leofdaeg admitted, hand falling protectively to his prize.

"It looks exquisite," said Hengist, eyes never moving from the weapon.

"It is, lord." Leofdaeg seemed to take a deep breath and then, with a smile that was obviously forced, he unbuckled the belt and held it out to the Saxon warlord. "You should have it," he said. "A gift, from your most loyal jarl."

Hengist grabbed the sword and slowly drew it from the scabbard, examining the blade closely, smile widening as he took in the fine details and understood just how incredible an example of craftmanship it truly was. "My most loyal jarl," he murmured to himself, looking at Leofdaeg at last and nodding before pushing the sword back into the scabbard and turning once more to Bedwyr. "Welcome to my fortress," he said happily. "Come, join me in my quarters."

Bedwyr opened his mouth to remind the *bretwalda* that he was bound, but one of Leofdaeg's men was already bending, seax in hand, and sawing at the lengths of rope that tied his hands and feet together.

"Up," the man grunted in a harsh tone, and dragged Bedwyr to a standing position.

For a long moment he remained in position, stretching out his neck and his limbs before he was punched in the back and made to follow the slowly receding figure of Hengist.

"Come on, keep up," the *bretwalda* called jovially back to them. "I have food and drink waiting. Well done, Jarl Leofdaeg, you have done well. Lord Bedwyr will be a most useful prisoner. Most useful!"

His words brought mocking laughter from Leofdaeg and the handful of Saxons who were escorting them towards Hengist's private quarters which, Bedwyr now realised, was not some old tent erected within the ruined old walls, but an actual stone building. Once it must have been an administrative centre where Roman clerks would keep records of visitors, and taxes, and whatever else the departed legions had thought valuable information.

Now it was home to Hengist, protecting him from the wind, rain, and snows that regularly battered the coastal settlement.

Lucky him, thought Bedwyr bitterly. He looked around, doing his best to appear stoic, seeing the large tents that most of the Saxons lived in when they were here in Garrianum rather than off destroying Britain. He noticed women, including many who were obviously slaves, working in the open, and cold anger began to replace his fear. The sea-wolves had done so much damage to Bedwyr's people, hurt so many people, and yet their leader lived like a king, or a Roman emperor, here in this grand stone building, served by captured Britons whose lives must be little more than perpetual torment.

If only Bedwyr had a weapon he would set about these tall, burly invaders and take down as many of them as possible before falling himself!

He had no sword though, and if he tried to take one from the warriors escorting him they would soon make him wish he hadn't. That would not do him any favours. If he was to escape from this, whatever it was, with his life and his body fully intact, he must remain calm and simply go along with Hengist's plans until a chance to get away presented itself.

Maybe Arthur would come for him he mused, a kernel of excitement growing inside. His friend was fiercely loyal and, when it was discovered that Bedwyr and his two guards had been waylaid on the road – with no sign of Bedwyr's body – maybe Arthur would know he was here and ride to his rescue.

It was not likely, he knew, and he steeled himself for what was to come as he was taken into the old Roman administration centre.

The place smelled strongly of men, Bedwyr noticed as he went inside. Sweat, leather, stale mead and ale, piss, even sex – these scents and more assailed his nostrils and he pictured the evenings

185

Hengist must enjoy with his most trusted captains and wenches in that musty interior.

He noticed an extremely attractive woman then, sitting in the corner of the main chamber, shrouded in the shadows cast by the sunlight coming through unshuttered windows. His eyes were drawn to the long, lithe legs and up to the slim waist and...He realised he was admiring the feared *volva*, Thorbjorg and his lust turned to disgust in an instant. He had seen what this witch was capable of when Arthur's army had faced the Saxons at Nant Beac just two years ago. No doubt she would claim she acted for the gods, but Bedwyr believed the woman to be evil incarnate, and he swallowed nervously, fear growing once again.

She did not speak, merely eyed him hungrily, or at least so he imagined, and he almost felt the blood draining from his body, as if Thorbjorg was sucking the very life from him for use in her black rituals.

"Bedwyr, friend, and advisor to Arthur."

Hengist's powerful voice brought Bedwyr's attention back to the centre of the room where the *bretwalda* had taken a seat. Two massive guards stood behind him armed with spears, ready to skewer the Briton, or anyone else, who posed a threat to their lord, and more of the Saxons took up positions along the walls. It was all designed to be intimidating, and it might have worked had Bedwyr not already been thoroughly terrified.

"You're probably wondering why we've brought you here," Hengist drawled, putting his feet up on a nearby table and gesturing towards a naked woman who stood in an alcove on the right. She hurried forward, breasts dangling as she bent to hand him a horn of mead before scurrying back to her gloomy corner.

"I assume you're going to sacrifice me to your pitiful gods," Bedwyr replied, and a strange joy suffused his being at the strength in his voice. Indeed, so confident did he sound that Hengist was visibly taken aback, turning with raised eyebrows to share a glance with the *volva* who gave a throaty chuckle in reply.

"A good guess," Hengist nodded. "He's one of the smarter Britons, eh, Sigarr?"

"Doesn't take a genius to figure out you needed me alive for some reason," Bedwyr retorted before the small man the warlord had spoken to could reply. "And, knowing your insane gods, it seemed obvious what that reason would be."

"Very clever," the *bretwalda* chuckled. "Honestly, we wanted Lancelot – Thorbjorg believes his blood would be the most powerful for her purposes. But we couldn't catch him, so, when we heard about you wandering around with only a couple of guards we decided to take you instead."

"Whatever, sea-wolf, do what you will." Bedwyr was happy that they had not caught Lancelot, even if it did mean death for him instead. "Your gods will never hold sway on our island."

"Oh?" Thorbjorg's voice, sibilant and oddly persuasive, came from the back of the room. "Why is that? You think Taranis, and Sulis, and Cernunnos, are strong enough to withstand our gods, just as your people hope to withstand Hengist's army?"

"No," Bedwyr laughed. "Because the Christians will eventually take control, and for all they talk of peace and love, their God is far less willing to share worshippers than any of our, or your, deities."

No one had expected that answer and a thoughtful, unhappy silence fell upon the room for a long moment. Eventually Thorbjorg cackled dismissively, and the gathered warriors joined in with her mirth although Bedwyr could see the worry on their faces. It seemed the Saxons had begun to fear the rapid rise of Christianity just as much as the likes of the Merlin and Bellicus of Dun Breatann did. Bedwyr was no follower of the White Christ, seeing the nailed God as a weakling in comparison to mighty Taranis, but invoking Christ's name had frightened the Saxons, if only for a moment, and Bedwyr was glad he'd done it.

"We will burn the Christians," Hengist growled. "Or crucify them if they prefer, like the fool they follow." His men murmured agreement and he set down his mead horn on a stand beside his feet. "You are ready to be a sacrifice then?" he demanded, his earlier jovial demeanour gone now. "To be Thorbjorg's plaything?" As if to emphasise his mastery over the prisoner, he removed his belt and replaced it with the one taken from Bedwyr, buckling it in place and admiring the fine sword that would now be his.

Bedwyr's mouth felt completely dry, yet still he had to swallow. It pained him to show his fear, but he could not stop the instinctive reaction to Hengist's threat. Feeling entirely impotent, he spat, "Our druids will make sure your blood rituals come to nothing, Saxon. Be sure of it."

"Your druids?" Hengist barked, smile returning to his bearded face. "You mean like Bellicus? He is probably dead already."

"Dead?" Bedwyr hated himself for rising to the bait but he couldn't help himself. Hengist's pronouncement had been made with some conviction, suggesting it wasn't just a throwaway comment.

"I sent one of my best warriors to Dun Breatann a few weeks ago," the *bretwalda* nodded. "With orders to find Bellicus and Duro and kill them."

"One man?"

Hengist smiled at Bedwyr's scoffing. "*Ja*, one man. The man who did away with your old Merlin. He has a better chance of passing unnoticed, deep into the heart of Damnonii lands, to find the people who murdered my brother, than a large warband would."

Bedwyr held his tongue, holding in the comment he wanted to make on Horsa. Clearly the brutal Saxon's death had upset the *bretwalda* deeply, but it would only bring extra pain to Bedwyr if he was to gloat about it.

Hengist saw the conflict within the Briton and smiled bleakly. "Bellicus, and Duro, are most likely being mourned by the people of Dun Breatann at this very moment," he said, draining the mead in his horn and holding it out for the naked slave to refill. "And soon, when Thorbjorg decides the time is right, you will follow them into whatever afterlife awaits you, Lord Bedwyr. Now, I had planned on offering you refreshments and treating you as an honoured, if condemned, guest, but I do not care for your company. Take him away."

Leofdaeg and his men came forward and roughly shoved him out of the building as Hengist and those left inside fell to celebrating his capture and the terrible fate that awaited him.

CHAPTER THIRTY-FIVE

Bellicus was not happy. In fact, although he'd managed to escape from the vengeful villagers without hurting them, or being injured himself, the merry dance that Saksnot continued to lead him on seemed to bring more pain and suffering with every mile they travelled.

In the afternoon he'd come to a farm and decided to replenish his supplies. He'd filled his water skin at a stream around midday but he hoped the farmers would sell him fresh fodder for Darac, maybe some meat for Cai, and a bit of cheese for himself since the stuff he had in his own pack did not look or smell too inviting thanks to the sun that had beat down on them all that day. It had been past time for a rest anyway, the druid had thought a little guiltily – he was sweating and uncomfortable but it was Darac and Cai that were having to do all the work. They deserved some time in the shade to cool down and ease their muscles.

He'd called out a greeting as he rode along the track from the main road towards the farm buildings but received no answer. All seemed quiet, too quiet, and Bellicus began to wonder if Saksnot was there, arriving just before the druid and causing mayhem. The thought had made him dismount and take his staff from its place on Darac's saddle, carrying it along as they approached the courtyard.

Immediately, the druid had spotted the dead man lying beside the hay bale and cursed under his breath. There was no need to warn Cai to be on guard for the mastiff had seen the corpse and the smell of blood and death would surely have alerted him that things were not right in that farm.

Saksnot had been there, that much was certain. With any luck the little prick was still around and Bellicus could do everyone in Britain a favour by sending him to his great Saxon mead-hall in the afterlife.

Bending to examine the dead man it seemed to the druid that he'd been killed fairly recently, perhaps even as recently as the last hour or two. He stepped warily across to the nearby barn, making sure no one was inside waiting to attack him but finding the empty stall where a horse must have been. Another oath burst from the druid's lips at that discovery – Saksnot could be miles ahead now if he'd ridden hard after killing the farmer.

189

Still, he'd promised Cai and Darac a chance to rest in the shade for a time, so he put the horse in the barn, securing him and making sure he was comfortable and had water to drink. Greedily, Darac supped at the full bucket on the side of the stall, looking like he was smiling as he flushed the water through his front teeth.

Content that his mount was safe, Bellicus murmured apologetically to Cai and the pair went swiftly but carefully towards the nearby farmhouse. As he peered in through the open front door the druid saw the second corpse, this time of an old woman with snow-white hair.

"What is wrong with that whoreson?" the druid had muttered, heartily sick of the terror and death that seemed to be left in the Saxon's wake everywhere he went. "What kind of threat would she have been to him?"

There might well have been even more killing then, for a couple of labourers had appeared from the adjoining fields and seen the dead man. When they noticed the massive druid they'd assumed Bellicus was to blame for the murder and, if it hadn't been for the terrifying presence of Cai, growling and snapping at the farmers, keeping them out of range of the druid's staff, it would have gone badly for them. Eventually, Bellicus was able to convince the men that he was not to blame for the crimes at the farm and they allowed him to rest in the barn for a time.

It soon became clear that Saksnot had stolen much of the food stored in the house, but the two labourers knew where more was stored, out the back in a low shed, and gifted Bellicus what they could spare. It was not much, and it was not the best quality, but it was better than nothing and would keep Cai's belly full for at least a couple of days.

Soon, Bellicus had bid the labourers farewell and taken to the road again, swearing to them that he would do everything in his power to see Saksnot face justice for what he'd done to the farmers.

The sun was still hot but not as bad as it had been around midday and Darac seemed quite fresh and well rested after his short time in the barn. Cai was Cai, full of energy and seemingly eager to continue their journey, loyally pacing Bellicus as they continued southwards, eating up the miles as evening approached.

He had no real proof it had been Saksnot who'd committed the murders at the farm but he knew it had to be the young Saxon. That meant Bellicus was still on the right track and, with any luck, would catch him before they came to Garrianum. The druid had been to the old Saxon Shore fort before, and he knew that it would be impossible to get inside if Saksnot made it there first. With that in mind he urged Darac into a canter, hoping to cover as much ground as possible before night fell and they were forced to set up camp.

And then, as he came down from the crest of a low hill, the land stretching out straight ahead, lit up orange in the sunset, Bellicus saw a lone rider. He squinted, trying to make out details on the figure that was a mile or so ahead. The druid had good eyesight, but the horseman was too far ahead to be sure if it was the Saxon. He kicked his heels in and began to close the gap, cursing as the road curved around to the left and his quarry was lost behind a stand of trees.

* * *

Saksnot knew it was the druid on the road behind him but he laughed grimly as he urged his mount into a gallop and careered around a bend in the road, effectively concealing himself from his damnably persistent pursuer. What to do now? It would be dark soon and even the druid could not see at night, surely?

Like the rest of the lands he had passed through on the way from, and back to, Garrianum, Saksnot did not know this area well. There might be the ideal hiding place within a few minutes' ride for all he knew but, given his limited knowledge and the urgency of his situation, he knew he must act quickly.

He gave the horse its head, practically flying along the road which was thankfully in good condition, until he saw a break in the trees and slowed for a better look. In the gap between the trunks he could see a well-worn path and knew it must lead somewhere. Since he did not think his stolen horse would be able to outrun the druid's larger, more impressive mount, Saksnot decided to take a chance and head into the trees, praying to Woden that Bellicus would ride on past.

He did not wait to check, following the path into the woods until they gave way to a clearing with a carved stone monument of some kind. So this was what the locals had worn the path away to visit.

Saksnot did not dismount but he looked closely at the strange thing and guessed it must represent one of the Britons' bizarre gods.

191

There was some kind of altar or table on the ground, with an upright block of stone depicting a figure holding sword and shield. It was an incredibly crude carving, and yet there was something about the circular eyes, slit mouth, and hanging genitalia that made the whole thing seem unutterably sinister.

A shiver ran down his spine and Saksnot knew he had to get away from that place. Bellicus would be in his element here and have a distinct advantage over Saksnot for Thunor and Woden would wield little power there in that foreign sacred place. Thankfully a second path, or perhaps just a continuation of the first, led on to the east and the horse plodded carefully along.

The foliage seemed to dampen all sound in the woods, creating an eldritch atmosphere that sent shivers along Saksnot's spine. He pushed on and came to a flight of makeshift steps leading down to a stream. The path continued on the far side, climbing upwards, and the warrior halted, desperately wondering what to do. The horse would not be able to walk down the steps – even a man would have to tread carefully or risk slipping. Of course, if Saksnot was to slip he would probably not suffer any injury other than to his pride but if the horse was to fall there was a good chance it would break a leg on the rocky bed of the stream below.

He could not go back and risk walking straight into his pursuer, and he could not abandon the horse. Even if he hadn't injured his own leg, he needed the animal to carry him quickly to his destination.

"What have we got here?"

The voice seemed to come from nowhere and it startled Saksnot's horse. The beast reared in fright and, unprepared, the young warrior slipped off, falling onto the grass, breath blasted from him. He grabbed the hilt of his sword and began to draw it from its sheath as he rolled and came up in a defensive stance. Or at least that was what he tried to do instinctively. Instead, his injured leg gave way as he was rising, and he squealed in pain, collapsing once more.

Two unkempt men were glaring balefully at him, apparently outraged by his presence as he tried once more to at least push himself to his knees but, before he could manage it he felt a foot cannon against the side of his head and then one of the men fell onto his back, dragging the sword from his limp fingers and pinning him to the ground.

"Who are you, boy?" the man demanded, pressing his mouth close to Saksnot's ear and shoving his face into the grass forcefully. Saksnot could not make out a word of the man's thick dialect, but he could tell by the cadence of the sentence that he was being asked a question. "Saksnot," he replied, making his voice high-pitched and as childlike as possible.

"Saxon?" the Briton growled in an even harsher tone and Saksnot realised he had made a terrible mistake. These men were natural enemies of his people and neither of them seemed inclined to simply pat him down and allow him to be on his way, even if they could converse with him and discover why he was in their domain.

The standing man kicked him again in the side of the head and he yelped angrily, dizziness threatening to make him vomit or even pass out. He felt the weight lift from his back and he was roughly hauled over and searched for any other valuables. They found the silver amulet he wore around his neck, slicing through its cord and discussing its possible religious significance. Slow realisation dawned on him as he stared up at his captors – these men were druids, or at least some form of priests or holy men.

They did not carry themselves with the same easy self-confidence the likes of Bellicus or the Merlin displayed, and they looked thoroughly grimy, as if they had little interest in personal hygiene. Hermits, perhaps, charged with guarding the hideous shrine in the nearby clearing.

"Up," one of them commanded, dragging him with surprising strength to his feet. The hermits might be filthy and, now that he was downwind of them, stinking, but they must be paid in good food for their service there at the shrine for they were both broadly built, and their eyes were clear and betrayed a keen intelligence.

The horse had run off, unsurprisingly, but the hermits didn't seem interested in the beast, instead forcing Saksnot to walk back towards the stone figure in the clearing. He took one step and collapsed, crying out as a searing pain lanced along his leg.

The hermits shared a nasty cackle with one another and reached down to grasp him under the armpits. They hauled him unceremoniously across the ground and the fear rose within Saksnot as they drew closer to the main road. What if Bellicus heard the commotion and came to find them? The hermits would naturally do what the druid told them.

He almost laughed at that. Bellicus was the least of his worries at that moment. He'd been robbed of his weapons, his amulet, the few pieces of hacksilver he carried, his mount was long gone, and he couldn't walk. Whatever these two lunatics had in store for him, he feared this might be the end of his adventures.

That fear grew as the Britons dragged him closer to the stone altar that stood in the middle of the clearing. The figure carved on it stared at him from those damnably sinister round eyes, but that was not the most frightening thing about it.

When he'd ridden past here before he had given the altar only a cursory glance. Now he could see there was a stone trough at the base of the thing, and it was stained the deep, unmistakable brown colour of blood.

Sudden understanding flowed through him and he felt his body grow limp with sheer terror. The hermits were going to sacrifice him to whatever god this horrific little stone idol was supposed to represent.

"Bellicus!" he screamed then, bucking and writhing ineffectually against his captors. "Bellicus! By the gods, druid, please help me!"

CHAPTER THIRTY-SIX

"I have a really bad feeling about this."

Arthur let out a long, heavy breath and glanced up at Lancelot who was anxiously chewing his upper lip. They were in the command tent, sheltering from the heat with welcome mugs of ale that had been somewhat cooled in a nearby stream. "It's probably nothing. I won't get too worried until we know more. Maybe they just got lost."

"Lost?" Lancelot returned with a disbelieving laugh.

"None of the three were very familiar with those lands. Perhaps it wasn't wise to choose those two to escort Bedwyr. Maybe we should have chosen someone local."

"All they had to do was stick to the main road. And that's exactly what they would have done," Lancelot persisted. "Bedwyr is no fool. He's also not impetuous – he's methodical, and measured, and sticks to the plan no matter what. I'm telling you, Arthur, they've met something bad on that road."

"Calm down, man," the warlord said irritably. They had been getting regular reports from Bedwyr who paid a messenger in each settlement he visited to carry news of his progress back to Arthur. They'd not had a report for some time now and, naturally, fears had grown with each passing day. "Maybe Bedwyr is fine, but his latest messenger got lost."

"Lost?" Lancelot demanded with another sardonic laugh. "How could someone fail to locate us? We have an army with us! We've been fighting Hengist's warbands all summer, it's not like we're riding around in secret."

"Fine!" Arthur cried, slamming his hand down on the camp table he used to lay out the simple maps he and his captains used to discuss tactics and forthcoming manoeuvres. His ale mug went flying, spilling what was left of the drink across the ground. He ignored it. "You can take a handful of men and retrace Bedwyr's journey. See if you can find him."

Lancelot nodded in satisfaction, but he came across and gripped Arthur by the shoulder. "You've been close with Bedwyr for a long time, and it pains me to worry you like this, but...I've been fearful ever since Leofdaeg ambushed me and my men. He wanted me alive for a reason, Arthur."

"Of course he did," agreed the warlord. "You were his slave, and you escaped. His ego was bruised. I mean, you ruined his sword-arm, Lancelot. Of course he wants to capture you alive, to torture you, enslave you, make an example of you. That has nothing to do with Bedwyr."

Lancelot looked down and ran a hand through his blond hair, shaking his head as he did so. "I truly hope you're right," he said quietly. "I truly do. I just fear the Saxons wanted to capture a high-ranking Briton, whether it was me or Bedwyr or someone else, for some twisted purpose."

His fear had infected Arthur deeply and the warlord stood up now, deep lines furrowing his brow. "I'd come with you"—

"Don't be daft," Lancelot broke in. "You need to command the army. Hengist himself might not be here, but the warband we've been fighting is big enough to cause a lot of trouble if you can't defeat them soon. No, I'll go and find Bedwyr, while you do what you have to do here. Don't worry, Arthur, I'll ride like the wind and be back before you know it."

"Ha, if only," Arthur snorted but he forced a tight smile onto his lean, bearded face, doing his best to remain stoic in the midst of another difficult month. Gods, when were months not difficult? The Saxons had even taken to causing trouble during the winter in recent years, allowing Arthur and his troops little respite. It was a hard life and one the warlord had sworn to put an end to by dealing with the sea-wolves once and for all no matter how long it took. "Listen, old friend," he said seriously, smile fading. "I don't want to lose you too. Don't take any chances. If Bedwyr and his escort have been murdered by some Saxon chief in one of our own settlements I want you to return here – alive! – and tell me. Don't be acting the hero, going in with your blade swinging. You hear me?"

Lancelot's crooked grin flashed for the first time since they'd started the discussion and he held out his arms in mock astonishment. "Me? Be a hero? When have I ever done anything foolish like that?"

"I mean it," Arthur retorted with almost a sad chuckle. "You come back here in one piece. We will deal with whatever is to come together, all right?"

Lancelot bowed, as a captain to his commanding officer, serious again. "I'll return soon, lord. Count on it."

They grasped forearms, both men perhaps wondering if this would be the last time they ever saw one another – such was the life of a soldier, after all – and then Lancelot turned and strode from the tent, calling for his horse and for volunteers to accompany him on his mission.

* * *

"Where was the last place we had a report from?" Lancelot asked, mostly to himself as he and five companions rode hard for the north less than an hour after his meeting with Arthur.

"Lord?"

"It was Durovigutum," Lancelot called over the pounding of hooves, answering his own question. "Any of you know where that is?"

He'd picked men not just for their martial prowess and experience, but for their knowledge of the lands between Arthur's camp and Bedwyr's expected journey, and he was rewarded for his foresight now.

"I know it, lord," one of his riders shouted, long hair streaming back beneath a finely crafted helmet. "I grew up nearby."

"Then lead us there! Make all haste, for every moment could be vital for Bedwyr."

"Aye, lord," the warrior replied, guiding his mount to the front of the formation, taking point as the horses thundered along the old Roman road, barely even slowing when it began to rain, hiding the horizon from view behind a grey mist that seemed darkly ominous to Lancelot.

It would have been folly to flog the horses, and not something Lancelot would ever order unless he knew for a fact Bedwyr was on the verge of being slaughtered by Hengist. The settlement of Durovigutum was not too far away and so the animals were sweating and tired when they came galloping along the main street rather than utterly spent.

"Where's the headman!" Lancelot demanded, knowing how impressive he looked in his armour, atop the chestnut mare he'd been given by Arthur for his loyalty. Even his hair, wet from the rain rather than shining golden in sunshine, had an effect on the village women who watched them pass and he couldn't resist returning their admiring smiles in spite of the seriousness of his mission.

"I'm the headman," someone called, and Lancelot turned his full attention on the burly, grim-faced fellow who appeared from a row of workshops. "What's wrong, my lord? Saxons?"

"Saxons indeed," the swordsman replied, raising a hand to stem the cries that were rising in response to the apparent threat. "No, none are attacking, rest easy. I want to speak with the Saxons who live amongst you," he confirmed. "The settlers."

"Ah, Taki's lot," said the headman. "He's the chief. You'll find them along there." He pointed but couldn't contain his curiosity, calling after the riders to ask why they wanted to speak with the Saxon villagers.

"We're looking for our friend, Bedwyr," Lancelot shouted back, not slowing his pace and seeing no reason to hide the reason for their mission. The more people that knew Bedwyr had not been heard from, the better.

No one volunteered any information however as they left the centre of the settlement and approached the section that had been allocated to the new settlers. Set a little apart from the main village, it did not take long for Lancelot to reach it, and to ride directly to the largest, most impressive building which he knew had to be where the Saxons met and conducted all their important business. All the different peoples had such a great hall, or mead hall, as the sea-wolves called theirs, and this looked a decent, if smallish, example.

An elderly man was carving a piece of timber near the doorway, slivers of wood flying as he worked the material. Rheumy eyes lifted to peer at them as Lancelot reined in his horse and jumped easily down to the ground.

"Where's your chief?" he asked the greybeard without preamble. He was not really a man for niceties, which was why Bedwyr had been chosen as an emissary to the Saxons rather than him.

The old man glared at him, clearly angered but, before Lancelot could upset him even further the hall door opened and a huge bear of a man filled the entrance. He was dressed like a farmer or a labourer, but Lancelot could tell from his stance that he'd once been a warrior, and the poorly-healed scars on his cheeks bore out the Briton's assessment.

"More of Arthur's men," said the newcomer, clearly as astute as Lancelot. "I am Taki, chief amongst my people here. What brings you here, so soon after Bedwyr?"

"Well met, Taki," said Lancelot, aware that this was someone he should keep on their side. The chief's tone when mentioning Bedwyr had been warm, suggesting the two men had parted on good terms. That was a good start, at least. "My friend, Bedwyr, has not been heard from in some days. Do you know anything about his whereabouts? Or where he was going after he visited you?"

Taki's face had become stern, almost thunderous, as he listened, and his eyes flickered for just a moment to the old man who continued to whittle away at the piece of timber that Lancelot could see now was the leg of a chair.

"Bedwyr was in good health, and good spirits, when he left here," the Saxon chief replied in a level, guarded tone. "We came to an agreement, shared food and drink, and parted on friendly terms. He was travelling next to Durobrivae, a village not far along the road to the north. I cannot tell you any more than that."

Lancelot listened, instinctively knowing that the chief was not being entirely truthful. He might have been on good terms with Bedwyr, but he was hiding something. For a second, the swordsman thought about forcing whatever it was from the burly chief – he might be built like the side of a house, but Lancelot was confident he could best the fellow. That would surely undo any good work Bedwyr's visit had done though, and aggression would probably not be well received by the rest of the settlers, some of whom were loitering nearby, watching what was happening.

"I thank you for your time, then." Lancelot nodded and turned away, quickly mounting his waiting horse. "If you hear anything else, send a messenger to Arthur, eh?"

Taki nodded slowly, and still his eyes strayed again to the greybeard who whittled idly away at the chair leg, an oddly smug glint in his watery eyes.

"To Durobrivae," Lancelot said to his riders and led the way back to the main road, picking up speed as they went.

When they had cleared the houses, Lancelot slowed, and turned to his men saying, "You lads ride on at a canter for a mile or so, then turn around and come back for me."

"Where are you going?" one called, but Lancelot had already jumped down from his horse and threw his reins to the man.

"Go! Before they notice we've slowed down!"

The riders were all veterans, used to obeying orders, and they did so now without further questions, galloping away from the Saxon settlement as Lancelot crouched low, doing his best to hide behind hedges and creep unseen back in the direction of the mead hall. He was at the rear of the hefty structure but, as he moved carefully, silently along the back wall and around the side, keeping to the shadows, he could hear Taki's great baritone voice raised in…what? Anger? Amazement? A mixture of both, Lancelot believed.

He paused, pressed against the wall, listening, hoping none of the Saxons who were hurrying towards the front of the hall would notice him.

He had picked up quite a bit of the Saxons' speech while he was held as Leofdaeg's thrall. Although 'Saxon' was a broad term that the Britons used to encompass all the diverse Germanic raiders and each had their own dialect, they did share many cultural elements and a broadly similar tongue. As he crouched beside the corner of the mead hall, Lancelot listened intently, picking out as much of the angry conversation as he could.

"I made an agreement with them!" Taki was shouting, clearly furious.

"And you should be ashamed of yourself!" came the harsh reply, although this voice was weaker and Lancelot knew it had to belong to the sullen old arse who'd been carving the chair leg.

"I am chief here, Fritigern," Taki raged. "And I make the decisions. I have allowed you to live with us despite the fact you're a troublemaker who contributes nothing to our community. We wish to live in peace, you withered old bastard, and you threaten us all with your actions!"

Other voices joined in, too jumbled for Lancelot to pick out, and he wished Taki would get to the point and reveal exactly what had befallen Bedwyr for that was surely the topic of this argument. Whatever the old man had done, it must have been heinous for it seemed the entire community of settlers was united against him.

"Hengist will soon take control of all these lands," the cracked, aged voice rose high above the others. "You would all do well to bear that in mind. Hengist remembers those who serve him faithfully."

"Betraying Bedwyr and his men will not be rewarded, you old fool!" Taki retorted, and Lancelot felt his breath catch in his throat as he finally understood what had befallen his friend.

"I've already been rewarded," the greybeard cackled, seemingly oblivious or immune to his fellow villagers' scorn. "Hengist gave me this."

Lancelot could not resist peering around the edge of the building. He saw the elderly warrior pull up his sleeve, revealing an emaciated, pale arm. Ludicrously clasped around the atrophied flesh was a bronze ring that must have been extremely valuable. Hengist had obviously valued the old man's actions very much.

"You condemned three men who wanted to befriend our people," Taki demanded. "For that? You look ridiculous! Give it to me!"

Lancelot watched as the huge chief bent down and easily bent the arm ring. Fritigern eyes were wide as he was so publicly violated and he tried to fend off the younger man, slapping at the questing hands as they inexorably removed the ring from his arm. His protests and flapping grew so frenzied that Taki eventually slapped him a resounding crack across the ear. He used an open palm but, even so, Lancelot winced at the noise of it and Fritigern collapsed sideways, mewling pitifully, withered arm shorn of its bronze prize.

"This will be traded to the Britons for grain and other supplies," Taki announced, holding up the ring so that the metal gleamed and the watching settlers' eyes seemed to shine greedily. Most had probably never seen, never mind owned, such a valuable trinket, but Taki's plan would benefit them all and it proved to Lancelot the chief was a man of honour.

The blond swordsman stepped out from his hiding place and walked towards the crowd, hands held out by his sides to show he was not holding a weapon or posed any threat to them. His sudden appearance was noted immediately, and Saxon voices rose in consternation, but he ignored them and headed directly towards Taki who watched him approach in silence, jaw set firm. The chief surely knew that if Lancelot was to report Fritigern's betrayal of Bedwyr to Arthur it could lead to the desolation of this entire settlement.

Of course, that made Lancelot a real threat to these people, and he spoke quickly before one of them decided to remove that danger by silencing him forever.

"You're a good man, Taki," he announced loudly and clearly in their own tongue, surprising more than a few of them. "You all are, apart from him." He jerked his head disdainfully at the furious old man who glared at him from the road, still clutching at his ear. "I will make sure Arthur, Bear of Britain, knows only he played a part in what's happened to Bedwyr."

Taki nodded, the relief plainly visible on his broad face and Lancelot, feeling more at ease, lowered himself onto one knee beside Fritigern and drew out his knife, placing it beneath the Saxon's jaw. He listened, waiting to see if any of the other folk in the settlement protested but it seemed the entire place was holding its collective breath as they watched the scene play out.

If any of them had been contemplating standing up for Fritigern they would have changed their minds as Lancelot's men rode back along the main rode just then, the heavy horses thumping into position so that no one could get past. Lancelot nodded to them in greeting and then shook his head, mutely advising the warriors not to draw their swords. Their presence was more than enough to remind the Saxons of his authority.

"Where is Bedwyr?" he demanded, pressing the point of his dagger into the jowly skin of Fritigern so that a trickle of blood ran down his neck.

Defiance flared in the old man's damp eyes and his lip curled in a vicious snarl. "Hengist has him," he said with obvious relish. Hatred for Britons, and probably everyone else at that point in his life, overcame the fear of dying and he tried to spit at Lancelot, although the saliva simply trickled embarrassingly down his own chin.

"What do you mean, 'has him'? You mean he's killed him?"

"I don't know," Fritigern admitted, and then he cackled nastily. "But I know he wanted to capture him alive. Hengist has plans for your friend."

"What plans?"

"No idea, but I doubt they'll be very pleasant for old Bedwyr."

He laughed again and rage flared within Lancelot. He was far more impulsive than Bedwyr and he did not hesitate, pushing the blade of his knife hard, upwards, into the sniggering Saxon's jawline and on into his brain. Blood gushed from the wound and Fritigern's eyes went wide with shock before Lancelot withdrew his blade and stood up, staring hatefully down at his handiwork.

There was total silence outside the mead hall and some of the gathered settlers made signs to ward off evil or to commend the dead man to the gods. The chief, Taki, merely grunted as though Lancelot had done him a favour.

"Do you have any idea why Hengist wants Bedwyr alive?"

Taki slowly shook his head, still looking in grim fascination at the body of the handyman. "No. Like the old troublemaker said though, it can't be anything good. Torture most likely, or maybe the *bretwalda* wants to enslave one of Arthur's noblemen?"

Lancelot digested that, remembering again how Leofdaeg's soldiers had tried so carefully to capture him too, even allowing him to escape rather than taking the chance of killing him. He did not really believe Hengist would go to all this trouble simply to make Lancelot or Bedwyr a thrall. Something else was going on, and Lancelot felt sick to his stomach at what his friend might be facing at that very moment.

"What now, lord?" one of his riders asked, perhaps feeling slightly exposed there, surrounded by Saxons when Lancelot had literally just butchered one of their own. Maybe Fritigern was universally disliked, but it was still, ultimately, 'us and them'.

"You spoke the truth when you told me Bedwyr had been heading to Durobrivae when he left here?"

Taki nodded at Lancelot's question. "*Ja*, lord."

"Then that's where we will go too, and see what there is to find, even if we're too late to do anything for our friends now."

"May your gods go with you," called the chief as Lancelot mounted his horse and led his warband northwards once again.

203

CHAPTER THIRTY-SEVEN

Bellicus realised the rider on the road in front of him had picked up speed and was opening a wider gap between them.

"It has to be Saksnot," he said, looking down at Cai. "He's noticed us coming and he's trying to get away again. Come on, we're so close now!"

The road curved a mile or so ahead, turning to the left and hiding their quarry from sight behind some woods. The path did not straighten out as the druid hoped when they reached the turn, instead curving around again, this time to the right so it was impossible to see how far ahead the Saxon might be. Or even if he'd continued riding hard along the road – perhaps he'd decided to veer off into the trees, either hiding from Bellicus, or, more worryingly, to set up an ambush.

Surely the sea-wolf would not do that? He was wounded and alone, while Bellicus was relatively fresh, uninjured, and accompanied by Cai. Perhaps if Saksnot had been allowed more time to properly set up a trap using a rope or some other clever method he might have chosen that course, but, as things stood, Bellicus did not really think there was immediate danger.

He did slow his pace though, partly to save Darac and Cai from blowing themselves out, but also so he could keep watch for his quarry. Saksnot must be utterly fed-up of this chase, and there was always a chance a desperate man could act in unexpected ways. Bellicus warily eyed the tall trees that grew right up to the road as they passed, half expecting to see the young Saxon launching himself from one of the branches at them.

"We're so close," he repeated in a low voice, hating the idea that their prey would somehow manage to elude them again when the chase was almost at an end. They moved on through the woods, Darac carrying him at a canter around each bend until, a mile or so further on, the trees gave way to more open, flat ground and Bellicus's eye traced the road ahead towards the horizon.

There was not a soul, either on foot or on horseback, ahead of them.

"Shit!" The druid brought Darac to a halt and scanned the land all around them, painstakingly searching for some sign of Saksnot. Nothing stood out – no movement, no unexpected colours clashing with the uniform greens and browns of the grass and foliage, and no thumping of hooves to give away the position of the Saxon's freshly stolen horse. Where was he?

"Well, he said," talking to Cai again, the mastiff peering up at him, head tilted as if he could understand the druid. "He's not ahead of us, so he must have gone into the woods somewhere. Can you find him for me, boy? Find."

Cai's ears jerked at the familiar word, and they turned to head back the way they'd come. Bellicus was hopeful that the dog might pick up Saksnot's scent – the man would be drenched in sweat after the day's melting heat after all – but Cai had never been the best tracker. He was more of a warrior than a hunter, rather like his master, but there was no other choice and Bellicus would not simply give up when he knew his quarry was somewhere nearby.

They went slowly, carefully, the druid inspecting each gap between the trees for some sign that a rider had recently passed that way. Every so often there would be a slight break between the trunks and a well-worn path would reveal itself and, at those points, Bellicus would direct Cai's attention there, watching for a sign that the hound had detected the scent of Saksnot or his horse.

Either no one had recently come by, or the mastiff simply could not smell them, for they continued back along the road northwards for quite some time before coming to an even wider, more obvious gap in the trees to their right. The road did actually split off here, going deep into the woods and, at last, Cai's nose went up and he sniffed curiously, walking towards the shadowy gap in the undergrowth. Watching his reaction, Bellicus slipped down from Darac's saddle and drew Melltgwyn – Cai's hackles were bristling along his back and the dog turned to look askance at the druid.

Something was off here. Perhaps it was the smell from the salve Saksnot had been spreading across his burns – Bellicus had noticed it immediately when they'd fought back in Dun Breatann – or maybe the Saxon was bleeding when he came into these woods, which wouldn't be surprising after he'd fought the farmer just a few miles ago. Certainly, something had spooked the mastiff.

Well, either they turned back and went home, or they continued to follow the druid's prey into these oddly foreboding woods.

Bellicus held Darac's reins in his left hand and led the way into the trees, feeling instantly a sense of isolation and something more sinister. He murmured a prayer of protection to Cernunnos, god of the forest, and remembered Peredur exhorting him to continue the hunt. He drew strength from his thoughts, and the feeling of dread abated somewhat as the trio moved deeper into the woods.

There could be little doubt Saksnot had passed this way before them. Hoofprints were impressed into the loamy soil of the path and the druid smiled. Only a fool would ride a horse at speed along an unfamiliar path through trees as thick as these – a fool, or someone terribly afraid of what lay behind them.

"Wait!" Bellicus hissed, staring at the rapidly darkening track ahead. Cai growled deep in his chest and they paused, blood beginning to pound at the prospect of one final battle with the Saxon who'd led them a not-so merry dance for hundreds of miles half the length of Britain.

The track must have come to a dead end, the druid surmised, forcing Saksnot to turn back and face them at last. He moved into a defensive stance, stepping ahead of Darac, sword held ready, Cai beside him, muscles taut and ready to spring at whatever threatened his master.

And then a man came striding towards them, heedless of the twigs he snapped as he walked. Bellicus watched him in surprise, taking in the man's appearance as he came closer, apparently oblivious to the travellers gaping at him.

Clad in a dark brown robe much like Bellicus's own, the man had a long, unruly beard that came to a point, and he wore an amulet on a thong around his neck. The massive druid squinted, trying to make out what the amulet depicted in the low light but, even as the man drew nearer, Bellicus did not recognise the strange face with round eyes and a gaping mouth – some obscure god the locals in these parts worshipped no doubt. There was a good chance he would know the deity's name if he was told it, for he had a vast store of such knowledge in his head thanks to the years of study he'd completed to become a druid but, from the crude depiction around the approaching man's neck, he was unable to place it.

"Oh!" The priest stopped abruptly as if only noticing the towering, robed figure before him, and the mastiff that gazed balefully at him.

Bellicus knew he was a priest from his manner of dress although that in itself did not endear the man to him. There were many such

206

'holy' or 'wise' men all across Britain – men who still followed the old ways, the old gods, but did not have the benefit of a druid's education or skills. Many of them were idiots, or charlatans who used their influence with gullible villagers to further their own ends, but they were at least preferable to the Christian priests and bishops who were a far bigger danger to the ancient culture of Britain.

"Have you seen a rider come along here?" Bellicus asked. "A Saxon."

The priest shook his head and his eyes moved from druid, to dog, and finally to Darac and the staff of office that was attached to the horse's saddle.

"You're a druid?" asked the man with a broad smile.

"Aye. Bellicus of Dun Breatann. I was once High Druid of Britain."

The man's eyes widened but it seemed to Bellicus that the reaction was exaggerated and not entirely honest. Perhaps the priest feared a real druid would interfere with his position in those lands, or perhaps he had simply never heard of Bellicus – this was an isolated place after all, and news didn't just travel slowly to the hidden corners of Britain, sometimes it did not reach them at all.

"What are you doing out here?" Bellicus asked, genuinely curious.

"Oh, we have a shrine nearby. I tend to it."

"A shrine to which god?" the druid wondered. "Or goddess?"

"Arawn," replied the priest, touching his amulet.

Bellicus had heard of that deity, knowing Arawn was associated with death but also hunting and the forest so may be some amalgamation of Dis Pater and Cernunnos. If the shrine looked anything like as hideous as the trinket hanging from the priest's neck it was not something the druid particularly cared to visit.

"And you've not seen a rider coming along this path?" Bellicus persisted, returning to the task at hand.

"Not today, no. Riders from the settlements nearby do come here – there was one just this morning actually, now that I think of it. A local merchant visited the shrine, but no horse or rider passed me just now. The path to Arawn's shrine is empty, my lord."

"Where does the path lead to?"

"Well, it goes past the shrine and onto the village. But there's a stream along the way and a steep flight of steps leading down and back up – your horse, or any horse, cannot pass that way."

Bellicus cursed. Some merchant had ridden along here hours ago and no doubt sacrificed a small animal to this Arawn – the blood from that ritual was what had set Cai on edge and they'd come in the entirely wrong direction. Saksnot had eluded them yet again! The Saxon's horse must be faster than Bellicus expected, remaining on the road south while the druid wasted time here.

"Would you like to pay your respects at the shrine, lord?"

"Eh?" Bellicus looked at the priest, confused for a moment, and then shook his head firmly. "No, my apologies but I must get back to the road. Here." He rummaged in one of the pouches sewn into his cloak and pulled out a small bronze ring of no great value, handing it to the smiling priest. "Offer that to Arawn for me. Maybe when I pass here again I'll come myself but, for now…"

"Of course, lord," the priest nodded, lifting his hand to usher Bellicus back to Darac. He watched the towering druid easily mount the horse, keeping a safe distance from Cai who did not seem to like the man very much. "May Arawn bless you on your journey."

Bellicus gave him a shallow bow in return and headed back towards the main road. When he reached it, he was dismayed to realise night was very nearly upon them and there would not be much time left to ride before they were forced to set up camp.

"Taranis, guide me," he murmured, looking up at the stars that were just beginning to appear in the darkening blue firmament overhead. "Arawn, even! Someone, lead me to that bastard Saxon, for I am heartily sick of this journey!"

Kicking his heels in, Darac sprang forward and Cai followed a pace behind. Saksnot might have evaded him again, but Bellicus knew exactly where the warrior was going. So they would continue south, all the way to Garrianum if necessary, and the druid meant to get as far as possible towards the Saxon Shore before the light faded completely.

* * *

"What happened?"

The priest strode back into the clearing where his companion waited, pupils like black pits in the gloom that was relieved only by the light of a single flickering oil lamp at the base of the Shrine of Arawn.

"The Saxon was right, someone was there!" the priest said, laughing in obvious astonishment and relief. "A druid! Massive he was, with a massive horse, and a massive dog too!"

"What?" The second man frowned, clearly not believing what he was being told.

"It's true, I swear!" the priest protested. "A giant of a man, name of Bellicus. Ever hear of him?"

His companion shrugged and gazed into the benighted woods to the left as he racked his brains for a memory of such a man. "No. What did he do?"

"He was looking for the Saxon," the priest told him, nodding at Saksnot who was still beside the shrine, eyes wide but bound hand and foot and gagged by a thick piece of rope.

"What for? Why would a druid – a real druid! – be looking for this piece of filth?"

"I think he was going to kill him."

"Well, that would make sense," the second man chuckled. "Did you send him on his way?"

"Aye. He didn't suspect a thing. Headed back to the road and galloped off into the oncoming night." The priest laughed at his deception and glanced at the stone figure beside them, bowing to it, and thanking Arawn for his assistance in sending Bellicus away without interfering in their work.

Saksnot mumbled something and the priest knelt, drawing out a dagger and placing the tip against the Saxon's eye, warning him not to shout for help as he'd done before. "You'd be wasting your time anyway, fool, that druid is never going to rescue you. There was nothing but death in his eyes when he spoke of you."

He pulled the rope roughly away from Saksnot's mouth and the Saxon gasped in desperation, "What are you going to do with me? If you let me go, Hengist will reward you very well." It was clear the Britons did not understand him, so he gasped out one of the few Brythonic words he knew, "Silver!", trying to make them understand what he meant.

The priest thought about it and then looked up at his companion. "Hengist," he repeated. "Another name I've never heard before. You?"

"Nope."

Dragging the rope back across Saksnot's lips, the priest stood up and smiled. "We have no need of wealth, Saxon. Arawn gives us everything we need, and, in return, we give him what he needs."

Saksnot watched as the priests drew out wickedly sharp knives and finally he guessed why he'd been taken captive. He thought of Thorbjorg, remembering rituals he'd seen the *volva* conduct, slaughtering captured enemies to honour the gods. He thought of the wide, petrified eyes of the victims as they drew their last, tortured breaths and he thought of his own reaction to the sight. He had gloried in those human sacrifices, enjoying the terror and pain suffered by the men and women who'd been sliced open while still lucid, screaming for release from their brutal ordeal.

Now he understood how those people had felt, and his courage failed him completely.

Jerking like a landed fish, Saksnot felt his bladder empty involuntarily as he strove to break free of his bonds, doing his best to scream through the gag, to cry out for help from Bellicus – from anyone! – but it was no use.

Arawn had claimed him, and the priests went about their work slowly and methodically, keen blades carving open his flesh and spilling his blood in the name of their monstrous god of death.

CHAPTER THIRTY-EIGHT

"They'll know we're coming," Gavo said, still not sure if Narina had made a wise decision.

"That can't be helped." The queen shrugged, guiding her horses around a curve in the road. She was not particularly fond of riding in the chariot, but the vehicle was undeniably impressive and struck fear into the hearts of an opposing army. "Besides, I hope Cunneda does get wind of our approach and comes out to meet us. In fact, I'm counting on it. It's time we put the Votadini in their place again, just like we did with the Picts."

Gavo smiled and shook his head. Narina had truly come into her own in the years since her first husband, King Coroticus, had died and she'd taken the throne. If any in Alt Clota had feared a queen would not be up to the task, she had soon disabused them of the notion and continued to do so now. Gavo just prayed that this latest move didn't prove to be her undoing for if Cunneda was to stand against them and win it would mean the end for the Damnonii people.

"You worry too much, Gavo."

The guard captain looked down at the third rider standing on the chariot's footboard. "And you two don't seem to worry enough, my lady."

Princess Catia laughed, cheeks ruddy from the wind that blew into their faces as they rumbled eastwards. "Have faith," she told him. "The gods are with us."

"And I'm glad they are," Gavo nodded. "I'm not quite so pleased by your presence, though."

"She'll be well back, out of any fighting," Narina said. "We've been over this, Gavo. I couldn't leave her in Dun Breatann again, not without you or Bellicus to look after her. Besides, if there's a battle with Cunneda and we lose…" She trailed off for there was no need to explain to them what that outcome would mean. The Votadini army would not simply strip their enemies' corpses of valuables and head home – they would march to Alt Clota and Cunneda would make Dun Breatann his, annexing all the Damnonii lands and becoming the most powerful king in northern Britain.

If Catia was left in Dun Breatann in that scenario, well, her life – what remained of it – would not be pleasant. Cunneda was not a particularly brutal king, but he would not hesitate to make a very public show of the defeated princess. Gavo gritted his teeth and pushed the unbidden images aside. That would not come to pass, he would make sure of it.

"What if Cunneda sends for help from his new allies?" the captain asked, moving the conversation quickly along.

"Hengist?" Narina frowned then, lips pursed, shook her head. "He must have enough to deal with in the south. I know Arthur's forces have been beset all summer by the Saxon hordes so I really doubt Hengist will have men to spare to send them up here to join the Votadini. Why would he bother? War between the Damnonii and Votadini will just mean fewer Britons to stand against him."

"True enough," Gavo admitted. "But we know Hengist despises us for killing his brother. You can never tell how such a man will behave."

"If he could spare an army to attack us, he would have sent that rather than the lone warrior that tried to murder Duro in his bed," Narina noted, shaking her head.

"Gods, I hope Bellicus catches that bastard and returns home soon," the captain muttered dourly. "I'd feel more confident if the druid was here with us."

"Stop worrying!" Catia repeated, playfully slapping the captain's arm.

He did smile at her, but his tone was stern as he replied, "You're twelve, lass. This is the first real campaign you've been on. You'll soon learn that worrying in advance is the best way to prepare for what might befall us."

Narina was smiling too, but hers had a touch of sadness in it and Gavo did not need to ask what she was thinking. She'd told him often enough that she hated how quickly Catia had been forced to grow up. Life as a queen, or a princess, was a privileged one, no doubt about it, but it was also hard in ways other people could never understand. If Catia was not as fearful of the coming days as Gavo, that was a good thing, and he grinned at the princess, pointing out a grey heron as it languidly rose into the air alongside them and sailed away to the south on its great wings.

The chariot was not moving fast for most of Narina's army was on foot. Only the noblemen and scouts were mounted so around two hundred spearmen walked, making the journey slower than Gavo would have liked. That was how armies worked though, and there was no way to cover the sixty-odd miles in less than four days. This was the final day, and they were almost at their destination. Dun Edin should come into sight by midday, the guard captain expected, assuming they were not held up on the road.

"Should we stop for a rest?" Narina asked him, looking back at the long column of troops marching in ragged formation behind them. "Give the ranks time to close up again? I don't like it when they're so spread out, Gavo. Feels more secure when we're grouped tightly together."

"I'm not so sure about a rest," Catia cut in, shading her eyes from the morning sun, her other hand gripping the edge of the chariot so hard that Gavo saw her fingers turn white. "But I do think we'll need to stop soon. Look, Mother."

Narina turned back to gaze at the road ahead, immediately spotting what the princess had seen and muttering an excited oath.

"What is it?" Gavo asked, mirroring the princess's movement and trying to shade his eyes to see better. "I can't see as well as you two. Is there something in the road?"

"Aye," Narina agreed, gently pulling on the reins and drawing the chariot to a halt, never taking her eyes from the front. "There's something there all right. An army, Gavo. The army of Cunneda, judging by the banner I see flying over them!"

213

CHAPTER THIRTY-NINE

Lancelot put his head in his hands and massaged his eyes, trying to ease the headache that had developed on the road back to Arthur's camp and only grown more intense when he met the warlord to deliver the news about Bedwyr.

Now, Arthur knew the full story and the two men sat in horrified silence, minds running wild with thoughts of what Hengist and Leofdaeg might be doing to their friend and what Bedwyr's ultimate fate might be.

"They're going to sacrifice him, aren't they?" the warlord asked in a low, hoarse voice. "That's why they wanted him alive. To spill his blood in praise of their gods." He trailed off and drew in a shuddering breath. "I can just picture that insane witch, Thorbjorg…"

Lancelot sighed and waved his hand, halting Arthur mid-sentence. "Enough," he pleaded. "Maybe that is what they have in store for Bedwyr, maybe Leofdaeg or Hengist simply wanted another of your friends as a slave. It would hardly be good for our army's morale to see one of your trusted advisors held as a thrall by the Saxons."

"Either outcome is horrific," Arthur grated, standing and running a hand through his shoulder-length hair. "I mean, from a selfish point of view, I would rather Bedwyr be allowed to live, even if it's as a slave. I'd prefer that to him being ritually murdered! But you know better than anyone what life as a Saxon thrall is like, my friend."

Lancelot shook his head, staring unseeingly at the wall of the command tent. "I'd rather be dead than held like an animal again," he admitted, reaching out and lifting the jug of ale that one of the servants had brought when he returned to camp. He filled his cup to the brim, swallowed the lot, refilled it, and again emptied it quickly.

"Are you all right?" Arthur asked, frowning. "You don't usually drink like that."

"Don't worry, it won't become a habit. I've got a pounding headache with all this and I'm hoping the ale will prove medicinal."

"I'm tempted to join you," the warlord admitted with a sad smile. "Wash away our troubles for a time. That would not help Bedwyr though, would it?"

214

"What would help him?" Lancelot asked, covering his mouth to belch.

"Rescuing him from whatever fate that bastard Hengist has in mind, be it thralldom or death!"

What choices were open to Arthur? He could try to forget Bedwyr – it was unpalatable, but a soldier faced death every day and the vast majority of Britons wouldn't miss that one man. There was no point in sending envoys to Hengist to try and make a bargain for Bedwyr's return – Arthur had soon learned the *bretwalda* was as likely to murder envoys as listen to what they had to say. Could Bedwyr be rescued somehow? Would it be worth the danger? Bedwyr was Arthur's childhood friend, but was that enough to risk the lives of others? And then Arthur remembered Thorbjorg and imagined the ritual sacrifice she would perform on Bedwyr. Even if her magic wasn't as successful as she must hope, the ritual slaughter of such a high-ranking Briton would galvanise the Saxon hordes, and push them to fight with even greater ferocity. For years now Hengist and Thorbjorg had sought to gain their gods favour – to bring about one terrific, final victory for their people. Bedwyr's blood might just convince Woden and Tyr to help the Saxons to that great triumph. It was a terrifying thought.

The familiar sensation of certainty suffused Arthur's entire being then, the same feeling he'd felt before when a plan that some might see as ill-advised or even insane came to him. Generally, he was guided well by his intuition, and he knew now that rescuing Bedwyr was the only option they really had.

Lancelot looked up in confusion, perhaps wondering if gulping down so much ale in a short span of time had made him so drunk that he was hearing things. "Rescue him? How?"

"We have an army, Lancelot. A bigger army than any Hengist can put together in the time we could be at Garrianum. Why not take the fight to them?"

"Perhaps we should have marched on Garrianum before now," Lancelot conceded, face flushed red as the drink and battle-fever took hold. He was plainly in firm agreement with Arthur's suggestion. "The sea-wolves have been pushing outwards for the past few months, striking in so many places that we've been unable to stop them all. Taking their main fortress might have given us a stronger footing."

"Indeed," Arthur nodded, stopping at the tent's entrance flaps to look back at his captain. "It won't be easy though. The last time we went there we'd just defeated Hengist's army in battle and had the upper hand. We chased them to Garrianum. This time they'll be better prepared, and we don't really know how many men they have there, or can call upon at short notice."

"Fair points, but this was your idea," Lancelot smiled.

"It was, but we should speak with our other commanders and listen to their counsel, I think, before marching the army to the east."

"Who cares what they think?"

"I do," Arthur laughed, knowing his friend was more inebriated than he usually allowed himself to get or he'd never have made such an arrogant remark. "I'm not a king, Lancelot. I need to have the agreement of the lords, and chieftains, and kings, and queens that I act on behalf of. They only agree to grant me troops if they feel they are somehow in control of me."

"They fear you," Lancelot noted. "Because you stand up to the invaders while they're content to cower in their own lands, letting you do the hard, dangerous work. Their own men who come to join your army end up feeling more loyal to you than to their own liege lords."

"Some of them, perhaps," Arthur conceded, not wishing to get into such a discussion at that time. Not when Bedwyr was in desperate need of their help. "Don't drink any more ale," he cautioned, wagging a finger at Lancelot, only half-jokingly. "I don't want you offending any of the noblemen when I bring them here." Without waiting for a reply, he went out and spoke to his guards, ordering them to send messengers to the various factions within the camp and have the leaders come to speak with him there in the command tent.

It did not take long for the men to arrive, quickly filling the enclosed space. Excited murmuring, ruddy faces flushed with excitement about this unexpected meeting, and the musky scent of soldiers who'd been on campaign for a long time greeted Arthur as he stood in the centre of the tent and looked around him. Qunavo was nearby, a steady, reassuring presence and Arthur felt a little guilty that he'd not brought the High Druid into the discussion earlier – Nemias would certainly have been part of it.

Putting aside that distraction, Arthur laid out the situation before the nobles and was met with enthusiastic nods of assent for his plan, but also some grumbles of discontent.

"Would you take the army to rescue one of us?" someone muttered. "Or are you just doing this because Bedwyr is your friend?"

Arthur had to think closely about that, and he considered ignoring the man's question. It had been one of the minor nobles who'd asked, and Arthur wasn't sure many others had heard him, so it would be possible to brush it aside. It was a valid point though, and he wondered how close to the mark the man had come. Was the warlord using his power to help his friend, putting the lives of everyone else in the army at risk purely for his own desire to rescue Bedwyr?

"You're right, Enda," he conceded, making the man's face flush as all eyes turned to him. "Bedwyr's capture is what spurred me to come up with this plan. Had it been you who was taken by the Saxons, would I have been so quick to suggest this course of action? Maybe not. I like you," he assured Enda. "And I value your counsel, your sword, and your friendship, but it's true, Bedwyr has been a companion of mine since childhood and the thought of him being tortured or sacrificed by Hengist and Thorbjorg strikes me deep in the heart."

Enda, a stout, red-haired young warrior of the Selgovae tribe, bowed his head, acknowledging both Arthur's honesty, and the compliments paid to him.

"However," Arthur went on, thoughtfully stroking a hand through his neat beard. "The emotion Bedwyr's plight engendered has perhaps opened my eyes to what we should have been doing all summer: taking the fight to our enemies, instead of following them around, trying to deal with the trouble they've been bringing to the settlements here in the eastern and central parts of Britain."

"Aye," an older warrior agreed with conviction. "I'm done chasing the bastards. Let's cut off the head of the worm and watch the body wither away!"

"Worms don't have heads," Kay noted quietly, drawing some laughter, even from the warrior who'd spoken up.

"You know what I mean," said the man, smiling. "Worm, as in dragon."

"Then, yes." Kay nodded firmly, placing his palm on the handle of his knife. "Let's ride to Garrianum and cut off that bastard Hengist's head!"

Cheers arose, and even Enda was smiling.

"Then we all agree? Rescuing Bedwyr from whatever dark fate the sea-wolves have in store for him is one of our priorities, but, ultimately, our mission is to take the war directly to Hengist, and to smash his army once and for all. Finish the job we started two years ago, and reclaim Britain for the Britons!"

"Britain for the Britons!" The chant was taken up, fists raised along with the voices of the warriors and Arthur joined in although the irony of it was not lost on him. Britain for the Britons was a nice slogan, easy to remember, satisfying to chant, but Bedwyr had been on a quest to welcome Saxon settlers to the island, and that was something Arthur could not afford to lose sight of. At this moment, however, he needed an army ready and willing to put their very lives on the line for an ideal – for the people, the mountains and the lakes and dells, and the old traditions of Britain.

"To Garrianum, my friends," Arthur roared, drawing his sword and raising it up. "To war!"

* * *

King Cunneda was furious, and Gavo could understand why. No ruler appreciated an enemy army marching into their lands, and Cunneda had, for a time at least, been Narina's father-in-law. Yet there she was, just a few miles from Dun Edin, the Damnonii army at her back as if she was spoiling for a fight.

Which she was, of course.

"What the fuck is the meaning of this?" the Votadini king raged as the leaders of the opposing factions faced one another. "How dare you come to my lands like this, Narina? An invading army? Really? I thought we were allies!" His face was as red as his great, fiery beard but the Queen of Alt Clota was not perturbed.

"Allies?" Narina laughed coldly. "You dissolved our trade agreement, Cunneda. What kind of ally does that?"

The Votadini king did not answer for a time. Whatever his reasons, he did not want to share them. Eventually, as the two armies glared across the field at one another, Cunneda shouted, "Breaking a trade agreement is no excuse to start a war. Are you insane, woman? Haven't you had enough of war these past few years? Your man, Coroticus, could start a fight in an empty house, but when he died I expected you to be a little more peaceful, less prone to acts of unwarranted aggression."

"You're right," Narina called back and Gavo was impressed, as always by her calm and her poise in such a stressful situation. Chin held high, she went on, "I am sick of war. But your son, Ysfael, dragged my people into one against the Picts, and now you plot against me. It's time you learned that the Damnonii should not be taken lightly, Cunneda! You, the Picts, and the Dalriadans, have all felt the force of my army over the years, yet still I find myself here, having to remind you of your place."

"My place?" the Votadini warrior demanded, turning to look at his men in disbelief before he addressed Narina again. "Who do you think you are, you little bitch? You're nothing but a skinny girl, riding around on that ridiculous chariot, thinking you're untouchable because you have old Gavo there, and Bellicus…" He trailed off, squinting curiously. "Where is the big bastard anyway?" His rage had given way to wariness, and he even looked over his shoulder, as though he feared Bellicus might sneak up behind him, despite the presence of his army standing there.

"You'll find out soon enough," Narina replied enigmatically, setting the others in Cunneda's front ranks murmuring fearfully amongst themselves. Did the Damnonii have some other army nearby, led by Bellicus? Gavo grinned at the consternation Narina's words had engendered in their foes.

"This is your last, and only, warning, Narina," roared the Votadini king, stepping back closer to his men and his waiting horse. "Leave my lands and go back to Alt Clota now, or we will attack."

Gavo watched Narina but she remained silent. Had she been a man, the captain was sure he'd have called some insult or threat to Cunneda – that was generally how things went, with each ruler vying for some supremacy, even just verbal, over their opponent before battle commenced. It was often quite ridiculous, with childish insults being hurled back and forth between two armies, and it could get even more insane if druids were involved. Gavo had seen mystics smearing themselves with shit as part of some bizarre ritual supposed to inspire terror in enemies. Thankfully Bellicus did not use those methods, and his wife, Narina, was similarly unlikely to become embroiled in a dick-measuring contest.

"Then attack, Cunneda," shouted the queen. She sounded assured and Gavo knew it stemmed, in large part, from the fact Catia had been escorted to the rear ranks of the army for her own safety. "Attack, or surrender and we can discuss terms for a lasting peace. One that doesn't involve me marrying another of your oafish sons!"

Gavo was not surprised to see the king's face flush red with anger again. It seemed Narina did not want this to end peacefully. He could understand her confidence, for the Damnonii army looked as though it outnumbered Cunneda's by almost two to one. Even so, Narina was not as brash or quick to anger as her first husband, King Coroticus. It seemed to the captain as if the queen wanted to send a powerful message here, not only to the Votadini people, but to everyone in Britain, and those who came from across the seas to raid there.

"What terms?" Cunneda demanded. He was not so furious, or so foolish, as to throw away a chance for peace without first looking for a compromise.

"The reinstatement of our trade agreement," Narina called, reasonably enough, Gavo thought. But she was not done. "And you will send us tribute every year – cattle, sheep, wool, tin, and also twenty young warriors who will serve in my border patrols."

The Votadini king stared at her as if he couldn't quite take in what he was hearing. Tribute? Gavo could see the wheels turning in Cunneda's head as he digested Narina's outrageous terms. Terms that might be delivered to the loser after a battle, not between two rulers of equal standing.

"Are you mad, woman?" Cunneda even laughed as he asked the question.

"You started a war with my people not so long ago," Narina returned levelly. "You, the Picts, and the Dalriadans – we defeated you all. Essentially, the throne of Northern Britain belonged to me, had there been such a thing. I see now that I should have imposed far harsher restrictions on you, but I was lenient, seeking allies rather than tributaries. So you will pay tribute to me from now on, Cunneda, and, on top of that, you will break any alliance you have with the Saxons."

"You are mad!" Cunneda replied, shaking his head, jaw set firm.

"Do you deny that you are working with Hengist?"

"The Saxons are slowly taking control of the entire east coast of Britain," spat the Votadini king. "I'd be mad not to try and live peacefully with them."

"So you broke our trade agreement to kiss Hengist's sea-wolf arse," Narina cried, making sure both armies could hear her words. "And what else did you give the Saxons? What else did you agree to do for them? You are a traitor to your people, Cunneda! Hengist's goal is to conquer Britain – you should be fighting them, not acting as their lackey!"

Even some of the Votadini soldiers were looking unhappily at their king now. Some of them had fought Saxon raiders and knew how fearsome they were. It did not seem wise to get into bed with the likes of Hengist.

"You know fine well that diplomacy is complicated," Cunneda shouted, looking somewhat anxiously at his warriors. "A king cannot fight everyone."

"So you chose to align yourself with the sea-wolves, going against Arthur and the southern kings who have been beset by Hengist's hordes for years now."

Gavo watched as Cunneda visibly swallowed; even at the distance between the two rulers, the Votadini king's consternation was evident.

"You are not fit to rule your people," Narina concluded. "Just as your son was not fit to rule over my people. You lack morals, and loyalty, and have sold yourself to Hengist without regard for the destruction that man will bring down upon you in the coming years."

Gavo was astonished by Narina's argument. She was so persuasive! In truth, he could hardly blame Cunneda for agreeing to an alliance with the Saxons, it made sense given the Votadini's position on the eastern edge of the country, where the raiders' boats plied freely along the whale road. And yet, the way Narina laid things out, Cunneda was a traitor to his own people, never mind the rest of the native Britons.

"Nicely done, my lady," the captain murmured, scanning the enemy shieldwall and seeing the discontent there in the shuffling feet and uncertain glances the warriors cast upon their own king.

"Hit them now," Narina replied softly. "While they're still trying to figure out if I'm right or not."

Gavo nodded, feeling the blood begin to thunder in his veins as he stepped out in front of their own shieldwall and raised his arms. "Prepare to attack!" he roared.

Cunneda looked stricken but he had been king for a long time and had seen many battles so it did not take long before he regained his composure and issued orders to his captains. Spears were lowered, shields raised, javelins that had been stuck in the ground before each soldier lifted, ready to throw.

"Dis take you, Narina, you fucking whore!" Cunneda shrieked as Gavo nodded at two of his biggest, most loyal men to escort the queen's chariot through the ranks to the rear of the army.

"Ready to throw!" Gavo called out, arm raised as he took up his place in the centre of the Damnonii line, feeling slightly breathless as the prospect of impending glory – or death – filled every fibre of his being.

Time seemed to slow almost to a complete standstill at that moment. Gavo watched Cunneda hurrying back to take up his own position with his men; he saw enemy soldiers panic at the thought of being ripped open by one of the iron-headed throwing spears, then steel themselves to do what must be done; he pictured his own wife and hoped he would see her again soon; and he felt the breath, strong and clear in his nostrils as he prepared to kill as many other men as it took to stay alive himself.

"Loose!"

The Damnonii line grunted and cried out almost in perfect unison and a terrible black cloud of javelins sailed up into the air. When it came back to earth mere heartbeats later there was a sickening sound of metal punching home in wooden shields, iron armour, and human flesh and bone. Gavo steadied himself, a fierce smile on his face as the screams of pain and horror came from their opponents, and then he remembered who he was, and what duties were his, and he roared, "Shields up!" as the Votadini line released their own deadly storm of missiles.

CHAPTER FORTY

"Pah, trade agreement! What use is that to a man? To a warrior?" Leofdaeg spat on the floor of Hengist's 'hall' in Garrianum and laughed mockingly at Siggar as some of the other Saxon jarls and chiefs joined in.

"An alliance is far more useful than your ruined arm, Leofdaeg," Sigarr retorted, face scarlet at being spoken to in such a dismissive manner in front of everyone.

"I'll still smash your teeth out, you wheezing little goat-turd, even with only one good arm!"

"Come on then!" Sigarr did not often lose his temper but his hatred for Leofdaeg got the better of him now and he stood up, drawing his seax from its sheath and gesturing with his hands for the other jarl to step forward. He had imbibed a little more mead than usual and it gave him courage, but it started to fade rapidly as Leofdaeg – a veteran of many battles – tried to charge towards him, being held back by the rest of the men who cheered and whooped in delight at the show.

"That's enough you pair of gibbering fools," Hengist snarled and, although he hardly raised his voice, it was sufficient for the room to fall silent, Sigarr and Leofdaeg staring murderously, breathlessly at one another, the promise of future violence hanging in the air between the rivals. "Sigarr brokered the deal with the Votadini at my request," the *bretwalda* growled. "He did well, and we will all benefit from it. More money in our coffers is always a good thing, especially in the midst of a war."

"Thank you, lord," Sigarr nodded, doing his best to speak between deep breaths so his words didn't come out in a rasping wheeze.

"In saying that," Hengist went on, "Jarl Leofdaeg capturing Bedwyr was nicely done, and, if Thorbjorg is to believed, will do much for our efforts to defeat the Britons for good."

"See!" Leofdaeg hissed at Sigarr. His arms were no longer pinned but he still stood as if he was being held back from attacking the smaller, older jarl. "You play the part of a diplomat, while I will be the warrior you always wanted to be."

"You think I always wanted to be a warrior who can only wield a blade with his left hand because some thrall smashed my sword arm?"

There was more cheering and laughter at the insult and Leofdaeg had to be restrained once more from attacking Sigarr who stood with a wry smile curling his lips, inebriated and knowing he was safe from harm. Even if his furious opponent did break free, Sigarr's captain, Cretta, would make sure Leofdaeg could not land a blow on him.

"Enough of this!" Hengist seemed to be the only one not enjoying the verbal sparring and his hefty fist slammed down, rocking the table violently. "You two, Sigarr and Leofdaeg, shut up, and sit on your arses before I have you both thrown into the sea!"

Leofdaeg was so incensed that it seemed for a moment that he might not have heard, or taken heed of, his superior's command. From somewhere in the room, though, came the melodious yet menacing voice of the *volva*, Thorbjorg. "Sit!"

Like the druids that served the Britons, the *volur* were given special training before going out into the world – training in herb lore, mythology, divination, philosophy, law, history, and more. How to use one's voice to manipulate people was a skill Thorbjorg had learned at a young age, honing and refining it over the years so now her simple, single word, barked with venom, made Leofdaeg collapse onto his chair instantly. The jarl looked astonished, but he remained silent even when some of the other men sniggered at him.

The *volva* came out from the shadows then, walking to the centre of the room as Hengist stepped back, allowing her to address the gathered warriors. She wore a necklace of glass beads, a lambskin cap, and a blue tunic with red sleeves that showed off her lithe figure. On her belt was a pouch with magical talismans inside and in her hand was a staff. Although no longer young, her appearance was striking and she captivated the men in the room.

"Bedwyr's blood shall be spilled three days hence," she told them matter-of-factly. "The moon will be right for the sacrifice. Four years I've waited for a suitable candidate to be given to our gods. Four years since that damn druid stole the girl from under our noses and we've had nothing but trouble ever since!"

Her words brought sheepish looks from those warriors who'd been there that night when Princess Catia was supposed to be sacrificed but Bellicus and Duro had rescued her while they blundered about in the darkness unable to stop them. The men who had not been there responded with angry murmurs, accepting her contention that all the defeats the Saxons had suffered in the intervening years would never have happened had the girl's blood been spilled that night. A princess, and daughter of a druid, was the perfect offering. Could the blood of a man like Bedwyr possibly be as powerful as Catia's?

Thorbjorg's fervour suggested she believed so, and Hengist's men were happy to follow her guidance in these matters. Bedwyr might not be royal, but he was one of the most powerful men in Arthur's army, and that made his life extremely valuable to the Britons.

"What will we do once the sacrifice is made?" Sigarr asked, feeling like he should remind everyone that he was there, and of as high status as anyone other than Hengist and the *volva*.

"We will crush Arthur and his army," Thorbjorg replied, leaning down to speak directly to Sigarr as though he was a dim-witted child. He flushed, not just at her mockery, but at the sight of her cleavage and her general proximity. She laughed and moved away, running her eyes across the rest of the men, smiling almost lasciviously, as though the thought of giving Bedwyr to the gods pleased her more than anything in this world or the next. "I will do my part as a conduit to the gods. You will all be expected to do your part by fighting and dying for our cause."

Sigarr was not sure he wanted to die for any 'cause', but he was not like most of the warriors within the chamber, as the rowdy cheers and oaths that followed Thorbjorg's proclamation proved. He growled and raised a fist so he didn't draw attention to himself, although he noticed Hengist watching him with an unreadable expression. Well, his cousin knew his strengths and his weaknesses – it was up to the *bretwalda* to make use of them. He listened in dismay though, as Hengist spoke directly to him.

"Leofdaeg will be in command of Garrianum while I am away with Thorbjorg."

Sigarr couldn't help glancing at his rival, who grinned back at him triumphantly.

"The two of you will work together, but Leofdaeg has more experience in military matters." The warlord glared at them in turn.

"No fighting amongst yourselves! If you can't get on with one another, I'll find some other jarls to take your places. Do you hear me?"

Sigarr's eyes met Leofdaeg's and the room was silent as they glared hatefully at each other. At last, Sigarr nodded. "I hear you, *bretwalda*. You can count on me."

"And me," Leofdaeg added, pushing his shoulders back, visibly proud to be named commander of the fortress for the duration of Hengist's short absence.

"Good. We won't be gone long. I'll escort Thorbjorg to the sacred site where she will sacrifice Bedwyr, and then the fate of Britain will be ours to decide."

"Are you all ready to reach out and grasp what I am offering you here?" the *volva* demanded, face set and determined as she glared into the eyes of everyone there, searching their souls for signs of fear or apathy and apparently feeling satisfied with their shouted responses to her.

"Then prepare yourselves!" Hengist cried. "Our time is at hand, my friends. Prepare your weapons – sharpen swords and spear points, mend tattered mail coats, polish helmets so they shine like fire in the sun, and make ready for a final, glorious battle!"

Even Sigarr could not help but be carried away by the *bretwalda*'s speech and he cast his mind ahead, to a few weeks distant, seeing himself laughing and revelling in the pain of hundreds of enemy warriors as the Saxon tidal wave washed across the island smashing all who stood in its way.

CHAPTER FORTY-ONE

Arthur knew the importance of moving quickly – Bedwyr would surely not have long to live if Thorbjorg planned to sacrifice him.

"When will she...do it?" he asked Qunavo as they rode at the head of the army, southeast, towards the Saxon Shore.

Qunavo did not hesitate in replying, clearly having thought about the answer in advance. "If she followed our ways, she might have performed the ceremony at Lughnasadh. But that is past now, and besides, the Saxons have their own traditions." He shook his head dejectedly. "The Autumn equinox would be a possible date, but that is a few weeks distant, and I do not think Hengist will want to wait so long."

"Agreed," grunted Arthur.

"So they will perform the ritual at the next full moon."

"Which is when?" the warlord asked a little irritably. Did he really need to drag everything from the new Merlin? The old one was much more forthcoming! By Taranis, Qunavo wasn't the worst companion, but Arthur missed Nemias terribly. Damn that Saxon scum that had killed him, may the gods deliver a suitable fate to his miserable carcass!

"In three days," said Qunavo, and Arthur wished he hadn't asked after all.

Three days...

"What will they do to him?" Arthur wondered, fighting the urge to kick his horse into a gallop. No point in him reaching Garrianum alone, he would simply need to be patient and match the army's pace, as hard as that was. "No, in fact, don't tell me. There's no need for me to know."

"I'm sure we'll not sleep imagining his fate," Lancelot muttered dourly. He'd been in a fine mood for the early part of the journey, but Arthur had noticed his enthusiasm wearing off as the reality of what was about to happen really struck home. Lancelot had honed his skills as a swordsman to the point that he was probably the best with a blade in all of Britain, but the youthful lust for battle and glory that so many warriors enjoyed no longer carried either man along in the way it once had.

They had all seen too much pain, too much death, too many friends and comrades maimed, screaming for their...

Arthur forced the bitter thoughts from his mind and looked ahead, taking in the inspiring view of the lands they travelled through. War was not the glorious adventure told of in countless poems, tales, and songs, but it was necessary at times, to protect the things people loved. And, gazing around him now, drinking in the sight of green fields and pastureland, glittering streams, and the little yellow and blue birds that flitted in and out of the hedgerows and juniper bushes, the warlord felt his sense of duty anew. He owed the people of Britain a land where they could be safe from the depredations of the likes of Hengist and Horsa. That was what he'd sworn to do, and he meant to uphold his oath.

First, though, he would find a way to save the life of his friend, Bedwyr.

"Can we do anything to…" Lancelot shrugged, at a loss for words for once. "I don't know. To help us get Bedwyr back alive? To defeat the Saxons when we reach their fort?"

Qunavo nodded. He was riding a grey mare and had taken to wearing a grey cloak. With his long white beard and light blue eyes he cut a striking, pale figure as they rode through the vibrant green summer-lands towards the Saxon Shore. "Have your hunters bring me whatever animals they can catch today. Alive. The bigger the better. We will have a feast tonight, and I will call on the power of the moon to disrupt Hengist's plans."

"Good," Arthur said approvingly. "I feel completely powerless here, so far away from Bedwyr and his captors. The gods at least do not suffer the same limitations as we do."

"Ask them to deliver that goat-humper Leofdaeg to me while you're at it, eh, Merlin?" Lancelot added without a trace of humour. "I think I would die content if I could repay him even a little for the horrors he wrought upon me when I was his thrall."

Qunavo did not reply other than with a shallow dip of his head. The gods could work miracles of course, but only they decided whether they would or not, no matter who asked or what they offered in return.

"Do you think this is a goose chase?" Arthur asked when they'd ridden a little further. His earlier melancholy had faded somewhat and, although his question was not exactly positive, his tone was lighter, and he watched his companions' faces with curiosity rather than resignation.

228

"Maybe," Lancelot conceded grudgingly. "But what else can we do?"

"Indeed," said Qunavo. "Besides, even if we can't help Bedwyr, if we can smash Hengist's hordes it might well end our problems with the Saxons forever."

Arthur agreed completely with that, and it was what kept him going when he thought of Bedwyr's plight. "We decimated his army at Nant Beac two years ago," he noted. "And we, perhaps naively, hoped that would be the end of things at that point. The *bretwalda* was able to call upon reinforcements from across the sea though, bringing more Jutes, and Angles, and all sorts of other skittering rats to his banner."

"There can't possibly be an unlimited supply of young warriors in those lands," Lancelot spat, taking out his waterskin and gulping down a long swallow. It was still hot despite the approach of the autumnal equinox that Qunavo had mentioned earlier.

"Precisely," Arthur said, also taking a drink and wiping beads of perspiration from his brow. "The Saxons are no fools. They follow Hengist because, thus far, he has led them well, despite us beating them on occasion. But if we can give them another crushing defeat, like that last one at Nant Beac, well, even if there are another thousand young Saxon men eager to win glory here in Britain, they won't answer Hengist's call again."

"We had Nemias with us then," Lancelot said glumly, before he seemed to remember who rode beside him. "No offence, Qunavo. Nemias knew these lands better than any of us, and he knew exactly how to deal with the likes of Thorbjorg."

"No offence taken," Qunavo said with a sad smile. Nemias had been a close colleague of his for decades, so he surely understood the loss everyone in Arthur's army felt now that the old High Druid was no longer with them. "Rest assured I will do what I can to offset the *volva*'s power though."

"We had Bellicus with us as well at that time," Arthur reminded his captain. "Shame he's not here now – he has past experience in rescuing captives just before Thorbjorg is about to sacrifice them!"

"I wonder where he is," Lancelot said thoughtfully, a fond smile lighting up his face. He'd enjoyed a few adventures with the giant druid, and Bellicus had played a part in helping him escape Leofdaeg's clutches.

"Probably enjoying a quiet life in Dun Breatann," Arthur chuckled. "Things seem to have quietened down up there with the defeat of the Picts. Bel will be enjoying the finest meat and drink, sunny days, and the pleasant companionship of Narina, Catia, and Duro."

"Aye, probably," Qunavo agreed. "Lucky bastard!"

* * *

Bellicus felt despair rise within him with every mile Darac covered. Even Cai seemed to look up at the druid in confusion, as though the mastiff could tell something wasn't right.

There had been no sign of Saksnot on the road for days now, since they'd lost the Saxon's trail back where that hermit had been hanging around in the woods. Bellicus had rode on, sure they would catch up with their prey eventually, or at least hear word of his passing from other travellers. They had not spotted the dishevelled rider ahead of them though, even far in the distance, and Cai had not seemed to pick up any scent of the man. Furthermore, when the druid asked people on the road if they'd passed anyone fitting Saksnot's description not a single one had. And it was not as if the youthful warrior was easy to miss!

No, Bellicus had slowly come to the conclusion that they had lost their quarry after tracking him for so many miles. It was utterly galling, and made him question his decision to continue the chase rather than returning home simply because 'Peredur' had exhorted him to do so while Bellicus was in a trance.

He was almost at Garrianum, he knew, and there would be Saxon patrols in the lands he was riding through soon enough. And for what? Saksnot had evaded him so what was the point in riding on? He might as well simply turn around and go back to Narina. How was Duro, he wondered sadly. Had his friend recovered from the wounds that Saksnot had inflicted upon him? What about Catia? The image of his beloved daughter filled his mind and he immediately felt happier as he imagined her sparring with older boys – men, even – and holding her own.

It started to rain then, and he pulled up his hood, muttering to himself. He would ride on until midday, he thought, then stop for something to eat out of the rain if he could find shelter. Then, unless by some miracle he saw evidence of Saksnot's passing, he would give up and start the long journey homewards. The thought of covering all those miles, of the strain it would put on his loyal animals, depressed the druid, but the idea of seeing his friends and family again went some way to cheering him.

It was not quite midday when Bellicus stopped for food and rest. The rain had not grown heavier, but it continued without stopping all morning so, when he noticed what seemed to be an ancient bothy just off the main road, he decided to take his meal there. The structure was not as old as he'd first thought and he approached it warily, in case other travellers had sought shelter there before him.

The bothy was little more than four walls with a large, ill-fitting door and a leaking roof overhead. It was enough to keep the rain from Bellicus and Cai for a while though, and Darac was content enough to stand outside grazing once the druid had fed him an apple. There did not seem to be any danger nearby but, even so, considering who he was, and how much the Saxons hated him, Bellicus decided not to chance a fire, instead eating some bread, and cold, salted meat which he shared with Cai.

He sat on the floor of the bothy, gazing out thoughtfully at the road. Was there any reason whatsoever to continue southeast? Was it possible Saksnot was just ahead of them, and they would catch the Saxon if they just continued onwards, perhaps at a faster pace?

No, that was more than unlikely. Bellicus had to accept that his quest had been one monumental waste of time and effort, and return to Dun Breatann empty-handed.

The rain was not that heavy, but it was quite noisy, dripping down from the damaged roof all around the bothy, but Bellicus thought he heard a higher pitched noise, like a child or a woman coming along the road, chattering loudly. He had packed away his ale skin and the food that hadn't been eaten but he sat watching the road, waiting for any travellers to pass by so they didn't notice him. He was sure that he hadn't imagined the sound for Cai and Darac were both looking towards the road, eyes watching to the right although trees obscured the view.

Soon enough a rider came into view, hood thrown up, head bent down as he plodded past just a short distance away from the bothy. The rider, a large man Bellicus judged, did not turn his head and close behind him came a second rider. Although both wore cloaks

231

dark with rain, obscuring what they wore beneath, Bellicus knew these were warriors. Round shields were attached to their mounts' which appeared bigger than most animals. The druid grasped Melltgwyn's pommel and stared silently as they moved past. The procession was not over however, as another two men followed the first pair, and then three more, and these ones carried spears as well as shields.

Bellicus examined the people closer – the furthest away was a man, hood up, but gazing ahead sternly, beard plainly visible. The rider nearest to the bothy seemed slighter though, a long, slim leg facing the watching druid, and she had a much smaller frame than the others travelling with her.

In a moment she and her bearded companion were past, and then another two riders went by, and another two.

Eleven of them – ten warriors, and a woman.

Bellicus gave them some time to ride on and then hastily grabbed his pack and ran out into the downpour, barely registering the rain as it blew into his face and made the straps slick as he attached his things to Darac's saddle.

He mounted the big black and looked at Cai to make sure the mastiff was ready to move. Then he hesitated, wondering what exactly he should do. Which direction to travel? Perhaps he should remain in the bothy until the riders, and the rain, had moved on?

His mind whirled as he examined each of his options and discarded them all. There was only one thing he could do: follow the warband that were riding to the northwest.

Saksnot might have escaped him, but it had suddenly become clear to Bellicus why Peredur had wanted him to follow this road for he had recognised some of the hooded, soaked riders who'd just passed.

"Hengist," Bellicus murmured as he guided Darac back towards the Roman road, carefully peering out. "With Thorbjorg. And I could have sworn one of those men was Bedwyr!"

Why would Arthur's friend be riding with the Saxon *bretwalda* and the witch? Bellicus had no idea, but he was absolutely certain Bedwyr would never betray Arthur, so that meant the Briton was Hengist's prisoner and, if that was the case, things would not go well for him.

What could Bellicus do about it? He was outnumbered ten to one, or two including the bold Cai. Ludicrous odds. As he moved back along the road his lips curled upward and he felt his blood, and the power of the gods, begin to thrum within him. He had been brought here for a purpose and now he knew what it was. Saksnot was not important – he never had been. Bedwyr was the reason Bellicus had come hundreds of miles southwards, and Hengist had no idea the warrior-druid was behind him.

He would find out soon enough!

CHAPTER FORTY-TWO

Although she was not a warrior herself, Narina had been involved in quite a few battles over the years. The warriors liked to know their commanders were not sending them to possible death while they sat safely in their strongholds, miles away from the conflict so, while Narina did not take up spear and shield, she did remain in her chariot at the rear of the Damnonii ranks, watching as the battle progressed.

"We're winning, aren't we?" Catia asked, face pale as she took in everything that was happening.

Narina glanced at her daughter and wondered again if it had been a mistake to bring her here at such a young age. Like the queen though, Catia had been forced to stand and watch as her people engaged in bloody warfare before – it simply could not be avoided when one's lands were surrounded by tribes and kings who coveted them. Still, Narina's own senses were reeling at the horrific sights of men horribly maimed and mutilated, the sounds of war cries and sobbing, and the sensation that her guts were about to consume themselves every time it looked like the Votadini soldiers might just break through the Damnonii line and come charging directly at the chariot.

Catia's observation had been correct though, and the queen nodded. "I'd say we're winning," she agreed. And, in truth, this was a relatively minor skirmish compared to some they had seen in the recent past. "With any luck Cunneda will surrender before too many warriors are lost."

Her words sounded hollow in her ears – a noble sentiment, wishing the men did not have to die, but who had commanded them to march there in the first place? Who had armed them and sent them into this battle, if not Narina?

She let out a heavy sigh, wishing it would take all her guilt with it, but she did not feel any better when she breathed in again and felt the tang of blood and shit in the air from the terrified men who'd soiled themselves as they fought desperately to live beyond this terrible day.

"I hope Gavo's all right," the princess said, standing on her tiptoes as if that would help her see through the ranks of spearmen before them. In the absence of the queen or Bellicus, Gavo would be at the front as the focal point of the army, inspiring the men to glory, or at least that was the idea. Narina often wondered if the thought of glory was soon forgotten once the bloodshed began, replaced by the primeval, instinctual need to simply survive.

"So do I," the queen murmured, wondering yet again if she'd made the right decision in coming here. She knew she had – the other kings and warlords that ruled in the lands bordering Alt Clota had to learn that they could not cross Narina. Especially with her being a woman – the likes of Cunneda did not respect her, or fear her, the way they feared another man. If she was to keep Alt Clota safe she had to prove that she could not be taken lightly. Like any ruler, no matter how large their lands, harsh decisions had to be taken – a hundred warriors dying today would hopefully save ten times that number in future months, perhaps averting another invasion by ambitious warlords when they realised a queen could be every bit as ferocious as a king.

Well, Cunneda was discovering that again today, Narina thought, and her warriors would not die for nothing. That, at least, was one lesson she'd learned from her first husband, Coroticus – never throw away lives without a very good reason.

"Mother!"

The queen jerked upright, reverie disturbed by Catia's frightened shout. She turned to look where the girl was staring and her eyes widened. Half a dozen men – Votadini men clad in the finest wargear and armed with swords and axes – were charging towards them from behind.

* * *

Arthur, Qunavo, and Lancelot rode slightly ahead of the main body of the army, close to the massive but incomplete walls of Garrianum, one of which had a great, black banner in the shape of a raven flying overhead. Whenever the wind blew, it seemed the great raven spread its wings in flight.

The Britons had faced very little resistance on the way there, for only the bravest – or stupidest – Saxon chief would stand against and army as big as the one Arthur had brought to the coast.

"Feels like I was just here," the warlord noted, gazing up at the helmets and spearpoints that jutted up over the crumbling fortifications. He smiled grimly, recalling that previous visit. "I can still smell the Saxon ships burning after we set fire to them just around the bend there."

"You have happier memories of this place than I," Lancelot grunted. "Not long before that day my entire warband, except Kay, was wiped out here and I was taken as a slave." He shuddered, gritting his teeth and glaring at the enemy soldiers who watched them from Garrianum.

Arthur looked at him but didn't really know what to say, so he said nothing and they continued to ride along the walls, noting large gaps, some of which had been barricaded with sturdy timbers and rubble, while others remained open. This had once been an impregnable fortress when the Romans had built it and manned its walls with their legionaries – now, the walls stood as an impressive monument to that time, but it was, in all honesty, a shadow of what it must have been like even just fifty years or so before. Locals had harvested much of the stone for their own buildings in nearby settlements, and the Saxons – who were far more skilled in the use of wood than stone – had done almost nothing to restore the place to its original condition.

Even so, Arthur dreaded trying to storm the place. He was sure he had enough men to do it, but he feared there would be many casualties when the Saxons rained down missiles on the Britons as they fought through the gaps in the walls. He wondered if Hengist hated losing men in battle as much as he did. Horsa, he was sure, cared little for the lives of those he commanded, seeing raiding and war merely as a means to write his own tale of battle fame and glory, but Hengist struck Arthur as more of a thoughtful, empathetic man than his dead brother. The warlord gave a little snort of amusement at his thoughts – who was he to guess what the *bretwalda* thought or felt? He did not really know the leader of the sea-wolves, he was basing his opinion of Hengist on hearsay, rumours, and his own hatred for the men who'd been ravaging the eastern edge of Britain for years now.

"Seems to me like Hengist is an arrogant fool who does not value the lives of his own men."

Arthur almost pulled his horse to a halt, so surprised was he by Lancelot's pronouncement. It was as if his friend had read his mind. "Why do you say that?" he asked.

"If you were to make this fortress your base here in these lands, what would you do first?"

"Shore up the walls," Arthur said. "Dig trenches outside. Rebuild those gates that are long gone."

"Exactly. Hengist has had an age to do all those things, yet he's never bothered. It's as if he doesn't care about protecting his own men. He believes he has the numbers to defend this place regardless of how many he loses as a result of the dilapidated fortifications."

"I was just thinking much the same myself," Arthur agreed, pointing to one large space where stone had been carted off by locals, probably to build a pen for pigs or to provide a foundation for some minor noble's hall. "It wouldn't take much effort, or material, to shore that up. But Hengist is no dribbling oaf, so I go with your first suggestion. He's simply arrogant."

"Or he believes in the power of the Saxon gods to protect this place," Qunavo suggested. "Who knows what rituals the *volur* have conducted here since they took control of the fortress? Those foreign gods will be more powerful here than anywhere else in Britain."

"Well, if Hengist thinks what's left of those walls, or his gods, will keep him safe he's in for a surprise."

"Indeed," growled Arthur as they turned and rode back to their waiting army. "And that's all to the good for us. Look, someone is on top of the walls, I think they want to speak with us."

Lancelot glanced up and Arthur saw the captain's face turn pale before his lips parted in a feral snarl. Leofdaeg stared out at them from atop the ruined gatehouse, the same arrogance Arthur had attributed to Hengist emanating from the jarl almost like a physical wave.

"What do you want here?" The Saxon called down, his voice confident and challenging. "I am Jarl Leofdaeg, Hengist's second-in-command, and I am in charge here. Now, be off, Arthur, before we come out and slaughter every last one of you."

"If you thought you could do that, you'd already be out here, Leofdaeg, you ugly sack of dog shit."

Arthur grinned at Lancelot's shouted retort, knowing his friend spoke the truth.

"Where is Hengist," the warlord bellowed before Leofdaeg could reply to Lancelot's insult. "Fetch him, you lackwitted whoreson. We're here to see him, not you."

"Hengist is not here," the Saxon called with obvious pleasure. "He's left me in command, so you've wasted your time travelling. Now piss off, you pair of squirrel turds, and enjoy your march home!"

The enemy warriors manning the walls cheered at Leofdaeg's words, believing he'd won the verbal sparring match.

"Never mind Hengist," Arthur shouted up, kicking his horse a little closer to the walls. "We're here for the Lord Bedwyr. Hand him over, and we'll do as you say and march away, leaving you to rut with your goats in peace."

Leofdaeg and his men laughed again. It seemed quite a few of them had learned to speak the tongue of the people they'd sailed there to invade.

"Bedwyr isn't here either," the jarl crowed. "He's gone off on a little trip with Hengist and Thorbjorg. You remember Thorbjorg? She's our *volva*, and she has plans for your 'Lord' Bedwyr."

"If those bastards don't stop that inane laughter I'll climb the walls right now, alone, and cut out their tongues," Lancelot muttered irritably.

Arthur was more interested in the jarl's claim that Bedwyr was not there in Garrianum. If true, they were too late to help their friend.

"You think he's telling the truth?" he asked Qunavo, ignoring the jeering from the Saxons, even when one of them launched a spear at them for it fell well short of their position.

"Probably. Thorbjorg may want to perform the blood sacrifice at some nearby place of power. Do you know of such a location?"

Arthur and Lancelot both shook their heads. "I'd expect there are plenty of places the witch would find suitable," the warlord replied. "The whole island is full of standing stones, dolmen, sacred wells and pools, groves…You know better than I, you're the Merlin after all."

Qunavo sighed. "I don't know these lands as well as I might. It's been a long, long time since I taught students about the holy places dotted around Britain. If I could speak with a local druid…"

"We don't have time for that," Lancelot broke in. "Face it, Arthur – if Bedwyr is not inside Garrianum, he might be anywhere, and, barring a miracle, we'll never find him. So, you have a decision to make."

Arthur looked at him, angry at his friend for forcing him to face reality. He turned away, silently staring up at the walls that seemed to mock him and his army – weak, crumbling, yet somehow still strong enough to stand in the way of the Britons.

"Did we bring our men here only to turn around and walk away?" Lancelot asked, tone neutral, as though he did not want Arthur to think he would judge whatever decision he made. It was very clear to the warlord what they must do, however. Regardless of whether or not Bedwyr was in the fortress, Arthur had persuaded the noblemen to follow him to Garrianum by promising they would take the fight to the Saxons and drive them into the sea, or into the arms of their gods in the afterlife.

"No, we will not walk away," Arthur said, looking up and seeing Leofdaeg still watching them. "We will take this fortress, and make everyone inside it wish they had never left their homes across the sea. Tell the men, Lancelot. Whatever happens to Bedwyr, Hengist and Thorbjorg will return from their travels to find themselves bereft of a home, and an army!"

239

CHAPTER FORTY-THREE

"They must have circled around us," Narina gasped, wishing Bellicus or Gavo were there. "Perhaps riding fast horses."

There were trees lining the road to the rear and it was there the enemy soldiers had come from, using the thick, summer foliage to conceal their approach.

"Get behind me!" Catia ordered, and Narina was shocked to see the girl had already drawn her sword from its scabbard. The blade seemed to shine, reflecting the daylight, and everything about the scene looked wrong to the queen. Her daughter had only seen twelve summers yet there she stood, weapon held in an unwavering hand, prepared to face six of the Votadini army's most dangerous warriors.

"Oh, gods protect us," Narina breathed, momentarily too terrified to think clearly, or do anything to save them. She could see the lines on the closest Votadini soldier's face now he was so close. The missing teeth in the side of his mouth as he snarled at the child barring his way. The pair of moles that were not quite hidden by his beard.

And then instinct took over and Narina jumped down from the chariot, ready to defend Catia, to use her own body as a shield to protect her daughter from the razor-sharp enemy blades. As she moved, she screamed for her own men to come to their aid, mentally berating herself for not doing so as soon as she'd noticed the Votadini warriors racing towards them.

Bellicus and Gavo were not there to watch for danger, but that did not mean no-one was looking out for their safety.

"Get back, my lady!"

A lean young warrior appeared in Narina's peripheral vision and she shrank back in fear before realising he was one of her own hearth-warriors. He did not look a match to the lead Votadini swordsman, but he was not alone, and at least ten of his comrades charged past the chariot, lining up in a small but hopefully impenetrable shieldwall.

The cries of rage from the thwarted enemy soldiers made Narina flinch – the sheer hatred and fury in their voices was animalistic and terrible, but it soon turned to grunts of exertion as the two sides came together.

The Votadini did not carry spears, presumably to allow them to move faster and without the great lengths of ash being spotted as they attempted to sneak up on the queen. They did carry shields, but the Damnonii warriors had the extra reach of spears, a massive advantage. It did not take long for Narina's hearth-warriors to carve their way through the attackers, leaving all six dead.

"By Dis, that was close!" the queen laughed, shock making her feel giddy and strangely joyful. "Thank you, all!"

The soldiers turned to salute her, every face a mask of steely determination, none betraying any emotion at all, be it fear, or even the triumph they must be feeling at having saved the lives of their queen and princess. The lean young man who'd led them bowed to her and then issued a command to the others. They spread out and formed a circle around Narina, Catia, and the chariot.

"You should get back on there," the warrior suggested, pointing the blood-coated tip of his spear at the chariot. "If Cunneda sends more men around here we might not be able to stop them from getting to you. If that happens, you must ride to safety."

"On that, Maelgwn?" Narina laughed softly, remembering the name of the young man who'd risen through the ranks quickly over the past couple of years thanks to so many soldiers being killed in the various battles. "The chariot's only good for flat ground. Try to pick up any speed on a field like this and the wheels will snap off. We'd be as well running!"

"Aye, well, maybe there's something to that," Maelgwyn smiled. "I've seen you run, my lady." He bowed deeply to Catia who was still standing with her sword held out, as though she was unsure whether the danger was truly over or not. "Your bravery is an example to us all, Princess Catia," he told her and turned to make sure no one else could creep up on them from behind.

Narina lightly touched her daughter's arm, nodding for her to sheath her weapon, and then the two stepped back up onto the chariot's footplate, looking towards the battle again in something of a stunned silence.

"We are winning," the princess noted, repeating her earlier assertion with more conviction as it became obvious Cunneda's army was not faring well. Sending his men around to try and kill

241

Narina was a last, desperate throw of the dice by the embattled Votadini king, but it had failed, and now the Damnonii warriors were closing in on the last few pockets of enemy resistance.

Narina was shaking and did not trust herself to reply for fear her voice would betray her terror. She gripped the edge of the chariot, and it shamed her to see Catia apparently calm and unmoved by their near-death experience. That feeling was exacerbated when Catia turned to see Narina's fright and the girl put her arm around her shoulders, drawing her in as if the princess was the mother – the protector.

"It's fine," Catia soothed. "I would have dealt with them."

It was an incredible statement and Narina opened her mouth to berate the girl before she saw the twinkle in Catia's eyes, and the wide grin, and she knew her daughter was putting on a front. The princess had been just as scared as Narina but had managed to hide it until the danger had passed.

"You're so brave, I'm proud of you," said the queen and the pair hugged one another tightly, only letting go when they noticed the sounds of battle had died away to almost nothing. And then Gavo's great bellow rose into the air in a cry of triumph and his men joined in lustily.

It was over, and Narina's Damnonii warriors were victorious.

They surveyed the battlefield, watching soldiers stripping the dead of valuables and weapons – an unpleasant but necessary and traditional task – while those enemy soldiers who'd been badly injured were put out of their misery.

"It's horrible," Catia muttered, tears in her eyes, and Narina was happy to see her daughter had not become desensitised to the horrors of war. Not yet, at least.

"It is," agreed the queen. "But it looks like we haven't lost too many men, and, thank the gods Alt Clota is safe again for a time."

CHAPTER FORTY-FOUR

Bellicus wished he knew these lands much better for he had no idea where Hengist and his company might be going. That they were taking Bedwyr somewhere for some dark purpose was obvious, and the druid supposed Thorbjorg knew of a place of power that would enhance her ritual, much as she'd sought to do when the Saxons tried to sacrifice Catia at the huge stone circle known as the Giant's Dance. The *volva* shared similar beliefs to Bellicus and the Order of Druids, and searching out sacred places to conduct rituals made as much sense to Thorbjorg as it did to any other mystic or priest.

But what sacred place were the Saxons riding towards? Where was it located? If Bellicus knew that he could ride on ahead and scout the land, maybe find some useful hiding place that would help him rescue Bedwyr, if such a thing was even possible given how many warriors guarded him. Not to mention Thorbjorg! Bellicus had been forced to deal with another *volva* just a few months ago, when Yngvildr had caused so much pain and suffering alongside Horsa in Alt Clota. Ultimately her power, her connection to the gods, had not proved enough to prevail over the Damnonii people despite her brutally sacrificing a number of innocent victims outside the gates of Dun Breatann, but Bellicus had seen how her black influence could cause terrible trouble for all she came in contact with. And Thorbjorg was an even more powerful *volva* than Yngvildr.

If Bellicus was to help Bedwyr he would somehow need to find a way to defeat, or bypass, not only nine warriors, but Thorbjorg as well. It was a daunting prospect, and one the druid suspected would prove impossible.

He also feared it would prove difficult to trail the Saxon party. Bellicus could not afford to get too close to them for, if noticed, he would be attacked. A giant of a man, on a black horse, with a war-dog for company? Every Saxon in Britain must know his description by now, given the trouble he'd caused them. And if Hengist somehow managed to capture Bellicus, the man the *bretwalda* held responsible for his brother's death, well, whatever they had planned for Bedwyr would seem delightful in comparison. Hengist would make sure Bellicus suffered greatly before being allowed to die, that was a certainty.

With all this in mind, the wisest thing to do would be to forget Bedwyr and ride home, allowing the Saxons to do whatever they had planned. Of course, Bellicus could not do that. He did not know Bedwyr particularly well – Duro knew him better, having journeyed with him two years before to recruit old Roman decurions to train Alfred's new cavalry units. But Bellicus could not simply abandon the Briton to Thorbjorg's sacrificial knife, it was not in his nature.

Besides, any ritual that strengthened the Saxon cause had to be disrupted. If the *volva* was allowed to carry out her plans it would only mean dire trouble for all the Britons, not just Bedwyr.

So, Bellicus guided Darac carefully along the road, Cai dutifully trotting by their side as the Saxons turned off the main Roman road and headed to the west along a narrow dirt track. The ground here remained mostly flat, so the druid was grateful that numerous trees of all kinds grew up along the path, allowing him to remain hidden from the enemy party's rearguard.

As it turned out, it was not quite as difficult to follow them as the druid had feared when he first set out after them at the bothy. Thorbjorg liked to sing as she travelled, and her voice, quite beautiful Bellicus was forced to grudgingly admit, filled the countryside as they covered the miles, making the damp, dull day rather more pleasant.

The druid wondered what Hengist thought of the woman making so much noise. While her voice was lovely, the singing might attract outlaws or other enemies. Of course, any group of bandits would need to have sufficient numbers to take on so many armed Saxons who were, undoubtedly, the elite of Hengist's hearth-warriors, but it did seem very strange, bizarre even, for a warband to journey through Britain in such a noisy fashion.

He noticed then that the singing was growing louder and hastily drew Darac to a halt. The Saxons must have stopped to rest and Bellicus might have stumbled right into them. Heaving a sigh of relief that he'd noticed in time, he dismounted and let Cai lie down for a time, while Darac drank fresh rainwater from a deep puddle. The druid stretched his own legs, relieving the stiffness that had set in over the ride. As he walked to and fro, he chewed a strip of meat from his pack and his thoughts turned yet again to Alt Clota. Was Duro on the mend? Was Catia enjoying interesting lessons with her tutors? And what of Narina? Whatever his wife was doing, he prayed she was happy, and enjoying a peaceful summer.

* * *

Cunneda's face was bloody, the result of a deep gash over his right eye that one of his healers had now bandaged. His lips were swollen too, as if he'd been smashed in the face with the rim of a shield or perhaps a Damnonii fist, but his shoulders were back, and he stood proudly as Queen Narina walked towards him. She had come in the chariot, cheered on by her victorious army while the defeated Votadini warriors eyed her sullenly. For her part she held her head high, nodding and smiling in gratitude to her men, thanking them for their brave service and promising them a share in the spoils of the battle. When she stood before Cunneda, Gavo was by her side.

The captain also had blood on his face, arms, and chest, but Narina could not see any injury at all and hoped the crimson stains were from beaten enemies. When he grinned at her she did her best not to recoil, for at least one of his teeth had been knocked out, although mercifully not the front ones. Still, the sight was jarring and might have been amusing had she not been seeing him after many good Britons had been killed.

Catia stood with her mother, and she was not quite so tactful. "Your teeth!" she gasped, eyes growing wide.

Gavo nodded, a wry smile on his face. "Aye, I'll be eating nothing but broth for a while, but it could be worse. There's men without hands or eyes over there, being tended to by the healers."

Catia's eyes fell and Narina knew the girl was both saddened and embarrassed by her reaction to the captain's injury but that was why the queen had brought her there – to learn. To learn how to deal with other kings and warlords, and how to deal with the terrible aftermath of a battle. Life as a princess was usually not so hands-on, or so concerned with martial matters, but Catia had made it clear ever since she'd been abducted by Horsa's Saxons that she would not live the coddled life of a noblewoman so…She would learn, and she would grow into whatever role was eventually handed down to her, whenever that may be.

All three turned their attention on the Votadini king then, examining his wounds, all apparently unsure what to say next. It was not in any of their natures to gloat the way many triumphant rulers would do after winning a battle, humiliating and mocking their humbled enemy, and Cunneda almost gave the impression he'd not lost at all with his straight back and steely gaze.

"Your men fought well," said Narina. "I'm sorry it had to come to this."

Cunneda did not reply but his shoulders slumped just a little, as though it was taking a great effort to maintain his stoic pose.

"We have defeated you again, my lord," the queen went on, speaking clearly and quite loudly but not harshly, simply matter-of-factly. "What would you suggest I do with you?"

That brought Cunneda's shoulders up again and his eyes blazed, hand falling to grasp his sword, fingers clutching nothing but empty air for he'd been divested of all his weapons by the Damnonii soldiers. "What should you do with me? You come to my lands, kill my people, and now what? Would you make a thrall of me? A plaything for your nobles to mock and amuse themselves with?"

"Oh, be silent, you fool," Narina barked. "I am not Coroticus, and even if I was, he'd have killed you and simply taken your head back to display on the walls of Dun Breatann, not kept you as his pet slave. I am wondering what I should do with you personally, but also with the throne of Dun Edin which is now mine by right."

Gavo was eyeing her, very clearly wanting to offer advice, but Narina didn't look at him. She knew he would tell her to kill Cunneda and place one of the Damnonii nobles in Dun Edin to rule in her stead, and she also knew that would be sensible, sound advice. But she could not command the king to be done away with – the man had been her father-in-law for a time and, although she did not feel any love for him, neither did she despise him. All she wanted was for Northern Britain to be a safe place for her people.

"You will come back to Dun Breatann with me, for now," she decided, ignoring Gavo's low groan. "You will be held with all due respect and comfort, as my prisoner, until I decide what to do with you long-term. We'll take ten of your highest-ranking noblemen too."

"Are you sure about this?" Gavo asked in a low voice. "We tried this before with the Picts, and it did not turn out too well."

"That was thanks to Cunneda's son, Ysfael," Narina countered, eyeing the enemy king archly. "And you say it didn't turn out well, but who rules the Picts now? Aife. She was one of those prisoners, and she is now our close ally."

"And my friend," put in Catia.

Gavo looked like he wanted to roll his eyes and throw up his hands in despair, but he was far too respectful and loyal to Narina to make such a public show of displeasure. Instead, he bowed his head and said, "As you wish, my lady."

"What say you, Cunneda?" she asked.

"I don't have much choice, do I?" he snarled. "I suppose it's better than having my throat cut."

"Much better," Narina agreed. "Take him into custody," she commanded two of her hearth-warriors, who moved immediately to follow her orders and led the deposed king away to the wagons at the rear of the army for transportation to Alt Clota.

"Who will rule in Dun Edin then?" Catia asked her mother.

"We'll discuss that this evening. For now, Gavo, the war is over, and I think you and your men have earned a drink."

CHAPTER FORTY-FIVE

Thanks to Thorbjorg's singing, which rarely let up throughout the day, and the constant pattering of rain on the muddy track, Bellicus was not detected and, at last, the sky grew even darker as the cloud-obscured sun decided it was wasting its time and dipped beneath the horizon for the night.

Apparently the Saxons were not the least bit worried about being attacked – why would they be? They were in the middle of nowhere after all – and even when the *volva* ceased singing for the evening the chattering of the warriors filled the silence of the woods. Bellicus tethered Darac some half a mile or so to the east and, taking Cai, crept back to the enemy campsite, finding a position amongst some hazel trees where he could see out but remain hidden within the undergrowth.

The Saxons did not go hunting or foraging for food – they had brought plenty with them, and the scent of woodsmoke and roasting meat filled the air once they'd started a fire and set up their tents. One large tent was shared by Hengist and Thorbjorg and Bellicus felt a little pang of jealousy as he imagined the *bretwalda* enjoying the closeness of the *volva* who, although into middle-age, remained lithe and alluring, carrying an unmistakable aura of power that most men could not resist.

Bellicus would have liked to sneak into that tent once night fell and deal with his two hated foes forever. The pair reminded him of Horsa and Yngvildr who had also shared a tent and sought to do nothing but harm, and the druid wished to see Hengist and Thorbjorg end up just as dead as the other two, but that was not his priority.

He was there to help Bedwyr, although as the camp grew darker and the Saxons settled down for the night Bellicus despaired of carrying out his mission. They might not be particularly worried about being attacked, but the enemy warriors set guards around the perimeter of the camp: one at either end of the road, and one who patrolled the whole area slowly and methodically, pausing often to peer into the gloom and listen for signs of anyone approaching. The druid had no doubt there would be three such guards all through the night as the nine, or eight if Hengist did not deign to lower himself to the task, would take turns to sleep and take watch duty.

It would be nigh on impossible to sneak past three alert warriors, never mind free Bedwyr and escape with him.

The captured Briton was not ill-treated, at least not while Bellicus was watching, but he did remain completely silent. Only Hengist and Thorbjorg attempted to converse with him but he ignored them, gazing into the dancing fire, and they soon grew bored, retiring to their tent and closing the flaps against the weather which had grown worse with the setting of the sun.

It was not cold, but the rain continued to fall, and the wind picked up, gusting hard every now and again and making the campfire blaze alarmingly.

Bedwyr was given a tent at least, presumably so the elements didn't kill him before Thorbjorg used him for her ritual, and he crawled into it not long after Hengist and the *volva* retired for the night. The prisoner's legs were tied together, and his hands were bound in front of him, but his tent was kept open so he could not attempt to undo the knots without being spotted. At least one of the Saxon soldiers had an eye on him at all times.

Of course, that might change when sleep overcame those who were not on guard duty, and exhaustion began to wear on the rest. Bellicus prayed to Cernunnos that that would be the case, or he would be as well heading back to Darac and leaving right now.

Not for the first time since he'd begun hunting Saksnot, Bellicus thanked the gods for his cloak. Being made from unbleached wool it was similar to the old Roman legionaries sagum –waterproof, and big enough for him to lie on the ground with some of the material over Cai so the pair remained mostly dry as the druid formulated a plan to rescue Bedwyr.

The weather would help, far more than a still, silent night would have, but, even with the wind and rain there seemed no way to reach the prisoner and remove him from his tent without someone noticing. The tents were all clustered fairly close to the fire, so it was not dark enough to sneak into the camp and speak with the prisoner, and even Bellicus and Cai could not take on nine hard warriors and a *volva* who knew only too well how to wield the sacrificial stone knife she carried at her waist.

Once, when the clouds cleared for a time and the rain eased off, Bellicus looked up and saw the moon high in the sky. He was reminded how close the glowing white disc was to being full and knew that, if he did not rescue Bedwyr tonight, he would be dead tomorrow.

But how? There were simply too many guards, and, even if he lay in the rain for the whole night, Bellicus feared no opening would present itself. These Saxons had been hand-picked for their skills, and they would not let down their guard for long enough to let the druid sneak into the camp.

One of the enemy soldiers came right up to the bush the druid was hiding beneath, and the sound of even more liquid splattering on the sodden forest floor told Bellicus all he needed to know. It would be easy enough to take out this warrior, reduce the Saxon warband by one at least, but then what? The dead man's absence would quickly be noticed and that would alert the whole camp that someone was trailing them.

When the Saxon had emptied his bladder and slowly wandered away, Bellicus touched Cai lightly and the pair moved like shadows, silently through the trees and around in a half-moon arc that brought them right up to the tent that Hengist and Thorbjorg were sheltering within.

It was much larger than the other tents, tall enough that a man could stand up inside it, and Bellicus had seen the frame being put together so he knew it was sturdy and constructed with timber and clever joints that would withstand all but the most intense gusts of wind.

"He's in there humping the *volva* and drinking mead while I'm out here getting soaked," Bellicus murmured to Cai, shaking his hooded head ruefully at the dog who cocked his head in turn and gazed at the druid as if he completely agreed.

It would probably be quite easy for Bellicus to wait until the occupants of the tent fell asleep and then slice a hole in the leather to slip through. The druid's blade would make short work of *bretwalda* and *volva* – Bellicus had participated in a similar mission not so long ago with Lancelot, killing the Jarl Leofdaeg's father in a tent very much like this one – but that would not save Bedwyr. Quite the opposite in fact, for the remaining Saxons would have no need for the prisoner and would simply slit his throat before doing their utmost to track down whoever had killed Hengist and the witch.

It was very tempting to remove the man who posed the biggest threat to Britain since the Emperor Claudius four hundred years before him, but Bellicus did not believe the gods had brought him there for that purpose. He was there to help Bedwyr, and he had to find a way to do that, not waste time fantasising about slaughtering Hengist.

The woods were almost pitch black even with the campfire crackling and hissing in the rain, so it was obvious when the candle – or whatever lit Hengist's tent – was extinguished. Bellicus crept even closer, pressing against the side of the tent and straining his ears, desperately hoping to catch some piece of intelligence – some whispered pillow-talk – that might help his cause.

He was rewarded almost immediately, thankfully, for he knew he'd need to get warm soon, or face catching a chill, and sneezing while one was sneaking around a Saxon camp was not advisable.

The muffled, low voice of Hengist came through the leather wall of the tent and Bellicus strained to hear over the patter of rain on the material and the foliage around him.

"Have you ever seen this sacred place we're going to?" the *bretwalda* was asking.

Thorbjorg's higher, more melodious tone was easier to hear, clearer and far less mumbled. "*Ja*," she said. "It's little more than two circular mounds. So old that grass has long since overgrown them."

Hengist was clearly not impressed, his snort reverberating through the tent. "Why are we going there then?"

"It might not be much to look at now, but it was clearly a major religious centre aeons ago. Old magic is often the best, if one is able to kindle its fire back to life."

Hengist's grunt of reply was less disdainful than before but did not sound like he was entirely convinced. "How much farther?" he asked. "I'm sick of the rain already."

"Another couple of hours riding in the morning and we'll be there." Thorbjorg told him. "I shall spend the day preparing the ground, and the prisoner for his sacrifice. We shall spill his blood when the full moon is high in the sky, whether she is obscured by clouds or not."

"Very good," the Saxon warlord said and his voice was easier to hear now, as though he was excited and it had made him speak clearer. "Speaking of spilling things, come here, my *volva*, and let me spill my seed deep inside you."

Bellicus rolled his eyes at Hengist's crude words, and made ready to slip away from the tent. The last thing he wanted to hear was these two rutting like the animals they were. Thorbjorg's voice came louder then, however, and the sound of skin being slapped accompanied her words as she apparently fended off Hengist's wandering hands.

"Get away from me," the woman scolded. "Are you stupid? You know my power will be more potent if I abstain from coupling. The strength builds up until the climax of tomorrow's ritual when it will be released in a mighty surge as Bedwyr's lifeforce is given to the gods as an offering."

"Oh, come on," Hengist objected, voice plaintive. Bellicus grinned, happy to know Hengist had been thwarted and would go to sleep frustrated, unless he decided to sort himself out. It seemed Thorbjorg was in something of a vindictive mood that night though.

"Go to sleep, Hengist," she commanded the *bretwalda*. "We must both conserve our sexual power for the ritual to be as potent as possible."

Hengist's angry reply was lost as Bellicus crept away from the tent, still smiling to himself. He did not think Hengist truly needed to abstain for any magical reasons, but he enjoyed the thought of the hated warlord lying there, frustrated, and as horny as a sailor in a brothel but unable to do anything about it.

When he was well clear of the camp and the patrolling guard, Bellicus made his way to where they'd left Darac pegged to the ground.

He felt good, and far less frustrated than Hengist he was sure. Although the druid was not familiar with this part of Britain, he did have extensive knowledge of the larger sacred sites that were dotted across the land, and he was sure he knew now where Bedwyr was being taken: Tir Ambre.

Tir Ambre was no longer used by the druids as a place of power – or so Bellicus had been taught years earlier. It was one of the many ancient sites that had become overgrown after generations of inactivity but was still revered by the locals as a magical area. What had drawn Thorbjorg to the place? Bellicus wasn't sure, but he did not believe there were many more impressive – physically at least – ancient monuments within a few days ride of Garrianum. There would be dozens of sacred groves, springs and pools with strange legends attached to them, and perhaps the ruins of Roman temples. The *volva* had her own reasons for choosing Tir Ambre but, ultimately, they did not matter to Bellicus. All that mattered was that he knew now where the Saxons were taking Bedwyr, and the druid could travel ahead of them, hopefully being able to prepare the area for a daring rescue.

They had almost reached Darac when a low growl came from deep within Cai's chest and Bellicus froze, placing a hand on the mastiff's neck. They stood stock still, as much a part of the woods as the hazels that grew up all around them, and listened.

A harsh whisper came to them and Melltgwyn was in Bellicus's hand, reassuring and empowering the druid who knew they must have been spotted by Hengist's soldiers, and followed to that spot. He bent to Cai's ear and murmured, "Stay," before he moved to press himself against the trunk of a thick tree.

CHAPTER FORTY-SIX

Footsteps came, louder now, as though their pursuers had lost the trail and were hurrying to try and find them before they escaped.

When the first man, tall, broad, and sporting a massive beard, stepped past Bellicus's tree Melltgwyn licked out in the darkness like the tongue of a serpent, plunging deep into the side of the Saxon. The astonished man was not even able to let out a scream as Bellicus's left fist came up, thundering against the Saxon's open jaw.

"Attack, Cai!" the druid hissed, and the sound of four muscular legs propelling a heavy body through the gloom filled the night air. There was a scream this time, as the dog's powerful jaws clamped around the second Saxon's sword arm, crushing fine bones and sending a wave of agony along the man's arm. His shriek of pain was cut off almost as soon as it was torn from his throat, as Melltgwyn, still slick with blood, came around in an arc and smashed into the screaming man's face.

There was a sickening crack as the blade struck home, sending the enemy soldier falling backwards, silent now, even though Cai was still tearing his forearm to shreds.

"Leave him," the druid said, and the dog reacted immediately, letting go of the Saxon and coming to stand beside Bellicus who was staring down at their handiwork. Despite the darkness, his night vision was good – far better than the Saxons' had been after spending their evening in the light of their campfire – and the druid could see the enemy warriors were quite dead.

"Shit," Bellicus breathed, wondering what this meant for them, and for Bedwyr. Were the rest of Hengist's soldiers searching for them as well? What would the Saxons do when they found the corpses of their comrades and realised someone was tracking them? It did not bode well for the prisoner.

The druid stood in silence again for a long moment but detected no sounds of other searchers combing the woods for them and he felt a little relief. If only these two had come after them, perhaps catching a glimpse of them as they retreated from the Saxon camp, then there was hope yet.

Bending, Bellicus lifted the smaller of the two men and threw the body over his shoulder. He began walking to the northwest, away from the enemy camp, and away from Darac, forging through trees and brambles that tore at his leggings and cloak. He ignored the undergrowth, dogged in his task as he moved and, at last, came to a stagnant, marshy pond. He actually stepped into the water, cursing as it soaked his foot but then smiling grimly as he realised this was the perfect spot to deposit his load, and he dropped the corpse with a splash that was swallowed by the surrounding trees.

Then he turned and hurried back the way he'd come, trying not to leave too obvious a trail. The second Saxon, the bigger man, was heavier than the first but Bellicus lifted him easily, great thigh muscles straining as he straightened and began the walk to the pool. It did not take too long to reach the place and Bellicus wondered if this body of water had once been viewed as a sacred place by the people who lived in these lands. Well, if it hadn't been, it was now, for Bellicus commended the second Saxon corpse to the embrace of the water and begged Cernunnos, god of the forest, to accept the two offerings.

There seemed nothing else to do other than to find Darac and head towards Tir Ambre. Part of the druid desperately wanted to return to Hengist's camp and find out what reaction the disappearance of two guards would engender amongst the Saxons, but that would be foolish. The first thing the sea-wolves would do would be to search for the missing men – hopefully not too far, and not too closely. They would surely discover Bellicus during any search and that would be the end of him and Bedwyr.

So the druid and his loyal shadow slipped through the sodden foliage until they reached Darac, silent and unbothered by his time alone although visibly pleased to see Bellicus. Soon, they were on the move, skirting the enemy camp.

If the missing guards had been discovered no sounds of consternation reached the three travellers as they made their way around and back onto the main road. With any luck the Saxons would believe their comrades had simply deserted, or had perhaps been carried away by some local nature spirit, never to be seen again. Such tales were as much a part of the sea-wolves folklore as the Britons, Bellicus knew, so it was not a foolish hope on his part.

Gods willing – Bellicus's gods that was – Thorbjorg would simply perform some warding ritual to placate the rest of the soldiers and then the party would continue on with their original plan to take Bedwyr to Tir Ambre.

There, Bellicus would be waiting for them, and now he would have two fewer enemy soldiers to worry about.

CHAPTER FORTY-SEVEN

"Alt Clota is undefended, and ripe for invasion!"

The current king of the Dalriadans, Domangart mac Nissi, sat in his hall high atop the fortress of Dunadd roughly forty miles to the west of Dun Breatann and listened with growing interest to the words of the merchant who'd just arrived there that afternoon. Domangart had come from Hibernia with his warband just a few months ago, finding Dalriada in a state of upheaval and disarray. The previous king, Loarn mac Eirc, had died when a seemingly innocuous wound taken fighting two raiders from Alt Clota – Bellicus of Dun Breatann and the former Roman centurion called Duro – became infected. Loarn's death had seen a number of would-be successors striving to take his place, fighting one another for supremacy and, ultimately, weakening them all. When Domangart and his fifty warriors had rowed across from Hibernia in their currachs they had instantly become the strongest faction in the nascent kingdom and, without much trouble, Domangart proclaimed himself king and took control of Dunadd.

"What d'ye mean, 'ripe for invasion'?" the Dalriadan ruler asked the merchant. "I've only just taken over this fortress and the lands hereabouts. You think I'm about to row my currach along to Dun Breatann and try to take that as well?" Domangart was no fool, and, although he was certainly ambitious, he knew very well that the Damnonii fortress, built atop an even bigger rock than Dunadd, was essentially impregnable.

"You don't have to take Dun Breatann," the merchant replied, clearly put out by the lukewarm reaction to his intelligence. His beard had been dyed bright red with goats' grease and beechwood ashes and he tugged irritably at it now. "You could just go raiding there. I'm telling you, lord, you'll never have a better opportunity. Alt Clota is filled with wealth!"

Domangart stood up, stretching out his neck which had grown stiff from sitting in his recently acquired throne. He was a stocky man, of average height, bald on top but with fierce grey eyebrows that gave him a perpetually angry countenance. He was in his forties now, but remained as ferocious as his appearance suggested, believing himself secure from danger within Dunadd, especially since his three adult sons, accomplished warriors in their own right, stood with him against all foes. They watched him now, silent, standing behind his throne, waiting for him to ask their counsel.

What the merchant suggested was tempting, Domangart could not deny that. Dun Breatann was famously wealthy, that was why so many different kings over the years had tried – and failed! – to storm the fortress. Why should any attempt now be different to those previous unsuccessful sieges?

"You said Alt Clota was undefended," the king said, wandering across to the firepit in the centre of the hall and basking in its glow. It might still be summer, but it was starting to grow chilly at times, especially atop Dunadd which was open to the elements. "What did you mean, exactly?"

"Queen Narina has taken her army east, to Dun Edin, leaving her lands open to attack," the merchant said, bobbing his head as if to prove he knew what he was talking about. "As you know, my lord, the Damnonii army have only just fought a war with the Picts and the Saxons. They won, but they lost a lot of men doing so."

"And Narina has foolishly taken what remains of her army and marched to attack Cunneda?"

"Precisely, lord," agreed the merchant.

"Why?"

"That I do not know. The workers at Dun Breatann's port did not want to tell me too much, and I did not want to push them for fear of making them suspicious. It's true though, Dun Breatann's garrison was practically non-existent when I was there unloading my currach."

"Narina is no idiot," Domangart murmured, walking back from the firepit to sit down once again on his throne. He liked sitting in that throne, it made him feel like a proper king. "I've heard enough about her to know she'll have left men to guard the walls, and someone competent to command them."

"That's just the thing though!" the merchant laughed excitedly. "One of Narina's commanders, Gerallt, was killed in the war with the Picts and Saxons, and the other one, Gavo, marched off with Narina to lead the army for her."

"Well, there's still that druid, Bellicus, and his centurion friend," Domangart said, holding out his hands, palms up. "I'm sure they know how to organise whatever garrison has been left behind in Dun Breatann."

"Bellicus hasn't been seen for days, maybe even weeks," the merchant reported. "That much is common knowledge. Word is, someone managed to break into the fortress and stabbed the centurion practically to death. He also hasn't been seen for a long, long time, and Bellicus is said to have gone riding off after whoever it was that attacked his Roman friend. I'm telling you, lord, this is the perfect opportunity for you to become King of Dalriada and Alt Clota. Two fortresses would be yours, Dunadd and Dun Breatann!"

Domangart's oldest son, Carvorst, still in his twenties but balding and stockily built like his father, stepped forward. "We don't have enough men to hold another fortress," he noted. "But if we were to conquer Alt Clota word would soon get around the other tribes here in Dalriada, and back at home in Hibernia. Warriors would flock to join us, father. The merchant is right – your name would become legendary!"

"And I would need someone to rule over at least one of the two fortresses, eh, Carvorst?" said Domangart dryly.

"Of course," his son replied without shame. "I would be happy to rule here, or in Alt Clota, whatever you decided, lord."

The king smiled. He was not daft – his sons were loyal to him but they, like every other soldier that had sworn fealty to him, expected to be rewarded for their service. An unsuccessful lord did not keep a warband together for long.

"This does seem like a good opportunity to expand our borders," Domangart conceded. "And it might mean an end to us fighting other Dalriadans, rather than the Britons. All the Scotti coming together under one banner. My banner!" He grinned back at Carvorst and his other two sons, nodding his head as his mind began to fill with possibilities and with the promise of true glory. Ruling Dalriada was one thing, but Alt Clota was a more established kingdom, with more people, more wealth, and more power to be wielded by whoever controlled those lands.

"You will, I trust, remember who brought you this news, lord?" the merchant asked. "When you become High King?"

"High King!" Domangart cackled at that, enjoying the feel of the words in his mouth and of the image of him, crowned and triumphant in the hall at Dun Breatann. "I will indeed remember you, my fine fellow. You shall become my trade advisor. In the meantime, how fast is that currach of yours?"

259

"Oh, it's fast, lord. The fastest!"

"Then get in it, and take yourself across to Hibernia, and spread the word there that King Domangart mac Nissi needs good fighting men to join him. Send them my way, merchant, with promises of golden arm rings, silver torcs, beautiful slave women, and lands of their own to farm! I will build one great kingdom here in Northern Britain," he slammed a mighty fist down on the arm of his throne and grinned around at his people who were gathered within the hall, although his beetling brows made it seem as if he was glaring at them all. "Now, where is that bishop, Dotha, that once served Loarn mac Eirc here? Bring him to me – we must pray to Christ for success. Are you ready to sail to Dun Breatann, my warriors?"

The cheers that came in response to his question were so loud the roof almost lifted off its beams in that great hall of Dunadd. Domangart might only have fifty men in his warband, but they were all great warriors, and soon they would earn immortality by becoming the first invaders to seize control of fabled Dun Breatann.

CHAPTER FORTY-EIGHT

Bellicus rode through the dark, allowing Darac to move quite slowly so the horse would not injure itself on some hole in the road or other obstacle impossible to notice in the gloom. Even at the reduced pace, it took less than two hours before the druid reached his destination. The rain had stopped at long last, and the clouds had parted to reveal the ripe, almost full moon, her light shining down on the centuried stone circle that must once have been an incredible sight. Now, there was little to see but mounds – Bellicus knew that if he could fly he would be able to make out the shape that the monument formed in the ground, and it would likely take his breath away for it was no minor site this. Of course, it was nowhere near as impressive as the mighty Giant's Dance with its towering stones and archways – Tir Ambre was much smaller than that, but similar in layout, and the druid tethered Darac amongst some trees and took a quick look around the site.

There were two circular mounds, one within the other, and at the centre there had once been timber columns that had long since rotted away. If only Tir Ambre had been constructed with the same bluestones as the Giant's Dance the site would likely remain intact even hundreds of years after its builders abandoned it. The druid could picture the site as it had once been, and, although grass had overgrown the entire place leaving just humps and depressions, Bellicus could feel the place practically humming with power beneath the layers of turf that concealed it.

No wonder Thorbjorg had chosen this site to sacrifice Bedwyr. To an untrained eye Tir Ambre was little more than a lumpy field, but to one tuned to the gods such as a druid or a *volva*, it was far, far more. It was a place of old, high magic, and a blood sacrifice here would harness that ancient power for the ritual's celebrant.

Bellicus shuddered at the thought, seeing in his mind's eye the Saxon hordes rampaging across Britain, suffused with the power of Thorbjorg's heinous ceremony. He could not let that happen – no matter what, Bedwyr could not die here in Tir Ambre.

Even if I have to kill him on the road, thought the druid. That would be preferable to allowing the Saxons to sacrifice him here. As unpalatable, as upsetting, as that thought was, the druid knew it might have to become reality.

He felt utterly drained and decided to get some sleep or possibly be useless the next day. It had been a long, eventful journey to reach this point, with one quest had falling by the wayside to be replaced by another, and it had taken a toll on him. He'd grown used to travelling with Duro and he missed the centurion's stoic, jovial companionship keenly at that moment. This would all be much easier with Duro by his side to help him prepare for what was to come.

Refusing to grow maudlin, he reminded himself of the two Saxon warriors he and Cai had dispatched that night, and that cheered him somewhat. It was always pleasing to remove enemies from the world.

Taking a last look around Tir Ambre, burning the topography of the site into his mind, he took Cai and they went to join Darac in the hiding place in the trees. It was not raining any more, but there was a chance it would start again, and he was damp despite his waterproof cloak, so he set up his tent and went inside. Cai came in too and their combined body heat soon had them feeling warmer and dryer.

Before he knew it, Bellicus was fast asleep, safe in the knowledge that Cai would notice anyone sneaking up on them.

When he awoke it was dawn and he felt quite refreshed, rather to his surprise. He could not remember having any dreams, but he was glad he'd come here and taken the lie of the land before resting. His sleeping mind had subconsciously sorted everything out, and he knew exactly how he was going to deal with Bedwyr and the Saxons.

"Cernunnos protect us," he murmured, looking up at the cloudy, grey morning sky. "This is not going to be easy."

* * *

Qunavo strode out to the front of the army of Britons and raised one leg, stretched out one arm to point at the walls of Garrianum, and closed one eye. Standing thus, he raised his staff high over his head, arched his back and let out an inhuman shriek that set the hairs rising on Arthur's arms. Even Nemias had never made such a blood-curdling sound in all the years he'd travelled as Merlin with the young warlord. It was shocking to hear that scream emanate from a man, especially since Arthur had absolutely no idea Qunavo could do such a thing with his voice.

Leofdaeg stood on the wall of Garrianum watching, pale faced and silent, as the High Druid, Merlin of Britain, walked up and down the perimeter of that southern wall, pointing his staff at them and snarling eldritch words that even the Britons could not understand. There was so much force, so much conviction, in Qunavo's speech and gestures that Arthur half expected bolts of fire to shoot out from the top of his staff and blow the old Roman wall to pieces. With each shout the Saxons cowered behind the crumbling stones, unusually quiet, which truly proved how spooked they were by the druid's show.

"This is fun," said Lancelot. He was lined up beside Arthur, a helmet covering his long, blond hair but his teeth flashing from beneath the finely shaped iron face mask. "This new Merlin is good."

"He is," Arthur agreed. "And it's all the better for the fact the Saxons don't seem to have any mystics of their own to counteract Qunavo's *glám dicenn* curses. It seems their *volva* really has travelled with Hengist and Bedwyr."

"Aye, bad news for Bedwyr, but good for us. With any luck we can smash these bastards, string Leofdaeg up from a tree somewhere, and then find Bedwyr before the witch harms him."

Arthur listened to his friend but did not comment. They both knew the scenario he described was the ideal outcome of this day's work, but they also knew it was almost impossible. The full moon was tonight, and that meant Thorbjorg would sacrifice Bedwyr once darkness fell upon the land. Could the Britons defeat the army encamped within the old fortress and then locate their captured comrade, all before the moon showed her pale, silver face?

He knew the answer to that, so he pushed aside thoughts of the approaching night and focused again on the task immediately at hand.

"Look, what's the arsehole saying?" Lancelot was pointing up towards Leofdaeg. "Can you hear him? This helmet makes me feel like I'm deaf, it blocks out so much sound."

"Cut your hair," Arthur suggested, smiling at his friend's shocked reaction. "Well, cut it around your ears at least."

"What's Leofdaeg shouting?" Lancelot asked again, pointedly ignoring Arthur's suggestion.

The warlord chuckled but focused his attention on the enemy jarl who was bellowing something at the soldiers beside him on the wall and then, as though those men had not given him the answer he needed, turned his attention into the fortress and shouted to the men hidden within.

"He's demanding someone come forward and counteract the Merlin's spells," Arthur said. "I think. It's hard to follow when he's speaking so fast, and so angrily."

He must have translated the Saxon's words correctly for, a short time later, when Qunavo was finishing off his impressive display, an enemy warrior climbed over the wooden beams and rubble that had been dragged across the ruined gatehouse and walked towards the Merlin. It was not the gait of a confident man, and Arthur shared an amused, expectant look with Lancelot, wondering how things would go but hoping to be entertained no matter what.

Qunavo stopped what he was doing and stood still, not moving a muscle. It was as if he'd become a statue, like one of the exquisitely carved Roman ones that might have adorned the streets of Garrianum a hundred years before. The Merlin had not been turned to stone though, and he called out to the Saxon newcomer to say his piece.

The Saxon was, presumably, some kind of spiritual leader. Not on a par with one of the *volur*, not even close, but the best Leofdaeg could call upon at this moment.

Arthur examined the man closely, seeing a portly, sweating figure with a scraggly beard, braided hair, and darting eyes. The warlord almost felt sorry for the Saxon.

"What's that in his hand?" Lancelot asked, lifting his helmet up so he could get a better view. "Is that…a stick?"

"I believe so," said Arthur, squinting at the brown thing in the enemy holy man's hand and shaking his head in wry amusement. "Maybe it's a magic stick."

"I guess it must be. Hopefully Qunavo is ready to defend himself against it."

The sea-wolf, plainly frightened of the situation he found himself in, raised his 'wand' which really was nothing more than a long twig he must have picked up on the way out of the fortress, and waved it around in the air. He called out some words Arthur couldn't understand although the warlord did pick out the names of Woden, Thunor, and Tyr before the man screamed and threw the stick at Qunavo.

It was a poor throw and the stick sailed well wide of the Merlin, much to everyone in Arthur's army's amusement, and Leofdaeg's fury.

"Kill him!" roared the jarl, hitting his hands against the top of the wall and sending a stream of dust tumbling to the ground below. "Kill the old bastard! Show him his gods have no power here. These are our lands now!"

Arthur cursed and started forward to protect the High Druid. This went against battlefield custom – holy men should not be harmed, physically, and the thought of losing a second Merlin to Saxon violence in the space of a few months enraged the warlord. What was wrong with these sea-wolves, by Dis?

The enemy warrior had heard his jarl's command and, although his face betrayed his revulsion at killing a representative of the Britons' gods, he took out a seax and sprinted towards Qunavo.

"Come back here!" Arthur called a warning to the Merlin. "Come back!" The warlord was heavily encumbered by his mail coat, helmet, and weapons and it felt as if he were running through a bog as he tried to reach the druid in time to protect him. Lancelot was also running, but they were too far away to close the gap in time, and Qunavo, well…

Qunavo had not turned to flee from the Saxon. Instead, Arthur watched as the Merlin reached into his cloak and took out a short-bladed knife. Seemingly without any fear or anxiety over the charging foe, Qunavo's arm came back in a languid, practised movement, and then flicked forward.

The polished blade flew like an arrow through the sky, so fast that the Saxon had no time to dodge aside before the point struck him, burying itself deep within his chest. Since the knife was not heavy it did not knock the Saxon backwards, but he did come to a staggering halt, gaping down at the hilt that was protruding from him, and the red stain that was slowly spreading across his tunic. And then, with one final, astonished glance at Qunavo, the Saxon collapsed to his knees, hand reaching up for the missile that had ended his life.

Only then did the Merlin give one last violent gesture towards Leofdaeg and turn to walk back towards Arthur and Lancelot as the Saxons either howled in anguish or stared gloomily out from the walls in silence.

It was never a good omen to come off worst in these pre-battle contests and to see one of their own cut down by the white-bearded old druid had rattled the Saxons who had not been prepared for an army to turn up at their non-existent gates.

"That was nicely done," Lancelot said as he walked past Qunavo to strip the fallen Saxon of his valuables and to retrieve the Merlin's knife.

"Ach, it was nothing," Qunavo replied, his Pictish accent stronger than usual as he returned to the army, face flushed with excitement. "We druids don't spend all our time communing with the gods. We learn how to defend ourselves too."

"Oh, we know that," Arthur laughed, following Qunavo and taking his place back in the centre of the shieldwall. "And with all this out of the way...Are we ready, lads?" he bellowed, looking along the line, and around at the ranks behind before repeating, "Are we ready?"

The Britons were indeed ready, and they followed Arthur as he led them in a charge towards Garrianum, full of confidence now that their gods were far more powerful than the Saxons' and would carry them to victory.

CHAPTER FORTY-NINE

Hengist had not spent a restful night in his tent. He'd been frustrated by the *volva* who seemed to delight in tormenting him by displaying her naked figure before she bedded down for the night without letting him touch her. And then, as he lay there with his throbbing member, wishing he'd brought one of his concubines or slave girls on the journey, the men on guard outside had raised the alarm.

Thoughts of sex had quickly disappeared as the *bretwalda* lifted his sword and charged out into the night to see the ruddy faces of his soldiers lit by the orange glow of the campfire. When he'd been told that two of their number had disappeared Hengist felt an icy dread grip him. He believed in Thorbjorg's powers, but he was always somewhat fearful of the native gods of Britain. These were their lands, not those of Woden and Thunor, and, no matter how many times the *volva* assured him that her power would protect them all, Hengist remained anxious whenever they performed rituals like the one they were riding to Tir Ambre to carry out.

How could two elite Saxon warriors simply disappear in the dead of night, in the middle of nowhere? What had become of them? Hengist sent four of the remaining men out, exhorting the other three to keep a close eye on their prisoner. Bedwyr watched them from within his tent, expressionless, although Hengist stared at him, wondering if the Briton had something to do with the missing warriors.

Bedwyr's bonds remained firmly in place though, so it was inconceivable that he could have done anything and besides, someone would have noticed him leaving the tent. Wouldn't they? Hengist eyed his own men suspiciously, imagining them falling asleep while on watch, and allowing the captive to do what he would under cover of the woods and the darkness. It was a ludicrous scenario though – Hengist knew these men well. They were his own hearth-warriors, and they would never doze off while guarding Bedwyr. Something else must account for two of them disappearing.

The search party had returned some time later with no news. Thorbjorg was no help, merely shrugging her shoulders disinterestedly when told of the worrying events. Hengist started to wonder if some supernatural agency – some agent of the local gods – had come from Tir Ambre and carried off his men to a terrible doom. The isolation of the camp, and the gloomy, dreich night did nothing to ease his fear and, with no alternative, he'd returned to the tent and lain there awake until dawn's light finally chased away the ghosts in his mind.

When he'd mounted his horse he was in a foul mood, upset by the loss of two good men who'd served him loyally, and by Thorbjorg's callous attitude to it all. She only seemed interested in her own thoughts, sometimes casting hungry glances towards Bedwyr as though she wanted to fuck the Briton, not kill him. Hengist was forced to remind himself that the *volur* were a law unto themselves, moon-touched, selfish, and far more in tune with the gods than with the other people of *Miðgarðr*.

The rain had at least stopped during the night so, as their horses carried them towards the sacred place that Thorbjorg had picked out for their destination the men rode with their hoods down, heads up, eyes searching the undergrowth for danger, every one of them nervous after the previous night's unexplained events.

Hengist consoled himself with the knowledge that Bedwyr was a true enemy nobleman – one of Arthur's closest friends and confidants. His blood would certainly power Thorbjorg's spells and bring the *bretwalda* the victory he craved. This would all be worth the trouble.

As they neared Tir Ambre Hengist looked at the quiet, proud man who rode between him and the *volva*. Bedwyr was not what he expected. Hengist had expected a brash warrior, full of bravado and threats and demands that he be allowed to face the Saxons with a weapon in his hand. In short, he'd expected someone more like Lancelot, the blond swordsman that Jarl Leofdaeg had taken as a thrall. Bedwyr was lean and muscular, and Hengist knew the man could fight, yet he seemed more introspective and certainly quieter and less arrogant than Lancelot. The prisoner had a dignity that was hard not to admire, even though his fear had been evident since the moment he'd been brought to Garrianum and told what his fate was to be.

Hengist could understand why Arthur valued such a man, and that was exactly what would make Bedwyr's death so potent. The reverberations of the ritual would be felt for many months, perhaps decades, in Britain. Hengist was sure of it.

"Lord!"

A shout came from the front of the group and Hengist sat up straighter on his horse, craning his neck to see why he was being called upon.

"Lord! You should come and see this. You too, lady."

"What now?" Hengist muttered bleakly, calling over his shoulder for the riders behind him to keep a close watch on their captive as he led Thorbjorg ahead, to where the road was widening out to reveal the grassy mounds of ancient Tir Ambre.

What he saw made the hair on his arms and the back of his neck rise up and he brought his horse to a slow halt as he took in the ancient, overgrown site that Thorbjorg had promised was filled with magic ripe to be tapped into.

"Someone has been here," he said, turning to the *volva* with an almost accusatory frown.

"I can see that," Thorbjorg shot back irritably and Hengist thought she was doing all she could to appear unruffled but not quite succeeding.

"Who?" the *bretwalda* demanded, still not willing to move forward and perhaps be consumed by Tir Ambre's dark power. "And why?"

"Some local druid, I imagine." Thorbjorg set her horse to a walk and slowly approached the grassy mounds. "This is a holy place, so it's no real shock that the natives still come here at times."

She dismounted and went across to the nearest of the items that had so frightened Hengist and the other warriors. It was the skull of a deer, recently propped up on a stick and facing the road. No one could see its presence as anything other than a bad omen, and possibly even worse. It was there to protect Tir Ambre from being defiled, and suggested that someone may have known of the Saxons' plans.

Added to what had happened the previous night, everyone in the group felt on edge and their eyes darted around the site and searched the foliage surrounding the overgrown mounds that had once been a pair of timber circles.

"What's that?" Hengist asked, poking at a group of twigs on the ground after he worked up the courage to come and join Thorbjorg.

"Don't touch it!" the *volva* shrieked, sending the warlord jumping back in fright. "It's a magical symbol used by the druids to ward off evil."

"What evil? Us?"

Thorbjorg did not answer, instead bending and murmuring some words of power only she could understand before slowly lifting the twigs and snapping them one by one.

"Set up camp," the woman commanded, calling back to the anxious riders. "And search for more of these symbols. If you find any, tell me."

The men did as they were told, some of them setting up the tents for they still had hours to kill before night fell and the full moon arose to herald the start of Thorbjorg's blood ritual.

"You fools would be as well huddling together around the witch and begging your gods for protection," Bedwyr said, surprising everyone for he'd hardly made a sound since their journey started. His features were tight, but he was taking grim satisfaction from seeing his captors thrown into disarray by the presence of a sun-bleached skull and few sticks fashioned into geometric patterns. "Our druids have been here, and their power far exceeds that of your woman."

Thorbjorg hissed something at Bedwyr and clawed at the air between them, but he simply laughed. Hengist was glad to see the man had finally found a backbone and decided to stand up to his enemies, even if it was far too late to do him any good. Still, the *bretwalda* was on edge as it was, without the Briton mocking them as well.

"Shut him up," he called to the two men guarding the prisoner and one stepped forward, punching his fist into Bedwyr's kidney. The Briton fell like a sack of grain to the ground, gasping and staring murderously up at the Saxon who'd hit him. "Keep your mouth shut, boy," Hengist shouted. "Or I'll see you beaten black and blue. Thorbjorg needs your blood flowing through your veins until the time is right to spill it, but you don't need to be awake, or have all your bones intact, while we await the moon."

Silence fell then, as Bedwyr wisely kept his mouth shut and the soldiers went about making the camp comfortable for warlord and *volva*. Two men went out to find a stream, returning a short time later with fresh water, while two others saw to the horses, and another set about cooking a hot meal for them all to enjoy. It would be a long day, no point in making it uncomfortable.

It eventually started to grow dark but, as one of the warriors walked around the perimeter of the camp he called out in alarm and Hengist ran to his side. On the ground was a pile of bloody offal and, within it, they could see the shining silver shape of a spear amulet.

"That belonged to one of the men who disappeared last night," the guard said breathlessly, gripping his spear and staring wide-eyed into the darkening countryside. "How did it get here? It wasn't there earlier – we searched all around the place."

Hengist swallowed. Could someone have sneaked up this close to the camp and deposited this horrific bloody message without anyone noticing? It was possible. But who, and how had they got the spear amulet, sacred to Thunor? It was yet another terrible omen and Hengist cast an anxious glance back at Thorbjorg, wondering again if this whole thing was a bad idea. He called her over and she performed a similar cleansing ritual to the one she'd done with the twigs earlier, moving the offal around and lifting the amulet with a stick before casting it far off, into the bushes.

"Someone is trying to frighten you," she told Hengist and the guard.

"They're making a damn good job of it," hissed the *bretwalda*.

"Calm yourself," she scolded. "If there were enough of them they would simply have attacked us. It must be just the one man, a druid who knows he can't stop us or challenge us openly. Do not fear him, but watch for him. If we can capture him, I will slice him apart by the light of the full moon, making my ceremony doubly powerful!"

Her easy confidence went some way to allaying the warlord's fears and he nodded to the guard. "You heard her. Tell the others to keep an eye out for a druid. Whoever brings him alive to Thorbjorg will have this." He tapped a gold arm ring that was worth a fortune, enough to buy a man a fine new horse and a full new set of wargear. "Now continue with your patrol."

The warrior gave a shallow bow and moved off, shoulders set, back straight, the promise of wealth giving him more courage than any spell the *volva* had cast thus far.

"If this is the work of a single druid the man has some set of balls on him," Hengist noted.

"They have total confidence in their gods," she said with a shrug. "It will be someone full of bravado, like Bellicus of Dun Breatann.

271

I wouldn't be surprised if it actually *is* Bellicus of Dun Breatann out there stalking us."

Hengist shuddered. "Why would he be here, so far from his home?" he demanded, angry at the woman for making him nervous all over again. "Besides, Saksnot should have killed him by now. Whoever is out there skulking in the bushes, it can't be Bellicus. It'll be some old greybeard, angered by our presence here in his sacred circles."

Thorbjorg smirked but did not reply to his pronouncement. "Whoever it is, I must prepare myself for what is to come. I will be in the tent, Hengist, do not disturb me for the next few hours, all right?"

"You will have peace," he vowed. "I will make sure of it."

She walked off, hips swaying, and he felt himself becoming aroused again at the sight of her, and the thought of what she might do for him once the sacrifice was complete. Past experience told him she would want him in her bed just as much as he wanted her the night before. Magic rituals always made her as lustful as a bitch in heat and his lips curled up in a smile as he pictured their lovemaking in his mind.

First though, he had to make sure that whoever was watching them from the darkness did not disturb them any more that night. No old mystic of the Britons would stop Hengist from claiming what was to be his.

With that thought, and images of the naked, writhing *volva* driving him on, he patrolled Tir Ambre, reassuring himself that he and his warriors would easily slaughter the druid if he came near.

At the back of his mind, however, a small voice asked how some old greybeard had managed to murder two of his elite hearth-warriors and dispose of their bodies without leaving any trace other than the spear amulet. That was surely not the work of a decrepit, elderly, holy man.

Could it truly be Bellicus out there, the towering young warrior watching, biding his time, begging the old gods of Britain to help him deal with the invaders?

"Let him come," Hengist spat, speaking out loud, challenging the shadowy trees as he walked around the camp. "Come to me, druid, if you're there, and let me repay you for what you did to my brother!"

CHAPTER FIFTY

As Thorbjorg had promised, it was a full moon that night and it hung high overhead as though watching the Saxons at work. Guards were positioned around the outer circular ditch of Tir Ambre, with orders to gaze out into the night and be prepared for any trouble from a druid or anyone else. In the centre of the ancient site the *volva* stood over Bedwyr who remained bound hand and foot on his knees, ready for his throat to be cut by Thorbjorg's stone knife. There would be nothing spectacular or impressive, visually, about this ceremony – the victim's neck would be sliced open and the blood would gush forth, nourishing the earth in honour of the Saxon god of the moon, Máni. Like the Britons and the Romans, the Germanic people had a wide pantheon of deities, male and female, but for this occasion, Thorbjorg and Hengist would dedicate Bedwyr's sacrifice to the full moon.

Bedwyr had tried to fight off his captors when they started dragging him towards the centre of the circular monument. He'd headbutted one of the guards, damaging the man's cheekbone, and then did his best to bite the ear off another before he'd been punched and kicked into submission and hauled into place before the sternly watching *volva*.

The campfire was extinguished, as Thorbjorg told the men that proud Máni would not want his light to be challenged by the puny flames of the Saxons' fire. This did not go down too well with the on-edge warriors who just wanted to get this whole thing over and done with. How were they supposed to watch out for trouble when they could hardly see the length of their own arm in front of them? they grumbled, but none did so openly.

As the time approached, Thorbjorg grew silent, standing completely still over Bedwyr, hands by her sides, gazing out from glassy eyes at the horizon. She did not flinch when an eldritch shriek split the air from somewhere nearby, but Hengist did.

"What the fuck was that?" he gasped, drawing out his sword and staring into the gloom.

"Be silent!" Thorbjorg hissed.

"But"—

"Silence!" the *volva* repeated.

273

Hengist swallowed and continued to stand with his sword in hand, fretfully watching the benighted land around them, wondering what manner of beast stalked Tir Ambre. Was it simply a single, old druid? Perhaps, but the *bretwalda* had never heard such a shriek emanate from the mouth of a human before. Maybe it was just a fox, they could make some bizarre noises…

Another, similar scream came from a different direction and again Thorbjorg seemed oblivious to it. Hengist knew she'd consumed some magical elixir to help her see the denizens of the other world flitting around them. That thought made him even more anxious and he wondered if those strange, invisible beings were the source of the noises. If so, they were there at his *volva*'s bidding, so he need not fear them, but he couldn't help being terrified. This was not a place for a warrior, and he prayed it would all soon be over.

"What's that smell?"

Hengist heard one of the nearby warriors muttering to a companion and the warlord sniffed the air, frowning. Sure enough, there was a pungent stench floating across Tir Ambre and Hengist retched for it was clearly the smell of rotting flesh. He tried to hold his breath for fear of inhaling the noxious fumes but could only do so for a short time before he was forced to suck in a great lungful of the stuff. Immediately, he felt light-headed and even more frightened than before and he wished he understood what was happening. He desperately wanted to ask Thorbjorg if this was all her doing, a part of her plan for Bedwyr's sacrifice, but he knew she would be furious if he disturbed her meditations again.

One of the guards on the periphery of the camp was sick then. Hengist could hear every retch, and every splatter as vomit landed on the sacred ground of Tir Ambre.

These soldiers were the elite, the very cream of his hearth-warriors, and they would stand in a shieldwall without fear even if they were vastly outnumbered. But there was something utterly terrifying about this place, and this ceremony, that had unmanned them all. Still, that was testament to the power the night held and, should Thorbjorg harness it correctly, Bedwyr's death would be used to bring Hengist all he desired. Britain would be his at last and the mounting terror of this night would soon be forgotten.

There was another high-pitched shriek, quickly followed by a bellow like that of some enraged bull and, since it was accompanied by the sounds of something large charging through the undergrowth just yards away it made more than one of the guards glance at their comrades and quietly question what they were doing with their lives.

"Should we check what that is?" the nearest guard called softly to Hengist. It was quite clear from the tone of his voice that he desperately did not want to check what it was, but would do so if ordered to.

Hengist appreciated the man's bravery, knowing he would never go into that undergrowth himself, even at the point of a spear. "No," he replied. "Whatever it is, as long as it stays away from us it can make as much noise as it wants."

"What do you think it is, lord?" the warrior asked.

"Probably just a stag," Hengist shrugged. "Ignore it unless it attacks us, which is highly unlikely."

"What about that smell?" asked another of the warriors. "It was like death or—"

"How the fuck should I know what it was?" Hengist retorted. "Stop acting like frightened children and do your duty!" He suddenly realised he still had his sword in his hand, betraying his own heightened sense of fear, and angrily thrust it back into its scabbard. Turning to Thorbjorg to command her to get a move on, he noticed she had raised her head to the moon and her arms were held out wide.

Máni was directly over Tir Ambre at last.

It was time to begin the ritual.

* * *

Bellicus stood behind an alder tree, staring out at the overgrown circular monument and catching his breath. The foliage was thick where he'd ran through it, crashing and making as much noise as possible, hoping one or two of the sentries might come to see what was happening. None had, but he took that as a good sign – they were probably too scared to leave their posts. The shrieking and bellowing he'd been doing was putting the Saxons visibly on edge and he smiled nastily, thankful yet again for his years of druid training. Qunavo and his other tutors had shown him how to use his voice in various different ways and he'd put those teachings to good effect this night.

275

The smell had been simple enough to create. The druid had come across the rotting carcass of a young hind trapped in a hunter's snare. The hunter had never collected the animal and, for some reason, perhaps the close proximity to the ancient sacred site, no other animal had come to eat the hind's flesh, not even the crows. Bellicus had taken the carcass and, when it grew dark, lit a small fire downwind of Tir Ambre. The smell produced – sour, acrid, and sickeningly reminiscent of rotten eggs – had drifted across the Saxons with, to the druid, satisfyingly amusing results.

Still, the fact remained that there were seven heavily armed Saxon warriors dotted around Tir Ambre and Thorbjorg was raising her arms, ready to begin her bloody ceremony. Bellicus would have to pray his preparations, and his plan – as insane as it was – would work, or it wouldn't just be Bedwyr's blood nourishing the earth that night.

Darac was positioned nearby, having been brought close to the sacred circle a short time ago. Bellicus knew he was taking a chance bringing the horse there – if Hengist had ordered his men to sweep the area for enemies, or to discover what was making all the noise, Darac would have been found and taken by the Saxons, leaving Bellicus without his means of escape. It was a chance he had to take though, and, thus far, none of the enemy soldiers had come close enough to notice his mount, black and silent within the trees.

They had not seen Cai either, as the big dog padded softly through the night beside the druid, eyeing him curiously when he made the eldritch noises that had terrified the nearby Saxons. He looked like he wanted to join in, and Bellicus thought about it – Cai's howl could certainly add to the atmosphere the druid was trying to create, but then again, they didn't want Hengist's men to know a dog was nearby…

Taking his staff from Darac's saddle, Bellicus ran his fingers across the bronze eagle that topped the polearm. That eagle had cracked the skulls and smashed the teeth of many enemies over the years, and he prayed to Taranis that a few more Saxons would be on the receiving end of its bludgeoning power this night.

"Ready, Cai?" he murmured, dropping to his knees and working on the mastiff who stood perfectly still, despite the strangeness of the situation. "Gods below, I hope this works."

The plan was quite insane, and the druid was well aware of that fact, but he could not see any other way to distract the Saxons, and Thorbjorg would kill Bedwyr any moment now. If the Britons were to survive this, Bellicus had to do something extreme, and do it very soon.

The *volva* had raised her arms over her head and the stone knife could be seen in her hand. Her movements were slow, languid, and told Bellicus that she had imbibed some concoction to allow her to commune with her gods more easily. Good, she would not be a threat and, with any luck, neither would any of the other sea-wolves around Tir Ambre.

Lifting his hand, the druid pointed at Bedwyr and murmured, "Protect him," in the mastiff's ears.

As he always did, the massive hound obeyed his master's command and, oblivious to his part in this insane scheme, ran towards the ancient place of power.

CHAPTER FIFTY-ONE

Hengist watched with great relief as Thorbjorg's knife rose into the sky over the wide-eyed captive. About bloody time, he thought, glad that this was all about to be done with.

"What the fuck is that?"

The scream of unbridled terror came from behind Hengist and he whirled, drawing out his sword again, squinting into the gloom to see what his guards were shouting about. They weren't just shouting either, they were running away in fright, damn them! *I'll have them flayed alive!* the *bretwalda* fumed. *By Máni's balls, I'll have every one of the craven bastards blood-eagled!*

And then Hengist's felt ice in his veins and he gaped at the nightmare vision that was running directly towards him. The rage he'd felt at his own men disappeared in an instant along with all thoughts of fighting this enemy that had been stalking them. He turned away and ran as fast as he could in the opposite direction, shouting at everyone else to do the same. Never before had Hengist felt such terror and he could not even look back over his shoulder to check if the hideous apparition was coming for him. All he wanted to do was run as far away as possible.

It was dark, and he stumbled more than once, whimpering as he forced his way into the undergrowth, not even feeling the brambles that ripped at his flesh and the branches that whipped his face and torso.

The memory of what he'd seen filled his mind's eye, spurring him to move even faster and with complete abandon, never once thinking of the sword in his hand.

How could such a thing, such a beast, come to be? His mind raced almost as fast as his legs as he cannoned off a tree, gasping but not falling as he continued on his way, deeper into the trees, praying that the thing could not follow his trail.

Shuddering, he finally forced himself to turn and look back, terrified that the scuttling monster would be right behind him. How could a spider grow to such a terrific size?

It had been a spider, there was no doubt of it. He'd seen the eight terrible legs moving in unison as the great, hairy body charged towards him, silent, its eyes glinting in the light of the moon.

Hengist had never heard of a spider growing as big as that, not even in the folklore of his homeland.

There came a scream from Tir Ambre and Hengist felt a wave of relief wash over him. He even laughed through his sobs of terror, knowing that the vile beast had attacked Thorbjorg so would not be coming after him.

The thought calmed him and he allowed himself to slow down, taking more care as he pushed through the foliage, the canopy of leaves overhead hiding the pale moonshine so he could not see where he was going or even truly know if he was going in a circle. He stopped, gasping for breath, and placed his back against a tree, gripping his sword tightly as he stared back in the direction the *volva*'s cry had come from.

What was the spider doing to her? He shuddered, imagining the beast biting her, making her struggles even more sluggish before it wrapped her in its silk, ready for consumption. What would the web of such a massive creature look like, he wondered. It must be absolutely monstrous in size, and he pictured animals and even men wandering blindly into the sticky material, becoming stuck fast and watching in horror, paralysed, as the eight-legged nightmare came for them...

As his fear started to dissipate the *bretwalda* wondered what to do next. He had to regroup with his men, find their horses, and escape from this accursed place. No wonder the Britons had allowed Tir Ambre to fall into disuse and become overgrown when it was haunted by a being like that spider.

Slowly, his mind went over what had just happened, showing him again the heavy body of the giant arachnid, and the legs that...bounced up and down? Was he remembering that correctly? At the time, in the darkness, he could have sworn each of those hairy legs had moved in unison, carrying the spider towards him with terrible speed, but now? Now he was not so sure. And then he realised the beast had only had two eyes, illuminated by the moon, its gaping jaws revealing a mouth full of white teeth.

"It was a dog!" he gasped. "Not a spider!" A myriad of powerful emotions surged through him at the realisation he'd been tricked: shame, fear, embarrassment, and anger, terrible, white-hot anger. Roaring a war-cry, the *bretwalda* charged back the way he'd come, hacking at the foliage with his blade, and howling at the moon when it finally appeared through the leaves overhead. "To me!" he bellowed as he came once more to Tir Ambre. "To me!"

* * *

Bellicus did not wait to see what effect Cai's appearance within the enemy camp would have. He knew there was not a moment to waste so he ran at the back of the great hound, staff in hand, Melltgwyn in its scabbard as a deadly backup should it be needed.

The first Saxon to spot Cai's approach reacted in an even more extreme fashion than Bellicus could have hoped, screaming in sheer terror and running away while calling on his comrades to do the same.

The druid had spent some time during the morning collecting twigs, long grass, and moss, and fashioning it all into six thick, bent 'legs' that he tied onto Cai's back. It all looked absolutely ridiculous in the daylight but quite convincing when night fell and everything in the world took on a more sinister hue. Bellicus wondered how he would react if he was one of the Saxons and he saw that monstrous apparition racing towards him from the undergrowth. There was something truly chilling about spiders that could terrify even the hardiest of warriors, something otherworldly about them, so it didn't really surprise Bellicus that the enemy soldiers were scattering into the night. The druid had once heard one of his mentors, Qunavo perhaps, suggesting that spiders were genuinely not from this world, but had come from some other realm, some other reality, and that was why humans found them so unsettling. Whether that was true or not Bellicus doubted he'd ever know, but when even a small spider could send a man scurrying off in fear, it was no wonder that one as huge as Cai had cleared a path directly through Tir Ambre to Bedwyr.

The mastiff had done as he was told to the letter, running straight for the prisoner, and the knife-wielding witch that stood over him in something of a daze. She did not even cry out when Cai slammed into her, throwing her backwards, stone blade flying into the darkness. She did, however, let out a tortured cry when the dog's teeth fastened on her wrist which she'd instinctively thrown up to protect her face and neck.

"By Dis, what is that?" Bedwyr demanded when Bellicus reached him and dropped his staff, taking out his own knife and hastily sawing through the ropes that bound the captive's forearms and ankles.

"My dog," replied the druid, letting out a whistle as he dragged the stunned Briton to his feet. "Can you stand?"

"I think so," Bedwyr gasped, then collapsed into the druid when he let him go. "Or maybe not."

"Try to get the feeling back in your arms and legs, my horse is coming." Bellicus turned, staff in hand once more, and stared around at the overgrown moonlit monument for returning enemies. None had come back yet but Darac was thundering towards them, a dark shadow, sleek and as fast as the wind.

"You should have put some extra legs on the horse too," Bedwyr laughed, although it came out more as a sob, betraying his terror at almost having his throat torn open in the name of Máni.

Bellicus didn't answer for Darac was already there. He helped Bedwyr onto the horse's back, roughly shoving the frightened man into the saddle before he turned and shouted to Cai. The dog appeared beside him almost instantly, eyes blazing with battle fever, and the druid used his knife to cut away the extra 'legs'.

He turned, intending to deal with Thorbjorg, but he couldn't see her in the darkness and there was no time to search. He took a deep breath, set his feet, and jumped up behind Bedwyr. It was a heavy load for the horse, but Darac was a thoroughbred and barely seemed to register the extra weight on his back.

"Ride," Bellicus commanded, and the big black exploded into motion, quickly picking up speed and galloping towards the road.

From the undergrowth just beside them Hengist appeared, sword flashing in the moonlight as he cried out, "To me! To me!" and then Darac was past, and Cai was at their side, and they were racing along the road for their very lives.

281

CHAPTER FIFTY-TWO

Bedwyr could not stop laughing as they galloped along the road. He was amazed to still be alive having come so close to dying. And to be saved by Bellicus in such a fashion? The tales that would be told about this night would make the towering druid a legend, as if he wasn't already fast approaching that status!

"Good boy, Cai!" the rescued warrior called over the pounding of hooves and wind rushing past. "Who would have thought you could be even more frightening than you already were?"

"I'm really not sure where we should go," Bellicus said into Bedwyr's ear, so the words weren't lost in the speed of their flight. "I was going home to Alt Clota when I saw you, but you'll be wanting to return to Arthur I expect."

"Aye, he'll be thinking me dead. I can't wait to see his face when I turn up with you, alive and mostly unhurt."

Darac carried them to the main road and, without any firm idea of where they should ride to, they turned right, heading southeast, simply because, in the moonlight, the road in that direction looked more winding and overgrown so would hide their passage better. For another two or three miles they raced, making the most of the level ground, and then Bedwyr guided the horse into the trees that ran alongside the road. When they were completely hidden from the view of any who might come hunting them, they dismounted and grasped forearms in greeting, both men grinning widely.

"Thank you, my fine big lad," Bedwyr said, bending to hug Cai ecstatically. The dog licked his ear once then stood stoically, allowing the man to make a fuss of him. At last, Bedwyr stood up and did almost the same thing to Darac, although the horse was not quite so accommodating. Clearly Bedwyr was overcome with joy to have survived Thorbjorg's murderous plan.

"What now though?" Bellicus asked, casting anxious glances back towards the main road. "Do we continue along the road and make our way to Arthur's camp? Is it even near here? Do you know the way? Or would we be better just hiding right here until Hengist and his lackeys piss off back to Garrianum and the road is safe again?"

Bedwyr shook his head, finally getting over his excitement and, from the look on his face, truly understanding just how fortunate he was, and the fate Bellicus had saved him from. "I know where Arthur's camp was a few days ago, but he had been talking about moving east. You know how it is, Bel. We go where the enemy is."

"Do you know these lands we're in just now?"

Bedwyr thought about that and then shook his head. "No. I'm not even really sure where we are. I was in something of a stupor for much of the journey."

"So there might be Saxon raiding parties nearby," Bellicus murmured, still eyeing the trees expectantly, fearing discovery by Hengist's followers. "Meaning the longer we stay here the more time the Saxons have to spread the word about what we've done, and to mobilise into hunting parties for us. If they bring dogs they'll easily pick up our scent."

"You're right," Bedwyr agreed. "We should move on. Take the first fork in the road that leads southeast, and follow that, hopefully, towards Arthur."

Darac and Cai were rested after their run from Tir Ambre so, although Bellicus felt guilty about making the horse carry both him and Bedwyr again, there really was no alternative. They would make much better time that way and, gods willing, would find a settlement as they travelled where they could buy a decent mount for Bedwyr.

It was not a pleasant experience, forging their way back through the trees in the darkness and rejoining the road. No one was in sight, but that didn't count for much – there could be a dozen enemy soldiers just a few paces away and they wouldn't be noticed if they kept to the shadows. There were no obvious sounds of nearby pursuit though, so the travellers headed east, praying that the manner, and speed, of their escape had left Hengist's warband too confused to quickly come after them.

They moved at a steady pace, not pushing Darac too hard, conserving his energy in case they were forced into another desperate gallop for freedom. Bellicus watched the sky, picking out the stars as they went, continually making sure the road was carrying them in the right direction and not back towards Tir Ambre. Small trails led off in all directions, but they ignored those paths, only heading to the south when a wider track presented itself to them. Such a road must lead to a settlement the men agreed, both uncomfortably aware of how vulnerable they were while sharing a single mount.

Once, the sound of shouting came to them across an open field and they gazed northwards, fearing they would see riders charging towards them, helmets and spearpoints glittering malevolently in the dim light. No one was visible though, for a row of trees obscured whoever was shouting and Bellicus, was seated at the front now, urged Darac to move faster.

Eventually, they came to a village that was little more than a collection of a dozen or so houses and workshops. No lights were visible but, as the travellers grew nearer they saw a man walking towards a barn. Bellicus hailed him and, after reassuring the farmer that they were not there to murder him, the druid handed over a silver ring in return for a small but young-ish mare, the tack needed to ride her, and some food for both horses. The farmer was pleased for he was getting the best of the deal by far, but Bedwyr was also greatly relieved to have a mount of his own and he profusely thanked Bellicus for the gift.

"Gift?" barked the druid as they returned to the road and continued on. "What d'ye mean 'gift'? You can pay me back once we find Arthur!"

"Taranis knows when that'll be," Bedwyr said. His earlier happiness at being rescued had worn off now and he continually glanced backwards. "Oh, by the way, do you have a weapon I can borrow?"

Bellicus handed him his knife in its sheath and smiled. "The gods will guide us to Arthur's camp, just wait and see. All will be well."

Bedwyr looked sceptically at him but then, turning back to the road, he cursed and took out the knife that he'd only just attached to his belt. "Look, Bel, they've found us!"

The druid had spotted the riders ahead too and he gaped at them in dismay. How could Hengist's warband have got in front of them? Did they know some shortcut?

"There's no point in running," he said, drawing Melltgwyn and looking down almost apologetically at Cai. "We're all exhausted, especially Darac and Cai. They've been on the road for days now. Are you fit to fight?"

Bedwyr's lip curled in a snarl and he gripped the knife firmly. "Aye, I can fight," he said. "And I'll welcome the chance to kill some of those bastards. They won't take me alive this time."

Bellicus nodded and they continued to trot along the road towards the enemy warband who had noticed them now and formed a line to block the way.

"Looks like there's only four of them," Bedwyr noted. "They must have split up. We can take four of them, eh?" He was grinning fiercely, no trace of his earlier fear evident now that he had a purpose, and a good weapon to defend himself.

"Aye, easy," Bellicus agreed, although he did not feel particularly confident, exhausted as they all were. He did not fear death, but he did feel sorry for Darac and Cai and hoped those two would escape, or at least not suffer ill treatment at the hands of the sea-wolves once the battle was over.

They drew near to the line of enemy warriors, seeing steely resolve in the armoured men's faces, and weapons readied in their hands.

"Bedwyr?"

Bellicus started, peering ahead at the rider who'd spoken in their own language, without a hint of a Germanic accent.

"Bedwyr, is that you?" the warrior repeated.

"Aye, who's that?"

"Brochmail! We come from Arthur, searching for you!"

"Brochmail! Gods, it's good to see you!"

It was obvious to Bellicus that Bedwyr recognised the man and it was also obvious that, with six of them now, and Cai of course, Hengist would be much less likely to attack them even if he managed to track them.

"Where is Arthur?" the druid asked.

"Attacking Garrianum," Brochmail told him. "We all feared Bedwyr would be dead, so Arthur decided to take the fight to Hengist and sent out a few parties like ours just in case we could find Bedwyr. It's a miracle to see you here. And you too, druid. What brings you to these lands?"

"We can talk on the way to Garrianum," Bellicus said. "Is it far?"

"No, if we cross the river rather than going all the way around we can be there in an hour or so."

"Then let's move," the druid said. "Gods willing, we'll get there before the battle has started. We've already pissed off Hengist tonight, Bedwyr, let's give him something else to cry into his mead about!"

* * *

"They'll have more men coming to join them, you know."

Leofdaeg chewed a piece of beef and looked angrily at Sigarr. "What of it?" he demanded.

"I'm just saying," the little jarl replied, palms held up, tone placating. "We are already struggling to keep them out. If they bring reinforcements, Garrianum may fall. Hengist won't be happy."

Leofdaeg masticated the beef with even more vigour, his expression dark as he glared at Sigarr. "What's your point, you little weasel?"

"We should send for aid ourselves," Sigarr replied, doing his best to keep his temper. He did not want to anger Leofdaeg more than necessary.

The temporary commander of Garrianum thought about the suggestion and did not seem to like the idea. Sigarr knew why: calling on other jarls to bring their warbands to the fortress might keep out the Britons, but it would mean even more rivals to Leofdaeg's position. It rankled him enough having Sigarr, Hengist's own cousin, vying with him for Horsa's empty place without bringing more arrogant, entitled, and aggressive Saxon chiefs there. If one was to perform particularly well Hengist might promote them over Leofdaeg.

"If we don't find more men from somewhere I fear Garrianum will fall," Sigarr said, raising his voice so the guards outside the room could hear him. Hengist should know that he'd tried to guide Leofdaeg – if the fortress was taken by Arthur Sigarr did not want any part of the blame.

Leofdaeg frowned, but he was not a stupid man and his eyes narrowed. "I see what you're doing," he growled. "But Hengist will never make you Horsa's replacement. You are too weak."

Sigarr swallowed, face flushing at the insult. He knew better than to challenge Leofdaeg at that moment however, for there was no one to break up a fight and, if that happened, Sigarr would not win. Even with one good arm, Leofdaeg was more of a warrior than he was.

"I am not even thinking of who replaces Horsa," he replied. "I just don't want Arthur to take Garrianum. I believe we must gather more men to help us, and I recommend you do so."

Leofdaeg chewed his lip, clearly torn. Eventually, he must have realised it would be far better for his reputation if he could keep control of the fortress, even if it meant sharing the glory with other jarls.

"Fine," he said. "I will send out a ship to take word to the nearest Saxon settlements along the coast."

"I can do it."

Leofdaeg's expression slowly changed, his frown becoming a broad, mocking grin. "So that's it," he murmured. "You want an excuse to run away from battle."

Sigarr opened his mouth to protest but realised it would be futile. Leofdaeg believed him a coward and a weakling – denying it would not make the man change his opinion. So he held his tongue and silently returned his rival's stare.

"Well, considering you share some of the same blood as Horsa and Hengist, it never ceases to amaze me just what a craven little shit you are," Leofdaeg said, standing up and placing his hands on his hips while shaking his head judgementally at the smaller man. "Well, someone has to go and bring us reinforcements and I would rather not lose a good soldier – Woden knows, we need as many as we can get at the moment. So it makes sense for you to go, since you're no use in a fight anyway."

Sigarr ignored the slurs, doing his best not to smile. Leofdaeg was wrong – he was not a coward, but he also had no intention of dying there in Garrianum if Arthur's army was to gain the upper hand and breach the walls.

"You can think what you like of me," he said with a shrug. "But I will do what I can to bring reinforcements here. As much as I dislike you, I would not see the fortress fall, even if it would mean an end to your influence with Hengist."

Leofdaeg's lip curled but he appeared too disgusted to even insult Sigarr any more. "Go, then," he growled. "Take your ship, and your crew, and find us more men to man the walls." He held up a warning finger. "Make sure you tell them that they will be well rewarded for their efforts, but also make it clear to them that I am in charge, and they will follow my orders."

Sigarr allowed himself to smile then. "Of course, my lord. You can count on me."

Leofdaeg's only reply was a grunt and Sigarr even gave a shallow bow before turning and stalking from the room.

He had used his cunning to engineer the ideal situation for himself, he thought as he hurried out of the stone building and made his way towards the shore where his ship lay waiting. If Garrianum did not fall to Arthur, Sigarr would be in no worse a position than he was just now. But if it *did* fall, he would not be there to feel the deadly bite of the Britons' blades.

He saw his captain, Cretta, lounging with the rest of his warband, cleaning and sharpening their weapons. "Lads, follow me to the ship! We have a mission! We've to bring our kinfolk from the nearest settlements along the coast."

Primed for action as they were with the ever-present threat of impending battle, the men were quickly on their feet and following the jarl to the shore, eager to do their bit for the war effort.

Let Leofdaeg revel in his command of Garrianum, Sigarr thought as his ship floated away from the besieged fortress. *Let him deal with Arthur. I will take my time bringing reinforcements and, gods willing, by the time we return, Leofdaeg will no longer be quite so smug!*

CHAPTER FIFTY-THREE

"Damn them!" Lancelot cried, slamming his fist on the table in front of him. "The bastards are taking everything we can throw at them, and dishing it out in return!"

The battle for Garrianum was not over as quickly as Arthur had hoped. Lancelot was the only Briton who'd been inside the old Roman fort in recent years and he'd been far too busy fighting Saxons back then to notice the layout of the place. Besides, even if he'd made an accurate mental map, there was no way to know how things had changed in the intervening period. Had Hengist added new timber walls? Choke points? Gates? Ditches? It did not seem likely to Arthur or his advisors given the ruined state of the main gatehouse, but, when the fighting started and the Britons had eventually managed to force their way inside it soon became clear that the Saxons had indeed made obstacles for attackers to deal with should they get through the damaged walls. Probably those obstacles had only been laid out within the past day, but they were quite effective in holding up the Britons and, eventually, forcing Arthur to call the retreat or face losing too many of his men.

Leofdaeg did not take part in the fighting personally, instead standing atop the walls, moving around them and directing his forces with the benefit of the higher vantage point.

"Come down and fight like a true warrior, you useless Saxon prick!" Lancelot had shouted at the jarl. The taunts did nothing to persuade Leofdaeg to stand against him though, and it was hardly surprising. Even when he'd had full use of both his arms, the Saxon had not been a match for Lancelot one-on-one. Not many of the sea-wolves, if any, were.

So the Britons used their missiles as best they could, casting javelins across the rubble barring their way, loosing arrows and slingshot at the defenders on the walls who did the same in return and, by the time the sun went down things stood much as they had before the battle started, only with fewer men in both armies.

The standoff suited Leofdaeg far more than it did Arthur. While the jarl might care little for the lives of the Saxons within the walls – few of them were his own sworn followers after all – Arthur hated losing even a single man, blaming himself for not leading them well enough to overcome the enemy defences. On top of this, the sea-wolves would undoubtedly have sent boats along the coast to call on reinforcements, and it would not be very long before they turned up and made it impossible for the Britons to capture the fortress. If there were enough Saxons camped nearby, and they joined Leofdaeg's army, there was even a danger that Arthur's forces would be wiped out completely, so finely balanced was the situation.

"We should leave here now," Kay counselled as dawn began to break and the noblemen came together in Arthur's command tent to discuss their plans for the day.

"He's right," another captain agreed sorrowfully. "We might force our way past the bastards' defences, but the cost would be too high in my opinion. The Saxons' morale is high, and they know they just have to hold out until reinforcements turn up to bolster them."

"While our morale is at rock bottom," added Kay, "and our men fear another day of throwing themselves against piles of wood and other detritus while the sea-wolves pick them off from high up on the walls with missiles."

"But we're so close to taking the place!" Lancelot argued, bowing his head tiredly and running a hand through his long hair. He looked like he'd barely slept, his eyes bloodshot, features drawn and pale, but clearly desperate to take the fight to their hated enemies again. "We might never have another chance like this."

"The whoresons will just come back another time, with more men, exactly like they did when we defeated them here before."

Lancelot rounded on the man who'd spoke, enraged. "So we should just let them do as they please, Aesibuas? Give in? Well, on you go then. You go out there and surrender to them, since they're unstoppable."

"Enough!" Arthur shouted. "We're here to fight Saxons, not each other. Any man who doesn't have the stomach for battle is welcome to leave, and take their warbands with them. I have been charged with keeping our enemies at bay, however, and I'll not be giving in without a fight, whether that be here and now, or days elsewhere in the future." He rested his eyes on Aesibuas, who was plainly upset at the suggestion he was a coward but not foolish enough to challenge Lancelot.

"This is not about having the stomach for a fight," Kay broke in, keeping his voice low, reasonable. "It's whether the cost of maintaining the siege, of attacking those walls again, is worth it, or whether we retreat and continue as we have been. Aesibuas is right – we beat the sea-wolves here before, but the bastards just come back with new ships, new jarls, new warriors eager to plunder our lands…Take a look at our men. They've had enough."

"We must continue," Lancelot snapped, shaking his head irritably. "That's the only way we'll win the war – persistence and determination. We have them at our mercy, cooped up behind those crumbling walls. True, we beat them here before, but they cannot have an unlimited supply of soldiers willing to come here, especially if those new recruits know their predecessors were soundly defeated not once, but twice."

From outside, the sound of Leofdaeg's voice carried to the Britons' camp, high and filled with amusement. "Where are you, Arthur? We're waiting here to greet your men again now that the sun has come up."

Lancelot stormed out into the morning, staring up at the jarl who jeered back from the safety of the fortress's wall.

"Come on, slave," Leofdaeg called to him. "Your army must have used up all your arrows and javelins yesterday. You left them all in here for us. For that, I thank you. Now when are you coming to reclaim them?" He hefted a short spear and shook it jauntily at Lancelot. "I've saved this one especially for you, slave. I even carved your name in the shaft, look can you see the runes there? No, it's probably too far away, but never mind, you'll get to see it up close soon enough, you preening peacock, when it's sticking out of your chest!"

The Saxons roared with laughter at their temporary commander's bravado, evidently fully accepting him as Horsa's successor and Hengist's new second-in-command.

Arthur followed his friend into the sunshine, feeling a hint of autumn chill in the air although it was a clear morning. They had gone amongst the army the night before and seen for themselves that the men were bitterly disappointed not to have captured Garrianum in that first day's fighting. Looking at the front rank of the shieldwall that had formed up while the captains were meeting with Arthur in his tent, he could see the morale had not improved any since the previous evening. Fighting Saxons was always a daunting task, but it was made even worse when the enemy had walls to protect them.

"Qunavo," he said to the Merlin who had come to stand beside him. "Can't you do something? Lift our men somehow? Give them back the belief they had when the fighting first started and they were filled with battle-fury? Kay's right – our army despairs of this stalemate."

The previous Merlin had been a stirring, inspirational figure who would surely have roused the beleaguered army without prompting, but Qunavo was a different man, a different druid, and his ways were not those of the departed Nemias, unfortunately. Perhaps, in time, Qunavo would grow into his new role, but that was not much comfort on this cool morning when the very future of Britain might well be at stake.

The Merlin was looking up to the sky, and he spun slowly around then, taking in everything. Arthur had no idea what the druid was doing but, when he'd finished his rotation, Qunavo nodded firmly to himself and said, "Summon the men from the tent, Arthur." So saying, he strode forward, staring up at Leofdaeg as Arthur called on Aesibuas and the other noblemen to come out and listen.

What would the Merlin do? What magic might he bring to bear that would give the Britons courage and resolve to once again assault Garrianum's walls?

"Britons!" Qunavo called, not shouting, yet making his voice carry effortless across the waiting ranks of Arthur's army. "You fought bravely yesterday, yet the Saxons remain within the walls of Garrianum."

This brought hoots of laughter from the enemy warriors who could understand Qunavo, followed by even more derisive jeers when they passed the word onto the rest of the sea-wolves. Arthur, like Lancelot and the rest of the Britons, watched the Merlin in confusion, wondering what he was doing.

"Should we attack them again?" the old druid called out, spreading his arms wide and keeping his back firmly to the fortress. "Can our gods bring us victory this day, or shall our enemies rout us?"

"This isn't what I had in mind when I asked you to do something," Arthur murmured, pitching his voice low so only Qunavo and those standing very close to them could hear.

The Merlin did not reply to the comment, instead lifting his arms even higher and raising his eyes towards the sun, closing the lids against the brightness as he spoke again. "Belenus, god of the sun, shine your light upon us, and guide us in our path this day. Should we attack these walls, or should we leave to fight again another day? Send us a sign, Belenus, sun god, Shining One!"

Everyone, even the Saxons, held their breaths for a long moment, gazing up at the sky in fear or expectation, wondering what Qunavo's exhortation might bring down upon them.

Arthur watched, a tight feeling in the pit of his stomach that only grew more pronounced the longer he stared at the lightening morning sky and nothing obvious happened.

Just as Leofdaeg opened his mouth to call out mockingly again, a shout went up from the rear ranks of Arthur's army. That shout was taken up by others, slowly rippling back towards the front row of warriors in the shieldwall and Arthur shared a questioning glance with Lancelot who was just as baffled as the warlord.

"What's happening?" Arthur asked Qunavo but received only a small smile in reply.

"By the gods, can it be?" Lancelot demanded in hushed, awed tones.

Arthur looked at him, seeing his friend's face light up in disbelief and joy, and then the warlord saw what had created such a sensation amongst his army.

"Bedwyr!"

Riding slowly past the far, northern end of the shieldwall came Bedwyr mounted on a horse. His face was bruised, but other than that he seemed healthy and in fine spirits as, eyes shining, he raised his fist and laughed along with the men in the ranks who were cheering his unexpected return.

Arthur couldn't believe what he was seeing. He had resigned himself to the fact that his friend must have been brutally murdered the previous night, with Thorbjorg spilling his blood in the name of her vile gods. Yet here was Bedwyr, smiling at him as he rode along the front of the triumphant shieldwall, alive and well!

Lancelot was laughing and Arthur realised he was too, then all three men were grasping forearms as Bedwyr dismounted and the young warlord dragged his miraculously returned friend into a bearhug as the entire army erupted in cheers.

"By Belenus," Arthur shouted with tears of relief in his eyes as he glanced back at Qunavo who was watching still with that small, satisfied smile. "You asked for a sign, and we have it! How did you know Bedwyr was coming?"

"The gods are not finished yet," replied Qunavo enigmatically, tilting his head to the north. He had not answered Arthur's question although, in truth, the Merlin seemed as amazed as anyone at what was happening.

Arthur craned his neck, seeing another rider coming along the flank of his shieldwall, this man much bigger than Bedwyr, hood thrown up so the warlord couldn't see his face. Then the horse rounded the front rank, and a great mastiff came into view, and Arthur was laughing again in astonishment as he recognised the newcomer.

"Bellicus! Bellicus! Bellicus!" The cry was started by Lancelot but within moments it had been taken up by every warrior in the army of Britons, including Arthur who gazed in wonder from Bellicus to Qunavo, wondering just how the pair had orchestrated this incredible moment.

"I asked for a sign!" the Merlin roared, addressing the army once their chant had faded away. "Belenus has given us a sign. Bedwyr is returned, unharmed, with Hengist's blood sacrifice thwarted. And come to join us in our fight against the Saxon invaders, Bellicus of Dun Breatann!"

He had not finished speaking but he gave up trying to be heard as the chants of "Bellicus!" were taken up again, the towering druid now dismounted and embracing Arthur, Lancelot and other warriors he'd fought alongside in the past. He was well known amongst the ranks, and well loved, and Arthur could see his men had been lifted by his, and Bedwyr's, appearance. Although the warlord was desperate to understand how they'd come to be there at that moment, now was not the time for explanations. They must make the most of the excitement, and the gods-given confidence flowing through everyone in Arthur's army.

"Form up men!" he cried once he could be heard. "Shields and spears at the ready! Today, with Bedwyr and Bellicus by our side, we take Garrianum back from the Saxon dogs! Are you with me?"

The reply was immediate, almost deafening, and Leofdaeg's face was pale and filled with fear as the besieging army moved towards the fortress, voices and weapons raised in righteous battle-fury.

CHAPTER FIFTY-FOUR

"Will you fight alongside us, Bel?"

The druid glanced down at Arthur, smiling at the warlord's shining eyes and flushed cheeks, the exact opposite of the expression that Leofdaeg wore atop Garrianum's gatehouse.

"I will fight, hopefully, but not here."

"Not here?" Lancelot asked, disappointment clear on his face. "Then where? This is where the battle is!"

"And your men are champing at the bit to get to it," Bellicus nodded, gesturing at the army marching behind them. "But Hengist and Thorbjorg are out there somewhere. They will be returning here soon, I'm sure, and I'd like to greet them when they turn up."

There was no time to hear the full story from the druid, but Bedwyr spoke up too, adding his voice to the plan. "Give us ten fresh men, Arthur," he begged. "And we'll make sure Hengist is never a danger to any of our people again."

"Go, then," said the warlord. "Choose your ten, and Taranis guide your spears, my friends. But when this is all done, I want to know the whole story behind this!"

"That I promise," Bellicus agreed. "But first we have to defeat our enemies."

The druid and Bedwyr made their way quickly back around the army, picking out ten good men as they went and commanding them to follow. Behind them, Arthur could be heard shouting, "Charge!" along with Qunavo's powerful voice calling on the gods to protect the Britons as the warriors moved forward and the fight for Garrianum began once more.

"You think we have a chance of ambushing Hengist?" Bedwyr asked as they rode, Cai ambling along at their side looking very pleased after being made a fuss of by the men in Arthur's ranks who'd grabbed the opportunity to pet the dog and take their mind off the coming battle for a moment.

"He only went to Tir Ambre to sacrifice you," said Bellicus. "That plan failed, so he will surely return here straight away. You heard them talking more than I did – don't you think the *bretwalda* and his men wanted nothing more than to come back to Garrianum as quickly as possible?"

"That's true," Bedwyr conceded. "They did not enjoy the journey, especially after you picked off two of their friends."

"They'll be here soon, I'm sure of it," growled the druid, grimly eyeing the surrounding lands, searching for signs of approaching horsemen. "And we'll meet them on the road and make a sacrifice of *them*, for the gods of Britain!"

As he spoke, he wondered yet again where Saksnot had disappeared to. Had the young warrior somehow made it back to Garrianum? Was he within the walls right now, standing beside the rest of the sea-wolves as they sought to keep Arthur's rampant troops from capturing the place? Or had he succumbed to his many injuries somewhere miles away from there? Bellicus feared he would never know and that thought irritated him greatly. Well, maybe one day he would find out but, for now, he had other matters to focus on.

They were approaching the Great Estuary which was fed by the Rivers Gerne, Bure, and Vividin and led directly out to the sea on the east. Bellicus and his companions had come this way earlier, paying some ferrymen to take them and their horses across the water at the narrowest point. Bellicus guessed ferrymen had always plied their trade here, back to Roman times and beyond, carrying men, animals, and goods to and from the nearby settlements and the forts along the coast. Nowadays, with the arrival of the Saxons, the ferrymen would make a good living doing the same as they'd always done, and, if the sea-wolves had any sense, they'd let the locals continue to work in peace for it benefited everyone. The druid had heard of ingenious Roman ferry boats that were actually powered by a team of oxen – he wished he could see something as impressive as that, but such technology had departed long ago with the legions.

There was also nowhere near enough boats to carry an army like Arthur's across, hence the long march they'd been forced to make around to the south, but there were enough to take Bellicus's small warband over the estuary.

"What do you think, Bel? Should we wait here on this side of the water? Or cross and set up an ambush there?"

The druid looked around and shook his head. "There's nowhere to really hide here. And besides, Hengist will see, or at least hear, the battle going on in Garrianum if he reaches this shore, and probably turn back until he finds out what's happening."

"Then we cross over. Look, that's handy, there's two boats coming this way now, they must have noticed us waiting."

Bellicus squinted, trying to see through the smirr of rain that had started a short time ago. He could not see the far shore, so how did ferrymen know to come and pick them up? The truth hit him as the pair of boats drew closer.

"That's Hengist!" he cried. "Hide, before they see us!"

The men scrambled, trying to find bushes big enough to conceal them and their mounts from view but it was too late.

"They've spotted us," Bedwyr groaned. "And probably heard the sounds of battle. Look."

All eyes were on the water as the boats slowly turned in a semicircle and headed back towards the opposite shore.

"By Dis, where are the ferryboats on this side of the estuary?" Bellicus cursed. "If there were any here we could give chase!"

But there were none, and there was nothing the Britons could do but stand and watch as Hengist and his company headed safely back to dry land; so close yet totally unreachable.

"Damn it," Bedwyr shouted, visibly distraught. He had so wanted to pay the Saxons back for what they'd planned to do to him but, with no chance of that happening now, he jumped back up onto his horse and addressed the others. "We might not be able to kill the *bretwalda* and his witch, but the battle still rages at the fort. Come on, lads, let's join Arthur, and help him make a great slaughter of sea-wolves!"

CHAPTER FIFTY-FIVE

Domangart mac Nissi had brought thirty of his strongest, most loyal warriors from Dunadd, making their way in currachs to the south until they were able to join the River Clota and paddle along towards Dun Breatann.

"By Dagda," said the would-be High King, forgetting he was a Christian now as he caught sight of the towering rock approaching. It was a fine, sunny day, with a soft breeze from the west, and Dun Breatann seemed almost ethereal as he took in its contours and the green lands that rolled away behind it. "Look how high it is. No wonder it's never been conquered."

"We will do it," his son Carvorst vowed, jaw set, hand resting on the head of the axe that was tucked into his belt. "And when the Damnonii army returns from fighting Cunneda they'll find us asleep in their own beds, our men manning their walls and gates."

Domangart pictured that as he gazed at the fortress, imagining himself on top of the vast rock, looking out over the river and the lands that would be his. Dalriadans would flock to join him there, helping him defend the place, and bolstering his position until he was strong enough to bring the rest of Alt Clota under his control. He laughed softly, impressed by the beauty of the fields and hills they were passing, knowing it would all be his soon.

It was almost impossible to believe. Domangart had been born to low status parents. It had been his own ferocity and recklessness in battle that had caught the eye of one warlord after another back home in Hibernia, allowing him to rise in rank and status and wealth until he took charge of his own warband. Ambition and determination had led him cross the water to seek fortune and fame in the lands around Dunadd and now he would reap the rewards his self-belief deserved. With his eldest son beside him, and his others remaining behind to protect Dunadd, nothing could stop him – Christ was with them after all. And hopefully Dagda too, he thought, still unable to completely shake off the pagan beliefs he'd held until fairly recently.

"This was a bold plan," said Carvorst, nodding his head enthusiastically as he too admired the sights of Alt Clota on both sides of the river.

"Bold," Domangart chuckled. "It is that. Foolish, some might say."

"No, Father, we've had reports confirming what the merchant told us: the Damnonii army is away in the east and only a few soldiers remain to guard Dun Breatann. Our plan is not foolish, it is bold, and it is genius!"

Domangart agreed with his son and the pair sat, near-mirror images of one another in looks and bearing, as the currach carried them ever nearer to their destination.

A mile or so before they reached the fortress the Dalriadan king raised his arm and pointed to the shore, portside. As agreed beforehand, the other currachs broke off, rowing for land where they would wait while Domangart's vessel scouted ahead.

"May God go with you," the warriors in the other currachs called, and the king grinned and waved in reply, beaming in the sunshine that reflected from the rippling blue waters. They were all eager to take the fortress, just as Domangart was, foreseeing a night of legendary drinking and debauchery as they celebrated a glorious victory over the depleted garrison of Dun Breatann.

"It's busy here," Carvorst noted, gesturing at the ships that were docked at the port beside the fortress.

"Aye, they do much trading, the Damnonii," Domangart agreed. "Vast wealth flows in and out of Dun Breatann."

"Should we disembark?"

The king examined the men and women he could see around the port. They did not look a threat – there were even children playing in the water and along the pebbled beach.

"Aye, I don't think anyone will attack us."

"Let them try," Carvorst growled, and his father smiled, seeing so much of his own nature in the young man. There was bravery there, although, the king had to admit, it did not take much courage to face up to the people on the port ahead for there did not seem to be a warrior amongst them.

The currach was guided in to shore, easily sliding up onto the beach with the tide, and Domangart spoke to the other three men who'd accompanied him and his son. "Wait here, lads," he commanded. "If we all go wandering about we'll attract attention, and things will go much easier if the gates aren't locked. I'd rather walk into my new home, than use the ropes we brought to climb the face of the rock."

"Aye," Carvorst agreed. "We don't even know if it's possible to climb into the place."

"Let's hope we don't need to find out. From what we've seen so far though, it really does look like there's no army within the fortress."

Domangart pulled his cloak about him, concealing his sword. Carvorst saw him doing so and followed suit, the pair walking nonchalantly towards some stalls that were setup a short way from the river. Merchants and traders hawked their wares as the Dalriadans approached, trying to sell them food, drink, spices, furs, bolts of cloth, and other, more exotic items. Carvorst stared at it all with wonder and even Domangart, who had travelled more extensively than his son, felt his pulse quicken as he thought of the riches to be made by taxing, or taking, these goods.

A vast empire, uniting the people from Dunadd to here in Dun Breatann and beyond was taking shape in Domangart's mind and he absently touched his sword through his cloak, knowing it would take much bloodshed to bring his dreams to reality, even if this fortress was likely to fall without much of a fight.

He glanced upwards, having to crane his neck to see the top of the two peaks. A lone raven soared over the highest one, letting out a great, raucous cry that made the hair stand up on Domangart's arms. Was it a good omen, or a bad one? He was not sure, although he was certain the bishop back in Dunadd would berate him for such superstitious thoughts.

His gaze travelled downwards, seeing merely rock and weeds for Dun Breatann was only inhabitable on the bottom, the top, and an inner section in the middle that could not be seen from where the Dalriadans stood. Eyeing the outer gatehouse, Domangart scanned the wall that was the fortress's first line of defence, and he paused, seeing a wholly unexpected figure there.

Nudging his son, the pair looked at the man who was gazing outwards, towards the market and across the river.

"Who"– Carvorst started to say, and then fell silent as understanding came to him.

Only one man would be standing on Dun Breatann's walls wearing a Roman legionary's cuirass and crested helmet.

"The fucking centurion!" Domangart hissed, turning his head away so as not to draw the attention of the former legionary. "Didn't the merchant tell us he was mortally wounded? Or near death at least? He doesn't look dead to me!"

Carvorst had also turned away, but he cast sidelong glances at the centurion who appeared tall and proud and, most worryingly, quite hale and hearty from this distance. "It doesn't matter," the young man murmured. "He's just one man."

"A centurion!" Domangart retorted. "*The* centurion. We've all heard the tales about him and the giant druid. That centurion is the man who killed Loarn mac Eirc, and the Saxon beast, Horsa. Dun Breatann was supposed to be without its army, and without a leader, but at least one of those claims I now see to be false!"

Carvorst shrugged. "A single man cannot stand against all thirty of us, father, calm down. We know the centurion was injured, that's why he's been left behind while Narina marched off to war. He can't stop us by himself."

A nearby trader called out, shaking an apple at them. Domangart took two of the red fruits, handing over a small amount of hack-silver in return. He had no appetite, but tossed one of the apples to his son and forced himself to eat, doing everything he could to seem like any other visitor to the market.

"Think of it," Carvorst went on, mouth full of the sweet, juicy flesh of his apple. "We walk in, kill anyone that stands in our way, and take the head of the centurion – with his stupid helmet still attached – and stick it over the gates for Narina to return to. We'll be legends, father! The men who avenged Loarn mac Eirc and conquered the unconquerable fortress of the Damnonii!"

Domangart smiled at his boy's enthusiasm, feeling his own excitement rise again. Carvorst was right – what could one man do against thirty experienced Dalriadan warriors?

"Come on then," he said, tossing the remainder of his apple away. "Let's get the rest of the men and—" He broke off, staring up at the top of the towering rock in dismay.

"What is it?" Carvorst demanded, cursing as he squinted upwards and noticed what his father had seen high on the eastern peak.

A row of spearmen was lined up, looking down over the wall, along the Clota. The sunlight glinted from burnished helmets and the sharpened tips of their weapons and Domangart could not help the feeling of despair rising within as he counted them.

"Seven," said Carvorst, tallying their number himself. "To add to at least another six or seven we can see on the lower walls here, and Christ knows how many more within the fortress."

They continued to scan the great lumpen rock, eyes running along the walls and walkways before settling at last once more on the gatehouse. The centurion stood there, straight-backed, helmet polished even brighter than the ones worn by his troops, and he was looking directly at them.

"Shit," hissed Carvorst. "He's spotted us."

"Come on," Domangart commanded, making no attempt to move away inconspicuously. He led his son at a fast trot back through the market, towards the river and their waiting currach, glancing once over his shoulder to see the centurion still watching them grimly.

"What are we going to do?" the young warrior asked, ignoring the curious, eager glances of their comrades at the currach.

"Do?" the king of Dunadd replied incredulously. "We don't have the men to storm the fortress, even if the gates remain wide open all night, and, I don't know about you, my son, but I don't fancy taking on that Roman in a fight to the death."

Carvorst hissed and Domangart gestured irritably at him to help shove the currach back into the water alongside the other warriors. As they jumped aboard and began to row back to the west Domangart felt utterly deflated, and understood his son's bitter disappointment. This was supposed to have been easy – a lightning strike against an undefended target that would bring them fame, power, wealth, land, and a base to go on and build an entire Dalriadan empire there in Northern Britain.

"We'll come back one day," the king promised to Carvorst and the rest of the men. "We just need to bide our time, not take unnecessary risks, and build our strength around Dunadd."

He spoke with conviction, or at least tried to, but he could see the other men in the little boat did not believe his vow and, as they picked up speed, he realised he did not even believe it himself.

* * *

303

On Dun Breatann's gatehouse, Duro watched, flint-eyed, until the two men – very clearly warriors, no matter how they had slumped their shoulders and tried to hide – ambled out of sight towards the river. He gestured to a nearby guard, a clean-shaven young man with slim shoulders who'd been temporarily promoted while the rest of the army was away with Narina.

"Lord?"

"See where they go," Duro told him. "And make sure they leave."

"Aye, lord. Who d'you think they are?"

"I've no idea," Duro growled, holding his tongue in check despite feeling the urge to snap at the young soldier not to ask questions when given a direct order by a superior officer. "But they didn't look like they'd come to market just to buy a couple of apples."

The warrior opened his mouth to ask something else, but Duro's brows came together in a warning frown and his stare was enough to send the younger man hurrying away, heading for the inner stairs that would lead him up and along the walkway that went around to the south-western edge of the rock. The walkway that the Saxon had climbed up onto when he'd almost killed Duro…

The centurion felt his jaw tighten at the memory – vague as it was – of that night. It had taken a long time for him to really start to regain his full sense of where, or even who, he was, and even longer for him to be allowed out of his sick bed. The Saxon had done a good job of attacking him but, praise Mithras, Bellicus had done an even better job of tending to his injuries. Still, when Narina and Gavo had taken the garrison and marched to attack Cunneda, leaving Duro as the most senior military officer in the fortress, he had not felt wholly secure. The rock was tall and steep, the walls sturdy, and the two gatehouses built to withstand even the most concerted attack, but the barely-healed wounds and the lingering pains in the centurion's body were a constant reminder that enemies were everywhere.

He glanced up but the helmeted, spear-wielding guards were not on the wall above him any more, having marched on to another section of the fortress, patrolling regularly, making sure there was a visible military presence within Dun Breatann throughout every day.

He wondered then if the two warriors that had been examining the fortress had spotted those patrolling guards high overhead and decided that whatever they'd been planning was a bad idea. Duro smiled for the first time in days at the thought – it had been his idea to setup those patrols, to deter would-be raiders while the main army was in Votadini lands.

He peered up again, seeing the raven, Uchaf, and then the spears of the guards as they returned to the wall high above, too high for anyone to make out any details of them other than their weapons and helmets.

The young warrior came hurrying back then, sprinting up the stairs to the wall where Duro stood.

"Well?"

"They got into a currach with a few other men and rowed away to the west, lord."

"Who do you think they were?" Duro asked, interested to hear the youthful officer's opinion.

"Can't say for sure," the man admitted. "But the others in the wee boat looked as much like soldiers as the first two. Dalriadans?"

"Keep an eye out for their return," Duro commanded. "And tell the rest of the guards. If anyone sees them, or any other currachs full of soldiers coming this way, the alarm is to be raised, our people brought inside, and both sets of gates locked, all right?"

The officer saluted, struck by the urgency in the centurion's voice. He scurried off once more to spread the word, trepidation and uncertainty apparent in his every movement as he spoke with the other guards in the lower section of Dun Breatann.

Duro watched him go about his business, feeling a little bad for the young man. The centurion did not really believe the men in the currach would return. On the contrary, he thought the raiders, if that's what they were, had spotted the spearmen patrolling the walls and decided Dun Breatann would not be worth attacking. He was also aware of his own burgeoning legend – thanks mainly to the stories and songs spread around by Bellicus – and the effect his mere presence might have on would-be invaders.

Chuckling at the absurdity of the situation Duro reached out and grasped the crutch that had been made for him. He grunted, feeling pain rack his body as he leaned his weight on the crutch and slowly, very slowly, made his way across the wall and down the walkway, moving more like a centenarian than a centurion. He might look as formidable as ever from a distance, but he could barely walk, never mind wield his spatha the way he had when he killed Horsa.

That was not the best of it though, he thought, thinking of the highly visible spearmen high overhead. Not one of them was a hardened warrior – two were literal children, some were old men, and the rest were women, all dressed up to look like proud, veteran soldiers from a distance.

Dun Breatann had to be the worst defended fortress in all of Britain at that moment, but appearances were everything – he'd learned that in his time with the legions, and again on his travels with Bellicus. If a few fake spearmen and the illusion of a stoic, heroic centurion was enough to deter raiders, so be it. Sometimes a fight could be won even without a blow being struck, if one was clever enough.

Such thoughts reminded Duro of Bellicus and he wondered where his friend was.

He smiled again as he entered through the inner gates of Dun Breatann, the few genuine warriors posted there saluting respectfully as he hobbled past.

Bellicus and Cai would be fine, the centurion thought, and they would return home soon enough. By that time, Duro's injuries would be healed, his body returning to its full strength, and then, well, Mithras-only-knew what adventures awaited them in the coming months and years.

Duro could hardly wait.

CHAPTER FIFTY-SIX

The army had fully made it inside the old Roman fortress by the time Bellicus, Bedwyr and their men returned. The sounds of fighting could clearly be heard, carried on the sea breeze to the druid who prayed for the safety of Arthur and his other friends along with every loyal Briton who was currently doing their best to drive the invaders from their lands.

Cai and Darac were left with the boys and old men who travelled with the army to provide cooking and other essential services but took no part in the fighting. Both the animals had done enough, carrying the druid all the way there from far-off Dun Breatann, and now it was time for them to rest in safety.

No respite for Bellicus though. "Come on, lads," he grinned, raising his staff of office so the bronze eagle pointed towards the fortress. "Let's show these bastards what happens to invaders in these lands."

He did not need to persuade them, they were already charging for the gatehouse behind Bedwyr before he'd finished speaking and he ran after them, heedless of the fact he had no shield.

Four Saxons had apparently decided they'd had enough of the battle and were trying to make their escape, climbing over the logs and other detritus that had been piled up in lieu of actual gates to protect Garrianum. Bedwyr set about the lead sea-wolf with the righteous fury that had been building within him since his capture away back near Durovigutum, hacking his sword down into the Saxon's breastbone so hard that it sliced halfway through his torso.

The other three enemy soldiers did not last much longer and then Bedwyr was leading the way across the rubble and into the fortress.

The sounds of battle assailed them as they pushed further within: screams; roars of rage and anguish and triumph; the ringing clatter of blade meeting blade; the dull thump of weapons striking wooden shields; the desperate shouts of command from captains and jarls. And all of these sounds were moving away from Bellicus and Bedwyr's group, towards the north, where the Great Estuary butted up to the northern edge of the fort.

"That's where their ships are moored," Bedwyr called out, moving faster now.

Bellicus remembered the layout well enough from his previous visit there, when the Saxon ships that were drawn up on the shore had been set alight by Arthur's men while the enemy soldiers looked on, shouting in impotent rage at the Britons who were destroying their beloved vessels.

"They're trying to escape," said the druid.

"Then we've won!" Bedwyr replied, laughing manically.

"Won this day," Bellicus agreed, hastening his own pace and passing the other men who did not have a stride as long as his. "But if many of the sea-wolves escape they'll just come back another time. Come on, we have to help Arthur kill as many of the bastards as possible!"

More enemy soldiers came their way, believing they had more chance of escaping through the ruined gatehouse than on the ships.

Not all of these foes were cowards – far from it in fact. They simply wanted to escape certain death, and they came at Bellicus and his comrades without hesitation, snarling war cries and lifting shields determinedly.

Bellicus was glad he'd chosen to wield his staff rather than Melltgwyn for the polearm's longer reach allowed him to smash the nearest Saxon's teeth well before the enemy was close enough to swing the axe in his right hand. The man fell back, mouth a gaping, bloody mess, too dazed to lift his shield as the druid brought the bronze eagle down on top of his skull. There was no time for the druid to catch his breath though, as another Saxon dodged close and swung his sword in an arc that would have bit deep into Bellicus's hip had it landed. Bedwyr was there though, slamming the boss of his shield into the Saxon's arm and sending him reeling back before he slipped and went down heavily. He did not get back up, for one of the other Britons thrust the point of his spear into his chest and a terrible cry of anguish split the air.

"Come on!" Bedwyr ordered, looking around and seeing no more sea-wolves to kill.

"Thank you!" Bellicus gasped as they started to run again. "You saved me there."

"Forget it! I'm in your debt, druid, and always will be."

The fighting had been fierce, as the scattered, tattered bodies of both Britons and Saxons proved but, as the small party neared the northern shore, they saw Arthur's warriors were in full control of the battle. Most of the enemy soldiers were already in their ships, or trying to get on board, to escape the charnel house Garrianum had become. Even the impressive banner in the shape of a raven had been torn down and set on fire by cheering warriors.

Bellicus saw Arthur sitting on the ground, a bandage being wrapped around his sword-arm by a healer as he watched events unfold with a somewhat dazed expression on his bearded face.

"How goes it, my lord?" Bedwyr asked, kneeling beside the warlord. "Are you badly hurt?"

"It's a long cut, but not overly deep," the healer said when Arthur didn't reply immediately. "As long as it's kept clean and wrapped tight it should be fine."

"Has he taken a head knock?" Bellicus asked, worried by the odd look on his friend's face.

"No," Arthur replied, seeming to come back to himself and throwing the druid a grim smile. "I'm just exhausted. That was a hard battle, Bel, but we're winning. The bastards are escaping though, look."

It was true, the Saxon ships were pushing out into the estuary, being rowed hard away from the frustrated warriors on the shoreline who wanted to put an end to the invaders forever.

"Shame we couldn't burn those vessels like we did before," Bedwyr lamented, sheathing his sword as it became clear there was no more need for it.

"Indeed," Arthur agreed, getting back to his feet with the aid of the healer. "It's not quite the comprehensive, crushing victory we wanted, but it's a victory nonetheless, and we must thank the gods for that. Did you find Hengist?"

Bellicus shared a look with Bedwyr, both men as disappointed in the result of their mission as Arthur was with the battle.

"We saw him," Bedwyr admitted. "But he saw us too, and turned the ferryboat around before they reached the shore. He's gone."

The men all walked towards the estuary as they were talking, joining the rest of the army who were standing screaming threats, insults, and curses at the departing Saxon ships. Bellicus looked around, nodding with some degree of satisfaction at the number of enemy dead, many of whom had been fleeing when they were cut down so hadn't even managed to injure their attackers.

"There he is!"

It was Qunavo who pointed towards the ships and every eye looked in the direction indicated. The ships that had left with the beaten Saxons from Garrianum were sailing directly east, but one vessel was coming down from the north, although it was making a turn to follow the others. In the stern two figures could be seen and, even at that distance, Bellicus could make them out as a man and woman.

"Hengist and the *volva*," Qunavo spat, softly beseeching the sea god, Llyr, to drown the entire enemy fleet. "They've escaped us again."

"It's another defeat for Hengist though," Bellicus reminded them all. "There's no way the Saxons will flock to his banner like they've done before. Beaten here, lost Garrianum, his brother dead and hung from Dun Breatann for the crows to feast upon, and Bedwyr still alive. All of that will lower his standing amongst the sea-wolves. It'll take him years to build his reputation again."

"That'll give us time to build on our new relationships with the Saxons who have settled here peacefully then," Bedwyr said. "I'd hate to think the mission that I started would be forgotten. It was going well until that whoreson Leofdaeg put an end to it, and it proved to me that there are many good Saxons out there, ready and willing to work with us, not against us."

Qunavo and Arthur both nodded, clearly in full agreement with Bedwyr.

"You really think Hengist is done?" Lancelot asked, stalking across the beach to join them, blond hair drenched in sweat but apparently uninjured.

"I do," Bellicus nodded. "And I'll write a song about his failures."

"Me too," Qunavo agreed with a nasty chuckle. "By the time we're done, the whole of Britain will be singing about Hengist's failures. No Saxon will ever want to follow him again."

"That's good," Arthur said, checking the bandage on his arm which was red from blood seeping through, but not saturated, thankfully. "I'd still rather Bel and Bedwyr had caught him though, and made sure he could never return to these shores."

"It's not all bad!"

The men turned at the sound of the baritone voice to see another of Arthur's closest companions: tall, blue-eyed Kay, dark beard bristling as he grinned at them and cried, "Look who I found!"

"Leofdaeg! I thought he must have escaped or been killed in the fighting!" Lancelot seemed to grow in stature as he faced up to the man who'd enslaved him and treated him worse than a dog. "It's so good to see you're alive."

The jarl stared at him fearfully and might have tried to escape if Kay hadn't held such a tight grip on him. A bruise was blossoming on his right eye, and he flinched when his captor moved, as though Kay had been the one who'd injured him. Or one of the ones, for now that Bellicus looked closely, he could see Leofdaeg was bleeding from the side, as well as from a wound on his leg.

"Where's the other little jarl that was gloating with Hengist over my capture?" Bedwyr asked the captive. "Sigarr?"

A bitter laugh came from Leofdaeg that was almost a sob. "He was supposed to bring reinforcements. No doubt the cowardly bastard simply sailed away to save his own hide. May the gods curse his bones!"

"May they curse every last one of you sea-wolves," Qunavo muttered, turning to Arthur and the others. "What will we do with him?"

"Torture him."

The Merlin shrugged at Lancelot's suggestion, and Bellicus eyed Arthur, wondering if the warlord would allow such a thing.

Leofdaeg seemed to believe it might happen and he tried to twist out of Kay's grasp, but the big man punched him in the kidney and tripped him up, dropping onto Leofdaeg's back with his knees and pinning him down as he thrashed about ineffectually, alternating between pleas for mercy and threats of violence.

"I won't stand by and watch a man being tortured to death," Arthur said eventually. "There is no honour in such a thing."

"Honour?" Lancelot blazed. "What honour was there in this whoreson spitting in my face every time he saw me? Or when he chained me up like a dog? Or when he pissed in my water cup? Or spat on my bread?" As he reeled off the list of charges he stepped closer to Kay and Leofdaeg, fists clenching and unclenching. "Or what about the times he punched me, kicked me, choked me, held

311

my head under water until I almost drowned?" He spun back to glare at Arthur. "Was there honour in those things?"

"Of course not," the warlord conceded. "And I'm not saying we simply let him go."

"Then what are you saying?"

"Leofdaeg will fight you for his freedom."

CHAPTER FIFTY-SEVEN

Lancelot's eyes lit up and his rage turned to steely determination as he glared venomously at Jarl Leofdaeg. "That suits me," he growled.

"How can I fight him?" Leofdaeg shouted, not even trying to move Kay any more. "I've been injured here, and my right arm is as good as useless thanks to him!"

"Your army is beaten, Jarl Leofdaeg," Arthur intoned calmly. "And you must pay for your crimes against the people of Britain, especially Lancelot. It's up to you if you want to run from him, or stand with a weapon in your left hand and fight for survival like a warrior. Let him up, Kay."

Leofdaeg had tears in his eyes as the weight lifted from his back and he slowly scrambled to his feet, staring at Lancelot with undisguised fear.

"Clear a space," the blond swordsman commanded, pushing his hair back and drawing his blade. "Where's my helmet, Leofdaeg?" he asked. "The one Merlin gave me, and you stole from me."

The jarl balked as though he couldn't bear the thought of losing the valuable helm, but then he must have realised he was about to die, and he spat at Lancelot although the phlegm did not travel very far. "It's probably back at the wall where I was captured."

"You!" Arthur shouted to one of the young lads who was carrying water for the injured Britons. "Go to the wall there and find Lancelot's helmet."

"What does it look like, my lord?" the boy asked.

"You'll know it," Lancelot told him, and the youngster sprinted away as though Dis Pater himself was chasing him.

"I need a weapon," Leofdaeg murmured.

Bedwyr walked to the nearby corpse of another Saxon and lifted the sword that was still gripped in the lifeless fingers, prising it free. "Here," he said, walking to Leofdaeg and throwing it on the grass before him.

The boy returned just a moment later and Lancelot beamed as his helmet was finally returned to him. It had been carefully made from two iron halves, with a central ridge, and decorated with gleaming brass plates. Neck and cheek guards were attached with straps and buckles, and Lancelot used his fingers to press down the leather liner before placing it on his head.

"This was a gift from Nemias, our old High Druid," he said solemnly. "He gave me this, and Bedwyr a fine scabbard."

"Which that bastard Hengist now wears!"

"Sorry, my friend," Lancelot commiserated. "Perhaps one day you'll get it back from him."

"Are we going to fight, then, or stand here gossiping like fish-wives?" Leofdaeg hissed, looking nothing like a man who wanted to fight.

"You," Lancelot retorted, "are going to die."

There was a circle around them now, as Arthur's army crowded around to see what would happen. Leofdaeg, self-proclaimed second-in-command to Hengist, swallowed and seemed to find some courage, his face twisting with hatred as he hefted the sword in his left hand and whispered a prayer to Woden.

Lancelot, resplendent in his shining helmet and chainmail, came forward, thrusting his blade at the jarl who parried it awkwardly. It was painfully obvious the Saxon was not naturally left handed, but Lancelot was not in the mood to play with him.

"Come on then, slave," Leofdaeg taunted, beckoning his opponent forwards, and Lancelot obliged, feinting, then altering the course of his blade, bringing it up across the jarl's exposed neck and tearing a terrible red line across it.

The wound spurted blood and Leofdaeg instantly fell to the ground choking and gasping, and the cheers that had went up from the army faded away as they realised the entertainment they'd been hoping for was already finished.

"It is over," said Arthur as Lancelot bent his head and thanked the gods for his vengeance. "It is over," Arthur repeated, shouting now so everyone could hear him. "And thanks to all of you, Hengist is gone, and Garrianum belongs to Britons once again!"

The cheers reverberated around the crumbling walls and Bellicus joined in as loudly as anyone. He had come south to hunt Saksnot, and, although that quest had ended in failure, he recognised now that the gods had guided him there for a greater purpose.

As the day turned to evening and the men opened barrels of beer and helped themselves to captured mead, Bellicus sat with Arthur, Bedwyr, Lancelot, Kay, and Qunavo and enjoyed the drinks and their company. It was a fitting, joyous end to a strange few weeks, he mused.

One friend was missing, though. How was Duro? Had the centurion recovered from his wounds, or had he passed over to the Otherlands?

The thought brought a lump to Bellicus's throat and he felt terribly homesick again, missing not only Duro but Narina, Catia, Gavo and the other good folk of Alt Clota. Were they safe? Happy?

"What's wrong, Bel?" Bedwyr, smiling, patted him on the back and refilled his cup from a jug of barley beer.

"Just wondering how Dun Breatann fares," the druid replied, forcing a smile.

"Ah, of course, you are feeling the pull of the road home, eh? Well." Bedwyr raised his cup in salute – he'd been told about Duro's injuries while they were escaping from Hengist and shared Bellicus's anguish for Bedwyr had also formed a close friendship with the centurion. "Stop worrying, my friend. Dun Breatann will be fine without you for a while, and Duro will be waiting, fit and healthy, and dour as ever, when you return."

The druid nodded and took a sip of his drink, trying to accept Bedwyr's words.

"Ever loyal, and worried for your friends and family."

Bellicus glanced to his right, wondering if Qunavo was being sarcastic. The Merlin was smiling, clearly inebriated, but his broad grin was sincere as he sat down beside him.

"Loyal and true, just like your father."

For a long moment Bellicus said nothing. He wondered if he'd imagined what Qunavo had just said, and replayed the words in his head, digesting them slowly, trying to make sense of them. Eventually, convinced he had not misheard, he turned to the older druid, who was sitting staring into the nearby campfire, eyes glazed, a contented smile on his lips.

Bellicus had known Qunavo since he was a child – the Merlin had been his tutor on the Isle of Iova off the north-western coast of Britain. Never once had the older man mentioned Bellicus's parents – they had been a mystery to him for as long as he could remember. He had tried asking some of the people on Iova about them but everyone professed ignorance and the youngster had no reason to doubt them.

For Qunavo now to drunkenly mention his father in passing was astonishing.

"My father?" Bellicus asked softly, watching Qunavo intently. "What of him?"

The Merlin turned to him and seemed to sober up in an instant. His mouth opened and he frowned before closing his lips and turning back to look into the dancing flames.

"What of him, Qunavo?" Bellicus persisted, voice hardening. He had never been particularly interested in his parents once he realised there was no way to discover anything about them. It had not seemed important, not when the youngster had so many other things to deal with. A druid's training was long and hard, and left little time for distractions.

Now, with the knowledge that his former tutor had known his father, it changed everything, and a burning desire to learn about his parents and his heritage began to grow inside Bellicus.

"Your father…" Qunavo sighed and trailed off, glancing quickly at the young druid before staring intently at the campfire once more. "Your father was a friend of mine."

"A druid?"

"No. A warrior. Very tall, powerfully built. Deadly. Much like you."

"What happened to him?"

"He went to Manu."

Bellicus absorbed that, shaking his head. "Manu?" He had never visited the island which lay in the waters between Britain and Hibernia and was said to be haunted by spirits and other fey beings. "Why?"

Qunavo's gaze turned downwards and he seemed to become lost in his cup, staring at the liquid within. It seemed this question had vexed the old druid for years. "Word had come from Manu," he said. "The Horn of Brân Galed had been found there, and seized by the king."

The Horn of Brân Galed was reputed to be a magical vessel that would fill with any drink a person desired. Such supernatural treasures were ubiquitous in Britain, or at least tales of them were. Bellicus had yet to see one of them in real life.

"The King of Manu was, and still is, a Christian," Qunavo noted. "Such a treasure would be wasted on him, and so King Drest sent emissaries to barter for the horn. Your father, being a formidable warrior, was part of the group. As was your mother."

Bellicus felt the hairs on his neck rise. His mother? Qunavo had known both his parents, and held it secret all this time!

"Why did my mother go?" he demanded, doing his best to stay calm in the face of these revelations. "Was she a warrior too?"

"No," Qunavo smiled. "Far from it. She was a Christian. Drest thought she might be able to persuade the King of Manu to trade the horn. Whether they did or not, I have no idea, for their party was never heard from again."

It was all too much for the exhausted young druid to take in and he sat back, mind reeling.

"Merlin!" One of the healers appeared from the darkness, face grim in the firelight as he addressed Qunavo. "We have need of your skills, lord. One of the injured men is beyond our help and"—

"I will come." The High Druid got to his feet slowly, long white beard almost tripping him in his befuddled state. He looked down at Bellicus apologetically. "We will talk more of this on the morrow," he promised. "I must go."

Bellicus nodded. He had completely forgotten the earlier battle, and the injured and dead, and even Arthur, and Bedwyr, and the other men around him. All he could think about was his parents. He tried to picture them in his mind, imagining what they might have looked like, who they might have been, what they might be like now if they had lived. And, most importantly, what had happened to them on Manu?

There had been many questions in his life. What had happened to Saksnot, for example? That was one he hoped to find the answer to eventually, but it did not really matter. Certainly, it paled in comparison to the question that now burned far brighter than the campfire within his imagination: What had happened to his parents?

Someone came and refilled the cups of the warriors around the fire. Bellicus hardly even registered their passing but, as he took a sip of the ale his thoughts turned once more to Alt Clota. He must return home and make sure all was well with his family, and his people.

And then he must take Duro and Cai and sail west, to Manu, to finally uncover the truth of his heritage.

AUTHOR'S NOTE

Unlike some authors, I don't fully plan out my novels – I will have an idea for the beginning and where I want things to end, but no firm outline for the things that happen in between. When I started writing *The Druid's Prey* it was always my intention to have Saksnot make it back alive to Hengist at Garrianum – so I was really surprised when the two hermits appeared and ritually sacrificed him to their god! Every so often something like that will happen for an author, when the book will somehow create itself, rather than the author being in control. At first, I thought it was just too crazy – how could I kill off the main baddie in such an unexpected fashion? But there's been a LOT of discussion lately about books being written by AI and how generic such books will end up being and, with that in mind, I decided that it would be wrong for me to change Saksnot's fate. Some spark of creativity, some piece of human (or even supernatural!) inspiration guided that section of the story making it a little more unique, a little less formulaic, so I went with it, and I'm glad I did. I do not use AI in any way to write my books and hopefully they are better for it.

One thing I DO is research heavily. I watched a review of one my books by some YouTubers recently and they made a comment that they thought I'd said I only used Wikipedia for research! I was amazed by that, because I often post photos of the sources I use to learn about historical periods so, for those who are interested, some of the books I bought recently and used to research *The Druid's Prey* were: *The First Kingdom* by Max Adams, *Germanic Warrior* by Simon McDowall and Angus McBride, *Anglo-Saxon Kings and Warlords* by Raffael D'Amatio and Stephen Pollington, and *The Druids* by Peter Beresford Ellis. These are in addition to the huge, and ever growing, library of books, audiobooks, and podcasts that help me steep myself in post-Roman Britain every time I start a new Warrior Druid novel. Wikipedia? Yes, I do use that as a jumping off point in plenty of cases. I think it's a great resource, but it's far from the only, or main, resource I use for research!

One really interesting thing I discovered during the course of my research was the ox powered boat that the Romans supposedly had.

Bellicus knows about them because they were written about in the 4th century *De Rubus Bellicis*. It's amazing to think of such technology and, if you're interested, there's a video and some commentary on the construction of a working model at the link here:
https://www.reddit.com/r/maker/comments/fyka8n/my_daughter_and_i_made_a_working_model_of_an/

I've used the term *Miðgarðr* throughout this book, because I thought it was more interesting then Earth or even Middle-Earth. The term apparently can be dated back at least to *Beowulf* in the 5th century, so I don't think it's historically inaccurate to use it.

My next project will be a fifth Forest Lord book, a sequel to *Blood of the Wolf*. I haven't written a full novel in that series for a decade so I'm a bit anxious about jumping back into the world of Robin Hood, but it should be fun. I also have a collaborative winter novella coming out this year which I'm working on with Matthew Harffy, so keep an eye out for that. We also recorded a rock song together

As ever, thank you very much for reading this book. If you enjoyed it please leave a 5 star review on Amazon/Goodreads as it really does help other people find my work.

Steven A. McKay,
Old Kilpatrick,
28th April 2025

ALSO BY STEVEN A. MCKAY & ACKNOWLEDGEMENTS

The Forest Lord Series:
Wolf's Head
The Wolf and the Raven
Rise of the Wolf
Blood of the Wolf

Knight of the Cross*
Friar Tuck and the Christmas Devil*
The Prisoner*
The Escape*
The Abbey of Death*
Faces of Darkness*
Sworn To God
The House In The Marsh*
The Pedlar's Promise*
The Christmas Gift*
The Heretic of Haltemprice Priory*

The Warrior Druid of Britain Chronicles
The Druid
Song of the Centurion
The Northern Throne
The Bear of Britain
Over The Wall*
Wrath of the Picts
The Vengeance of Merlin

LUCIA – A Roman Slave's Tale

Alfred the Great trilogy

**Titles marked * are spin-off novellas or short stories.
All others are novels.**

Acknowledgements

Thanks to my cover designers, More Visual for their eye-catching work on the artwork for this novel. Thanks also to my beta reader, Bernadette McDade and David Baird, and editor, Richenda Todd. The map of Britain was created by me using Canva – I know it's not very good, but readers seem to like maps so I thought I should make some up.

Printed in Dunstable, United Kingdom

66342822R00190